Property

of

LADY OF THE SNAKES

Rachel Pastan

LADY OF THE SNAKES

HARCOURT, INC.
Orlando   Austin   New York   San Diego   London

www.HarcourtBooks.com

Library of Congress Cataloging-in-Publication Data

Pastan, Rachel.
Lady of the snakes: a novel / Rachel Pastan.—1st ed.
p.   cm.
I. Title.
PS3616.A865L33 2008
813'.6—dc22   2007009586
ISBN 978-0-15-101369-2

Text set in Electra LH
Designed by April Ward

Printed in the United States of America

First edition
A C E G I K J H F D B

For David

LADY OF THE SNAKES

CHAPTER ONE

DURING JANE'S miserable twenty-hour labor, she thought a lot about Masha Karkova, who had died in childbirth in 1884 along with the baby she was carrying. Jane's pain was in her back, and she crouched moaning on the rug in their tiny living room waiting for Billy to come and get her, and later she screamed staggering up and down the hospital room with its pastel prints and floral curtains, like a decent hotel only with cupboards that opened to reveal sterile pads and stainless steel. Dying seemed a likely outcome—much likelier than producing a child. As she cried Billy's name she wondered if Masha had cried out for Grigory, and if so what he had done. Not pressed a tennis ball into the small of her back the way Billy was doing, the way they'd been taught in childbirth class.

Not that it helped.

Nothing helped. Not the breathing or the shower or the shot in her arm. Billy held her face in his hands. "The baby will be out soon," he said. His face and the smell of her own sweat were all there was until the next contraction seized her. They coaxed her onto the bed and told her to push and she did, and the hospital gown came loose and the nurse kept tying it shut again. Who cared? Who cared who saw what now, or how many doctors, interns, medical students trooped in and out like packs of dogs?

How distraught—ruined!—Billy would be if she and this baby died. Jane could picture him in the cemetery, his threadbare black socks showing beneath the cuffs of the tight suit he'd worn to his mother's funeral. Oh, the pathos of those socks. "Billy," she said, partly wanting to comfort him and partly to remind him of the names they had chosen for their child in case she died, though of course he would remember. Billy looked at her with a drawn, serious face, but now the doctor was talking. The pushing, which was only supposed to take an hour, had been going on for three, and they were going to try to vacuum the baby out with some kind of extractor. The medical staff didn't seem to be worried about Jane anymore, only the baby, and that frightened her more than anything. The bright lights made yellow and purple starbursts float in front of her eyes. She didn't want to die, as Masha had died; but surviving if the baby didn't was a kind of hell she hadn't imagined before. The thought seeped sulfurously through her veins and she couldn't obey when Dr. Mooney told her, yet again, to push. She shut her eyes against the lights, but then Billy cried out and she opened them again. And there she was: Margaret Levitsky Shaw—Maisie—covered with mucus and blood, a full head of black hair sticking up on end. The room smelled of the ocean and of rust.

The nurse wrapped the baby in a blanket and gave her to Jane, a bundle so light it seemed to weigh less than the completed chapters of her dissertation. The baby's face was startled, her brow wrinkled, her head battered from the hard journey. Where had she come from? Jane thought of the passage in Grigory Karkov's novel *The Lime Trees* when Yelizaveta and Sergey have their first child. For a moment she got lost inside the memory of that scene, the dim chamber with candles and hot water and the baby crying, and she forgot where she was until Billy said, "You were great, Janie! You were a force of nature."

Jane was back in the room again, uneasy. She had missed the first moments of her child's life because she had been thinking about the Karkovs.

For a couple of days after Maisie was born, Billy got a substitute to take his classes and he and Jane lounged around admiring the baby. Wrapped in a blanket, smelling of skin and cotton and souring milk,

Maisie slept in the bed between them. She was all face and bundled receiving blanket, her eyes a wide dark newborn blue, her tiny nostrils flaring as though she were considering the scent of the world. It was impossible to stop looking at her, trying to take in the fact of her existence. She was a new continent they had discovered, their private India, curled on her side like a bean and breathing noisily. Every few hours she woke up to mew and nurse. If she wouldn't go back to sleep after nursing, Billy carried her around against his chest and crooned to her. One night (the second? the third?) Jane watched him—really watched him, as though he were a movie or a rare specimen of wildlife that had wandered in. She watched his tall frame move back and forth across the room, his sweet face thinned by exhaustion and scrupulousness, his thick, once-blond hair as soft as cat's fur. More hair curled across his chest, and the baby clung to it with her brand-new fingers, while light from the streetlamp leaked in around the blinds. Jane lay in the rumpled bed propped up on pillows, knowing she should use the time he was giving her to sleep. But he was so beautiful and strange carrying the baby that she couldn't shut her eyes. He seemed taller, as though he had already grown into this new role, and his face wore a more tender expression than Jane had ever seen on it. She was glad—even relieved—to see how clearly he loved their daughter, but at the same time a hiccup of uneasiness ran through her. She felt that she was on the outside. She felt she might cry, as she had cried twice already today, exhaustion hollowing her out and a powerful brew of hormones shooting poisonously through the emptiness. Jane didn't cry often, and the feeling of tears in her eyes was almost as foreign as that of the milk on her nipples. She didn't like the way so much emotion had moved in, a guest who'd left all the faucets dripping. Who was this Jane from whom unfamiliar liquids seeped, who lay beached like a whale against the pillows? Who was Billy with his darkening hair and his pale, broad shoulders hunched protectively over the baby? Maisie emitted quiet, intermittent squeaks like a smoke detector letting you know its batteries were running down. The light fell irregularly across the room in pale yellow strips through which the man and the child passed and passed again, swaying, gilded, dusty with light.

Jane's graduate student friends came by with flowers, plastic pastel keys, stuffed animals, Chinese food. Sitting on the couch, Jane nursed the baby and ate Szechuan shrimp. She was glad to see them, to be reminded of who, until a few days ago, she was. She was glad, too, to get a chance to show Maisie off, and she liked seeing Billy hand out beers and brag.

"Don't be fooled by her apparent ignorance," he said of the snuffling baby with her plump cheeks and paintbrush hair. "She's extremely bright. She understands Russian already."

"Of course she knows Russian," said Catherine, a second-year student, a thin young woman with bright copper-colored hair who worshipped Jane a little. "Jane's been reading Karkov out loud to her for nine months!"

Jane patted Maisie's back, trying to get her to burp. The baby's head wobbled against her shoulder, and Jane lowered her face to feel the silky hair against her skin. "And Karkova, of course," she said. She was writing her dissertation on Grigory Karkov's heroines as versions of his wife, Maria Petrovna Karkova, and much of her material came from Karkova's diaries, which had been mostly ignored since publication of an excerpted edition in 1970. Masha was Karkova's pet name, used by those who knew her intimately. Jane used it only in the privacy of her own head.

"How long till you get back to Maria Petrovna?" Jane's officemate, Laura, asked. She knew that Jane's heart lay with the diaries. Jane would have liked to write her dissertation on them directly, but her adviser, who was not interested in feminist points of view, hadn't allowed it.

"Maria Petrovna is always with me," Jane said grandly. "Did I show you guys what Shombauer sent?" Shombauer was the adviser, an elderly German, the first woman ever to get tenure in the department. Jane handed Maisie to Laura and got up slowly, the episiotomy stinging. She hunted around among opened packages and stacks of journals and balled-up sweaters and extra receiving blankets until she found an old-fashioned silver rattle engraved with Maisie's initials. "Isn't that something?" she said. "Isn't it so Shombauer?"

"A peace offering!" Laura bounced the baby in her arms. Jane watched Billy watch Laura as she held the baby with one hand and reached for her beer with the other. Laura's sweater had slipped down to reveal the thin burgundy strap of the kind of bra Jane had almost forgotten existed.

"I won't drop her," Laura told Billy.

"Why a peace offering?" Catherine wanted to know.

"Laura means Shombauer's whole attitude when I told her I was pregnant," Jane said. She imitated her adviser's Hamburg accent, not very nicely: "'I thought you vere dedicated to the verk!'"

Everybody laughed.

"Karkova had six children and ran Dve Reckhi and copied out Karkov's books and wrote those amazing diaries," Jane said. "And Shombauer thinks I can't write a dissertation and take care of a baby!"

"She doesn't know how good a husband you have," Billy said.

Jane smiled at him. Maria Petrovna had had a notoriously bad husband. When he wasn't writing his novels with their unflattering portraits of her, he disappeared for days at a time, cavorting with peasant girls as though determined, in this arena at least, to compete with Tolstoy.

Maisie looked uncomfortable in Laura's arms. She turned her birth-battered head from side to side and smacked her lips.

"She wants to nurse," Jane said.

"Didn't you just nurse her?" Laura asked, handing the baby back.

Jane felt a sting, as though Laura had criticized her. What did Laura, with her thin bra strap and her round recreational breasts, know about anything? "Her stomach is the size of a walnut," she said lightly, lifting her shirt and unsnapping the nursing bra, pushing the pad out of the way. She was glad to have Maisie back in her arms where she belonged. Nothing was sweeter than holding her daughter, except for all the times she longed to put her down.

The baby latched on unevenly and tugged hard. Jane grimaced, unlatched Maisie with her pinkie, tried again. Billy brought her a cushion to rest her arm on. Embarrassed by the production, Jane went on talking about Shombauer. "I thought she'd guessed. I was sure it was written all over my face. But no, she had no idea, she was completely shocked!" The still unaccustomed tingle of milk moving through her and the awkwardness of holding the baby in the right position made it hard to keep the thread of the conversation. She thought of her adviser with her pale eyes and her thick accent and her soft, white, fluffy hair that conveyed a false impression of grand-motherliness. At heart she was hard and uncompromising; Jane knew that. Jane had always admired her for it. She spoke six languages, wore expensive suits, gray shoes with straps across the instep, large gray pearls at her neck. When Jane had said she was pregnant, Shom-bauer's eyes had gone cold and inhuman so that she looked suddenly like a fish, a dangerous fish, maybe a barracuda.

"Pregnant," she'd spat. Her mouth puckered as though the word itself were sour.

"Yes," Jane had said. In the low plastic student chair, she'd felt ill and bloated and slightly dull-witted. Her jeans were unbuttoned under one of Billy's T-shirts and her feet were already swollen inside her tight leather boots: three months along. She looked up at Shom-bauer across the oak desk. "But I'm ahead of schedule on my re-search. Even if I have to slow down for a month or two, I'll be fine."

"Fine," Shombauer repeated. "Fine." She let the word hang in the air between them.

Jane looked at all the books on the long shelves, hundreds of books that Shombauer had read, analyzed, critiqued, written. She felt the weight of them in the room, smelled the dusty smells of paper and glue, just like in her father's office back in California when she was a child. She had always loved the smell, but now she had to breathe through her mouth so it wouldn't make her sick.

Shombauer looked at her hard with those cold eyes: pale stones. "You can't serve two masters," she said, leaning forward, her hand resting palm up on her desk, gray and thin. An old woman's hand. "It's not possible!"

Jane sat up straighter. "I'm my own master," she said, and Shombauer leaned back again in her chair.

"Of course," she said, and smiled. It was a thin gray-pink smile, like a scar.

Now Catherine said, "It's not easy to surprise Shombauer."

Jane's huge granite breast ached like an arm that has fallen asleep as the baby sucked. She felt tired, suddenly, and would have liked to lie down.

Catherine held the silver toy out toward Maisie, who, never pausing in her sucking, eyed it warily as it winked and clanked. Laura began to talk about trying to catch a movie.

"Don't go yet," Jane said, although she felt if she shut her eyes she would fall asleep.

"Tell us a Maria Petrovna before we go," Catherine said.

"How about the one about the pigeons, Janie," Billy said. "It's nice and morbid."

Jane made a face, but she liked that one, too. In the middle of the night when Maisie screamed inconsolably, it was good to know others had also experienced this despair in the face of what one was told brought so much joy.

"This is from right after her first child was born," she said. "'He is an angel, but my mind is so black with suffering that I can hardly bear to look at him. Grisha does not even know he is born yet—his son with his father's black hair and pale knowing eyes! I have sent Ivan

Stepanovich to look for him, but he is nowhere to be found...' And then, 'Just gazing at the child's tiny face, so like his father's, makes me want to climb up on the roof with the pigeons and throw myself into the street!'" She quoted in English since Billy was there, but she could have done it in Russian equally well. She had a gift for the language and translating came easily to her. She'd been surprised when she got to graduate school that it wasn't like that for everyone. Russian was another medium; speaking it was like swimming in a rough salty ocean instead of the bland turquoise swimming pool that was English.

"That's interesting," Laura said. "Do you see a lot of that suicidal ideation in the diaries?" She stretched, exposing her firm, tanned stomach, her silver navel ring with its onyx bead. Jane's own stomach was white and soft and bulky as a pillow, mottled with blue, the purple-black seam of the linea nigra barely faded. Her hair was stringy and she had dark circles under her eyes. She looked to see if Billy was looking at Laura, but he was making faces at the baby over Jane's shoulder.

"Not that I can think of," Jane said.

"Let us know if you start to feel like that," Catherine said. "We'll make sure you get Prozac."

"I'm okay," Jane said. "Though I was kind of preoccupied with death during the labor. I kept thinking about how Maria Petrovna died in childbirth."

Billy put his arm around her.

"Karkova died in childbirth?" Catherine said. "I don't remember that." She was more interested in Akhmatova than in the male novelists, but she was sharp.

"Yes," Jane said, leaning back into the warmth of Billy's arm. "She was pregnant with what would have been their seventh child." But suddenly she wasn't sure. Usually she was confident in her recall of fact. She wondered whether her confusion could be related to the hormones.

Catherine shrugged, losing interest. The light was fading outside the apartment windows. It was time to go.

Laura got up. "Maybe she did commit suicide," she said, putting on her coat. "If she wanted to throw herself off the roof after one kid, imagine how she felt at the prospect of seven!"

Catherine carried the plates into the kitchen, came back, and kissed Jane. "Are you all right? You look exhausted," she said.

"I'm fine," Jane said, yawning. "I just need to catch up on my sleep."

But after they left and Billy took Maisie so Jane could get some rest, she couldn't sleep. She lay on the rumpled sheets of the bed that was no longer ever made and thought about what Catherine had said. She knew she couldn't possibly be wrong about the way Masha had died, but nonetheless the need to confirm it drove her out of bed and across the hall to her study. She would sleep better after she had looked it up.

The study was a tiny room, hardly bigger than a closet, dominated by a poster of the Kremlin domes. The secondhand desk was littered with the jade figurines her father had brought back from China when she was a child, little dogs and long-billed birds and smiling men with braids. Books in English, Russian, and German crammed the brick-and-board shelves, and papers were piled everywhere. She dug out a copy of James Delholland's biography of Grigory Karkov, sat on the floor, and opened to the passage on Masha's death.

> By 1884 the publication of *Dmitri Arkadyevich* was five years behind him and still Karkov was not near to producing a new novel. The manuscript for the book he was at work on in the early 1880s has been lost; after the death of Maria Petrovna in the summer of 1884, he abandoned it in favor of the story of an itinerant pilgrim of the kind that occasionally wandered through the countryside around Kovo. This work, as we shall see, is much concerned with death (and the related issues of

folk cures, superstition, and spiritual redemption), doubtless provoked by the sudden passing of the novelist's wife.

Maria Petrovna, confined with her seventh pregnancy, died on August 2, throwing the household into a state of grief and confusion. Maria's sister, Vera Petrovna Lensky, who came to Dve Reckhi from Moscow to help care for the children as well as to attend her sister's funeral, wrote to her friend, the Countess Lydia Stogova, "You have never seen anything like the sorry state of affairs here! The children, poor darlings, weep and stare and refuse to bathe. Katya is so upset she will speak to no one. The servants go around with tears streaming down their faces and spill the soup. And as for my brother-in-law! He has shut himself up in his study and refuses to come out. I have never seen a man so destroyed by grief. What will become of this family, I don't pretend to guess."

Jane closed the book and shut her eyes, her tired brain trying to make sense of the passage, which seemed to raise more questions than it answered. Delholland did not, after all, come out and say that Masha had died in childbirth, though that was certainly the implication. What did "confined" mean, exactly? Why did people still employ coy language to talk about childbearing? She thought of her own obstetrician, who had used language to obfuscate in a different way, speaking of the "discomfort" of labor.

But even if Masha hadn't died in childbirth, there was no reason to believe she had taken her own life. There were lots of ways to die, especially in 1884 in the middle of nowhere. Diphtheria, scarlet fever, influenza. Vanya, Masha's sixth child, had died of pneumonia just two years before his mother's death, when he was only four.

Jane had thought she'd known how terrible a blow that must have been, but now that Maisie was born, she felt the horror of it in a new way, in her bones. Masha had not written much about her feelings—or anything else—in the months following Vanya's death, but Jane recalled this passage:

I would have thought my Vanyushka's dying—and my own subsequent collapse—would have driven Grisha to the other side of the Earth to escape. But in fact he has been at dinner every night, Anya says, pale as death and hardly touching the soup but scolding the children if they fail to eat, or forget their table manners. Forms of behavior are what we have to fall back on when the pit of Hell gapes, he says, and I am grateful to him for having any idea of how to proceed, as I have none.

U menia net was the Russian for the last phrase—literally, nothing is with me, nothing in my pocket, nothing in my house. *Net.*

U menia net, Jane thought, curling up on the floor among the stacks of books and the dust bunnies, her head resting on the Delholland biography. Was it possible—was it?—that after two years of trying, Masha had given up the struggle to proceed with life? *Could* she have killed herself? Jane thought about it, making an effort but failing to imagine it. Suicide just wasn't possible for the Masha Jane knew, especially not with a child inside her on the verge of being born.

And yet Jane found her mind could not quite let the idea go. Who, after all, could say what another person would do? And how scholarly was it to assert that she knew Masha so well—so intimately—that she could rule out the possibility? Might Masha have found, at the moment of crisis, that she could not bear to bring another child into the world? Another hostage to fortune; another baby to replace Vanya, who could never be replaced? And what if she had experienced postpartum depression with her other babies, as the passage about throwing herself off the roof suggested? Could the anticipation of that, too, have deranged her? *I have none*, Jane thought again, and the words, written over a hundred years before, made her shiver.

And if it *were* true, after all, it would certainly open up some interesting literary possibilities. Each chapter of Jane's dissertation explored how a female character from each of Karkov's five major novels could be read as a version (seldom a flattering one) of his wife.

The protagonist of Karkov's final novel, *Lady of the Snakes—Dama Zmiev* in Russian—had required a somewhat tortuous argument: that she was a kind of anti-Masha, embodying the freedom and power that Masha, as a married woman of her time, could never have. The narrative described the woman (she was unnamed throughout the novel) leaving her five children in the middle of the night and wandering across the countryside as a mystical healer, ministering to the peasants. She carried live snakes in her basket and cured the sick. At the end of the book, she committed suicide. Could Karkov actually have modeled the Snake Woman's death on his wife's? How neat—and what an extraordinary scholarly scoop—if he had.

Poor Masha! Jane thought, as she had thought so often before. The journals revealed a woman of warm intelligence, enormous energy, a sharp eye for the natural world, and a haunting, lyrical prose style. How had a woman like that survived the life of constraint and restriction fortune had dealt her, stuck in the provinces, mired in her traditional role? Not that she wasn't lucky in many ways. She was a member of the upper classes; she had servants and clothes to wear and good food to eat. The estate might be losing money, but actual poverty wasn't a threat.

Nevertheless, Jane thought. Nevertheless. Nineteen years of living with an unfaithful, irascible husband; of looking after a large family (making clothes, ordering meals, supervising education, nursing the sick); of managing the sprawling, unprosperous estate; of being her husband's scribe (making fair copies of the scribbled drafts of three of his novels at night so he had clean pages to begin with the next morning); and then losing a child on top of all that! I might well have killed myself, Jane thought, under the weight of it.

And certainly, if Masha *had* taken her own life, the family would have done everything they could to conceal it. Maybe the evidence of the cause of death had been destroyed and that was why Delholland's sentence was ambiguous. Why, after all, if Masha had died of some common disease like influenza, had Delholland not just gone ahead and said so?

I'll have to look into it, Jane thought, drifting off to sleep on the floor with all the lights on, as soon as I can find the time.

Billy went back to work. In the mornings he set the alarm for 6:30 and was out the door by 7:15, clips around his ankles to keep his cuffs out of his bicycle chain, having downed two cups of coffee, a yogurt, and a piece of toast. Jane had to drink milk—five cups a day, the doctor said. She forced herself, trying not to picture the hot udder of its origin. She'd spent the summer she was twelve on a farm in the San Joaquin Valley, but the close straw-and-manure smell of the barn had sickened her, and she'd kept her distance from the cows. Now she more or less was one.

This morning Maisie nursed at five and then blessedly went back to sleep till almost eight. Jane nursed her again and then got out of bed and carried her down the hall into the kitchen. The little table was covered with newspapers, empty cups, wilted flowers in a carafe. She thought of Masha, of her description of the dawn, gray and silent and grim as a cat hunting. She thought of Masha's rants and recriminations against Grigory, out all night somewhere, Katya ill and little Nikolai teething and Grigory's mother and sister visiting from Moscow. And here was Jane, fortunate in her good husband and free of visiting relatives (her mother, in from California for a few days, had stayed in a hotel).

But still, Jane's life was transformed as suddenly as a plot of land was transformed by a developer. *This is what women's lives are like*, she thought with a start in the dim kitchen, her bare feet cold against the linoleum. It had never occurred to her—not really—that women's lives were still so deeply different from men's. Now she saw it, and it shocked her. She had thought the world had changed since Masha's day, but here it was, its iron demands the same as they had always been. She had thought she would not live as Masha had lived, always for others, but now this was her life: nursing and walking, eating cheese and crackers with a free hand. Changing diapers, changing her own milk-soured shirts. Sitting in the glare of the blank computer screen in a spare half hour. At night she slept in bursts with the baby wedged between her breast and Billy's back, her nightgown pulled up to her neck. Just finished nursing, ready to nurse again. Home alone with Maisie, it was impossible to get anything done. She couldn't understand it; the baby slept eighteen hours a day. Still, six o'clock found Jane in her bathrobe on the old brown couch exhausted and hungry, the baby curled against her chest or latched on to her nipple, which had been stretched so much it looked like a caterpillar.

Maisie wanted to nurse all the time. She liked to sleep in Jane's arms. She hated the bassinet with its quilted lining and screamed when Jane put her in it, her face going red and her fat limbs flailing. No matter how deeply asleep she seemed to be, the minute her back was cradled by something unbreathing, she knew it and startled awake. "Clever baby," Billy said, but he didn't have to hold Maisie while trying to open a can of soup, or read the mail, or go to the bathroom.

Jane tried working with Maisie on a cushion in her lap, but it would slide, and it was hard to hold her arms up over the baby to reach the keyboard. She tried holding Maisie in one arm and writing longhand but her words slipped diagonally down across the page, unintelligible. Her back ached. Her mind felt damp and boggy. "Peanut," she crooned. "Radish seed." She rubbed her cheek against the baby's downy hair, kissed her feet, held her close. "Mommy needs to get some work done. Why won't you sleep?"

Maisie mewed like a kitten and yawned, her whole face caught up in it, her startled eyes seeming to wonder what was happening. Already those eyes were changing color from that deep ocean blue to a paler, odd bluish brown like the outside of an oyster shell. When she looked at Jane, her gaze was steady and thoughtful as though she were on the verge of comprehending who Jane was. No one had ever looked at her like that before.

In the evenings, when Billy was in charge, he put Maisie in the bassinet and let her scream.

"How can you leave her there?" Jane asked, coming in from her study to stand in the doorway.

"She's screaming anyway. What difference does it make where she does it?" Billy said, looking up from his lesson plan or his magazine, or the bowl of cereal he was eating since no one had made dinner.

"It makes a difference," Jane insisted.

"Sometimes people need to be left alone," Billy said. "Even babies."

Maybe he was right. Maisie was certainly calmer with him. Why was that? How could Maisie, at one month of age, even distinguish one person from another? Although Masha claimed her babies could always tell her apart from the wet nurse who had nourished them from their first hours: "If Kostya turns to Yelizaveta Pavlovna with delight as though her round white breasts were twin moons, still he turns his face to my face as though I were the sun, bringing light and warmth and joy." Jane did not feel that Maisie absorbed joy from her. The baby looked at her with the same troubled, anxious expression with which she regarded the rest of the world, as though the street, her crib, and her parents were all seeded with explosives and you never knew when something was going to go off.

Maisie had not been a planned child, but Jane and Billy were married; they were old enough. They had met in college, in Thad Everhardt's Karkov seminar. Billy was an English major dabbling in Russian literature. He liked Karkov, but he wasn't a devotee like Jane, who banged on his dorm room door early one Saturday morning in December of their freshman year, her dark hair studded with snow, her eyes alight. "Get your boots on," she'd said, and dragged him outside, where the year's first snowfall had already blanketed the streets.

They had been friends then, not quite dating, but her mittened hand held on to his all the way up to the quad, where she let go to pull a book out of her pocket. It was *Dmitri Arkadyevich*, the Sigelman translation, which they had been assigned for class.

"Listen to this," Jane said, and she read out loud: "'As he stood in the street and watched the first flakes float down from a sky the color of goose feathers, Dmitri Arkadyevich felt his heart lift and swell until it seemed to fill his chest with a passionate fluttering. . . .'"

When she finished the passage, she held out her arms to watch the flakes catch in the palms of her mittens. "I love it!" she said. "It snowed exactly once in my whole childhood. We really only knew about snow from TV."

"We used to build snow forts," said Billy, who had grown up in Connecticut. "Me and my brothers. Snowballs, ice balls. We used to hide in the bushes until the bus stopped at the corner, and when the driver opened the doors, we'd throw our snowballs in and run."

"That's terrible!" Jane put her hand to her mouth and tasted the pure cold, her tongue pushing through the snow to the wool of her mitten, which tasted so different, so animal.

Billy laughed.

Laughing transformed him. His muscles relaxed and his face opened up. Other people were like that, Jane knew, with insides and outsides, like geodes, but with her, everything was on the surface. "My brother never did anything like that," she said, thinking of Davis with his comic books and his chemistry set. She could feel Billy watching her, feel his eyes fixed on her. He was so close she could see the individual snowflakes landing on his short, blunt, dark eyelashes. When he kissed her, she kept her eyes open and he did, too. His eyes were pale blue mixed with gray, and his lips were cold at first, but in a minute they were warm, and to her surprise her own chest, like Mitya's, filled with a passionate fluttering as she and Billy stood kissing in the snow.

———

It was November, the year was winding down. Each day was the coldest Maisie had ever known, each night the longest night. Jane was at her desk one evening working on 1873. It was a bad year for the Karkovs. They were in debt, and Masha's youngest sister, Sofya, died of scarlet fever. Words poured out of Masha as she grieved—memories of Sofya as a baby blowing kisses from her pram, as a little girl splashing in the river, all dressed up for her first ball. There was a long description of the funeral: the icy rain, the family huddled together watching as the box was lowered into the muddy earth. It was clearly the model for the funeral of little Igor in Karkov's novel *Silent Passage*. "And then the wind came up and rattled the skeletal oak leaves still clinging to the branches of the trees that lined the cemetery wall. The sleet hissed against the coffin as the men lowered the ropes. It was unbearable to leave her there, alone in the cold and wet," Masha had written, and Karkov's novel, too, mentioned the skeletal oak leaves and the sound of the sleet.

Distracted by the noise of the television through the closed door, Jane got up and went into the living room, where Billy sat on the couch watching the basketball game, the baby in her red onesie curled like a bug on his chest.

"You've got to see this, Janie," Billy said. "Two minutes left and the Celtics are down by five."

Jane's eyes were filled with tears, her mind caught in the wet Russian graveyard with the cold rain and the mud and the wind whipping the heavy branches of the trees back and forth, everyone clutching their hats and weeping. "Maria Petrovna's little sister died," Jane said. She was partly crying for herself, too, though she could hardly admit it: for how hard her own life felt to her, even though she knew herself to be lucky. Lucky! Only twenty-five and already she had a good husband, a healthy child, a promising career. What was wrong with her that she didn't feel her own luck? That she had felt happier before—before Maisie—was a truth too awful to acknowledge for more than an instant before shutting it out again. The days dragged on, hour after tedious hour, watching Maisie like watching grass grow. She didn't *do* anything. She slept and ate and fussed and looked around. She needed Jane—profoundly, entirely—but not because of who Jane was. It was Jane's arms and breasts Maisie needed: her animal warmth. Jane might as well have been a wet nurse. The fact that she loved Maisie, that she would without hesitation step in front of a moving car for her, was irrelevant. What kind of a mother—of a person—was she, to feel this way? Better to cry for Masha and the dead.

Billy stretched his long legs out into the middle of the room, his big Converse All Stars planted firmly on the rug. "They all died," he said.

Jane wondered if he was thinking of his own mother. Sofya died, Jane thought; they all died. Billy's mother, also named Margaret, had died two summers after they graduated, and one day this infant Margaret would die, too. She looked at Billy, but his eyes were still on the television. Maybe he wasn't thinking of his mother. His face was set in a laconic concentration that was similar to the expression he wore during sex. Sometimes he seemed to disappear inside his skin as if inside a locked room. If Jane asked what he was thinking, he was likely to smile and shrug and say, "Nothing," or else to mention sports. Jane wondered if, as she did, he missed the time they used to have just to be together, talking or going to the movies or riding their bikes around the reservoir. She was afraid to ask him. For the first time there were things about herself she didn't want Billy to know. So she, too, she supposed, was locking herself away.

Outside the window a few flakes of snow swirled around the streetlight. Jane thought of the passage in *Dmitri Arkadyevich* that she had read to Billy that December morning when their life together was itself a white, blank field of untrodden snow; when Karkov had still been her hero rather than the ambiguous figure he had now become—charming, immensely talented, volatile, faithless.

It wasn't until her second year of graduate school that Jane had discovered Karkova's diaries, which had been published only in a slim, highly abridged edition and never translated into English.

Slowly she saw how Karkov had taken Masha—the facts of her child-hood and her physical person, her joys and terrors, even the stutter that sometimes plagued her in society—and twisted them, showing everything in its worst light, to create the character of Olga in *Dmitri Arkadyevich*, the only one of his novels critics ever compared to Tol-stoy. At the same time, he took the best of himself for Mitya—poor Mitya, who married Olga Petrovna, the beautiful woman who tor-mented him with her sly stupidity, with her jealous fits and her hypochondria!

When Masha read *Dmitri Arkadyevich* (she had been his copyist for the first three novels, but this book had been transcribed by a bright peasant boy from the estate), she wrote in her diary:

> *Well, I have read it. At first I wept for myself and for what people will think. And indeed they will consider it true, or mostly true. But what is odd is that as I read I was so drawn into the story that I ceased to care that this was how Grisha saw me, or that he would expose us to the world in this manner. He is a cat bur-glar for art, sneaking around in the dark. He would steal any-thing for his work—words, secrets—whatever he could get his hands on. He is like a sponge, soaking up the nectar and blood of life and wringing it out on the pages of his novels.*
>
> *I do not mean that to sound so cold and terrible. Despite everything, I admire him. There is no question he is a great genius.*

It was when she read this that Jane's heart began to harden toward Grigory Karkov and open toward his wife.

The light from the television flickered as the basketball game went into overtime and the baby slept and the steam rushed into the radiators, and Jane's thoughts gathered like a great wave.

"Billy," she said. "I'm never going to finish if we don't get some-one to help with Maisie!"

The words seemed to hang in the air, visible, spelled out in neon. It was as close as she could get to saying what she felt: that she would die if she couldn't finish her thesis, and that not finishing seemed increasingly likely. Even as each day saw her work pushed along a little further, the amount *not* done seemed to yawn wider still, until she felt she was teetering on the edge of a precipice of mental dullness and misjudgment, of things undone.

Maybe it was just the lack of sleep.

Billy nodded. "I was thinking about that, too," he said.

And just like that, Jane's heart lifted. The canyon at her feet shrank to a muddy ditch. His words unlocked her, made her feel again that he knew her, that they were traveling through life together on the same tidy ship, standing at the rail and seeing the same view: hills and valleys and shadowy, unknown forests.

"It'll be good for Maisie," Billy said. "To have someone else besides just us in her life."

Of course it would! Jane thought. Why did she assume that what was good for her would be bad for her daughter? What kind of oppositional nonsense was that? The warmth she felt for Billy was liquid, pervasive: very much, in its physicality, like her love for the baby.

She sat down next to them on the couch and leaned over to press her nose into Maisie's head, feeling the steady thrumming pulse, breathing in the clean astringency of soap and the ripe peach smell that seemed to be the essence of her. She stretched out on the sofa, thinking how lovely it would be to work without one ear always cocked—to dive deep down into the ocean of Masha's world like the swimmer she was. No more of this wading, this dog-paddling she'd been doing. She thought how much she loved Billy, and how far she had come from the house on Euclid Avenue where her parents had their own spheres (his the third-floor study with its view of the backyard and the tops of the Berkeley Hills, hers the kitchen, the living room, the cluttered front porch). She was ready to embark on the adventure of her own existence as soon as she could get a little more sleep.

CHAPTER TWO

WHEN MAISIE was almost two, they moved to the Midwest. Jane landed a job at the University of Wisconsin, and Billy was accepted to the law school there. Jane was going to replace Otto Sigelman, the man who had almost single-handedly rescued Karkov from a waning reputation. Not that Karkov had ever exactly had a place in the pantheon. His novels sold briskly in their time, and they were well regarded, but he was never considered to be in the same category as Tolstoy and Dostoyevsky and Turgenev—or even Goncharov.

That began to change in 1963 when Sigelman published *Second to None*, his brash, brilliant, aggressively argued study of Karkov's work. Over the next ten years, Sigelman was everywhere, giving papers on Karkov from Boston to Paris and Istanbul and retranslating, as well, the two best-known novels, which appeared in shiny new editions fronted by his incisive and entertaining introductions. Sigelman was a bigger-than-life figure, a Hungarian-Jewish émigré who had made his way to America by sea, stowing away at the age of sixteen (so the story went) on a rat-infested cargo ship ferrying a load of shoes to the stinking port of Wilmington, Delaware. He had worked his way up into New Jersey as a janitor, a newspaper hawker, a dishwasher, and a busboy, attending school at night until he got a scholarship to Rutgers University. Eventually, amazingly—through native brilliance and enormous effort—he found his way to graduate school at Columbia. There, working with Leon Novitz, he achieved the nirvana of a Ph.D. Once arrived he made his mark: he shone. He charmed everyone with his accent, his erudition, his smiling arrogance, his searing commentaries and luminous translations. His life seemed a metaphor for the times, for postwar America. It had been an early student of his—probably also his lover—who had edited the diaries of Maria Petrovna after they came to light in the hands of Karkova's great-granddaughter Galina Pisareva, who had escaped from the Soviet Union with her parents as a child.

When Jane got the phone call about the job, she went to see Shombauer in her office with its creaking oak floors and silver-framed certificates and shelves of books and bowls of fresh flowers. As she came in she noticed that the head of a freesia had fallen onto the carpet, but she stepped carefully over it, leaving it where it lay. Shombauer liked everything to be in order—every footnote, every reference, every flower. There was nothing to be gained by pointing out a flaw.

"Good for you, Jane!" Shombauer said when Jane told her the news. "I'm so pleased." And she looked pleased: pleased for Jane, and pleased with herself for having a protégée who'd landed such a good position. "Wisconsin, eh? I thought Otto Sigelman would never retire!"

"I'm looking forward to meeting him," Jane said. "I decided to study Russian after I read his translation of *Dmitri Arkadyevich*. Not that he'll probably be around much."

"I'm sure he'll be poking his nose into things," Shombauer said. "You're young and bright. He'll take an interest. It could be useful for you, too, as he still has a lot of influence. Just don't talk to him about your so-called literary interest in Maria Petrovna."

"Why not?" Jane said, more impatiently than she meant to. The first thing she planned to do after she got out from under Shombauer's supervision was to write a paper on Karkova. "It's because of him that the diaries are in print at all."

"But only as ornament," Shombauer said firmly, raising her voice to make sure Jane remembered who was who here. "Only to burnish Karkov's reputation. Otto was always sorry there were no riveting literary memoirs about Karkov of the sort, for example, that Nadezhda Mandelstam wrote about Osip. This was the best he could manage."

"I think Karkova's journals might stand up to Nadezhda," Jane said boldly.

Shombauer frowned. "That's exactly the sort of thing you shouldn't say to Sigelman," she said. "I remember some years ago at a conference in Stockholm, that woman Danielson gave a paper about Sofya Andreyevna's journals, talking about them the way you proposed to write about Maria Petrovna's."

Jane said nothing, though in her opinion Sofya Andreyevna — Tolstoy's wife — was hardly much of a stylist. She certainly wasn't in Masha's league.

"I remember at the bar afterward," Shombauer went on, her silver rings glittering, the heavy pearls she wore at her ears dragging down the pendulous flesh. "Otto was ridiculing the paper and Danielson and especially the diaries. 'Worthy only to keep company with shit!' I believe he said."

Jane must have looked shocked, because Shombauer smiled.

"He always had a memorable way of speaking," she remarked. "And he's destroyed more careers than—" Shombauer cut herself off, but Jane wondered if she had been going to say "than I have."

Rather than live in campus housing, Jane and Billy flew out to Madison over the summer and bought a house: brown shingles with a wide, weedy front lawn. Marigolds and zinnias were planted along the weathered rail fence, and the front yards all along the street were crowded with flowers and tricycles. Neither the houses themselves nor the lots they sat on were large, but Jane felt almost as if she were moving to the country. The whole city with its lakes and wide views of the sky and its smells of algae and grass had an expansive feeling about it after the ancient brick and dirty streets of New England, the way the buildings there crowded in on each other like jungle plants jostling for light.

Their first night actually living in the house, after the moving truck left and Maisie was asleep, Jane and Billy sat on the back steps looking out over the little yard: dandelions, a scraggly rosebush, a small pear tree with a few hard pears on it, an overgrown hedge of blackberry brambles and jewelweed separating them from the neighbors on either side. It was a beautiful late summer evening. The sky towered over them, a pale luminous blue shot through with gold. Somewhere a marching band was practicing. Jane, sitting a step below Billy, leaned back against his legs and said, "There's a passage in Maria Petrovna about walking through a meadow where she talks about a great calmness descending. She says, '*Derev'ia shevelili list'iami*... The trees shook their leaves like young goats shaking the buds of their new horns—and the river surged over the rocks—and I felt that I myself was a river, with life surging through me.' And then something about seeing her role in the scheme of life: 'mother to my children, mistress of my household, and, above all, child of God!'"

"Is that how you feel?" Billy asked. "Like a child of God?"

Jane laughed. "I feel something. Filled with a great calmness, the way she says. Like this is a good place."

Billy picked a pebble off the steps and tossed it across the yard. It hit the arborvitae at the back of the property and disappeared. "Everything you feel," he said, "did Maria Petrovna feel it first?"

She turned and looked at him. He was smiling.

"I hope not!" she said.

"I hope not, too," Billy said.

She took his hand in both of hers. "For instance, I love you more than she ever loved Grigory."

"That's not a terribly high standard," Billy said. "He was an asshole."

"People love assholes," Jane said lightly. She kissed his hand, his long fingers, his bony knuckles. She didn't want to argue, especially not on their first night. She wanted them to be happy. She moved up to the step he was sitting on and kissed him, and he kissed her back.

The sky had faded rapidly from blue to purplish gray and was moving on quickly to charcoal as though to help veil the million distractions—boxes to unpack, floors to sweep, neighbors to meet and lectures to prepare and textbooks to buy—that might make their minds wander just when they ought to be thinking of nothing but each other. Since Maisie was born, they no longer made love the way they once had, working up through all the rainbow shades of touch. Instead, sex had become a white blaze: intense, rushed, the entire scope of their sensual relationship compressed into a taut kinetic coil. Jane pulled Billy down from the stoop onto the dark lawn, pulled him on top of her, saw with pleasure that a few stars had pricked through the blackness over his head. The wind moved in the trees in their yard and the yards around them. The grass beneath her was prickly after the long dry summer, but Jane didn't care. It was theirs: their grass, their pear tree, their pink, scraggly rose.

One of the most exciting things for Jane about her new job was how close it brought her to Chicago, the city where so many Karkov papers were housed. One of Grigory and Masha's sons had fallen in love with the daughter of an American diplomat and followed her back across the ocean in 1899, all the way to the Midwest, and he had arranged for many of Karkov's drafts, notes, and letters to be housed in a special collection of the Newberry Library. It was a scandal at the time, taking it all out of Russia. Later, in the sixties, Galina Pisareva—descended from the Karkovs' daughter, Katya—had donated Masha's diaries as well, so that the writings of the two progenitors were now once again housed under the same roof. Jane hoped to get down to the Newberry before too long. Funded by a grant, she had done a lot of research there the spring before Maisie had been born, and she'd taken other, shorter trips both before and after. The later visits were mostly for fact and reference checking, but she had looked a bit, when she'd been there most recently, into the idea that Masha might have taken her own life. She hadn't found anything definitive in the diaries, no death fantasies or glaring symptoms of depression. There were a few passages that were suggestive, but nothing you could be sure about. For example, in reference to Grisha's infidelity:

I thought I had ceased caring about it long ago. I thought I had come to understand him—even to accept him—with all his faults and mortal failings, that after all this time I finally felt free to be myself without reference to him: apart from him. That his foul actions in no way diminished me.

And yet now the cycle is starting over again—the awful spiral that starts on an ordinary summer afternoon and ends in Hell. Grisha disappears after dinner. I catch a glimpse of him from an upstairs window strutting down the road in the direction of the fields with his gun, and somehow I know where he is going. I tell myself it may not be so, that he may return for supper with a brace of snipe slung over his shoulder. But at supper his place remains empty, as I knew it would.

"Where is Papa?" the children clamor.

"Out shooting," I tell them. "He won't be back until very late."

And he is not. The zala clock strikes twelve, it strikes two. The moon comes up. I cannot sleep. Soon, the sun, too, rises.

And now, at last, as though ushered in on the first golden rays, he comes. I hear the door. I hear his stealthy footsteps stealing up the stairs. I get up from the bed, pull my dressing gown around myself and open my bedroom door just as he is creeping past, as quietly as he can.

For a moment, seeing me, he freezes like a fox in the henhouse caught in torchlight. His black eyes glow and there is straw all over his clothes and in his hair. A smell rises from him as though he had swum hard in a salty sea.

And then he laughs! Ha-ha—he cannot help himself! He is giddy with hilarity—abashed, but deeply pleased with himself. He revels in everything, even in my catching him.

For what, after all, can I do? Nothing! He knows this. I know this. I am bound to him as a martyr is bound to the stake, while he is free as a hawk.

Or this brief fragment, written shortly after Nikolai's birth:

When I was a young woman, it seemed to me that I could shape my own destiny, but now it seems that destiny has overtaken me. Sometimes I struggle against it like a hare caught in a trap. Sometimes I feel like two women—two souls—struggling together in one body, and I wonder which of them is going to triumph in the end, the one that finds peace in the great blue sky God shows us; or the other one.

Still, there were hundreds of pages of the diaries nobody, as far as Jane knew, had yet read carefully. She had broached the subject of suicide with Shombauer, who had asked, reasonably enough but very sharply, "And your evidence is *what?*" She had e-mailed the biographer, Delholland, who had e-mailed back, "Although it's true that death certificates from Kovo from that era have been largely destroyed, I am confident that Maria Petrovna died in a manner relating to her well-advanced pregnancy," a reply that did not inspire as much confidence as Jane might have wished, but that was, nonetheless, hard to argue with. She had put the idea away then, feeling she had pursued it as much as she could for the time being. Finishing her dissertation to Shombauer's satisfaction turned out to be more work than she had anticipated, and even with babysitting (they could only afford part-time), Maisie slowed her down more than she liked to admit.

Now, however, as an assistant professor faced with the task of turning the dissertation into a book, she allowed her mind to play over the possibility again. If she *could* prove that Masha had died as the Snake Woman had—if a letter existed, for instance, that hinted at it; if unpublished parts of the diary not yet scrutinized by Jane painted a clear picture of depression—that could be enough to write at least a speculative chapter. Coupled with the argument that Karkov was unlikely to break his pattern of basing his female protagonists on his wife, such a theory, if argued convincingly, could significantly boost her chances of publication.

For the first few weeks of the semester, though, it was all Jane could do to keep her head above water, lecturing, consulting with teaching assistants and undergraduates, going to meetings. She tried to get to know her busy colleagues: the chair, John Lewin, with his thin, harried face and walrus mustache; Carmen Bilinsky, who had a joint appointment in Slavics and religion; Franklin Donovan, the white-bearded, Birkenstock-wearing Sovietologist; and the others. She had a pleasant office with a view of the lake and more bookshelf space than she could at the moment begin to fill. She had never had her own office before, a place to work where nobody could come in without knocking; a heavy wooden door she could lock and pretend not to be there the way Otto Sigelman did in the office next door. Even though he was emeritus, he seemed to come into the office most days of the week. Jane could hear him moving around sometimes, hear his mini-blinds rattling open or shut, and then someone out in the hall would knock and he would be very quiet until they went away.

On one of the first days of the semester, Sigelman was coming out of his office just as Jane was going into hers. He frowned at her, his shirt wrinkled under his shabby jacket, jowls waggling, blue eyes rimmed with red. She could see why the graduate students called him the Old Bulldog.

"Professor Sigelman," she said. "I'm Jane Levitsky." She held out her hand. He took it in his broad, fleshy, cold one, lifted it to his lips, and kissed it.

"Ah," he said. "The young Jew."

For a moment she couldn't believe he had said it. He held on to her hand, caressing her palm with his big sclerotic thumb.

"Yes," she said. "And you're the old one."

He laughed, showing crooked yellow-brown teeth. "Indeed. I'm very old—a hundred and ten at least! But I still know how to appreciate a pretty face." As he stood grinning in her doorway, Jane saw that smoke was gently wafting up from his jacket pocket.

"Are you on fire?" she asked.

He looked where she pointed, then turned to scowl up the hallway where Krista, the department secretary, was pinning notices to a bulletin board. With a hand on her arm, he escorted Jane firmly into her own office and shut the door behind them. "Sit down," he said, and took a seat himself without being asked. From the pocket he removed a pipe and lifted it to his lips. "I can't smoke in my own office anymore," he said in the heavy accent that made it sound as though his mouth were full of caraway seeds. "I've been busted for it too many times."

Jane sat down behind her desk. She straightened a pile of books and shunted loose pencils into a drawer as though this were high school and she would be graded on neatness. "What can they do to you? You're already retired."

"Yes, but they can make things tiresome."

"How's that?"

"They want me to give up my office." Sigelman sighed. "Space is tight. The graduate students are always complaining. Graduate students!" He spat the words out. "In my day you were lucky to get a carrel in the library, but nobody complained!"

"Surely they wouldn't evict the leading Karkov scholar of the twentieth century," Jane said, smiling.

He looked at her suspiciously and then decided to laugh, throwing his head back, his jowls wobbling. "Times change," he said. "I'm known mainly for the translations now, and even those—who knows? Not so many people read Karkov anymore. They're looking for new authors. Women. Minorities! If you could find a few limp poems by a female Tatar, imagine to what heights you could ascend."

"I can't imagine people are going to stop reading *Dmitri Arkadye-vich*," Jane said seriously. She loved all of Karkov's books, even *Prince Leopold*, which most people found ponderous.

"It's too long. Professors are afraid to assign it."

"*Dama Zmiev*, then." *Lady of the Snakes.*

"*Dama Zmiev*," Sigelman said with distaste. "Hardly my favorite."

Jane had a special place in her heart for *Lady of the Snakes*, the only one of Karkov's novels that, in her opinion, contained a truly complex and intelligent female character. "When did you last read it?"

"I don't know. 1968?"

She laughed. "You might want to try it again. It has wonderful stuff in it. Descriptions of the countryside that are almost hallucinatory, and all that creepy superstitious stuff about the snakes. The portrayal of peasant life is unlike anything he ever did before."

"Yes, yes," Sigelman said. His pipe had gone out, and he reached into the capacious pocket and pulled out a teacup, into which he emptied the bowl. Then he filled the pipe again with fresh tobacco and lit it. He got up from his chair, walked around Jane's desk, and stood, leaning against it, regarding her. The smells of pipe tobacco, wool, and age were overwhelming: powerful, repellant, and yet somehow magnetic, too, suggestive of the past and of secret knowledge. Sigelman reached out and picked up Jane's hand, cupping it in his own large tobacco-stained one. She could feel his hot, sour breath on her face. "Perhaps sometime you will come over to my house and we will have a long talk about Karkov, eh? Drink a bottle of wine. I will make goulash for you! You like goulash?"

Jane pulled her hand away gently. "Who doesn't like goulash?" she said.

Sigelman studied her. "You know," he said, "for a while it wasn't clear the department would be able to keep my tenure line. Karkov, as I said, is going out of fashion."

Jane smiled uncertainly. "I'll take that as a challenge," she said.

He nodded. "So you should," he said, his rheumy eyes fixed on her. "Listen: I'm known for not mincing words. I'll tell you frankly that I didn't like that article you wrote about Amalia Nikolaevna in *Silent Passage*. The one that suggested that Karkov was a misogynist and went on and on about the wife."

"I never said 'misogynist,'" Jane said. "I would never use that word about Karkov. It's too reductive."

"So it is." He nodded again. "I'm glad you agree."

Jane thought of what Shombauer had said, how Sigelman could be useful to her, how he could be ruthless. She'd be careful, she thought, but she wouldn't pretend to be somebody she wasn't. "He married Maria Petrovna, after all, didn't he?" she said. "He chose a smart, complicated woman, when he could have had anybody." This was true, though Jane often wondered whether Karkov had regretted his choice, whether Masha's intelligence and complexity were what had driven him into the arms of the dairy maids.

Sigelman smiled. "Yes, though she was only sixteen at the time," he said. "Maybe she wasn't too complicated yet."

"Sixteen was older then than it is today," Jane said. She was happy. How wonderful to be an assistant professor with her own office passing the time discussing the Karkovs with Otto Sigelman, of all people!

"So was thirty-five," Sigelman said. "What was life expectancy? Even when I was a child, fifty was considered ancient."

"Not that Karkov had done much writing yet, when they got married, had he?" Jane said. "Just *Country Days*." *Country Days*, a collection of sketches of rural life, had been published to substantial acclaim, but it wasn't in the same league as his later work. "It's as though he needed Maria Petrovna for the novels."

"You mean she was his muse," Sigelman said, drawing out the vowel so that the word sounded sarcastic, though that might have just been his accent.

"And his copyist. Editor, too, perhaps. Her assistance was practical as much as inspirational." Amazing how much she had done, Jane thought for perhaps the thousandth time. Here she was herself, having moved, like Masha, from the city to the country, swamped by new responsibilities, trying to be half as productive as Masha had been under the harsher circumstances of a more primitive world. She thought of Masha at sixteen, fresh from her parents' comfortable house in Moscow, accustomed to callers, concerts, dances, and conversation, moving to Dve Reckhi, Karkov's provincial estate, with no idea what she was getting herself into. Masha had read *Country Days* with its lyrical descriptions of haying, of the changing light in the birch grove, of the singing of the peasants and their picturesque, blasphemous festivals. In one story a young girl wept as she washed laundry in the fast-running Vaza River. Elsewhere the return of the geese over the thawing March fields was used as an image of the indomitable spirit of the Russian peasantry. All of it was engagingly written and true enough, as far as it went.

But the day-to-day reality of provincial life was very different. The uncomfortable beds of Dve Reckhi; the incredible heat; the obtuseness of the servants; the swirling dust of the yard; the stink of the chicken house; the dull, endless expanse of the hours unbroken by a single carriage passing on the Kovo road: how could she have had any conception of it beforehand? She tried to absorb it, tried to make friends with Anya the cook, and the maids with their crooked teeth, and the stable boys (old men, really) with their dirty beards and bloodshot eyes and their way of looking straight at her when they ought to have looked at the ground. She read books and sewed a little and tried to teach Anya to make the dishes she liked. Grisha was out all day doing she had no idea what, and sometimes half the night, too. And when she broke down and wept and told him how unhappy she was—and how nothing in *Country Days* had prepared her for this life—he laughed and ran a hand through her dark hair as though it were a length of silk he had bought at a good price.

Razve ne znaesh' raznitsu mezhdu iskusstvom i zhizn'iu? he had asked her: Don't you know the difference between life and art? She wrote in her diary, "It was as though he had slapped me. It had never occurred to me until that moment that there was any substantial difference."

She had known him less than a year when she wrote that. How could you marry someone you'd known only a few months? Jane and Billy had known each other six years before they got married. They had first slept together, however, only a week or so after their first kiss in the snow. Billy's hair had been pure blond then and shaggy, hanging down to the frayed collars of his shirts. He hadn't grown into his height yet and his chest was a narrow, pale expanse she liked to kiss her way across, making his eyes shut and his jaw go slack. Almost any way or place she touched him (his cheek, the bony small of his back) made him first smile, then reach for her and pull her so close it was as though he were an amphibian who breathed through his skin, and she was his source of oxygen.

Neither of them had much experience with sex then. For Jane there had been the high school boyfriend in his mother's station wagon, and also a boy she'd met freshman week, a mistake, whom she passed afterward in the library or the dining hall with barely a nod of recognition. Billy was the first person who made Jane feel it was *her* body he wanted—her particular round, pink-tipped breasts to run his tongue across, her wide buttocks (which she had been embarrassed by before) to squeeze—rather than any woman's body or girl's body. He was the first person whose open eyes she looked into during orgasm, the first person who paid attention to her face when he touched her to see what made her smile or moan. It was only later, after they were engaged, that she realized (assuming things in their lives went well, that they both lived to a ripe old age and so on), she would never have this kind of sex—grown-up sex—with anybody else. She might never even see another man naked, except in the movies.

Not that she wanted to. Still, it was strange to think about it.

Things might not have turned out this way. After they graduated from college, Billy had moved to Japan to teach English in a small city two hours from Tokyo. He and Jane corresponded, but he would probably have stayed on for a second year if his mother hadn't gotten sick. Theirs might have become just a college relationship, memorable because you grew up so much in those intense years, but not much more than that. Once Billy had been in Japan for five or six months, it was hard for Jane to remember the specificity of his presence. She looked at his photograph over her desk and could see only the shapes and colors on the paper—the half moon of his hair already turning brown, the pale blue rectangle that was his shirt, his eyes dark circles surrounded by grayish rings—not the person they represented. And then there was the biology graduate student she sometimes had coffee with (though she told him she had a boyfriend, and coffee was as far as it went). By the spring, when Billy's letters arrived—long letters with detailed descriptions of the landscape—it sometimes took Jane two or three days to get around to opening them.

But Billy's mother did get sick, with metastatic breast cancer. He came home in June and spent two months watching her die, cooking for his father, sitting with his mother with the TV on, both of them pretending that they weren't thinking about her body rotting away minute by minute. He told Jane about this when he visited her, which he did every couple of weeks, spending twenty-four hours in her bed: sleeping, making love, reading. It was as though she fell in love with him all over again that summer—or not again, exactly, but anew, because Billy seemed to have become a new person. Adult, tragic. Stoical. Here she was, living essentially the same life she'd lived in college— a student life—and in the meantime Billy had penetrated another culture, been penetrated by it. Was being penetrated, now, by death.

Still, he needed her. He needed her more than he had before, to ground him. To tie him to life. And she was happy to be able to do this for him. It made her feel grown up, and necessary, and it tied *her* to life as well—life outside the library, outside the pages of books. When they made love now, it was not more passionate than it had been before, but it was somehow more serious. Billy's body had filled out—maybe that was part of it—and when he gripped her shoulders and thrust himself inside her it felt more definite, as though he had decided for sure that this was what he wanted. His certainty and his man's body, and the sense she had that he knew her better than anyone else in the world, made Jane feel as though her body was the land and he was the sun, warming and lighting her. Making her visible.

Billy's mother died at the end of July. In August Billy found a job teaching at a local prep school and moved in with Jane. A year later they were married. How foreign it all would have seemed to Masha, who had married early, had a clutch of children all in a rush, and died when she was barely thirty-five.

"Oh," Sigelman said now in Jane's brand-new office, waving his pipe in the air. "I wouldn't overrate Maria Petrovna's influence. Karkov was a great man! Great men manage to make their genius known, whatever the circumstances."

Old, hairy, yellowed and bent with age, he eyed Jane malignly, fitting his pipe between his teeth. It was hard not to think he was talking about himself.

There was a story about Sigelman that went around the department. It was told to Jane first and most memorably by a graduate student named Felicia Noone, a tall young woman with a long nose, bright green eyes, a cascade of curly reddish gold hair, and the awkward long-legged grace of a flamingo. Felicia had stopped by early in the semester to introduce herself and to invite Jane to join SLAV, the Slavic Ladies Association for Vice—a drinking group made up of Felicia and the other women graduate students in the department. Felicia sat in Jane's office in an oversize Wisconsin Badgers football jersey, her long thin legs crossed in faded jeans, and told Jane how, when he was teaching, Sigelman used to swear all the time in his lectures.

"It was 'hell' this and 'fuck' that, every other minute," Felicia said. "And then one day a student, this girl from some small town upstate, raised her hand. 'Professor Sigelman,' she said. 'I'm not used to hearing that kind of language. I'd appreciate it if you didn't use those words.'"

Felicia paused. She wasn't pretty, but there was something compelling about her, a showy sensuality that made people look twice. Jane was the newest hotshot in Slavics, and Felicia clearly had her sights on her for a dissertation adviser. She leaned forward and rested her elbows on Jane's desk before going on.

"So Sigelman says, 'What? Not used to it? Not used to the word *fuck*? Well, fuck, fuck, fuck, fuck, fuck, fuck, fuck! There. Now you're used to it!'" Felicia leaned back in her chair and laughed, her many mismatched earrings catching the light, shattering it into shards across the walls.

Jane couldn't help smiling.

CHAPTER THREE

ON TUESDAY Jane missed the 5:03 bus because a student stopped her in the hall with a question. When she got home (twenty-two minutes late), Maisie and Elise, the babysitter, were sitting on the floor in the tumbled living room coloring on scrap paper as the sallow light faded. Elise was a pleasant, spacey, even-tempered twenty-something who had worked for one of Jane's colleagues the year before. Getting her had been a great piece of luck. If Maisie regarded Elise at first with narrowed, suspicious eyes, Elise did not appear to mind. She approached Maisie with a careless toss of her long hair, a casual smile, and a dirty canvas bag filled with coloring books and plastic beads. Jane loved the way Elise seemed to feel so comfortable in her own pale, plump skin, the way she loved to build cities and zoos out of blocks, and how readily she laughed. The way she was with Maisie was the way Jane would have liked to be.

Almost two years old now, Maisie had developed into a dramatic, mercurial girl who liked to dance and to wear dress-up clothes, and who was happiest when everyone was looking at her. She could be dazzling when she was in a sunny mood, with her big brown eyes and golden-brown curls and her obvious delight in human interaction—making faces, playing clapping games, singing "The Wheels on the Bus." She could also throw impressive tantrums when she didn't get her way. She liked books, the square cardboard kind with bright pictures, and though she preferred to have them read to her, she would also sometimes sit with a stack of them, turning the frayed pages slowly and babbling to herself as though she were reading, which never failed to please Jane—perhaps inordinately. Jane, who had spent most of her childhood curled up with a book in her closet or behind the jasmine bush in the yard—the places she was least likely to be interrupted—worried about what it meant when a child needed so much adult attention. Was it just the way Maisie had been born? Or could she tell how short her mother's patience was for peekaboo or games of pretend, and was she always therefore in need of reassurance that Jane loved her—reassurance in the form of Jane's undivided attention? Was Jane spoiling her by giving in to her demands, or was she making her insecure by too often and eagerly turning away? Sometimes Jane thought one thing, sometimes the other.

Tonight crayons were scattered all over the floor along with discarded drawings, books, dolls, Legos, plastic dinosaurs, Cheerios, and sticky crumbs of toast. The blue rug was covered with fish of all sizes and colors, cut out of construction paper. Maisie, wearing silky yellow pajama bottoms and wrapped in a spangled scarf, wriggled among them giggling wildly while Elise, wearing a Greek fisherman's cap that had once belonged to Billy's father, stood over her with a string tied to a long Tinkertoy pole, casting. Every evening it was the same, Jane's first glimpse of her daughter going straight to her heart like an explosion, and then the painful process of moving from one self to another, from professor to mother, like a silvery fish heaving itself onto land to become a frog.

When she heard the door open, Maisie looked up, registered Jane's presence, and rolled onto her back, arms and legs flailing ecstatically. "Mama! Mama!" she cried. Jane stepped out of her boots, dropped her bag, and picked the squirming child up. Nine and a half hours was too much time apart. She held Maisie close, absorbing the sweet animal presence of her, and Maisie pressed her face violently, passionately, into Jane's collar in return. She smelled of peanut butter and crayons. Jane kissed her sticky cheek, and Maisie curled up into a ball in Jane's arms like a satisfied cat, the long scarf slipping off to reveal the T-shirt Billy had given her, sky blue with the Japanese character for "happiness" on it.

"Sorry I'm late," she said to Elise. "I missed the bus."

"That's all right," Elise said, but she already had the fisherman's hat off and her jacket on. "Bye, Maisie!" she said.

"Let's wave," Jane said as Elise went out the door and down the warped front steps. "Elise will be back in the morning."

"Lise!" Maisie cried, wanting the sitter now as passionately as she had wanted her mother the moment before. She wanted everyone she loved with her always; who could blame her for that?

When Elise could no longer be seen through the window, Jane carried Maisie into the kitchen. It was getting late and Jane was hungry, and she needed five minutes to get dinner together. "You play with these things, okay?" She knelt down and tried to disentangle Maisie, to distract her with the pot lids and cake pans in the bottom drawer.

Maisie clung harder. Her sharp fingernails dug into Jane's arm. "Mommy uppy!" she said.

"Yes," Jane said, "Mommy's giving you uppy. But I need to put you down so I can make dinner."

Maisie pulled at Jane's sweater and burrowed her head into Jane's neck. "Mommy uppy," she insisted.

It was hard not to want Maisie to act less like a two-year-old sometimes. Jane lugged her back out into the living room and shook her off onto the couch, where she lay on her back with her thumb in her mouth while Jane turned on the TV.

Back in the kitchen, Jane filled a pot at the sink and set it to boil for spaghetti. She chopped and sautéed an onion, added a jar of tomato sauce. The room was drafty, dingy. One of the bulbs in the ceiling fixture had gone out and the wan, watery, grayish-yellow light made the scarred countertops and scalloped curtains and striped wallpaper look tired and moribund. Once Jane had enjoyed cooking. Now they ate pasta, sandwiches, fried eggs, canned soup. There was something mean and paltry about a life of pasta and sauce out of a jar. It wasn't the kind of life Jane wanted.

The front door opened and Billy called, "Hello!"

"Hello!" Jane called back. She took out the lettuce and found the bag half-full of damp, brown liquid. The refrigerator was like a marsh, pungent with pockets of moisture and unexpected flora.

"Hello there," came a loud familiar voice. "You like cartoons, do you?"

Billy must have brought Vince Steadman with him. Vince was a friend of a friend of Billy's. He'd gone to UW law school ten years earlier and now worked for the university, and Jane and Billy had seen him several times since they'd moved to Madison. He was a big man with black curly hair and a black beard. Divorced, no kids. Jane dumped the spaghetti into the pot, set the timer, and went out into the front hall where Maisie, all smiles now, was perched in Vince's arms.

"Hello, Jane," Vince said.

"Hello, Vince." Jane turned off the television. She was embarrassed by the dirty, chaotic room, the child parked in front of *Arthur*. Why hadn't Billy called to warn her he was bringing someone home? He kissed her and she pecked him back, then, contrite, put her arms around him and gave him a better kiss.

"I invited Vince for dinner," Billy said.

"It's only pasta," Jane said.

Vince bounced Maisie in his arms. "Hey!" He opened his eyes wide. "What's this?" He pulled a penny out of her ear. "Oh my, my goodness! Did you know this was there?" he asked her, astonished.

Maisie grinned. "Again," she said.

Vince Steadman took a penny out of her other ear. Maisie squealed with delight, her shiny curls bouncing and her wide brown eyes lit up. You would have thought she was the easiest child in the world.

"Dinner will be ready in a minute," Jane said, tossing toys into milk crates, turning on lamps.

"Great," Vince said. "I'm hungry! Are you hungry, Maisie?"

"Hungry," Maisie agreed.

"You don't mind my holding on to her, do you?" he asked Jane.

"Of course not," Jane said. "Keep her. Take her home with you!"

"Would you like to come home with me?" he asked Maisie. "See my house? My kitchen? My tropical fish?"

"One fish, two fish," Maisie said, knowledgeably.

The timer rang.

"That's the spaghetti," Jane said.

"I'll get it," Billy said, but Jane was already halfway to the kitchen. She dumped the pot out into the colander and boiling water splashed onto her arm.

"Fuck," she said, and thought of Sigelman as she grabbed a piece of ice to hold against the burn.

Over dinner Billy and Vince exchanged law school gossip. "I'm not ambitious like Billy," Vince told Jane, refilling his own wineglass. "I'm not out to save the world."

Billy smiled. "I don't want to save the world," he said. "Just enforce a couple of reasonable regulations." He planned to be an environmental lawyer, maybe work for a nonprofit.

"Sue the pants off a big polluter or two," Vince said.

"Pants!" Maisie said, banging her spoon on her high-chair tray.

"She doesn't miss a trick," Vince said.

"We think she's brilliant, of course," Billy said half jokingly. "She knows what a burro says and a snow monkey and a giant squid."

"What does a giant squid say, Maisie?" Vince asked.

Maisie wiggled her arms and legs the way Billy had taught her and made choked glugging noises. Vince laughed. Maisie crowed with pride and began going through her repertoire: polar bear, squirrel, hummingbird. It was hard to tell what they were unless you already knew, but Vince applauded each one. Maisie was in heaven. She banged her spoon on the high-chair tray, and it slipped out of her fingers, bouncing away and landing on the floor, bits of gooey starch flying everywhere.

"Oops!" Vince said. "Very messy!"

"Oops!" Maisie echoed, delighted, and brushed both arms across her tray, sweeping what was left of her dinner to the ground to please him further.

She could clean up the mess, Jane thought, or she could ask Billy to do it. Or she could wait and see if he thought of doing it himself. She thought of Masha always entertaining Grigory's guests: local farmers and travelers; his mother and siblings, of course, who came to stay for months at a time; but also distant cousins; and young acolytes who sought him out in threadbare coats, their apprentice stories clutched under their arms. Karkov didn't encourage them, but they wouldn't leave of their own accord, either. Masha had to beg him to send them away.

"Billy," Jane said, "your daughter needs a bath!" There was so much to be got through tonight before she could get back to her desk: the dinner dishes, Maisie's bath, the struggle over the soap. Pajamas, toothbrush, story, night-light, the door open not too much but not too little.

"Thanks for dinner," Vince said, appearing to take the hint. But when Jane came out of the kitchen ten minutes later, Vince and Billy were still talking.

"Billy," Jane said, "do you want me to give Maisie her bath?"

"No, no," Billy said. "I'm happy to do it."

Why did he sound like he was doing her a favor?

Billy took Maisie out of her chair, excused himself, and carried her upstairs, but still Vince Steadman didn't go.

"That's a terrific little girl you've got there," he told Jane. "Bright and beautiful. She's going to be a stunner."

"We like her," Jane said. She was trying to hold on. It would be ridiculous to fall apart now, when he was almost out the door.

"I mean it. She's really great. I don't know how you can bear to leave her and go to work in the mornings."

"Yes," Jane agreed. "Mornings are tough."

"No, really," Vince said seriously. "If I were you, I'd quit my job and stay home with her."

Jane kept on smiling. "Somebody has to make a living," she said.

He laughed. "Right," he said. "Absolutely."

When he was finally gone, Jane went into the kitchen and tried to do the dishes. Instead she stood before the running water, shaking with rage. She thought about the recent letter from her father, who had lived in Hong Kong since Jane was fifteen and with whom she'd maintained a steady paper-and-pen correspondence. In the letter, inquiring about Jane's job, he had described his own first semester of teaching, at UC Santa Cruz in 1966 before Jane was born. "On the weekends we, the junior faculty and their wives, had little dinner parties," he wrote.

I remember walking home from campus in the evenings, feeling how lucky I was to be embarked on my career. Your mother, I think, was happy, too, having a garden that bloomed year-round and a baby (your brother) on the way. Despite how things turned out for your mother and me, and despite all the hard work, I recall those Santa Cruz years as some of the happiest of my life.

When Jane climbed into bed, Billy was reading. "Is the child asleep?" he asked.

"Yes."

"I would have put her to bed."

"It was my night." Jane switched off her light.

Billy put down his book and switched off his light, too.

"You can keep reading," Jane said. "It won't bother me."

"That's okay," Billy said.

They lay there, both of them wide awake in the dark. After a while Billy moved closer to Jane and kissed her. Jane knew these kisses: rafts launched across a river. It wasn't passion that fathered them but a desire to have things be all right between them; but things weren't all right. She was rigid with anger, and when he touched her his hands registered only dimly, like the glow of lights from a distant neighborhood.

Sometimes it seemed to Jane that Billy and Maisie were always reaching for her body, as though they thought she was a tree laden with fruit. Didn't he know how early she had to get up in the morning?

When had she started counting hours of sleep as more valuable than sex? When she had to talk coherently and engagingly to a room full of bored-looking undergraduates first thing in the morning, that was when. Outlining the lectures was the kind of labor she was used to, but delivering them was something else. It was like swimming: exhilarating, exhausting. It left her breathless, her limbs rubbery, sweat trickling under her clothes. What had the university been thinking of, hiring her to do this? They'd tossed her into the classroom the way children used to be tossed into the pool to teach them to swim. She'd thought her knowledge and her confidence, her passion about the work, would get her through, but it seemed something different was required.

"Why did you invite Vince for dinner?" she said, trying to speak neutrally but hearing the knife edge under the words.

Billy sighed. "I don't know, Jane," he said. "I like him. I thought you liked him."

"I like him fine," Jane said. "That's not the point."

"I'm sorry it didn't work out," Billy said.

He turned over and lay still, either asleep or pretending to sleep. Jane squeezed her eyes shut, squeezed her hands into fists. How could you fight with someone who wouldn't fight back? Or who fought back only with apologies and silence. How did people like Billy survive their lives, pressing everything down, holding it in — anger, frustration, irritation, and fear compressed like compacted garbage?

She got out of the bed.

It was cold in the house, cold in her study. Boxes were still stacked against the wall under the window. She opened one and took out a pile of books, looking for her English copy of *Dmitri Arkadyevich*, which she needed to reread for her survey course in nineteenth-century Russian literature. She found it near the top, a tattered paperback poorly repaired with masking tape. The margins were penciled with notes, question marks, and scribbles, many of which she could no longer decipher. Some of the interior pages were coming loose.

Jane opened it at random.

Mitya was on the train, on his way home to Moscow after living abroad for years. A group of men was joking with him in the dining car, telling him how he would hardly recognize his country anymore, teasing him for speaking Russian with a French accent: "We may not have the fine wines you have grown used to in foreign lands, or the witty conversation," one of them said. "But the girls! In Russia, the young girls are still as sweet and innocent as a breeze from the countryside. That's what a young man needs—a fresh Russian flower to take to his breast."

How Mitya had blushed, hearing that. How he had promised himself such a wife to make up for the long, lonely years of exile. Though of course he would find himself, a couple of hundred pages later, with a different kind of wife entirely. Jane thought of her conversation with Sigelman, how she had told him that she believed Karkov had married Masha for her intelligence. Was there a day when the reasons you'd married someone became precisely the things about them you couldn't stand? She was thinking of Billy's scrupulousness, his patience, his glacial calm in the face of a flat tire or a screaming child or a geographical upheaval, or even a death.

She turned some pages.

But try as he might, Mitya could not get his mind to focus. The more he tried to concentrate, the more his mind seemed to rise up free from his body and roam about the house. Here was his old aunt in her sitting room by the fire with her icons and her broderie anglaise. Here was the cook, half drunk in the kitchen,

plucking geese. Here were the sleeping dogs, paws twitching, in their warm kennels. And here at last (although he wished mightily to avoid the sight of her) was his wife, Olga Petrovna, sitting alone in her chilly bedchamber before the mirror, her lovely eyes—brilliant as sapphires—regarding their own reflection in the cold glass. Here she was, the woman to whom he had bound himself for life in the heat of a passion he understood now to have been a kind of conjurer's trick. What he had taken for love was an illusion, an empty bubble. A deceit foisted on him by the devil, or by the ice-woman herself—it scarcely mattered which. For him, they had long since become interchangeable.

Jane tucked her freezing feet up under her, her heart aching. She had forgotten this, the stark horror of Mitya's agony, which grew worse as his lust for his wife ballooned even as he came to despise her. She was stupid and petty, jealous and cold. She took lovers under his own roof; she frittered away his money; she bore him no heirs. And yet Karkov had created Olga Petrovna so that she shared his own wife's looks, her age and upbringing, even her patronymic. Could Grigory really have seen Masha that way, as a woman of ice?

She pictured Masha with her lovely oval face and her thick hair, sailing through the big house like a ship, her gold rings glinting. This was the woman she had grown into after the hard early years had toughened her. What was Jane growing into? She didn't want Masha's life: deeply domestic, circumscribed by children and meals and sewing and visitors. She refused such a life, she refused to be Masha—but all the same she envied her energy, her good humor, her patience and calm.

She turned the page. Here was the scene in which Sasha, the young girl Mitya falls in love with late in the story and tries to seduce, is walking out into the meadow on a summer morning. It was a passage Jane knew she must have read before (although it was unmarked by her pencil), but time had wiped it from her memory:

As Sasha walked through the long grass that by afternoon would have fallen to the peasants' scythes, she felt a great calmness descend over her. The wind shook the branches of the young apple trees, which looked like goat kids shaking the buds of new horns. The brook, swollen with rain, surged over the rocks, and Sasha, with the beginnings of a new life inside her, listened to it, sensing instinctively, in the way of women, her kinship with the world—the brook and the apple trees, the lark in her nest, the flowers in the grass that would soon be gone. She could not have put this feeling into words but sensed it as a rightness. She saw clearly her role in the scheme of life—wife, mother, mistress of the household, child of God—and that deep, unconscious knowledge was like a wellspring, filling her with joy.

Jane could not believe it. She read the passage over again, and then she read it a third time. Then she got up and rooted through her boxes until she found her copy of Masha's published diaries. There it was, more or less as she had remembered it, the passage Jane had quoted to Billy that first night in Madison, sitting on the back steps:

We walked in the meadow through the long grass that would soon fall to the peasants' scythes, and a great calmness descended over us. The trees shook their leaves like young goats shaking the buds of their new horns—and the river surged over the rocks—and I felt that I myself was a river, with life surging through me. Inside the house the million details—the clothes to be sewn, the meals to be ordered, the accounts to be sorted out, Vera Alexandrovna's temper to be soothed, and always at the end of a long day Grisha's scribbles waiting to be deciphered, interpreted, and copied—buzz around me like wasps. But out in the air I am calmer—I am myself. I seem to see clearly my role in the scheme of life—mother to my children, mistress of my household, and, above all, child of God. And I feel able to do what is required of me with joy.

Jane's eyes moved back and forth from the novel to the diary and back again, translating, comparing. Masha hadn't worked on *Dmitri Arkadyevich* with her husband. It had been copied by Anton Bek, the gray-eyed peasant boy Karkov had plucked from the fields when he found out how well he could read and write. Masha hadn't seen so much as a draft of it until it was published. Karkov could have talked to her about what she had thought and felt, except that Jane was quite certain they were not, at that point in their marriage, having that kind of intimate conversation. The only alternative was that he had read Masha's diary—read it and stolen what he had found there! Tolstoy was known to have mined Sofya Andreyevna's diaries, but for content only, as far as Jane knew; he hadn't lifted whole sentences practically verbatim. She remembered what Sigelman had said: "I wouldn't overrate her influence." What would Sigelman—what would Shombauer—say to this?

The moon rose and the house grew colder. How must Masha have felt when she found out? Jane thought of all the ways Karkov had used his wife—all the ways men had used women for centuries: for sex, for meals, for clothing, to take care of relatives and visitors. The world *had* changed a great deal, thank god, even if it still had a long way to go.

Something startled her then—a sound that she could not at once place. It was a kind of bleat from behind her that, turning, she realized was Maisie in her room across the hall. She looked at the clock and saw that it was almost one. It was cold and still in the study, dark except for the pool of lamplight on the desk. Maisie bleated again, softly. Jane switched off the lamp and went to stand beside her door. She turned the knob and crept into the room where the girl lay with her eyes shut, squirming, her bottom in the air. Jane resettled the blanket and stroked the warm bird-boned back. She could feel the rigid muscles relax under her hand. Maisie turned onto her side and clutched her stuffed duck, her knees tucked up to her chin and her hair splayed across her face. She was so perfect, Jane thought, when she was sleeping.

CHAPTER FOUR

OVER THE NEXT few weeks, Jane used what scraps of time she could scrounge to look for more concurrences between Masha's diaries and Karkov's novels. It was late November and freezing cold, though it hadn't snowed much. The grass lay brown and shriveled along the pitted sidewalks, and ice crept slowly out across the lakes. In Jane and Billy's house the storm windows rattled in their frames. Through them they could see the narrow yard, the chain-link fence lined with frosted arborvitae, and the cold black stone of the Moravian church beyond.

Jane read and reread the slim published volume of Masha's diary excerpts, as well as the printouts of the passages she had typed into her laptop when she'd been doing her dissertation research. She finished *Dmitri Arkadyevich*, trying to keep Masha's words in her head as she read, but nothing jumped out. She began to doubt she'd found anything in the first place and had to go back several times and look at the concurrent passages side by side. Whenever she had the words laid out in front of her like that, the excitement returned and she felt sure she couldn't have stumbled on a single instance of something, nor some random accident or illusion of translation. (She'd looked up the passage from the novel in the original Russian to make sure.) But by the next day, the uncertainty would be back.

There was no time to reread any of Karkov's other books. The end-of-semester push was on for both Jane and Billy, and on top of that, Maisie was having trouble sleeping. It seemed to have started suddenly, but maybe it wasn't really sudden. Maybe it had been coming on for weeks. In retrospect the somnolent whimperings and the extended bedtime rituals—the repeated, plaintive calls for more kisses, for forgotten stuffed animals, for the exorcism of shadowy monsters behind the door—were perhaps not events in themselves but coming attractions for the horror movie that was playing now.

Now Maisie was up two or three times a night and sometimes more. It was like having an infant again, the upstairs hallway a nightmare path more familiar in the dark than in daylight, buzzing with dream fragments and the endless refrains of recorded lullabies. Jane and Billy were beyond tired: they were exhausted, haggard, fuddled with fatigue. Falling behind in her work, Jane worried about tenure, even though she wouldn't be up for it for years. Still, what if she had moved her family halfway across the country only to fail them? What if they had to pick up and move all over again? She pictured herself at some third-rate university in Tuscaloosa or Albert Lea, teaching four preparations a semester. She could see the sparse, understaffed library, smell the odor of low standards and mimeograph machines. Otto Sigelman stopped by to smoke his pipe in Jane's office now and then, and he seldom failed to make some sly, gleeful comment about new hires who lost focus and failed to make the grade.

"A couple of years ago we had an assistant professor, Sarah Darling," Sigelman said one afternoon, crossing one stumpy leg comfortably over the other, his thin gray hair sticking out in all directions the way Maisie's did first thing in the morning. "Very serious girl. Very hardworking, though I personally didn't think she was too smart, Princeton or no Princeton. Short hair—cut like a man's, you know—and lots of earrings, everywhere. Not just in her ears either, from what I understand." Sigelman paused to suck on his pipe and squint nearsightedly at Jane, who kept her expression carefully neutral.

"The students fawned on her, as you might expect. The girl students worshipped her and the boy students wanted to fuck her. Well, maybe the girl students wanted to fuck her, too, who's to say, and as it turns out they would have had a better shot at it—ha! At least until poor Sarah fell in love with a theater professor from Superior. Superior—can you imagine! She didn't even teach drama, this northern love goddess. She taught *acting*. As though anyone attending UW Superior could have the slightest chance of success as an actor!"

Here Jane could not resist interrupting, "Didn't Arnold Schwarzenegger go to UW Superior? Or was it Stevens Point? You'd have to admit he's *somewhat successful*."

Sigelman lowered his scraggly eyebrows. "If by successful you mean wealthy," he said, "I wonder how you rate your chances of success in any field."

"When and if I become a full professor, I expect to be able to afford a decent car," Jane replied, but Sigelman ignored her.

"Poor Sarah Darling," he continued. "She started spending all her time on Interstate 94 and, of course, in bed, rather than doing her job. In what morsels of time she had left over, she was writing a book, a study of images of women. By which she meant body parts. Breasts and vaginas as seen in, I don't know, flowers, teacups. Snowdrifts. That kind of crap. Of all people she picked me to show it to! She wanted my advice."

"Which was?" Jane asked. She looked up at the clock on the wall, wondering how long Sigelman was planning to stay. His pipe was almost out, but sometimes he didn't notice.

"I told her it scarcely mattered that the windows didn't open up here on the fourteenth floor, because she had already as good as committed suicide!" Sigelman's face lit up at the wit of his own remark, his eyes glowing with malicious light. Then he took his pipe out of his teeth, frowned, dumped it out into the teacup he'd placed in readiness on Jane's desk, and began to fill the bowl with fresh tobacco. "You didn't like my story," he said, glancing up at her.

"Oh, was I supposed to like it?"

"You're not an idiot," Sigelman told her. "That's a compliment! You just need to work on a thing or two."

"You mean, like my sense of humor?"

Sigelman coughed and spat into his dirty handkerchief. Outside the window the sky was already growing dim. Lights were coming on in the concrete and brick buildings spread out below. Cars crept by on University Avenue, headlights sallow in the afternoon gloom. "Maybe you missed the point of the story," he said. "The point is—"

"I know what the point is," Jane said.

"The point," Sigelman said, "is that nineteenth-century literature was written by men, mostly about men, and largely for an audience of men."

"And that anyone who disagrees with you is by definition a fool," Jane added.

Sigelman smiled his ugly smile. "Poor Sarah," he said again. "She was a nice girl, really. And not unattractive. A love affair of that kind is almost never a good idea for a young scholar. Sex itself, of course, can loosen the body and focus the mind. I personally have found frequent sex to be conducive to some of my best work."

"Are you making an offer, Otto," Jane said lightly, "or just trying to see if you can make me uncomfortable?"

Sigelman laughed.

Despite all the things that were distasteful about him, Jane liked Sigelman. The way he talked was a knife stuck in the balloon of academic-speak, and keeping up with him conversationally was exhilarating. Her other colleagues were pleasant enough and not unfriendly, but the truth was they bored her a little with their gossip and their chatter about conference hotels and their children's soccer leagues. As though determined to convey that they were just ordinary people despite their Ph.D.s, they seldom talked about literature. Jane preferred Sigelman, cranky as he was, who (when he wasn't indulging in cautionary tales) would talk about *The Lime Trees* or *Dmitri Arkadyevich* for an hour or more, sucking on his pipe, his eyes moistening, as though the characters were old friends from better days. Sigelman, who was almost never boring.

"Yes, sex is all right," he said again. "It's love you have to watch out for. Obsessive love. You're probably safe, though, I'd guess. Happily married how long now? Four, five years? Long enough for the dullness to set in."

Jane didn't answer. *The dullness,* she thought. It sounded dire and inescapable, like the scurvy, or the change.

"If you're going to be obsessive about anything, it had better be your work," Sigelman advised. "That's the most rewarding thing, anyway."

"What are you working on, Otto?" Jane asked, quite ready to change the subject.

"I'm pursuing an idea or two," he answered vaguely, running a hand across his brown scalp. "Of course, what one wishes for at this point is new material. The archive at Pushkinskii dom, the Leninka, the Newberry, the Beinecke (not the same, of course, since Alexis died)—everyone's been through them all. Everyone scrabbling like dogs over the same old bones! Still, Stephen Olen will die one day." Stephen Olen was the grandson of Grigory and Masha's son Konstantin, the one who had married the American diplomat's daughter and smuggled his father's papers out of the country.

"What about Galina Pisareva?" Jane asked.

Sigelman waved the name away. "She's got nothing," he said. "I should know."

He clearly wanted her to ask about this, so Jane let it pass. "But you think Olen might have some papers of interest? I thought the family had donated everything long ago."

"I'm willing to bet he does," Sigelman said with a cold voracity, his blue eyes glinting like chips of ice. "Difficult to know for certain as you can hardly get a civil word out of the man. Still, I hear his health is poor."

Jane sat up straighter, bothered by this remark as she had not been by his misogyny or his attempts to shock her. She wondered suddenly if she had underestimated him.

"So, Sarah Darling didn't get tenure?" she said, rearranging some papers on her desk, trying to convey the air of someone with much to do, which she certainly was.

"Well, it was a close thing," Sigelman said. "In the end the department decided not to recommend her by just one vote." He held up his stubby forefinger, its horny nail cut short and blunt like the butt of an ax, to show her: one.

That night Billy had a late review session and didn't come home for dinner, and after the review session he called to say he was going out for a beer with a couple of other students. After she put Maisie to bed, Jane began rereading *War and Peace*, which she would be teaching the following week. She loved Tolstoy, but she also resisted her own feelings of admiration, resenting the way he'd had the world at his feet while Karkov—admittedly not quite as talented—had always gotten so much less attention than he deserved.

Tonight, though, it was hard to concentrate. She found herself feeling about the book the way so many of her students did: nine hundred thirty-six pages! How was she supposed to get through all of *that*? It was unbelievable how much time and energy teaching, and the preparation for teaching, required. Certainly it was satisfying work some of the time, but it wasn't where her heart lay. She longed for the Christmas break when she could finally get down to Chicago, get her hands on the actual volumes of Masha's diaries. It was hard not to daydream about what she might find there: evidence of suicide, or more passages that Karkov had stolen, or who knew what? If nothing else, Jane had an idea for an article about images of nature in Masha's writing and how her descriptions of animals (birds, snakes, deer, mice) reflected the place of women in nineteenth-century Russian society. "The Bird in the Nest" she could call it. There were a few passages in the published excerpts and in her notes she could use, but there was no substitute for concentrated work at the archive itself.

The moment Billy walked in the door Jane said, "I'm thinking about going down to Chicago for a few days during the winter break!" As soon as the words were out of her mouth, she knew they had been the wrong ones. Why hadn't she said hello first? Why hadn't she gotten up from the couch and kissed him? "Hello," she said belatedly. "Did you get a lot done tonight?"

This, too, seemed wrong, implying that it was only all right for him to be gone all evening if he had used his time productively. (But if she'd asked, instead, "Did you have fun?" wouldn't that have been just as bad, suggesting he was out pleasing himself while she was at home stuck with the household drudgery?)

He looked at her sharply. Or maybe the look wasn't really sharp but only seemed so. It was five degrees outside and he had walked up from the bus stop, so his face wasn't as mobile as usual: maybe that was all it was. His face was changing as he approached thirty, thinning out so you could see the structure of it, the bones asserting themselves beneath the flesh.

"Speaking of the break," he said, "I'm going to do a three-week internship at this environmental law firm. Vince introduced me to one of the partners."

"Oh!" Jane said. "That's great!"

A dream seemed to have found Maisie. There was a repeated nightmare in which a tiger (Maisie pronounced it "tigow") played a starring role, and also a box, though Jane could never get any clear idea what kind of box it was.

"Do you think it's a big box?" she asked Billy. "Open or closed?" They were in bed, reading for a few minutes before they slept. That was all they did in bed, lately: read and sleep.

"What difference does it make?" Billy said.

The brown reed shades moved noticeably as cold air seeped in around the windows. Cobwebs hung from the corners of the ceiling, and the heavy secondhand oak bureau listed on the warped floor. In the distance a train whistled.

"I'm just wondering," Jane said. "What do you think she's actually frightened of? Monsters? Ghosts?" Did Maisie know about ghosts yet?

"She's frightened of the tiger and the box," Billy said. He turned a page of his magazine, his voice strained with the effort of patience.

"But what do they *mean*?" Jane persisted. "What do they signify?" Stop talking, she told herself. Just close your mouth.

"Jane," Billy said. "It's not a literary dream. It's just a plain old nightmare." He tossed the magazine on the floor and switched off the light.

The moaning and the rattling grew louder as Maisie, like a hiker with a bell traversing bear-infested woods, tried to ward off the dangers lurking behind the trees. The fiery-eyed dream tiger and the mysterious, implacable box.

Jane threw back the covers to get up.

Billy reached out and held on to her arm. It might have been the first time he'd touched her all day, and she found to her distress that her instinct was to flinch.

"This is insane!" he said. "She needs to go to sleep!"

"She can't sleep!" Jane said. "She's afraid."

She got up and pulled her bathrobe around her as she strode down the hall. The cold floor squeaked under her bare feet, like ice getting ready to crack. Jane lifted Maisie out of the bed. "*Sshh,*" she said. "Mommy's here."

"Tigow, tigow!" Maisie cried. Tears streamed down her face.

Jane sat in the rocking chair and held Maisie close. What was wrong with Billy? What cold chunk of adamant had lodged in his chest where his heart used to be? "*Sshh,* sweetheart," she said. "There's no tiger."

"Tigow," Maisie said, pitifully.

"No, no tigows," Jane said.

"Not *tigow*!" Maisie wailed. "Tigow! Tigow!"

"Tiger," Jane said.

"Wight." Maisie sank like a rag doll against Jane's chest, a mollified god.

Jane had lunch at a coffee shop on State Street with Felicia Noone to discuss Felicia's thesis, which Jane had agreed to supervise. "But you can't cover all Karkov's female characters," Jane warned when Felicia sketched out her ideas, heavily influenced by Heldt, about how women in Karkov were idealized and demonized simultaneously. "Why don't you focus on three or four?" She envied Felicia, who, like Sigelman, could spend every moment on her work if she wanted to. Not that she did want to. She had other ways of spending her time. Sometimes Jane wanted to take her by the shoulders and shake her. She remembered how, when she was pregnant, hours would slip away while she dozed in a hard chair in the stifling library or stared at the computer screen, unable to bring her mind to bear on the words floating there like foam on the surface of the ocean. How terrible it had been—time lying all around her and she unable to gather it up, to make it hers, to put it to any decent use! Time like fruit left rotting on the vine.

"It's so hard to choose," Felicia complained loudly, meaning among Karkov's heroines. "I always want all the ice-cream flavors. All the lipstick colors." She wore a black leather miniskirt over gold lamé leggings, a tight black sweater without a bra, combat boots. Her lipstick was a dark bluish purple, the color of a bruise.

Jane laughed. "That's why I don't wear lipstick. It saves energy choosing."

"Yes." Felicia smiled slyly. "But I can see you want everything, too. Kids, husband, career. The whole superwoman thing."

Jane took a bite of her sandwich. "Think about Maria Karkova," she said. "She did twice as much as I do, and she was pregnant the whole time she was doing it. Pregnancy," she went on, "is like spending nine months with a chloroform handkerchief in front of your face."

Felicia laughed.

"Six children," Jane said. "Just think about it!" She wondered what Masha would make of contemporary women with their skimpy clothes and their extraordinary freedoms. Who would she be more like if she lived today and had today's choices—Jane, with her tailored slacks and her tight schedules and her fidelity, or Felicia?

Felicia shrugged. "Everyone did it in those days. Even the Snake Woman had five."

"The Snake Woman is a character in a book," Jane said.

"So's Karkova," Felicia replied.

"She was a real person."

"Sure. But we only know about her through books. Her diaries aren't objective."

Jane knew this, of course. Furthermore, because Karkov showed his characters from the outside and the inside, coherently, with an awareness of audience, there was a sense in which his fictional women would always seem more real than Masha. Masha's diaries were rich, tangled, private, sometimes cryptic. They were a jumble of fragments, like a box full of shards of colored glass that were supposed to make up a mosaic. How much of a sense of a person could you get from that?

And yet Jane felt she had a strong picture. There were early photographs of Masha looking solemn, her hair pinned up and her oval face dusky, eyes looking directly into the camera: curious, lively. Jane could picture her striding through the meadow along the river, her hair coming loose from the tight bun, a child holding each hand and more children trailing behind. "Look," she'd say, pointing out a moorhen's nest she'd spotted, eight perfect eggs nestled inside, pale buff with darker brown speckles. She'd tell the children about the habits of the moorhen, what it made its nest out of and how it found its food.

Jane could picture Grigory almost as clearly, tall and thin as a knife, black hair gleaming, white, strong teeth gleaming, too, when he spoke. "I'm going out," he'd say, or: "Keep the children quiet—I'm working."

Felicia finished her extra-tall chai and stood up. She seemed to take up a lot of room in the narrow coffee shop, and Jane was aware of eyes turning toward her. "I have to go by my place and feed the snake," she said. "Want to come? My car's just around the corner."

"You have a snake?"

Felicia smiled. Her strong white teeth gleamed like the snow that was just beginning to fall in fat wet flakes outside the window, leaving dark splotches on the frozen streets. "I was in the pet store, and they had this python. I was thinking about the Snake Woman. I thought maybe, if I had my own snake, I could understand her better. Get inside her head."

"Karkov didn't have a snake," Jane said. "He just made it up."

Felicia hiked her big red leather purse higher onto her shoulder. "I know," she said.

Jane pulled her coat on and followed Felicia out onto the sidewalk.

Felicia's car was actually parked about eight blocks away. Jane wrapped her scarf around her head and leaned into the wind all the way up Gorham Street while dead leaves and bits of litter skittered down the pavement. Snow whipped around them as they walked, settled in their hair and on their sleeves, insinuated itself damply under their collars. The sky lowered, yellowish gray, and the air smelled of car exhaust and lake ice. Jane had never seen a big snake close-up. When she had first read *Lady of the Snakes*, she had been appalled and fascinated by the descriptions of the serpents wrapping themselves around the heroine, coiling around her arms and through her hair. Why had Karkov chosen snakes? What had drawn him to their ominous, unblinking malevolence, their creeping silence, their quick black forked tongues? With what misogynistic malice did he imagine them into being, slithering across a woman's throat and breasts and bare belly?

Felicia stopped in front of a new bright red Celica convertible and unlocked the doors with the remote.

"This is your car?" Jane said in surprise. She put her gloved hands to her face and breathed into them, trying to thaw her cheeks. She was going to have to get a warmer coat.

"Boyfriend's. He's out of town this week." They got in and Felicia blasted the heat.

"So," Jane said. "Who is he? The boyfriend."

Felicia pulled out of the parking space and switched lanes without signaling. "His name is Douglas," she said. "He's a sound engineer. A nice-enough guy, but a little young for me."

"How young?"

"Twenty-six. I know I'm only twenty-five, but I think I need to be dating older men. Guys in their twenties don't know who they are yet. They don't know what they want."

Jane thought this was funny. But then she thought of Billy, who was only now settling into his life.

Felicia turned the wipers to high, peered through the snow. The car sped on through the slick, unfamiliar streets.

She parked in front of an old frame house on the east side. The rusting fire escapes were white where the snow had begun to stick. Jane followed her up the stairs and through a battered door into a living room furnished in familiar graduate-student style: ripped armchair, lumpy futon couch, orange crates overflowing with CDs, books everywhere. And on the floor, clothes and empty yogurt containers and diet soda cans. Chipped and mismatched dishes filled the sink beyond the breakfast bar.

"My roommate is a slob," Felicia commented, disowning responsibility. She dropped her red purse by the door and pulled a small box out of it. Something was scuffling around inside the box. Jane followed Felicia behind the couch where a long aquarium lay against the wall, hidden from view. "It's warmer back here," Felicia explained. "Snakes need to stay warm. And besides, this way Karin doesn't have to look at it."

"Karin is your roommate?"

Felicia nodded. "She had kind of a fit when I brought the snake home."

The tank, which was about four feet long and lined with newspaper, was illuminated by a large heat lamp that cast an eerie orange glow. The snake lay along one edge, doubled back on itself like a bobby pin. It was black with white blotches, as long as a person was tall and as thick around as Jane's arm. Its eyes were two eclipsed moons.

"Isn't she gorgeous?" Felicia said. "You know I have something for you, don't you, baby?" she crooned. "A nice fat rat." She laid her hand on the screen that served as the snake's roof, and the snake raised its head a fraction of an inch, its tongue flicking.

"How do you know it's a female?" Jane asked. She started to take a step forward, then changed her mind. The truth was the sight of the snake made her skin crawl. It was alive, and yet it was so dead looking, so still and cold. Its scales were rough like bark, though even a tree looked more alive, she thought, than this creature that seemed to have crawled out of the forgotten swamp of a different age. What was it doing in this shabby apartment on a freezing afternoon in Wisconsin? What would it do when it found out it didn't belong here?

"I don't, really. But I don't know that it's a male, either."

"What's its name?"

"She doesn't have one."

Like Karkov's Snake Woman.

Jane stared at the python. She thought of the Snake Woman with her basket of serpents, walking barefoot along the dirt roads from village to village, curing the sick. Sleeping in ditches. "It's not quite like having a dog, is it?" she said.

Felicia tossed her hair back over her shoulders. "Lots of people have strong reactions to her. But she's just an animal," she said.

An animal, perhaps, but an animal with a voluminous résumé. Medusa and Satan, the cobras of the Egyptian pharaohs. Cleopatra's asp. Ravenous sea serpents. The winged serpentine dragons of the Chinese dynasties.

In Russia there was a folk tradition identifying the serpent with the stovepipe of a peasant's house, connecting the inner world of the hut with the outer world of the field and forest. The snake was a guardian. It was an umbilical cord. Jane watched Felicia's python move inside its cage. The front end moved forward and the tail went back, so that it slid itself apart from two directions. "Are you going to take it out?" she asked.

"No, no," Felicia said. "Don't worry. She gets room service." She unhooked the screen. "Come here, sweetheart." She took the terrified rat out of the box and dangled it by its tail, lowering it into the tank.

The snake struck. One moment she was sliding slowly across the newspaper and the next she was in the air, the head of the rat in her jaws and three or four coils around the body, squeezing it dead.

"My god!" Jane said. "Aren't you afraid it's going to miss and get you?"

Felicia smiled.

CHAPTER FIVE

AT LAST December arrived. Christmas, with the monthlong semester break, glittered on the horizon like a mirage. Amid the blizzard of exam sessions and papers and final conferences, Jane made reservations for the three of them to go to California, where the temperature, according to the computer, was fifty-eight degrees.

Jane's mother lived in a cramped two-bedroom condo in the Berkeley Flats. The big house on Euclid Avenue with its Mission oak cabinets and Mexican tile floors had been sold long ago. Jane and Billy, Jane's mother, and Jane's brother, Davis, had their Jew's guilty Christmas dinner jammed around the kitchen table, while Maisie moved Cheerios in careful arcs around the tray of her borrowed high chair.

Two years older than his sister, Davis—now a soft-money physicist at Stanford—had always been a loner and a science geek, devoted to his chemistry set and his robots, his comic book collection. He and Jane had never been particularly close. He'd never been particularly close to anybody, as far as Jane could tell. She'd met a number of physicists over the years, and mostly they were ordinary-enough people who had girlfriends or husbands and remembered to get their hair cut. It was only her brother, it seemed, who conformed to the stereotype (though he didn't wear glasses). He lived alone in a one-bedroom apartment and he worked late a lot, but he seemed happy enough in a nerdy, low-expectations way.

"I keep thinking I should apply for a job like yours," he told Jane, mixing a thick pat of butter into his boiled potatoes. "There's zero security with soft money."

"You should," Jane said. "Absolutely."

"Only I can't see myself standing up in front of all those people and talking every day. It's kind of a drawback." He smiled the thin, dry, self-deprecating smile that always made Jane feel a pang of helpless, protective love.

"I think you'd be a good teacher, Davis," their mother said. "You're so patient."

Was she implying that Jane wasn't? Or that patience was Davis's only strength? The moment lengthened awkwardly while Davis's fork scraped across his plate and Jane wondered if everything she ever said to Maisie would, eventually, be taken as a criticism. Now, though, Maisie sat cheerfully oblivious in the high chair. She looked up from her Cheerio art and drummed her bare heels against the rungs. "Bread?" she asked, reaching out toward her grandmother and opening and shutting her dimpled hand. "Ga-ma, bread?"

Jane's mother's face lit up, and she handed Maisie a piece of bread. Davis looked at his niece as though he'd just noticed she was there, and Billy helped himself to more chicken, and Jane felt her breath move just a little more easily through her body. Maisie smiled her radiant smile and bestowed airy kisses all over the room.

The best part about the trip was the easy way things were with Billy, who joked with her mother and tickled Maisie and asked Davis surprisingly knowledgeable questions about string theory. He was good at making people comfortable. He was a good father. It was easy to forget in the roar of daily life, but out here on the edge of the continent, Jane remembered again how lucky she was to be married to him.

Christmas night, after the dishes were washed and her brother had gone home and Maisie was asleep in the port-a-crib jammed between the two twin beds, Jane said, "Next year let's just stay home for Christmas." Billy had stripped down to his boxers, and she could see the cycling muscles in his legs, the fading tan line at his bicep left over from the summer.

"Yes," he said, "that's a good idea."

"And let's get a big tree of our own. Wisconsin seems like the place to have a big Christmas tree. Maybe we could put candles on it, like they do in Scandinavia."

"Too dangerous," Billy said.

"Okay. But lights. Tinsel."

"Fine with me." He reached out and stroked her hip.

"I think we should celebrate all the holidays," Jane went on. She touched his chest, took her hand away. Put it back. "I don't think we've been doing enough celebrating."

"Not nearly enough," Billy agreed. He slid his hand around to the small of her back, pulled her toward him.

"Groundhog's Day, even," Jane said.

Billy stroked her hair, the hair she had never learned to brush regularly and so had cut short at nineteen and worn that way ever since — the same way her mother wore hers.

"Did you know that Groundhog's Day used to be Candlemas?" he said. "February second. The day John baptized Jesus."

Jane pulled away just enough to stare at him. "How do you know that?" she said.

Billy smiled. "I know all kinds of things," he said. "You shouldn't underestimate me."

There was a pause while they both considered whether that was what Jane had been doing or not.

New Year's Eve, Jane and Billy had been invited to a party by Jane's chair, John Lewin, but they couldn't get a babysitter. Instead they organized a last-minute gathering of their own. They vacuumed the rug and put the piles of newspapers on the back porch and swatted the cobwebs out of the corners. They hung chili pepper lights along the archway between the living room and the dining room. Jane wasn't comfortable inviting any of the Slavics faculty, who were presumably going to the Lewins', but Billy called up some law school students and their next-door neighbors, Kurt and Melinda, and Jane sent an e-mail to the members of SLAV. Katie Axelrod showed up with her medical school boyfriend, and Felicia came as well, somewhat late, wearing a sleeveless, sparkly gold polyester dress and matching shoes. Wrapped around her neck like a stole, she wore the python.

"You said to bring a date," she said, smiling slyly as she watched Jane eyeing the snake. "You didn't specify gender, or species."

Jane smiled back. She couldn't see the point of making a fuss. Besides, conversation (except for a knot of law students arguing about politics) had largely subsided. Kurt, who was in computer programming, and Melinda, who was a fourth-grade teacher, had been cornered near the narrow stairs by Vince Steadman, who was telling them about the time he got arrested for trespassing at the ELF facility; Katie Axelrod and her boyfriend were sitting on the sagging brown couch by themselves; and one of the young law students was in the toy corner by the windows trying to distract Maisie, who was upset because Kurt and Melinda's kids were playing with her plastic pizza and trying on her hat collection. Maybe the appearance of the snake would catalyze things, bring the disparate groups together.

"I'll introduce you," she said. "Though I can't introduce the snake, I guess, since it doesn't have a name!" Jane was feeling giddy from two glasses of champagne. She was ready to be amusing, amused—brought out of herself. The reptile lay heavily across Felicia's shoulders, thick as an arm. It was black and white as though camouflaged for the shadows of a snowy forest (though certainly it wasn't made for snow). When you looked more closely, you could see that the white was slightly yellowed, like teeth. The muscles bulged under the rough skin, the scales looking less like armor than like stitches of an old, loosely crocheted afghan. It exuded a compelling mixture of power and decay.

"Of course, every other python in Madison is named Monty," Felicia said.

"Are there many other pythons in Madison?" Jane asked. "Maisie, sweetie, come over and look at this."

"Dozens," Felicia said. "Especially in frat houses."

Maisie, who had retrieved her plastic fire helmet from the head of one of the neighbor boys, padded over.

"Look at the snake," Jane said, holding Maisie by the shoulders at what seemed like a safe distance. "Isn't it beautiful?" Though *beautiful* wasn't exactly the word. Impressive, certainly. Startling. Even disturbing, the way it emerged from under Felicia's hair and lay across her pale, freckled shoulders.

Maisie was entranced. "Snake!" she said, and bounced up and down in her red pajamas, her face alight.

The neighbor children, Josh and Adam, ran over, almost knocking down the coat rack.

"Wow!" Adam said. "That's so cool!" He was ten.

Felicia smiled down at him tolerantly. "I'm glad you like her," she said.

"Don't touch," Jane warned the boys, who were crowding close to Felicia.

"It's okay," Felicia said. "You guys can touch her if you want to. She's very smooth." The boys petted the snake where it hugged Felicia's hip. "Wow!" Adam said again, and Josh echoed, "This is awesome!" The snake lay so still and torpid, it might have been dead.

Felicia pulled her hair back and tied it into a knot so more of the snake's body was visible. Not to mention her own body. The boys' parents came over to see what was going on, and Katie Axelrod and her boyfriend got up from the couch. Kurt wanted to know what the snake ate and where it was native to, and the CD changed from the Talking Heads to something older and jazzier, and Billy came out of the kitchen with a tray of spanakopita. As he set the food down on the table, the chili peppers blinked on and off all around him, lightening and darkening his body as he stood with his back to Jane.

"More food, everybody!" he said, turning. He was wearing a midnight blue shirt and a thin black tie and the new shoes he'd bought for his upcoming internship. His face was freshly shaved.

Maisie reached out and stroked the snake's skin, then jumped back in delight and squealed. She reached out again but Jane pulled her away. "That's enough," she said.

Jane saw Billy register Felicia and the snake. His eyes narrowed and he moved toward them through the archway, ignoring one of the law students who was trying to speak to him.

"Billy," Jane said, trying to behave as though she hadn't noticed he was upset. He always looked more handsome when he was angry. His nose seemed straighter and the gray of his eyes got darker and stormier. "This is my student Felicia Noone."

"Is that a boa constrictor?" Billy asked.

"Python." Felicia smiled at him, a flirtatious, challenging smile, shifting the snake across her bare shoulders. Her lipstick was coral orange, and her eyelashes were thick with mascara, very black against her white skin. Her slightly protuberant green eyes glowed. "I guess you're Mr. Levitsky," she said.

It might have been the first time anyone had called him that. He smiled back at Felicia, but Jane could see how tight his face was.

"You can't have the snake here," he said. "I'm sorry."

"Oh, she's not dangerous," Felicia said. "Don't worry about *her*." She ran her hand along the black-and-white skin, caressing it.

Maisie was jumping up and down. "Look, Daddy!" she said. "Look, look!"

"Well, I am worried," Billy said. "If you're comfortable keeping something like that as a pet in your own house, that's your business. But bringing it here—with lots of people, and children, and all—

is something else. In my house anything that might happen is my responsibility."

How much like a lawyer he sounded already! Rational, cautious, self-righteous. "Oh, Billy," Jane said. "It'll be okay. You can see it just lies there!"

"She's very docile," Felicia confirmed.

"Lookie, lookie!" Maisie shouted, pulling on her father's leg.

"I see, sweetheart," Billy said. "But the snake has to go. Now." It was the same voice he used with Maisie when she misbehaved.

Felicia shrugged. "The serpent is everywhere despised," she said, and looked around for her coat.

Maisie started to cry. "Snake!" she wailed. "I want! I want!"

Jane picked her up. It was hours past her bedtime. "Say good night, sweetie," Jane said.

Maisie laid her head on Jane's shoulder, suddenly spent. "Night, snaky," she said.

Jane carried her up the steps.

Downstairs the New Year's party lurched on like a bulldozer through the dark, cold night, plowing a relentless track into the new year.

The next week the temperature dropped well below zero, making it painful to breathe. When Jane took out the trash after dinner, the stars glittered in the black sky like chips of ice. In the morning the thermometer rose only to five above. The sky was enormous, a brilliant crystal blue that seemed to rise up forever. The wind blew, gusty and fierce, off the frozen lake, cutting through thick down coats, under scarves, nosing in between the stitches of woolen gloves. *Siberia*, Jane thought, riding home from work on the city bus in the early darkness, grateful for the heat blasting out of the vents but wishing she had a long hooded fur coat and fur-lined boots. The temperatures were supposed to moderate over the weekend and rise to a balmy twenty-five by

Monday when she was leaving for Chicago. She thought of the thick silence of the Special Collections room at the Newberry, how she could sit at the heavy tables touching the actual pages Masha had touched: white fields where the tracks of the diarist's pen lay like footprints across the snow, leading the reader back into the past.

The bus had passed the car repair place now. Jane pulled the cord. She lurched to her feet and down the steps, out into the brutal cold. The thin, glacial air seemed to fill her chest with frost. She put her head down and trotted awkwardly, lugging her satchel, up the icy street, past the Mitchells' and the Fromms' and the Petersons', narrow two-story houses outlined still in Christmas lights. The yards were white with snow, packed down by dogs and children in some places, in others clean and drifted, marked only lightly with the delicate three-pronged prints of birds.

From outside her own brown undecorated house, Jane could see Maisie and Elise through the living-room windows. They sat together on the couch, Maisie in Elise's lap, their heads bent together over a book. All the indoor lights were on against the winter evening, bathing them in a yellow glow and shining off Elise's long black hair and Maisie's brown curls. "Hello, girls!" Jane said, coming in. She peeled off her coat and dropped her satchel on the stairs, absorbing the warmth of the house into her chilled limbs.

"Mommy!" Maisie crowed.

"I have something to tell you," Elise said.

Jane thought something must have happened to Maisie. She picked her up and looked at her, but she seemed all right.

"What is it? What's wrong?"

"I got a new job." Elise pulled her long black hair back over her shoulders with both hands and knotted it. She looked like a different person suddenly, all plucked eyebrows and gold-studded ears.

"What do you mean?" Jane thought she must have misunderstood. She needed Elise. Maisie needed her. Elise could not desert them.

"I'm sorry! I should have told you sooner," Elise said. "Maisie is great and everything. It's just, I'm thinking of going back to school. I don't know what I'm doing, really, but part-time is definitely what I need for now." She smiled apologetically, and all of a sudden Jane saw her not as an indispensable piece of her own requisite luck but as a twenty-two-year-old with a disordered, casual life—the kind of life Jane herself had never had.

"Oh," Jane said with an effort. She knew she had to say something. "What's your timetable?"

Elise smiled again. "This is it," she said. "This is my last day."

It took all Jane's concentration to keep the explosion inside her chest from showing. "Perhaps you could stay just one more week? Sitters usually give more notice."

"I know, I know. Like I said, I'm really sorry." Elise wrapped a long red-and-white checked scarf over her head. She didn't have a hat. Her black ski jacket stopped at her waist.

It was hard to know how to say good-bye to her. Jane was bewildered, and as far as Maisie knew, Elise would be back on Monday. Was that okay? Should Jane make Elise stay and explain to Maisie what was happening? There wasn't any time to think it over; Elise was opening the door, letting in the cold.

"Let's wave," Jane said automatically.

They stood, waving, by the front window as Elise walked unhurriedly down the frozen street, her breath billowing behind her in great white gusts. Not seeing them. Not once looking back.

Billy got home and started to cook dinner while Jane was upstairs giving Maisie a bath. When they came down, Billy was standing in the kitchen holding a cleaver, a clove of garlic half-chopped on the cutting board. Its pungency mixed with the smells of olive oil and wet boots.

"Elise quit," Jane said.

"What?" Billy turned from the stove. "Why?"

Jane shrugged his question away. "We have no child care, as of right now."

"Didn't she give any notice?" Billy said.

"No notice at all."

Billy's jaw tightened. He lined up the big glinting blade and hacked through the garlic, each stroke of the cleaver leaving a mark in the wood, then dumped it in the pan, where it sizzled fiercely in the smoking oil.

Jane watched Maisie stepping into Billy's big boots that sat dripping by the back door. "We'll have to find someone else," she said. "I'll look as soon as I get back. Can you miss a week at McKinley?"

"Are you joking?"

Now it starts, Jane thought. Her research time set against Billy's responsibilities—not to mention the money he was earning. It wasn't as if classes were in session yet; it wasn't as if she had to teach. "Don't blame me," she said. "This isn't my fault."

Maisie had got both the boots on and was tramping gritty slush across the linoleum with a look of serious concentration. Jane understood what was going to happen. Either Billy would refuse to miss his week of work, or he would offer to forgo it—to anger the firm and let down the client he'd been assigned and give up the salary they needed—and Jane, if he did that, would decline his offer. She could see, as if it were written up somewhere, in some public document, that she would.

Maisie was out the kitchen door, tracking muddy slush all over the dining-room rug.

"Maisie! What are you doing!" Jane called.

Maisie's face went cautious and thoughtful. She froze in her tracks for a moment.

Billy put his knife down. "Although it is true that you hired her," he said.

Maisie took another deliberate step.

"Stop it!" Jane yelled at Maisie. The smells of garlic and chicken and wine seemed out of place in a room with so much anger. "Stop it right now!"

———

Instead of going to Chicago, Jane spent the next week visiting day-care centers. She had decided not to look for another sitter. Maisie needed to be with other children, she thought, and Jane needed the stability of child care that wouldn't quit or call in sick. Redirecting her frustration, she approached the task with her usual compulsive organization, calling everyone she knew to ask for recommendations, talking to the various directors over the phone, narrowing down her alphabetized list.

The actual visiting, however, was a shock. Jane had never been to a child-care center before, and at first she couldn't tell if her horror grew out of this unfamiliarity, or if the places were, indeed, horrible. It wasn't that any of them seemed dangerous or cruel, although she knew there were such places. Nor was there any particular mode of horror. Each terrible child-care center was terrible in its own way.

The first place she went—recommended by her pediatrician—seemed big and institutional. Babies were lined up in cribs in the wide front windows like merchandise, although surely it was so they could amuse themselves taking in the view. Nobody else was amusing them. The three toddler rooms opened off a carpeted hallway, each identically furnished and arranged, their closed doors decorated with identical paper snowflakes. "We recently got a fifty thousand–dollar grant for our playground," the admissions director told Jane, but Jane, sensing a kind of compulsive, super-orderly replication at work, wasn't listening.

At the next place, the director showed Jane the enrichment activities: counting beads, alphabet letters for coloring, cards for matching. Classical music played. Small children crouched on mats, busy with something. They didn't look unhappy, only quiet and intense. Jane thought this was the kind of place designed to appeal to parents like her, overachieving academic types, but it filled her instead with a creeping horror. Wouldn't there be enough constructive tasks later on in life? Enough quiet intensity?

"What about playing?" she asked.

"Of course they *play*," the director said.

The third place was dingy and sad, and at the fourth, the chirping, condescending brightness with which a teacher told Jane, "Brian is our problem child. But we're working on that, aren't we, Brian?" chilled her. She had thought it would be helpful to have Maisie along and be able to see her response to each place, but Maisie seemed to like them all. She had no idea why they were there, but she got into the car cheerfully every morning, asking, "Where we going today?"

"We're going visiting," Jane told her.

"I *like* visiting," Maisie said. What she liked were all the new toys—plastic telephones, little people, buses, jumping frogs, big wooden lofts.

At last Jane found a place she liked. The Chestnut Lane Children's Center was decorated with posters of children playing, height marks, seeds sprouting in plastic pots, collages bulging with paste, photographs of babies, muddy finger paintings. It was messy without being decrepit, noisy but with a feeling of cheerful, controlled chaos. Jane liked the director, a loud-voiced, heavy woman who greeted the children by name as she showed Jane around. "Hi, Benjamin! Hi, Leo! Hello, Kinesha, Tyler, Stevie, Jessica! The children are happy here, as you can see," she said. "Well, not all the time! But we help them learn to get along. To communicate when they're angry or sad. It's hard work. A full-time job for them and for us." She must have given this speech a hundred times, but still she sounded like she meant it. They were in the preschool room, and Jane watched two children fighting over a yellow truck.

"It's my truck!" one yelled. "I had it first!"

"I had it before!" the other cried. "I just put it down for a minute!"

The teacher, reaching onto a shelf, produced another identical truck from a shelf, and the boys stopped screaming.

"Of course," the director said, "sometimes the solutions are kind of simple."

But when Jane asked about signing up, the director said, "Unfortunately, we're full right now. But I'll put your name on our waiting list. We usually have openings in September."

"I don't know what we're going to do!" Jane said at dinner that night as Maisie turned her sippy cup upside down and tugged on the spout. Drops of milk sprayed across the tray. "Moo, moo," she said.

Billy took the cup from Maisie and turned it right side up. "That's not to play with," he said.

"We went to the Children's Museum and she milked a big plaster cow," Jane explained. "You bring a child up in Wisconsin, that's what you get." She loved the way Maisie had made the connection to the sippy cup, the actual milk.

Billy watched Maisie turn the cup over again. "I thought we'd get a progressive politician," he said.

"Well, I'll bet it's organic milk," Jane said.

"Oh, ganic!" Maisie yelled. "Ganic, ganic!" She bounced up and down in her seat.

"So," Billy said to Jane, "what's your second choice?"

Jane tried speak calmly. "There is no second choice," she said.

The next day after breakfast, Jane took Maisie to the toy store at the mall and let her pick out a little set of figures in a box. There were knights and dragons, pirates on rafts, shepherds and sheep, peasant women in kerchiefs pushing carts of vegetables. Maisie chose one with a bride, a wedding cake, some fiddle players, and a lot of fancy tables and chairs.

"How about this one?" Jane said, holding out the sheep scene, but Maisie stuck by the bride.

They drove over to campus and walked along the icy sidewalks to Jane's building. Going at Maisie's pace, it took twice as long as when Jane walked it alone.

In Van Hise no one seemed to be around. The lights were dim in the Slavics hallway, and all the doors were shut. Jane helped Maisie open the box and take the figures out of their plastic bags.

"Dis one has pretty hair," Maisie said, sitting on the floor near the window where the low winter sun slanted in, casting a watery parallelogram of light. "Dis one has a feather. Dis one has a purple hat." She arranged the bride and her entourage in a small phalanx, admiring their accessories.

Jane sat at her desk and opened the volume of selections from Masha's diaries. If she wasn't going to be able to get to Chicago, perhaps she could find enough here for the nature paper at least — enough to hammer out a sketchy draft to be filled in later. Also she needed to start preparing her classes for the upcoming semester; really, she should have been halfway done by now.

"Mama," Maisie said. "Who dis lady?" She stood against Jane's knees and pushed the bride into Jane's face.

"Sweetie," Jane said. "I can't see it if it's so close." She looked at the figure of the bride with her tight white dress, her tiny white shoes, her white plastic veil that snapped on and off. "That's the bride," she said. "She's getting married."

"But what's her *name?*" Maisie wanted to know.

"I don't know," Jane said. "What do you think it is?"

"I'm asking you!" Maisie said.

"Careful of the book," Jane said. "Maybe Lucy?"

"No," Maisie said. "Not Lucy."

"Tracy?"

"No."

"I don't know, honey," Jane said. "You can name her anything you like." She took Maisie's hand and led her back to her spot on the floor. "What a pretty cake," she said. "Do you think it's chocolate?"

They set up the table and chairs. Jane slipped back up to her desk.

Masha was writing about how the snow had twice delayed her journey:

I will not be surprised if one of these years it snows in July. Snow is the soul of Russia made visible. Still, I will be glad when the grass in the meadow is up to my waist and the sun draws the flowers up out of the ground like young girls with ribbons in their hair drawn into the ballroom by the strains of a waltz.

"Mama," Maisie said. "Mama, Mama! It vanilla cake. Vanilla!"

"Yes," Jane said. "Vanilla." She lost her place and ran her finger down the page, trying to find it.

"Mama, I like vanilla cake," Maisie said.

"I know you do," Jane said. "So do I."

"I like all kinds of cake," Maisie said.

An entry caught Jane's eye:

Before Katya was born, I longed for her arrival the way a child longs for a lovely toy. I couldn't imagine how she would trans-form my life any more than a creeping caterpillar can imagine what it is like to be a butterfly—soaring over the emerald fields, but battered and sent tumbling by every breeze.

"Mama!" Maisie said.

"Maisie!" Jane said. "You play with your toys! Mommy's trying to read."

"No!" Maisie said. "No, no read!" She shook her head, making her curls fly.

"Yes," Jane said. "Mommy has to get a little work done. Then we'll have lunch."

"I want lunch now!" Maisie said.

"Soon," Jane said. "It's almost lunchtime."

"Now!" Maisie yelled. "I hungry now!"

Jane took a deep breath. She looked at Maisie clutching the plastic bride in her hand. She shut the book with a slam.

"I'm hungwy!" Maisie cried. "I need vanilla cake! Wight now!"

"Maisie!" Jane said sternly.

"You never gimme vanilla cake!" Maisie said, starting to cry. "Only appa-sauce!" Her articulation dissolved along with her self-control.

Jane found she could easily picture her at eight or twelve or fifteen, a big girl with a wild bramble bush of hair, wailing inconsolably for attention, or cake, or whatever sweetness her parents were denying her then.

She picked Maisie up and bounced her against her shoulder. There was some candy someone had given her in the top drawer of her desk. "Maisie," she said, "do you want some chocolate?"

Maisie stopped crying and looked at her mother. She nodded.

Jane set Maisie down in her desk chair and opened the drawer. Out in the hall, she could hear footsteps. Then came the arthritic scratching and rattling of Sigelman trying to get his key in the lock.

"Fucking door," she heard him mutter. "Goddamn fucking hands!" Then he poked his head into Jane's office. "Oh-ho," he said. "Who have we here?" He looked at Maisie sitting in the desk chair. "That's your daughter, eh, Levitsky? She looks good enough to eat." Stout and stooped, he made Jane think of Rumpelstiltskin.

"That's Maisie," she said, thinking of the miller's daughter trading her firstborn child for the magic of straw spun into gold.

"Hi, Maisie." Sigelman waved his thick fingers at her.

Maisie looked at Sigelman. "I got a chocolate bar!" she said.

Sigelman laughed.

"Want some?" Maisie held out the gooey mess.

"That's all right," Sigelman said. "You go ahead."

"Okay," Maisie said.

"So," Sigelman said to Jane, "you survived your first semester. Congratulations."

"Did I survive it?" Jane said. "Maybe I'm just a ghost of myself."

"Oh, come on—it wasn't that bad," he said. "It's not that hard, really. Teaching."

"I guess not," Jane said. "If you don't care very much."

He liked that. "You've discovered the secret!" he said. "And why should you care? The students don't. I hope you're doing some real work over the break."

"Yum-yum," Maisie said, trying to make eye contact with Sigelman again. "Yummy chocolate."

"I was going to go down to the Newberry," Jane said, "but my babysitter quit."

"Want some?" Maisie offered again, holding out the bar as far as she could toward Sigelman.

"I was going to ask you," he said, ignoring both Maisie's offer and Jane's mention of Elise, "if you saw that Leighton is giving the keynote at AATSEEL. Who picked him, that's what I want to know? That chicken kisser was a student here in the seventies, and even then he didn't know his ass from a groundhog's hole."

"She didn't even give any notice," Jane said. "And Billy's working, and you would not believe some of things I've seen this week at various centers. The misbehavior chart!"

"He no want," Maisie told her mother. "No want chocolate."

"There aren't any standards anymore," Sigelman said. "For example, when's the last time you heard of a paper getting rejected by JSSL?"

"Who sends their kids to those places?" Jane said. "It's utterly beyond me!"

"Jane," Sigelman said in a colder tone. "If you insist on talking to me about your child-care problems, I'll be forced to tell you about my hemorrhoids."

Jane stopped short. She had heard him use that tone before, but never with her. She looked down at Maisie and saw that she had gotten chocolate all over her face, in her hair, and on the edge of the desk.

"All for me!" Maisie said, bouncing in her chair.

"And I wouldn't blab it around the department, either," he went on, turning to go. "It doesn't present you in the most professional light." He banged the door shut behind him.

"Too loud," said Maisie, who was frequently reminded not to slam doors.

———

That night at dinner, Billy said, "I asked around at McKinley. Jenny Lawrence sends her daughter to a family day care she likes, and she says there's an opening."

"I don't know," Jane said. After a full day of trying to work with Maisie around, she was feeling desperate, but she didn't like what she'd heard about family day cares. "Do you know what the ratios are in those places? I think it's eight to one. And there's no supervision. I mean, if something—goes on—there's no one there to see." She imagined hitting, yelling, sexual abuse. You were a fool if you pretended these things didn't happen.

"There's no supervision at home, either," Billy said. "With a babysitter. And Jenny Lawrence says this woman only takes six kids. Besides, what else are we going to do?"

Jane thought of what Sigelman had said: *It doesn't present you in the most professional light.* "Fine," she said at last. "Only you go visit this one."

Billy went the following day on his lunch hour, reported back by phone from his office that it fit the bill. Clean, breakfast and snack provided. Only five children, as promised—Maisie would make six. The provider, Mrs. Vlajic, was cheerful, friendly, enthusiastic.

Jane agreed, but she found she did not trust Billy's judgment, though he would have trusted hers as a matter of course.

CHAPTER SIX

 MRS. VLAJIC lived in a little one-story house in an old manufacturing neighborhood near the railroad tracks. The front walk was cleared of snow and ice, and the stoop was swept. Around the back of the house, Jane could see a blue toddler slide and a plastic turtle sandbox half buried under snow.

It was only just after eight, but three other children were already there. A boy and a girl, preschoolers, sat on the floor in front of a television watching *Barney*. An infant dozed in a bouncy seat, its head tilted at an uncomfortable-looking angle. The house was clean and spare, if somewhat dark, with fake wood paneling, small windows, and dull mushroom-colored carpeting that had seen better days. It smelled of peanut butter and disinfectant.

"I'm Jane Levitsky," Jane said. "This is Maisie. You met my husband, Billy Shaw."

"Of course!" Mrs. Vlajic was a short, stocky woman in her forties with thin hair pulled back in a ponytail and an apron over her dress. When she smiled, she showed small discolored teeth. "I was just getting breakfast." Jane followed her back into the kitchen. Aqua-green plastic bowls were ranged on a tray with a box of off-brand sugar-coated flakes, a plate of banana slices, and a carton of milk.

"The kids like to eat this," Mrs. Vlajic said. "Kids always eat good for Mrs. Vlajic." She spoke English with a strong accent that was superficially like Russian, but with distinctly different vowel sounds. She was a Slav of some sort—possibly Serbian—but Jane had never paid much attention to the southern Slavic languages. Billy had thought the fact that Mrs. Vlajic was Slavic would make Jane disposed to like her, but so far Jane didn't like her.

Still, you couldn't judge an entire day care on what was served for breakfast. Jane looked around the kitchen. Beige, aging appliances. Speckled linoleum. Baby locks on the cabinets. Decals of Donald Duck. It was spotless.

"I have two cribs here." Mrs. Vlajic pointed to a door. "For the babies. Older kids sleep on mats. I wash sheets every day!"

"Sometimes Maisie won't nap," Jane said, finding herself choosing small words and speaking slowly. "Sometimes she's too excited. She wants to play."

"All my kids nap," Mrs. Vlajic said. "I tell them they need to rest to grow strong."

Maisie clung to Jane's neck, her brown eyes fixed warily on Mrs. Vlajic.

"She's never been in a day care with other kids. It may take her a while to get used to being here," Jane said. Surely Maisie could sense Jane's horror. She put her hand on her daughter's back and tried to exude confidence.

Mrs. Vlajic poured cereal into the bowls. She clattered spoons onto a tray. "She'll be okay." She smiled at Jane. "You don't have to worry. Baby will be fine with Mrs. Vlajic! I've had lots of babies here in this house, happy babies." She picked up the tray and walked back into the front room, her step lively.

Jane followed. Mrs. Vlajic hadn't said Maisie's name yet, and Jane wondered whether she remembered it.

The two preschoolers looked up from the TV as breakfast was delivered. "Yum," said the girl. "Frosted flakes!"

"I already had breakfast at home," said the boy, a skinny, dark-haired kid with a worried face.

"You eat again for Mrs. Vlajic," Mrs. Vlajic told him brightly. "You need food to grow up big and strong!" She set bowls on the floor in front of the children, leaving the TV on.

"Are these all the toys?" Jane asked, looking at the few worn stuffed animals, the jack-in-the-box, the plastic train.

"More in the closet." Mrs. Vlajic indicated a door in the corner. "We get out later."

Jane nodded. She knew she was a snob. There were certain things she liked, certain cultures in which she felt at home. Who was to say this wasn't a fine place? A warm, caring, happy place where children were well taken care of. Billy thought it was. Billy, who was less hampered by academic blinders, who was a more generous person. Who liked people more than she did.

Mrs. Vlajic stirred cereal around in a bowl for Maisie, pulled a bib out of her apron pocket, and came forward to pull it over Maisie's head. Maisie pushed the bib away.

"Don't be like that!" Mrs. Vlajic exclaimed. "We have fun here! You come to Mrs. Vlajic." She held out her arms, but Maisie, who had been told she was going to a new place to play while Mommy and Daddy worked, buried her head in Jane's neck and held on.

"Mommy has to go," Jane said. She felt sick.

"Come on, baby," Mrs. Vlajic said cheerily. "Do you like frosted flakes? Do you like Baby Bop?"

The place was clean, and Mrs. Vlajic was energetic and cheerful. She waited with her arms out. A clock ticked on the wall. Jane had half an hour to get to campus, park her car, hike up to her office, find her notes.

"You'll be fine, Maisie," she said, brightly, horribly, hypocritically, into Maisie's lovely ear. She kissed her and brought her over to Mrs. Vlajic. Maisie screamed. Mrs. Vlajic held Maisie tight while Jane peeled off her daughter's arms. Maisie grabbed with desperate fingers—Jane's shoulder, her shirt, her hair. The two preschoolers watched, distracted from the television. The infant startled and woke up, looking around in a dazed way, and began to hiccup. "Mama!" Maisie wailed, drowning out Barney's kids singing "This Old Man." "Mamamamaaa!"

Jane scuttled out the door. Behind her she could hear the sitter's voice: "Baby will have a good time! Don't worry!" Jane started the car, drove half a mile, and then pulled over to the side of the road and sobbed.

An hour later, standing at the lectern in the hot classroom under the lights, her eyes puffy, her face pale and strained, Jane's mind shut down right in the middle of the lecture. In front of her, forty students shifted in their auditorium seats, rattling papers, yawning, sipping take-out coffee. She had a note to talk about issues of translation in Pushkin's classic novel in verse, *Eugene Onegin*. She stood silently before them with her mouth open, waiting for the words to come.

The silence stretched itself out. It spun a cocoon around the classroom, thick and cottony. Someone sighed. Jane shifted her weight to the other foot. Could Maisie still be crying? In her mind she saw the paneled room, the carpeting, the television.

In the front row, a student in a green-and-gold Packers jacket cleared his throat loudly, and suddenly Jane was back in the room, talking. She skipped translation and plunged straight into Pushkin's death in a duel on a January day in 1837. Blood on the snow.

When he died, Pushkin had been thirty-eight years old, not so much older than Jane was now. But oh, how much he had done!

After lunch Felicia came into Jane's office and pushed a book across her desk. "It's an encyclopedia of snakes," she said. "I thought I'd try to figure out what kind the Snake Woman was carrying."

Something was wrong with the heat in the building. It never seemed to switch off. Jane was sweating in her wool turtleneck, but Felicia kept her big army surplus jacket on, bell-bottoms and scuffed Doc Martens showing underneath.

"What makes you think they were some particular kind of snake?" Jane asked. She enjoyed the sessions with Felicia, but lately she had begun to suspect that provocative ideas were more interesting to her advisee than the truth. "I would have assumed they were an imaginary amalgam. Ur-snakes. Chudo-Yudo." Chudo-Yudo was a monster-dragon of Russian folktale, a skin-shedder.

"Possibly," Felicia said. She wore her hair pulled back in a braid, and you could see her face better than you usually could—long nose, green eyes, hardly any cheekbones to speak of. She wasn't pretty, it was the hair that fooled you: red-gold curls halfway down her back. "But the descriptions are so particular and detailed."

"You're supposed to be focusing on the lady, not the snakes," Jane said mildly.

"I don't know that you can separate them," Felicia countered. "The Snake Woman is a witch figure, a *ved'ma*, a Baba Yaga. Baba Yaga is associated with snakes."

"Yes. But again we're talking about mythological snakes. Dragons, really."

"Karkov takes the mythological motifs and puts them into natura-listic settings."

Something strange was happening to Felicia's coat. The material along her shoulders seemed to shift, bunching itself up, rising and falling in a long undulation. Then a blunt black-and-white head emerged from Felicia's sleeve.

"Don't you ever leave that thing at home?" Jane asked, trying to sound nonchalant.

The forked tongue flicked. The mouth seemed to sneer at Jane, its white lips drawn back. The thick body glided out onto Felicia's knee until about three feet of it was showing, the rest still hidden in the big, bulky olive-green sleeve. The snake stopped with its head raised, posed like pictures Jane had seen of cobras. It looked as though it was watching her.

"What's it doing?" she asked.

"She's okay," Felicia said. "She likes to see where she is sometimes."

"What's wrong with just leaving her at home in her cage?" Was Felicia trying to *be* the Snake Woman?

Felicia smiled. "It's really quite a trip," she said. "Walking around, going to class, going to the library, with this big python inside my jacket. And nobody knows!"

"What if it escapes?" Jane could easily imagine it gliding down to the floor and across the room, slipping behind the bookcase or into the bottom drawer of the filing cabinet.

"Actually," Felicia said, "she did get out last week. Just briefly. She pushed the top off, but I've gotten stronger latches now."

"My god!" Jane stared at the thick, ugly body of the python, the bulging eyes with their vertical slits. "How did you find her?"

"She hadn't gone far. She'd found the radiator and curled up next to it. It was no big deal." Felicia shifted and the snake began to retract itself upward, back inside her sleeve. Again the heavy material of the coat bunched across Felicia's shoulders.

"What about your roommate?" Jane said. "Did you tell her?"

A flicker of uncertainty crossed Felicia's face. "She was there," she said. "The radiator was in her room, actually."

"I'm surprised she didn't move out!" Jane said.

Felicia shrugged. "The lease is in her name," she said.

The whole situation was appalling, and Jane didn't want to talk about it anymore. It seemed inevitable to her that it would happen again, stronger latches or no. How much control could a young woman exercise over a full-grown python? "Do you have any new work to show me?" she said, her voice harsh — not her own voice, but still familiar, somehow.

"Not exactly," Felicia said.

"Why not? What have you been doing with your time?"

Felicia just looked at her, as though to say that Jane didn't really want to know.

"Friday," Jane said, still in the voice that wasn't hers. But she recognized it now: it was Shombauer's voice.

———

Billy and Maisie were already home when Jane got there. Maisie was watching television while Billy got dinner ready. She sat in a corner of the couch holding her stuffed duck, her face peaceful in the flickering light, one sock on and the other lying on the floor. Jane dropped her things and picked Maisie up, held her tightly. "I missed you!" Jane said. "How was your day? Did you have a good time?"

Maisie moved her head so she could still see the television. "Ssh, Mommy," she said, putting a finger gently against Jane's lips. "I'm watching dis."

After her bath Maisie fell asleep on the rug in her room. That had never happened before. Jane put her in the bed and pulled the blanket up. Back downstairs Billy was sitting on the couch, studying. Jane sat down beside him and let her head fall back against the cushions. "She fell asleep on the floor," she said.

Billy marked his place with his finger and looked up. "Well, it's tiring," he said. "Being somewhere new."

"How was she when you picked her up?"

"Fine. They were having snack."

"How much TV do you think they watch over there?"

"We let her watch TV," Billy said.

"Not *Barney*."

"What's wrong with *Barney*?" Billy said.

"What do you mean, what's wrong with it?" Jane said. "It's aesthetically bankrupt!" She hated *Barney* with its condescending, saccharine, specious attitude toward learning, as though learning were not something perfect and inherently desirable, like a ripe peach, but a tasteless supermarket fruit that had to be sugared to go down.

Billy laughed.

"She gives them frosted flakes for breakfast," Jane said.

"And fruit," Billy replied. "And milk. Anyway, I used to eat frosted flakes."

"I didn't."

"You. You grew up in Berkeley," Billy said. He put down his book and put his arms around her.

Jane leaned against him. "She screamed so much when I left her this morning," she said. She wished she knew if he really felt all right about Mrs. Vlajic's, or if he was just putting a good face on it.

In the morning Maisie started screaming as soon as Jane took her out to the car after breakfast. "Where we going?" she cried. "I don't want to go dere!" She thrashed and wept. Jane felt hopeless and also angry with Maisie for putting her through this. At the sitter's house, Maisie screamed and held on. Jane wanted to shake her, to throw her down on Mrs. Vlajic's awful plaid sofa and run. Instead, she spoke calmly.

"You'll be fine, sweetheart. Mommy has to go to work. I'll see you tonight, I promise. Daddy will pick you up."

Maisie screamed. The other children watched. Mrs. Vlajic smiled and held out her stubby arms.

Jane checked her mailbox in the department office and found the big, dusty snake encyclopedia filling it up.

"What's that?" asked John Lewin, on his way through with a cup of coffee.

"Felicia Noone is taking a detour into zoology," Jane said.

"How's her dissertation coming?"

"Not bad. She's very bright." Jane flipped through the book. The text was dense, but the photographic plates were clear and startling. There were pictures of snakes with their pink mouths wide open, snakes slithering along beaches and dangling from tree branches, snakes devouring jelly eggs with tadpoles visible inside. Snakes emerging from papery-looking snake eggs. Snakes shedding. Snakes eating other snakes.

John Lewin peered over her shoulder and grimaced. "Very bright is one thing," he said. "Good judgment is something else."

Did Otto Sigelman have good judgment, Jane wondered, looking at a picture of a snake with a mouse tail drooping from its lips. Was it really a prerequisite for good scholarship, or did Felicia just make Lewin, with his big mustache and his khaki pants and his bow ties, uneasy?

Billy said, "It's normal for a kid to take a while getting used to a new sitter. What do you expect?"

He said, "Do you want me to bring her in the mornings?"

He said, "She probably stops crying the moment you're out the door. Isn't that what Mrs. Vlajic says?"

It was, in fact, what Mrs. Vlajic said. Furthermore, it was what Jane's own ears told her—Maisie's screams following her out the door and then ceasing mysteriously when Jane was halfway down the walk. Nevertheless, she was certain Maisie spent all day crying. Not playing, not eating, although every day Mrs. Vlajic returned Maisie's lunch box empty—yogurt, cut-up apples, chocolate chip cookies, all gone. "All Mrs. Vlajic's kids are good eaters," Mrs. Vlajic said. But Jane knew she must throw the food away.

Still, after a while Jane had to admit that Maisie was settling down. Waking up in the mornings, she still said first thing, "I don't want go dere today," and when Jane dropped her off, she still cried, but there was a kind of perfunctoriness about it, as though even she were getting tired of the performance.

Jane's hatred of the place, however, continued unabated. It grew, if anything—as if to compensate for Maisie's increasing acquiescence.

Felicia kept asking Jane if she had looked at the candidate snakes in the snake encyclopedia yet, so Jane lugged the book home. Maisie saw it on the coffee table and looked with awe at the picture on the cover, a long green snake dangling from a tree. Gingerly, she ran her hand across it.

"Careful," Jane said. "That's not our book."

"I'm careful," Maisie said.

Jane went into the kitchen. When she came back, Maisie was still looking at the snake on the cover.

"What its name?" she asked.

Jane opened the book and found the cover photo information. "It's a parrot snake," she said.

"Parrot," Maisie repeated. "What that one?" She pointed to another picture. "What that one?" Her hands starfished across the pages.

"Ring-necked snake," Jane read. "Calico snake. Stiletto snake. Black mamba."

"Mamba," Maisie repeated carefully, looking up at Jane to make sure she got it right.

Jane sat down on the couch and pulled Maisie onto her lap. "Let's see what it says about the mamba," she said. " 'After the king cobra, the black mamba is the largest venomous snake in the world.' Wow, Maisie, what do you think of that?"

Maisie leaned back into Jane's embrace. Her warm, hard little body fit perfectly against Jane's chest. "The mamba is the *queen* cobra, then, Mommy," she said, and Jane laughed.

It seemed to snow every day in February. Snow inched up the trunks of the trees, accumulated on windowsills and telephone wires, piled itself in great drifts against buildings. There was so much snow, there wasn't anywhere left to put it when Jane shoveled the driveway in the morning.

Maisie's hair was getting long and wispy. Jane tried to keep it out of her eyes with barrettes, but the hair was so fine the barrettes slipped out. They were all over the house, yellow and pink and turquoise plastic bows. Maisie's hair was as soft as silk and curly, the clear, golden brown color of maple syrup. Out the window the snow had begun to fall again in big, soft, clumpy flakes. It was hard to believe it would ever be spring.

"Sit down," Jane said. "Let's get that hair out of your face."

Maisie stopped in the middle of the room. She looked at Jane, then pulled her hair down in front of her eyes and nose. "I like it," she said.

"Maisie," Jane said.

Maisie peered out between the strands and took a step backward.

"Come on, silly goose," Jane said. "We'll play beauty parlor. It'll be fun."

Maisie looked at her with disdain and took another step back.

"We'll play dog groomer," Jane amended. "You be the puppy."

"No," Maisie said. "I'm not a puppy. I'm a snake! *Hissss.*" She threw herself down on the floor and slithered.

"Okay," Jane said. "I'm the snake groomer. Slither over here and I'll make you nice and neat."

"Snakes don't got haircuts."

"Oh, come on, Maisie," Jane said. "It'll take five minutes! Anyway, snakes don't have hair, do they? If you want to be a snake, yours will have to go."

Maisie thought about it. "Yes," she agreed. "Cut it off!" But she drew the line at sitting on the chair Jane offered her. "Snakes don't sit."

"Fine," Jane said.

She got a sheet from the closet and spread it on the floor. Maisie wriggled over on her stomach. Jane sat beside her and carefully snipped the soft curls until the hair was a little less than shoulder length. It was hard to tell if the sides were even, but she did the best she could. "Okay!" she said. "We're done, snaky."

Maisie reached up and tugged on her hair. "It not all gone," she said.

"It's much, much shorter," Jane said.

"No!" Maisie said. "Too long! Too *long!*"

Jane cut some more, feeling doubtful. She intended to cut a kind of pageboy, but she made it too short on one side and then on the other, and by the time she got the sides reasonably even, it would have been nearly impossible to cut the hair any shorter even if Jane had wanted to.

Maisie, putting her hands to her head, was pleased. "I'm a queen cobra," she said, and slithered across the room, bits of hair scattering. "I'm a ma-ma-mamba!"

Jane fetched the broom. *It will grow back,* she told herself, sweeping up the brown wisps, seeing how dead they looked, lying in the dustpan.

"It'll grow back," she told Billy when he got home, even before he had a chance to say anything.

Maisie, still on her stomach, wriggled over to his feet and hissed fiercely. Melting snow and grit from his boots soaked into her clothes.

"My god! What happened?" Billy said.

"She wanted it short," Jane said.

"Well, she got her wish," Billy said. "When's dinner? I'm starving."

Jane went into the kitchen to get a pot for pasta. In the other room, she could hear Maisie hissing excitedly.

"Guess what I am!" she said.

"I have no idea," Billy said. "A naked mole rat?"

"A mamba! A mamba!"

"Oh, good. I've always wanted my own mamba."

Jane found the damp half of an onion in the fridge and chopped it. Billy's voice, though tired, had an affection she seldom heard in it anymore when he talked to her. These days when they smiled at each other, Jane felt the strain in her face. She was aware of a distance between them even during sex, which they had rather perfunctorily every week or two, as though not to make love would be to admit something about the state of their marriage that they weren't ready to admit. Even so, when their eyes caught in the dark while their bodies heaved and groped and thrust, they would look quickly away from each other, like strangers whose eyes meet accidentally on a train.

———

A couple of days later at pickup time, Mrs. Vlajic met Jane by the door and put a hand on her arm to stop her from going into the living room, where the kids were watching cartoons. "There is a problem with the girl," Mrs. Vlajic said. She had stopped calling Maisie "baby" lately and begun to refer to her as "the girl." Jane didn't know what it meant, but she didn't like the way it sounded. It was the term her grandmother had used for the woman who came to clean.

"What problem?" she asked warily.

Mrs. Vlajic glanced through the doorway at Maisie, who was sitting on the floor next to Laurie, the blond preschooler, who never went anywhere without a Barbie doll. She lowered her voice. "She pretending to be a snake." She drew out the last word with a kind of appalled wonder. "All the time! She doesn't want to play anything else. I say, You want to play with dolls? You want to watch a video? She says no, she only wants to play snake! She lies on her belly and crawls around."

Jane breathed again. "She's just playing," she told Mrs. Vlajic, whose brow was furrowed with worry or disapproval. "She's interested in snakes. It's just pretend."

"Pretend," Mrs. Vlajic agreed. "But I never saw a girl pretend like this! Every day same thing. Snake! It's very—" She broke off, apparently unable to find the word she wanted in English.

"All children go through stages," Jane said. "This is just a stage."

"It's not right," Mrs. Vlajic said. "For a little boy, okay, I can understand it. But not a little girl. Little girls pretend to be mommies, they play house. They play sisters, kitties, babies. They aren't snakes."

Jane stared at her. *I knew!* she thought. *I knew!* "Little girls can play anything little boys play," she said.

Mrs. Vlajic shook her head. "It's not right," she repeated. "Girls who want to be boys grow up and get into trouble." She stared at Jane, a long, hostile, unblinking stare.

"You don't tell children what to play," Jane said. "If Maisie wants to pretend to be a snake, that's okay with her father and me!"

The children had noticed something was going on. Laurie put down her doll and stared with naked interest. Thomas, the skinny boy, watched more covertly, his eyes just clearing the back of the couch. Maisie ran over to Jane and clutched at her knees.

"Why you cut her hair?" Mrs. Vlajic said, touching Maisie's head. "Such beautiful hair, like a princess."

"It got tangled," Jane said.

"So—you brush it," Mrs. Vlajic said sharply. "Now she looks like a boy."

"She looks fine!" Jane said. "Lots of girls have short hair!"

"Maybe you wish you had a boy," Mrs. Vlajic suggested. "Maybe you try to turn her into one."

Jane stared at the babysitter, at her shrewd frown and her wrinkled apple face, her thick, clean beige apron, and her old blue Keds. She reached down and took Maisie's hand. "We're going," she said. "We won't be back."

"What?" Mrs. Vlajic said, suddenly angry. "You take her? You don't like what I say, you quit?"

"That's right!" Jane said. "We quit."

"You own me two weeks' payment!" Mrs. Vlajic shook her finger like a storybook stepmother. "It's in the contract!"

Jane picked Maisie up and held her tight.

"I'll send you a check," she called over her shoulder, hurrying down the plowed walk.

Jane thought Billy would hit the ceiling when she told him, but he only grew more still. He was often still, lately, as though he were consciously setting himself apart from the turmoil of the house, the flurry of cooking and bathing and laundry, Jane's quick footsteps ringing out, and Maisie trotting or slithering around the rooms scattering toys behind her—even the windows rattling in the brisk February wind.

"Anyhow," she said. "I know we're stuck now. I can get home by noon tomorrow if you can stay home in the morning. And then at least we have the weekend to deal with it. I'm sorry if you think I acted hastily."

Billy picked up his glass of water. He used to drink iced tea, grapefruit juice, coffee, beer, but lately (except at breakfast) he only drank water. What was that about? Purity? Was he watching his weight? "It's done," he said. His voice was calm, cold. It was like a stream icing over.

"If you had been there," Jane said, "you would have seen why I had to do it. I knew she was like that, underneath! I knew it."

"Jane," Billy said, warningly. "You told me to take care of it, so I wish you wouldn't start blaming me now."

"I'm not blaming you," Jane said.

"After all, I didn't blame you for Elise."

"Elise!" Jane cried. "What was wrong with Elise?"

"She never cleaned up!" Billy said. "She was hugely spacey! She quit with no notice!"

"Maisie loved Elise!" Jane said.

Jane had loved Elise. Right this moment she felt she had loved Elise more than she had ever loved Billy.

In the morning Billy stayed home so Jane could teach her class. Because she didn't have to drop Maisie off first, she actually got to school early for a change. The halls were quiet, office doors shut, the only sound the hum of the fluorescent lights. She stopped outside the graduate student office to leave a note for Felicia canceling their afternoon meeting. She dug in her satchel for a pen but found instead, among the books and papers, a wooden doll, a Matchbox car, a plastic container of cereal, a mauve crayon, and a bottle of Tylenol. As she crouched down in the hallway to empty the satchel on the floor, a soft noise came from behind the cartoon-plastered door. Jane looked up. Something seemed to shift inside the office. There was a thump and a scuffling.

Jane knocked softly. "Hello?" she called. "Is anyone there?"

"What?" a voice said from the other side. A hoarse, tentative voice, but Jane recognized it.

"Felicia?"

"Hold on." More scuffling, and then the sound of something heavy bumping into something else. There was a rustling, and Jane thought she heard a zipper being zipped.

"Felicia?" she repeated. "Is that you?"

"Hold on. I'll just be..."

Finally the door opened. Felicia stood in the doorway, pale and rumpled in ripped jeans and a heavy sweatshirt, her hair everywhere.

"I was just going to leave you a note," Jane said. She thought she had never seen Felicia looking so tentative and flustered, so equivocal. So almost ordinary.

"Oh, okay. I just—got in early."

Jane looked past her into the crowded, windowless office that four students shared. It was close and stuffy in there, barely enough floor space for all the desks. Posters sagged from the yellow cinder-block walls: forest glades, famous writers, an artistic rendering of the Cyrillic alphabet. The desks were ugly, metal, scarred, and unmatching, covered with books, folders, Xeroxes, dried flowers, clocks, computers, photographs. A large, dusty plastic plant sat in one corner, hung with red and silver Christmas tree balls. In another corner a large backpack and a duffel bag leaned against a filing cabinet.

"Did you *sleep* here?" Jane asked, aghast.

Felicia sat down in a scuffed wooden chair. "The snake escaped," she said. "Karin flipped. She kicked me out. So." She pulled her hair back and knotted it behind her neck. "The snake was stronger than I thought," she admitted. "She pushed her way out of that cage. Even with the latches on!"

"Did you find her?"

Felicia shook her head. "She could have got back into a wall, gotten outside. Probably she's dead. Someone will find her, frozen in a gutter. Imagine that."

Jane, who had thought Felicia's decision to get the snake an irresponsible stunt that would end more or less this way, was surprised to hear real sadness in her voice. "Don't snakes hibernate?" she asked.

"Not pythons. They're tropical."

Jane didn't want to think about either a live python loose in Felicia's house or a dead one frozen in the snow. "What are you going to do?" she asked.

Felicia leaned back in her chair with her long legs stretched out in front of her. She looked at her boots. "I don't know. If it had been last month, I could have stayed with Douglas, but." She shrugged and looked up at Jane. With her protuberant green eyes and her receding chin, she looked like a beached fish.

Jane thought about how cold the weather was, ice clinging to every twig and wire. She knew how tight the Madison housing market was, how little money graduate students had. She had been a graduate student herself, after all, until very recently. And Felicia was her student. "You could stay with me," she said. "Until you find someplace. We have a finished basement, a futon. There's even a kind of a bathroom down there."

"I—"

Jane thought Felicia had begun to say "I couldn't," but then stopped herself. Her nod was so slight it could have been a twitch. Her face wore a mask of brittle nonchalance.

"You don't have any babysitting experience, do you?" Jane asked.

"I have four younger brothers," Felicia said, with some disgust.

After class Jane drove Felicia to the house. The car hummed down the wet street. The weather was warming up. Jane thought about offering Felicia a deal. Felicia could watch Maisie fifteen or twenty hours a week, and in exchange she could live in the basement rent-free until the end of the semester. They could work out a schedule. She'd have to discuss it with Billy first, but the possibility filled her with hope. With three of them, they could juggle the working week.

She hoped Billy would think it was a good idea, but she was having a hard time lately guessing what Billy would think about anything.

At the house Billy and Maisie were sprawled on the couch, watching cartoons. It was lunchtime, but Maisie was still in her pajamas and Billy looked as though he hadn't showered yet. He got up when they came in, leaving the television on.

Jane explained, briefly. "Felicia will be staying for a few days," she said, daring Billy to object.

"Without your snake, I hope," Billy said.

"There is no more snake," Jane said.

"Hey, Maisie," Felicia said. "Do you know what kind of snake you can eat for dessert?"

Maisie looked at her blankly, then shook her head.

"A pie-thon," Felicia said. "Get it? A pie-thon?"

Maisie giggled.

CHAPTER SEVEN

JANE COULDN'T SAY it was a mistake to have invited Felicia to move in. It certainly solved her most pressing problems. The schedule they settled on had Felicia taking care of Maisie nearly twenty-five hours a week. Felicia was done with class work, and she wasn't TA-ing. Besides writing her Ph.D. thesis, babysitting Maisie was her only job. In a way, Jane thought, it was the same as it had been for Jane herself—writing her thesis and taking care of Maisie, when Maisie was an infant. Only Maisie was more fun now than she had been then, and Felicia was getting paid.

Maisie adored Felicia. Jane wasn't sure why this surprised her, but it did. Felicia was very good with her, and this surprised Jane too. She invented complicated games of make-believe and organized art projects involving shaving cream and food coloring, or tin foil and scissors and cardboard boxes—projects that made huge, thrilling messes. Felicia always cleaned up the messes, too, often long before Jane got home, so the only way Jane knew what had gone on was if someone told her. She would never have known about Felicia and Maisie putting on bathing suits so Felicia could body-paint them from head to toe if Maisie hadn't said at bedtime, "I look good blue, but next time I'm gonna be purple."

Jane wasn't sure exactly what about this bothered her or exactly why. It wasn't as though body paint was harmful, and she'd never said Felicia had to tell her everything.

And now spring break—incredibly—was less than two weeks away. Jane would finally get to take her trip to Chicago. While she was there, she thought she might look up her old friend Helen Landis, who had been the graduate student teaching assistant in Jane's college Turgenev class and had encouraged Jane to pursue her interest in Russian. Helen had gotten a job at Northwestern straight out of graduate school, and Jane had e-mailed her for a while until the responses dried up. A first-year professor now herself, Jane understood it.

It was cold in Jane's study, always colder upstairs than down in this house, which didn't make any sense. The laws of nature seemed to be reversed. "We'll be walking on the ceiling soon," Jane had said to Billy the other day, but Billy hadn't laughed.

Tonight Jane sat at her desk and took out her address book, an old, tattered volume decorated with photographs of objects from the Hermitage collection: ornate silver samovars and bowls carved out of amber, diamond tiaras, jeweled eggs. Relics from the age of opulence. Russia was such a vast, abundant country, and its associations were so multiform: tsars and armies of faceless soldiers, countless miles of wheat, blinding blizzards in Siberia. Ravaged Jewish shtetls, chandeliers in the subways. Jane loved Russia's contradictions and its extremes, its superstitions and its incomprehensibly vast geography. She loved its language, rich and deep and guttural, amazingly expressive. In part, of course, the Russia she loved was gone, as the Karkov estate was gone, bulldozed to build a toothpaste factory. But as long as she and people like her—Shombauer and Sigelman, Helen and Felicia, too—continued their work, it would not entirely vanish from the earth.

Jane hadn't talked to Helen in years. She dialed the number in her book but wasn't surprised to get the recording saying the number wasn't in service. Next she tried e-mail.

Dear Helen,

I wonder if this address still works. I feel a little as though I'm launching a message in a bottle. My own e-mail is new, courtesy of the University of Wisconsin where I'm in my first year as an assistant professor! So much has happened it's hard to know where to start, but I'll be in Chicago from the 14th–18th and hope perhaps we could get together, and then I can tell you more easily how strange and tangled life has become, the wonderful things (like the job) seemingly inextricably linked to the less wonderful things, like having no time and being exhausted and feeling I can't manage this, that the juggling pins are about to hit the ground.

Did you know I married Billy Shaw? I think you did. Now we have a daughter, 2½, amazingly articulate and so much her own self. I'm anxious to catch up with you and hear about your work, and maybe get some hints about how to manage this crazy life. Academia is certainly not the quiet, meditative, monastic world it is sometimes portrayed as being. More like trying to think clearly while strapped onto a roller coaster.

Hope all is well, and that I'll see you soon!

Fondly,
Jane

In the morning, when Jane switched on her computer, she found the following message waiting:

Hi, Jane!

How lovely to hear from you out of the blue! I only have a moment, but of course we must see each other. Why don't you stay with us in Evanston? Life here is ridiculously hectic, but it would be great to have you. Congratulations on your job!! I'm sure you're wonderful, however uncertain you feel. And of course congratulations on your daughter. Sounds like as much has changed for you as for me. Sorry things are hard! No easy solutions. We'll talk it all over. Let me know exactly when you're coming, and I'll send address and directions.
—Helen

The day before Jane's trip, Maisie caught a cold and wandered blearily around the house with a dripping nose. Jane gave her orange juice and heated up chicken soup, but Maisie turned her face away from the spoon. She didn't have any appetite. Jane wondered if she should cancel Chicago (again!) and stay home. Did Maisie need her? What did *need* mean in this context? Was it more like a plant needing sunlight, or more like Jane needing a cup of coffee at three in the afternoon? What did other mothers do when things like this happened?

Jane didn't know. She didn't know who to ask. She could talk it over with Billy, but then if he said she should stay, she'd have to stay. And, after all, it was only a cold. Maisie had had a dozen colds in her short life. Jane mixed cinnamon into a saucer of sugar for cinnamon toast, hoping to tempt Maisie to eat something, then washed her hands. It might be only a cold, but Jane didn't want to catch it. She cut the toast into four even triangles and brought it over to the table, where Maisie had put her head down as though she were exhausted.

"Mama," she said, and sniffled. "Ma-ma-ma-ma-ma..." The word dissolved in her mouth into pure lament.

No, it would never be banished, Jane saw—the guilt, and the worry about what the right thing was. You could pluck it the way she plucked shiny leaves of goutweed by the driveway, but the blind white roots always thrust up more.

The next morning Jane woke Maisie early to say good-bye, holding her close and smelling her sweaty hair while Maisie yawned and rubbed her eyes. She coughed, a sound like a small engine trying to start up.

"Bye, Maisie. I'll see you on Friday, okay?"

Maisie coughed again and laid her head against Jane's chest. "Okay," she said sleepily, barely awake. There were no tears, no wailing; no protest of any kind. That was something to be grateful for, Jane told herself.

———

It was bright and cold in Chicago. On the windy sidewalk in front of the Newberry with its measured marble arches, Jane paused with one hand on her head to keep her hat from blowing off. She had spent most of one summer here years ago, but the building looked different now, its cornices weighted down with snow and its fountain turned off, like an old friend who has aged since last meeting. Jane, too, had aged, of course. She could empty her pockets of children's flotsam as she had that morning before catching the bus, but she could not stop herself from being changed, the way a new shirt is changed by going through the laundry. Standing in the frozen park across the street, she dug out her cell phone to check on Maisie, but no matter what she did the screen stayed blank. She must have forgotten to charge it. Trying not to think what a bad mother she was, she climbed the long, low steps to the door. The sun sparkled off the icy railings. The week lay before her like a blank white field of snow.

The diaries were small cloth-bound books, nearly square at four by five inches, each containing ninety-two sheets of creamy paper. There were twenty-six of them, filled with Masha's assured, angular Cyrillic script, each one in its own archival folder neatly labeled with the dates. There were some blots and crossings out, but not many, and to Jane this made the quality of the writing all the more remarkable. This was no revised, reconsidered, ultimate version, as Karkov's novels were, but a first intuitive draft.

Jane sometimes wondered whether Marlena Frey, who had edited the diaries for publication, had even bothered to read them all. Had she just scanned the pages for Karkov's name and included the entries that contained it? Was her Russian as fluent as Jane's? Had she felt the pull of Masha's language or of the picture of a particular, deeply felt life unfolding? Had Delholland or any of Karkov's other biographers? Had Sigelman sat in this chilly, high-ceilinged room (already Jane was wishing she'd worn a warmer sweater) with volume 10 or 20 or 25 resting on a book pillow before him, a cloth book weight (book snakes, they were actually called, because of their shape) holding the pages open? It was possible, but she doubted it. She felt strongly that she herself was the first reader ever to appreciate Masha's writing—or even to try to read it carefully—but she was determined she wouldn't be the last.

Masha had kept diaries sporadically starting in 1862, when she was thirteen and living in her parents' lively household in Moscow. The entries for the first years mostly described balls and parties and squabbles with her sisters in fairly pedestrian, melodramatic language. It was not until 1865, during her courtship with Karkov, that her language became more original, her entries more regular, and her thoughts more interesting. From then on she wrote faithfully, never lapsing for more than a month or two.

Jane turned her mind to the ambiguous circumstances of Masha's death. She thought how unhappy Masha had been after Konstantin was born and again after Katya's birth. She thought how hard it was for her, Jane, to manage life with just one child—how despite the sweetness that she felt so intensely some of the time, despite love, motherhood wore you down.

And yet except for a few entries shortly after the births of the first three children, motherhood *didn't* seem to have worn Masha down much. She seemed, if anything, to have grown into it, to have become accustomed to the fit. One might have thought that the birth of twins (Alexy and Pyotr in 1874) would have been a difficult time, but Masha seemed to flourish after their birth, writing, for instance:

The autumn is so warm and clear that the children are outside from morning to night, even having their lesson under the lime tree. Pyotr has just learned to sit up and, naturally mild and easygoing, he is content to listen to his brothers recite history for half an hour at a time! While Alexy, who cannot sit, wants me or Yelizaveta to dance with him all day and far into the night by way of compensation. It bothers her rheumatism, but I like to do it. It's beautiful weather, these October days, for dancing.

If Masha had committed suicide, it seemed to Jane that Vanya's death must have had a lot to do with it. Vanyushka was her darling, the child she nursed herself, having finally given up the conventional wet nurse. He was the one who always seemed to come to her with a kiss when she needed one, the quiet, watchful boy who wanted everyone to be happy. The year after his death had been a dark one, indeed, but eventually Masha seemed to have forced herself back into the light, for the sake of the children if nothing else. But maybe she found, after all, that she couldn't keep it up. Maybe the prospect of another baby who would seem to replace Vanyushka was too much for her.

Or maybe, Jane thought (reminding herself again that a scholar lived by evidence, not intuition, and that evidence was something she did not yet have)—maybe seven had just proved a mortally unlucky number for Masha. Numberless women, after all, had died in childbirth over the millennia. She tried to quiet her busy mind and just read, to let the river of words carry her. There would be plenty of time for judgments later.

On her previous trips to Special Collections, Jane had focused on a few particular periods in Masha's life: 1866, when she was a new bride (like Yelizaveta in *The Lime Trees*); 1876, when she was a sometimes distracted, extremely busy mother of five (as was the careworn, shrewish Lyudmila in *Prince Leopold*); and 1882, when Vanya died (as the child Igor had died in *Silent Passage*). Now she meant to begin at the beginning and work her way methodically through, taking notes in three categories into three different folders on her laptop: one for passages that were reminiscent of passages in Karkov's novels; one for animals and other nature references; and one for despair. After that she would look at Karkov's correspondence around the time of Masha's death and see if there were any clues there.

She could not resist, however, beginning by opening the volume containing most of 1878, which was probably the happiest period of Masha's life. She had overcome her early dislike of the country and found her footing as a provincial lady with a house full of children and visitors and servants. Konstantin was twelve, Katya eleven, Nikolai nine, the twins four, and Vanya still a babe in arms. She wrote in her diary frequently that year, long entries about family life in the house and animal life in the meadow, and the writing showed good humor and tolerance even toward Grigory. She seemed to have found not only her balance but also her voice; perhaps they were the two sides of the same coin. Even when something did ruffle her, like her glamorous sister Varya Petrovna Lensky visiting from Moscow with her four children, she kept her sense of humor and perspective.

That May, with the Lenskys in the house, there were picnics and expeditions, swimming in the Vaza River that ran, wide and shallow, at the bottom of the meadow. Katya adored her older cousin Alexandra, who was sometimes nice to her and sometimes wasn't. There were tears and tantrums. Katya's relation with Alexandra was in some ways an echo of the relation between the grown-up sisters. Varya traveled in the most exclusive circles in the capital. Her clothes were expensive. She wore a great deal of jewelry. Masha's country life—comparatively impoverished, with half a dozen noisy children always running in and out, needing things, scheming, quarreling, and growing out of their clothes, with little social intercourse and no culture at all except what they could generate themselves—was foreign to Varya, who could not prevent herself from commenting on what she considered Masha's coming down in the world.

"Before Varya came I never gave a thought to what I wore," Masha wrote.

I put on whatever was to hand and clean. Now I find myself wasting precious minutes worrying which dress would be best—which is not too unfashionable, not too often mended, not too "country," as she said of the blue I was wearing the day they arrived. Oh, what nonsense! This is country life, and if Varya doesn't understand that, it is no excuse for my behavior.

Jane could picture Masha standing in front of the mirror over her dressing table, holding up first one dress and then another. She could see her brow furrowing as she settled on the gray, then changed her mind and put on the blue after all, listening all the time to the voices out in the corridor. Was Varya giving impossible orders to the servants? Were any of the children crying? She could see Masha fumbling to catch a stray lock of hair in a comb before hurrying out of the room again in the mended blue dress, hot and irritable, hoping she'd manage to let her sister's comments slip by.

What would it have been like to have a sister? Jane had often wished she'd had one, someone to talk things through with; to confide in about motherhood and work and even, perhaps, about her marriage. But Masha didn't seem to have confided in Varya. She had had a closer relationship with her younger sister, Sofya, but by 1878 Sofya was dead.

After a satisfying if not earth-shaking afternoon, Jane took the El and then the bus to Helen's house, a large brick colonial on a pretty, quiet street in Evanston. The sycamores and oaks were bare now, and the sidewalks glittered with cold. Snow shovels stood at the ready on the porches or by the front steps. The snow itself was dingy and pocked, packed down by dogs and children's boots. Partly melted and then frozen over again and again, it had the worn-out, exhausted look of a young mother who's been awakened too many times in the night.

Jane rang the bell. Footsteps pattered on the other side of the door which was thrown open by a small boy.

"Hi," Jane said. "I'm Jane."

"Jane who?" the boy asked. He had shaggy brown hair, pale skin scattered with brown freckles, and a serious blue-gray stare.

"Jane Levitsky. I'm a friend of your mom's."

"You can come in," the boy said. "My mother is busy at the stove right this minute, so she couldn't come to the door."

Jane stepped into the house. "Thanks," she said, putting her bag down. The pale green carpet in the entryway spread off to the left into a spacious living room furnished with yellow couches and round scallop-edged occasional tables. The floor was scattered with toys and books, videocassette cases, a violin, balled-up socks, several pillows, and a red plaid sleeping bag.

"Jane—is that you?" Helen called. "I'm back here!" Her voice sounded the same as Jane remembered it, clear, loud, enthusiastic. She might have been projecting to the back of a lecture hall rather than calling from the kitchen through the intervening rooms. Behind the living room there was a linoleum-floored playroom with a large TV and shelves full of games and art supplies and all kinds of toys. There was a big cage with two parakeets in it and another with a brown lop-eared rabbit, half blocking the pass-through to the kitchen.

"There you are," Helen said as Jane skirted the rabbit cage. "Of course I was right in the middle of browning the chicken the moment the bell rang! But Michael is very good about the door. Thank you, Michael. Sorry about the mess. I never notice it until someone comes in, and then I remember how awful it is." She smiled warmly and hugged Jane hard with her soft arms.

"What a lovely house!" Jane said. "So roomy. How long have you lived here? What smells so incredible?" She was starving, she realized. She looked at Helen. Her smile was the same, as were her sharp gray eyes, but her body had gone from rangy to thick, and her pale hair, once cut as short as a boy's, was now long and streaked with gray, tied back with a pink scrunchie. The black jeans and faded T-shirts had been exchanged for drawstring cotton pants and a loose print blouse.

And how about me? Jane wondered. How have I changed?

Helen laughed. "It's just chicken," she said. "Come in, sit down! I'll be done in a minute. Do you want a drink? A glass of wine? Iced tea? Michael, go find your sister and both of you please set the table."

"I can't," Michael said. "I haven't practiced yet."

"You can practice later. Go."

"But I didn't practice yesterday," Michael said. "You didn't remind me."

"Later!" Helen said, not angrily but impatiently, waving him away as though he were a pesky insect. And then to Jane, "You found us okay?"

"Yes," Jane said. "Only I forgot how big Chicago is. So huge and freezing! I feel like I've trekked across Antarctica to get to your neighborhood. I hope it's okay I left my sled dogs tied up outside."

"Of course!"

A pot on the stove began to boil over, and then the baby started to cry and had to be fetched, and the smoke alarm went off when Helen opened the oven door, so there wasn't much of a chance to talk before dinner.

At last the table was set and the food laid out, and the family assembled around it. Helen's husband, Paul, whose entrance Jane had missed in the confusion, was a man of medium height—perhaps a shade shorter than Helen—with curly black hair growing thickly around a bald spot, and a ruddy, scrubbed-looking face above a neat beard. Jane remembered vaguely that he was some kind of doctor.

"Nice to meet you, Jane," he said, shaking her hand over the oval table set with laminated place mats showing views of Mount Fuji and cherry trees in bloom. "Levitsky, eh? Descended from the tribe of Levi! My cousin married a Levitsky. Nice guy, an engineer. Carl, from Boston. He wouldn't be your husband's—I don't know—second cousin or something, would he?"

"No," Jane said, digging hungrily into the chicken with olives, the salad, the fragrant rice pilaf. The food was delicious. She wondered if they could possibly eat this well every night. "My husband's last name is Shaw. I'm the Levitsky, and I don't have any relatives named Carl that I know of."

"Abby, please stop kicking the table," Paul said, and then to Jane, "I just assumed it was your married name."

"I have noticed that more women are going back to changing their names, even in academia, " Jane said.

"Like me," Helen said, cutting up bits of chicken for the baby. Jane looked at her in surprise. "I thought you kept yours."

"I did for a while, until Abby was born. But I got tired of having to explain who I was all the time, to doctors and teachers and people."

"No wonder I couldn't find you under 'Landis,'" Jane said, spreading butter on a piece of warm bread. (Helen couldn't have *baked* the bread, could she?)

"She's Helen Williams now," Paul said, smiling at his wife. "A whole different person."

"Better or worse?" Jane asked meaninglessly.

"Oh, better, I hope!" Helen said. "Better all the time."

"I guess I might have thought about changing my name if Billy had had a more interesting one," Jane said, which wasn't true. "But not for Shaw."

"And yet it's amazing how many things you end up doing that you never imagined considering," Helen said, almost dreamily. "Me, quitting my job, for example! Who would have ever guessed I'd do that?"

"You quit your job?" Jane said. She was stunned. "You're not working anymore?"

"I told you a lot of things had changed." Helen looked in Jane's direction without quite catching her eye, her expression bright, misty, faintly nostalgic. "I quit after Abby was born. I just decided I'd had enough of it. Not the work, but the politics and all of that. And as I got older, of course, I had less energy. It got to the point where I couldn't be up all night with a baby and still do a decent job teaching in the morning."

"You gave up *tenure?*" Jane was aghast.

"Well, the fact that I *had* tenure made it easier! No one could say

I quit because I wasn't good enough." Helen's expression hardened slightly, as though a soft filter had been pulled away from a camera lens. There were lines in the corners of her eyes and pouches around her mouth.

Jane couldn't think of anything to say.

Helen put some rice on the baby's high-chair tray and cut a piece of chicken to slivers. Her own food, neglected, cooled on her plate. "I tried working part-time after Michael," she went on. "The department didn't like it, but they said okay, one year, part-time. But I just couldn't manage it! Even teaching only one class, I couldn't get any research done. Well, I didn't want to. Michael was so amazing, hours would just pass—days would pass. Where did the time go? And then I got pregnant with Abby, and after she was born things were just impossible!"

"Abby was an impossible baby," Paul said, smiling at his daughter behind his beard. He had finished his chicken leg and helped himself to another.

The little girl scowled.

"She cried all the time," her father teased.

"Did not!" Abby said.

"Yes, you did," her brother said. "You just don't remember."

"No I didn't!"

The baby began to fuss. She thrust her head back against the padding of the high chair and flung her spoon to the floor. Helen got up and lifted her out of her seat and bounced her.

"Don't you miss it?" Jane asked, her voice barely audible over the baby's clamoring and Abby's angry protesting and the racket of the birds, which had started squawking in the next room. "Don't you miss having a career? An intellectual life?" She had been going to say "your own life," but she managed to stop herself.

"Not much. I think of this as a stage. My housewife stage. I had my intellectual stage; who knows what will come next? The kids will grow up eventually. Leonora will be in kindergarten in four years!" Oblivious to the commotion all around her, she ran a hand through her hair, which in this light looked as purely blond as when she had been a graduate student, living in a bare room without a rug or a comfortable chair, existing on cheese sandwiches and oranges. When Jane had wanted to be exactly like her.

CHAPTER EIGHT

AFTER DINNER Jane helped Helen clean up and get the children ready for bed. Paul was in and out of the kitchen making coffee, helping Michael find his violin music, making Abby wash her face again after she'd already washed it once. He got down on the floor and chased the baby, who, although she had been yawning, was wide awake and giggling by the time Helen came to put her to bed.

Helen didn't seem to mind. She seemed to like the chaos. Part of Paul's role in the family seemed to be to create it—riling up the children, leaving coffee cups everywhere, putting on CDs and turning them up loud so he could hear them all over the house. Another part seemed to be criticizing the chaos created by others. He yelled at Michael and Abby for leaving their shoes in the middle of the floor and for not brushing their teeth right away when he told them to. He told Helen the dishes weren't clean enough and that she should call the dishwasher repairman, and that the book he was reading had disappeared, and that something had to be done about the state of the garage.

"Don't talk to me about the garage!" Helen said good-naturedly. "I always park in the driveway. I never even go in there."

"Well, you'll be shocked when you do, Helen. It looks like a tribe of pygmies has moved in."

Listening to his loud, complaining, complacent voice, Jane felt a great tenderness for Billy, trekking with her across the vast, unknown, often treacherous territory of a marriage of equals, braving its geography of unwashed laundry and refrigerator shelves crusted with flecks of dried milk. Paul seemed like a nice man and a good father, and Helen seemed happy with him, but Jane was glad to have a different kind of husband. Once again she resolved to remember to appreciate Billy, and to be more patient, and to be nicer to him. It had been a tough year for both of them; it was time to make things better. She excused herself to call him, to say hello and to see how Maisie was, but the line was busy.

Helen asked Paul to put the children to bed. "Jane and I need some time to talk," she told him. "But don't keep Michael up all night reading to him. He has school in the morning."

"But we're at such a good part in the book," Paul said.

"And don't forget to set his alarm clock," Helen said. "We'll be in the sewing room."

Sewing room? Jane followed Helen up the plushly carpeted stairs and down the hall to a small room furnished with a shabby wicker love seat, an old-fashioned writing table, a sewing machine, and a bookshelf packed tightly with pattern books and Russian novels. Helen sat down on the love seat and slipped off her shoes.

"I've taken up sewing, as you see," she said. "I like it. My grandmother taught me when I was eight, and I made a little checked skirt that I wore everywhere. I was so proud of myself."

"My mother sewed a little, but she never taught me," Jane said. "Or I never wanted to learn, maybe." She was uncertain how to talk to Helen now that she saw how different their lives were, really: what different choices they had made. Was Helen a different kind of person than Jane was, or than she had been when Jane first knew her? And if she was, did it matter? Jane wasn't sure.

"I'm teaching Michael," Helen said. "He made a little drawstring bag to keep his Yu-Gi-Oh cards in."

"I still can't get over the fact that you quit your job," Jane said. She hadn't meant to say it, but there the words were, bursting out of her mouth. She took a sip of her coffee and looked at Helen, then down at the polished yellow floor, the faded kilim rug, the dust along the baseboards.

"Well, it was a big decision," Helen said.

"Huge," Jane said.

Helen pulled her knees up under her on the love seat and frowned thoughtfully at the gingham curtains. "I'm glad I did it, though," she said. "I'm not saying it would be right for everyone. But I kept running up against those things you mentioned in your e-mail. Too many balls to juggle! Too many things that were supposed to be indications of success feeling like burdens. I felt like I was walking around with all these weights strapped to me. Pulled down all the time."

Jane didn't say anything. She could see that Helen was only telling her own story the way she saw it.

"I might go back and do some teaching someday," Helen said. "You never know." Her gray eyes grew misty as though she still thought that all the possibilities of life were open to her.

"Sure," Jane said. "Why not?" But she knew, as Helen must, too, that "doing some teaching" was not the same thing as having a career.

"I just thought you should know that it's an option," Helen said. Her gaze was suddenly sharp again. "That's all. That you don't have to continue doing something, just because you started out doing it."

There it was, Jane thought. She smiled and shook her head. "It's not an option for me," she said.

"It took me a lot of years before I let myself consider it," Helen said.

"Did it." There was a pause. Then Jane said, "So, this used to be your office, I bet."

They looked at each other. The moment stretched out, not hostile exactly, but tense, weighted with the decisions each of them had made, or might make. On the other side of the door, Mahler blared, voices shouted to be heard over it, a telephone rang and no one picked it up; but up here it was relatively quiet, and the lamplight was soft. Jane thought how grateful she was to have somewhere to go to-morrow, that the library waited for her. That Masha, like a lover, waited for her, making demands as any lover would. Sleeplessness, sacrifice, devotion. She knew that she could never do what Helen had done. She could never give Masha up.

"Anyway," Helen said, her tone shifting, acknowledging that the subject had gone as far as it was going to go. "You're only in your first year. That's the worst, really. Everything's new—every single prepara-tion, every day! And you don't know the culture of the place yet. I re-member feeling like everyone was judging me every minute and also that they were ignoring me. Surely both of those things couldn't have been true." She smiled and Jane smiled, too. "But Madison's a great school," Helen went on. "It's a great department. Isn't Otto Sigelman there?"

"Retired," Jane said, glad to move on to a different subject. "Thus, the job opening."

"So, you're the new Sigelman! How exciting."

"Yes," Jane said. "Sigelman's really something. He still has an of-fice in the department, so I've gotten to know him a bit. I like him, actually. He can be nasty and foul-mouthed, but I like him. He's in-teresting. And he really cares about the work."

"Sure," Helen said. "He's a lonely old man. What else does he have to care about?" She pulled out the scrunchie and shook her head so that her hair spilled across her shoulders. In this light the gray was very prominent, but there was something sensual about the way the hair fell around her face and down her back.

"It's more than that," Jane said.

"I've only met him once or twice at the occasional conference," Helen said. "But I've heard things."

"There are a million Sigelman stories," Jane said. "He attracts malicious gossip, but I haven't seen anything I'd call dishonest or destructive."

Helen shrugged. "Even if only some of it's true, it's bad enough."

"He knows more about Karkov than anyone alive," Jane said, more sharply than she'd meant to.

There was another pause.

"Speaking of Karkov," Helen said. "I suppose you heard that Stephen Olen died."

Jane put down her cup. "No," she said. "No, I hadn't! I'd heard he was ill, that was all." Who was it who had told her that? Oh yes, Sigelman.

"Just a week or so ago," Helen said. "I heard it from someone I keep in touch with at Northwestern."

"Isn't that a shame," Jane said, and after a pause she asked, "Do you think it's true that he had some of his great-grandfather's documents? Things that were never donated?"

"Maybe." Helen yawned. "It's nice to hope so, I guess. But even if he does, one doubts if it would shed any light on the work."

"Everything sheds light on the work," Jane said.

The house was quiet when they brought their empty coffee cups down to the kitchen. Helen pressed the button on the blinking answering machine. "We can't seem to get to the phone half the time, even when we're home," she said.

Billy's voice, so unexpected in that tall, dim room, startled Jane and filled her with longing. "Hi, this is Billy Shaw. I'm trying to reach Jane. Please ask her to give me a call when she gets a chance. Thanks." In the background the clattering of dishes, someone coughing. Maisie, coughing.

Jane looked at her watch. It was well after eleven. If Billy was asleep, she didn't want to wake him. "I'll call him in the morning," she said.

But in the morning, everyone overslept. Jane was awakened shortly after seven by the baby crying. She must have been on a different floor because the sound was faint and thin, but nonetheless Jane was immediately awake, the covers thrown back and her feet on the floor before she realized where she was, and that the baby could not possibly be her baby. Then came footsteps and Helen's voice in the hall rousing Michael and Abby. "It's late, hurry up!" she said. "You'll be late for school!"

Breakfast was a rushed chaos of toaster waffles and orange juice. Jane drank coffee and tried to make herself useful fetching syrup and clearing plates. Helen, in an old blue kimono and slippers, looked tired and kept apologizing.

"It's not usually this bad," she said. "I guess I forgot to set my alarm, but normally Leonora's up at six anyway!"

"It's fine," Jane said. "You should see us at our house."

"Helen!" Paul called. "Where are my brown shoes?"

"Mommy," Michael said. "You didn't sign my math test."

"Jane," Helen said, "if you're ready by eight, Paul can drop you at the train."

The day before, Jane had been so impatient to start working that she'd barely glanced around the reading room. Andy Quinn, a Slavics guy from Minnesota whom she knew from occasional conferences, had said hello, but Jane had greeted him distractedly, and he'd let her get back to work. This morning, however, she looked around while she waited for the desk assistant to bring her requests. It was early. Andy wasn't there nor anyone else she recognized. As she looked at the handful of bent heads, the twiddling pencils, the glowing laptop screens, a sudden wave of happiness unfurled inside her. It rolled across the room, a warm current, and she thought that she'd rather be here, in this reading room, which hummed soundlessly with diligence and discovery, than anywhere else in the world.

By lunchtime Jane had reached October 1873, when Karkov had gone to Moscow to see about the printing of a new edition of his first novel, *The Lime Trees*. On October 10 Masha wrote:

I hope he will do some things while he is there besides merely attending to business. He is so gloomy, it sets the entire house-

hold on edge. Even Auntie Anna Borisovna, half-blind, sweet-tempered, and indulgent as she is—the ribbons on her cap always bright, like spring flowers—mentioned that she thought the change would do him good. "Grisha seems rather grumpy," she said with a kindly smile one afternoon after he had been to see her. Harsh words, indeed, from that old lady!

Jane went back and read the entry again. What had stopped her was only a little thing, but still it sent her scrambling for her Russian-language copy of *Dmitri Arkadyevich. Half-blind, sweet-tempered, and indulgent, the ribbons on her cap always bright, like spring flowers* ... All around her at the long tables, her fellow scholars turned pages with care, made notes, coughed, shifted in their chairs. What were they finding? What were they hoping to find? Would their disciplines be revolutionized by the work they did here? Would their own careers—their own lives—be changed? Did what happened in this room touch the world in any way? As Helen's doctor husband touched it, by saving people or by failing to save them; as Billy hoped to with his law degree; as Karkov had with his novels.

Anna Borisovna was Karkov's great-aunt, and she had lived at Dve Reckhi all her life. She had never married, and she never, apparently, bothered anybody. Masha almost never mentioned her. It seemed she never did anything worth mentioning, except at Christmas when she played carols on the piano. Jane thumbed through *Dmitri Arkadyevich* until she came to the passage about the death of Nastasia, Mitya's mother-in-law, a kindly old lady who never thought ill of anyone, least of all her cold-hearted daughter Olga, Mitya's wife. Nastasia had come to her daughter for a long visit that spring and stayed on into the summer. Karkov wrote:

Nobody minded, her mild presence upset nobody, except perhaps Olga Petrovna, who seemed to prefer not to be reminded of the past—of the fact that she had once been a tender, defenseless child, or that she was the daughter of such an ineffectual mother. She would have preferred to deny her bond to the sweet-tempered, indulgent old woman whose cap ribbons were always bright, like spring flowers.

Was it an obvious trope, ribbons like spring flowers on an old lady's cap? Was it a Russian cliché that Jane was for some reason unfamiliar with? No, no, it couldn't be. Holding her breath, Jane lifted the book snake and gently turned the page. She put the weight down again, trying to remain calm, to be skeptical, but her heart began to beat fast as she read (just as she'd known she was going to) that Anna Borisovna, like Nastasia, soon suffered a bad fall.

October 19

Some days she is lucid. Other days her mind wanders and she addresses herself to people who aren't there. Or at least, we with our feet firmly planted in this world do not see them. It is possible, I suppose, that they exist simultaneously with us but invisibly, their voices whispers of breath against our ears that we take for a breeze, or the reverberation of a door shutting.

October 21

Today Anna Borisovna was lucid for several hours in the morning and asked to be moved to the little room at the top of the staircase. We protested. Wouldn't she miss her view of the orchard! And it is drafty up there in the attics, no matter how well the windows are chinked. But she was determined. She smiled her sweet, humble smile and told me she didn't want to die in this big, sunny room that we would want to use for other purposes. She didn't want her death to taint it for us. And so we moved her—Ivan Stepanov on one side, Grisha on the other. We carried up her icons and made her as comfortable as we could.

In chapter 36 of *Dmitri Arkadyevich*, Grigory Karkov had written of Nastasia:

> On the last day of July they moved her, at her request, to the little room at the top of the staircase.
>
> "Please," Mitya had begged. "Won't you miss your view of the orchards? The plum trees are such a deep purple, and you can watch the children chasing the birds away. Besides, it's drafty up in the attics!"
>
> "No, Dmitri Ivanov," the old woman said, smiling faintly, her face seeming as smooth and unlined as a child's in the early morning light. She did not want the shadow of death to hang over the cheerful room, which they would want to use later for other purposes, and for once in her quiet life she was quite insistent.
>
> They carried her icons up and made her as comfortable as they could.

Jane's eyes moved from the printed page to Masha's diary and back again. She felt as though she'd broken through the surface of the world and found another world, shadowy and haunting, waiting underneath. Carefully, so as not to break the spell, she turned to the next entry and read Masha's thoughts on Anna Borisovna's death.

October 27

Anna Borisovna died last night, peacefully, in her sleep. We all miss her—her warmth and calmness, her kindness, her quiet, lovely blue eyes. She asked for so little and left such a little mark on the world! No children or household of her own. She leaves behind nothing but our love for her, and our memories— which for the children will begin to fade before very long.

Often I have envied her peaceable nature, but now that she is gone it seems a terrible thing to have left the world with so little mark upon it. Is it not perhaps better to storm and rage like Grisha, and yet to leave such a legacy as he will leave? Works of genius that will never be forgotten. Of course, it is more difficult when you are a woman.

Still, even the lark bequeaths us her song.

CHAPTER NINE

AROUND NOON Jane was startled by the touch of a finger on her shoulder. She looked up to see Joyce Winterson, the grande dame of Russian folk literature. In her stretch pants and bright blue beads, with the warm smile she always had for you whether she remembered who you were or not, she looked more like an eccentric grandmother than the publishing dynamo and star Stanford professor she was.

"So good to see you again, dear," she said to Jane. "I thought it was you when I came in, but I didn't want to disturb you. You had that absorbed look. I hate being interrupted, don't you? And yet the only way to avoid it, I find, is to work in the middle of the night. No one ever calls between one and four! Well, except my daughter Julie, but she's living in New Zealand and she can't keep track of the time difference."

"I can't work in the middle of the night," Jane said. "I wish I could."

Joyce smiled. "You're still young," she said. "You have plenty of time to develop insomnia."

Joyce was having lunch with Andy Quinn, who must have come into the reading room, too, while Jane was engrossed in the diaries. Joyce invited Jane to join them. "You can't do good work on an empty stomach," she said, patting her own plump middle. "I tell my internist, each of these extra pounds is a *Slavic Review* article!"

"Thank you," Jane said. "I'd like to."

The sun was out and the banked snow was melting, dark trickles spreading across the sidewalks. The sky was so blue it hurt to look at it, and the air was stirred, damp, suffused with the smell of earth. Joyce strode along, leading the way. Her leather coat flapped in the wind, and her gray hair was wild, her bright red lipstick unevenly applied.

It was warm in the dingy Polish diner with its scalloped paper place mats and metal napkin dispensers, its heavy chairs with patched vinyl seats—something of a relic in this neighborhood of sushi bars and high-end coffee shops. Steam fogged the glass doors.

"The pierogi melt in your mouth," Joyce said. "And I dream about the potato pancakes!" She slung her big lumpy purse over the back of her chair, flung off her coat, and lit a cigarette. "Jan!" she exclaimed as the waiter approached. "How's your wife? She must have had that baby by now! What was it, another boy? Send her my regards. I'll have the golabki, please, to start with. Andy? Jane? Stuffed cabbage for everyone?"

The waiter beamed, poured water, brought an ashtray, disappeared. Andy blew his nose into a rumpled handkerchief and produced pictures of his children.

"Thomas is the older one. He's four," Andy said. "Ben is twenty-two months." He passed around a snapshot of the two boys posing with Santa Claus.

"How sweet they are!" Joyce said. "They change so fast at that age. A new milestone every hour, practically!"

"My daughter's just between them," said Jane, who hadn't thought to bring along a photograph. "She's two and a half."

"You could betroth them," Joyce suggested. "Not that it would matter, of course. I tried so hard to convince Victor, my oldest, to marry my neighbor's daughter. A beautiful girl—and wouldn't you know it, she became a radiologist! My daughter-in-law the doctor, it might have been, but he wouldn't even ask her out. I was young then and still thought I could influence them, but of course you can't. Still, I kept trying, with Lily and Julie. By the time Luke came along, I had finally given up. Beaten into submission!"

"How many children do you have?" Jane asked.

"Just the four." Joyce took a long drag on her cigarette.

"My god!" Jane said. "How did you manage it?" She looked at Joyce, whose work she had always admired, with a new respect. Four children!

"God only knows," Joyce said, flapping her hand to disperse the cigarette smoke that gathered around her head, remarkably similar in color and texture to her hair. "Harold was out of the country half the time, consulting about communications systems. Well, I had a live-in nanny for a while. And I always only cooked once a week. Soup or chili. Sometimes meat loaf. When that was gone, we lived on cereal and peanut butter until it was Saturday again. The kids were all very self-sufficient. They learned to put themselves to bed because I would get involved in something and forget, and they always wrote their own homework excuse notes. They had my signature down pat. When I think about it now, it horrifies me! But they all grew up, one way or another. Though I notice none of them is jumping right into having children of their own."

The food arrived.

"People are having children later these days," Andy said as Jan, the waiter, set down the plates of watery, pale green cabbage studded with gray bits of meat. "My wife and I were both thirty-eight when Thomas was born."

"It's not that." Joyce shook a flurry of salt over her plate. "They're absolutely petrified of parenthood!" She dug into the food as though she hadn't eaten for days. "What are you working on, Jane?" she asked through a mouthful of cabbage.

Jane did her best to describe her research without mentioning either the concurrences or her questions about Masha's death. Just the fact that she was looking at the diaries as texts of interest in their own right was enough to raise the bushy eyebrows of Andy Quinn. "Karkova was very interested in folk figures," Jane said, knowing this would interest Joyce. "She wrote about the peasants' beliefs. About Baba Yaga, and snakes sucking the rain from the sky."

"A common but intriguing idea," Joyce said, running a piece of bread around her plate. "Very ancient. It probably goes back to the Neolithic Eye Goddess, the rain spinner, whom we sometimes see represented as a snake. Also as a frog or a butterfly—anything that transforms itself. Parthenogenetic. The goddess-as-snake can give rain or withhold it, just as she can give fertility or withhold it." She stuffed the piece of bread in her mouth, wiped sauce from her chin.

"Funny you should mention the rain," Andy said. "I've just been rereading that wonderful tale of Karkov's, 'The Little Rain Cloud.' That's the one where the boy finds the snake in the dried-up streambed, but instead of killing it he befriends it, and the snake brings the rain that saves the harvest."

Jane put down her fork. "I'd forgotten that story!" she said. "What I remember is the one where Baba's snake-dragon servants kidnap a youth on the night before he's going to marry a maiden."

"That's right," Andy said. "And the maiden has to rescue him from Baba Yaga's hut before she eats him."

"Baba Yaga's always threatening to eat everybody," Jane said. "But she seldom seems to actually get around to it."

"Still, the skulls on her fence presumably came from some-where," Joyce said.

"Living skulls, with fire for eyes," Jane said.

"Poor Baba Yaga!" Joyce said. "Always hungry! Always bony-legged, no matter how much she eats."

"She certainly eats a lot," Andy said. "Enough for three men, enough for ten men. There's always something in her oven."

"Yaga the destroyer!" Joyce went on. "Queen of the Underworld with her iron teeth and iron breasts—fingers floating in her soup!"

"And yet," Jane objected, "she's also the beneficent mother. She gives horses, and guidance. She presides over the birth of children."

"Yes, sometimes," Joyce conceded, running a hand through her hair with a sigh and lighting another cigarette. "But I always think she's happier as the carnivorous crone. Nurturing can be so exhausting! Besides, she gets to fly through the night in her mortar, sweeping away her tracks with a broom. Who wouldn't want to do that?" Her eyes fell to her empty plate, and she looked around for Jan. Smoke seeped delicately from her nostrils.

"In one journal entry," Jane said, "Maria Petrovna talks about snakes eating their young to protect them, and how humans might want to do that, sometimes."

"I always thought Maria Petrovna had a ruthless streak," Joyce said. "Don't you find that, Jane?"

Jane shook her head. "No. She's strong, certainly. She protects her children and she runs the household and so on. But I think of her as essentially nurturing. Deeply maternal." She thought of Masha regally sweeping through the big house with her head held high. But was that the right image? What about Masha sitting tensely at the long dining table while Grigory's endless visitors made sycophantic remarks? Or lying awake at 2:00 A.M. wondering if Grisha was going to come home that night? What about Masha and Karkov in bed, conceiving one of their many children? No, no—her imagination balked at that.

Joyce ran her finger around her plate. "That's the image she creates on the page," she said. "But think about Olga Petrovna."

"That's fiction!" Jane objected. "Karkov's fiction. And, besides, Karkova never expected an audience for her diaries."

"Every writer imagines an audience," Joyce said. "Even if it's only an audience of one."

It was midafternoon by the time Jane and Andy got back to the Newberry. Joyce had left them after lunch, saying she had some shopping to do.

"She always does that," Andy said as they hurried back up Walton Street. "An hour in the archive and she's done. Wait and see, she'll get three articles out of the work she did this morning!" He shook his head admiringly.

"Maybe she uses magic," Jane suggested. She thought of Joyce laboring away in the dead of night, as the magic doll in the Russian folktale had weeded Baba Yaga's garden and picked the dirt out of the witch's wheat under the light of the moon.

That afternoon—or what remained of it—Jane noted two more particularly striking entries about snakes for inclusion in her "animals" folder.

June 28

The peasant is no friend to the snake. He fears and loathes the sturdy viper in whatever vestments, whether the rusty-red of the earth, the dull brown color of the muddy river, or the cold, clear black of a moonless sky. Considerably smaller than her harmless cousin the grass snake, the viper is marked by a zigzag trail running down her back like a ribbon of black lace. Along each side she bears a series of roundish spots, as though some child had marked her up and down with sooty fingerprints. And on her head is stamped the form of a small, shadowy heart.

August 12

So much superstition living alongside so much faith! Some will give their last kopek to the priest when he comes through the village, sanctifying unions that may already have borne the fruit of two or three children. Others dispense with Christianity altogether and worship the old gods. For them, the rivers and streams are full of rusalki and other nymphs, and the moon waxes and wanes at the pleasure of the old Baba.

Yesterday I found a snake living under the chicken coop. Ivan Stepanov will kill it when he finds it, but I cannot bring myself to mention it to him. For Evil dwells among us—who dares to deny it? It is only through the Devil that we can know that God exists, for we see the works of Satan everywhere around us, while God has hidden His face.

No more concurrences, however, or evidence of despair.

"Ten minutes for items from the vault," came the call of one of the desk assistants.

Jane looked up and was surprised to see that she was one of the last readers left. Andy Quinn was gone, as was everyone at the tables close to hers. Hastily, she gathered up her belongings, separating her own papers from the archive materials. Getting to her feet, she flipped through the last pages of the volume she had been reading, skimming to get a sense of what came next. The pages did not flow evenly under her thumb, however, but flopped together at the end. Something was behind them. Something was jammed between the last page and the cover. Jane flipped to the back to see what it was and found that some papers had been wedged in, age adhering them to the inside cover. Brittle, yellowed pages, folded into quarters. Jane eased them free and unfolded them carefully.

Masha's handwriting.

"Dear Varya—"

Jane's eyes skated over the first few sentences, taking nothing in. It was a letter, apparently, from Masha to her sister at court in Moscow.

"Items for the vault," the desk assistant repeated.

June 11, 1884

Dear Varya,

I received your letter yesterday, and although I thank you for your kind offer, I cannot spare Katya just now. It is true as you say that she has been through a difficult time these last months—largely through my own fault, as no one knows better than I! But it seems to me that to send her away just at the moment is not the best course. We have wasted already too much time each trying to make his own way through the darkness, and now I feel strongly that we must hold together. Nor can I satisfy your other concern and account to you for my recent illness or what you call my "peculiar behavior."

You inquire as to whether the "entire incident" has passed from my mind, but it has not. In fact, every detail of those days seems burned into my memory, and I am convinced I will never forget a moment of it. I do not, of course, talk about it with anyone, but it haunts me — as though it underlay everything as I move about the house. The hard dirt road seems to lie just under my shoe at every step. I remember the first night when I awoke in the dark and the room seemed to pulse with the sound of a voice so deep it was beyond hearing except as a kind of distant thunder. I rose from my bed and drew the curtains. The light of the full moon flooded in, and so I did not need even a candle to dress.

Outside it was cool and the wind moved the new leaves of the birches. I walked across the lawn and out into the meadow and down to the river in the dark, my feet seeming to know where they would go. It did not feel like walking, but rather as though I were gliding through the whispering grass. Yes, yes, the grass said with its ten thousand tongues, as I moved through it in the dark down to the water's edge.

At the river, the water was black and gleamed like obsidian in the moonlight. I sat down on a rock and watched it — moving and yet seemingly still, like the earth itself, which feels solid under our feet, yet which we are told is actually a sphere of rock and fire spinning through space. I thought how cold the water would be if one plunged into it — a searing cold like fire that would cleanse me at once of misery and mortality — and for a moment it seemed that this was what had called me out of my warm bed — the dark voice of the river.

After I had sat there for some time — minutes or hours, I could not say — I saw something rising out of the dark water. It was like an emanation of the water itself — a gliding blackness which slid up onto the bank and paused, then coiled and lay still. It was a snake — a large one. Probably it and I, if laid side by side and nose to nose, would have covered just about the same amount of ground.

"Ma'am?"

Jane looked up. The desk assistant stood in front of her, a young man in a blue shirt smiling apologetically.

"Yes?" Jane blinked, seeing him indistinctly. It was as though she were in a fish tank and he were outside the glass.

"It's after five thirty. All materials from the vault need to be returned."

"Yes," Jane said automatically. "Yes, I'm done." Her eyes slid down to the page again.

It seemed to me that the snake was watching me—waiting to see what I would do. It flicked its forked tongue in the moonlight as though it would taste what sort of creature I was. It raised its head and, although remaining as silent as the moon, it seemed as though all the sounds of the night—the wind in the grass and the creaking trees and the cold water flowing over rock—were funneled through it, and I picked it up and put it in the basket I was carrying. The snake was

"You need to stop, now."

But Jane couldn't stop. The sound of Russian roared in her ears like the ocean into which the drab syllables of English fell like pebbles.

The snake was heavy and silken like a woman's breast—and yet strong and muscled too, like a *muzhik*'s back. And so I felt that I had found what I

A cold hand touched her arm. Jane looked up to see who had gotten into the fish tank with her. It wasn't the rosy-cheeked desk assistant but an older man—perhaps fifty—gray-haired with pale, graying skin and a beaky nose, his eyes sharp behind his red metal-framed half-glasses. "I need you to return the material *now*," he said.

Jane stared at him, blinking in confusion. "I just—" she said.

"Now."

She folded the letter and put it on the table, coming to her senses. "I'm sorry," she said.

She took the El back to Evanston and walked from the station in a daze. Masha had, apparently, left the house secretly in the night, just as Karkov's Snake Woman had! She had found a snake by the river and picked it up. What had happened to her after that? How was it possible? It had never crossed Jane's mind that parts of the Snake Woman's story *other* than the suicide might have had any basis in fact, but apparently they had.

And what was the letter doing in the diary? Jane wondered about this as she turned the corner and saw the lights glowing in the window of Helen's house, none of the curtains drawn, the house ablaze like a beacon in the darkness. Could it have been put there in later years by an unknown hand? Was it only a draft? Had it, possibly, never actually been sent?

Immediately inside the front door, Helen was waiting for her. She was talking, but Jane had missed the beginning of the sentence and couldn't follow what she was saying. Her tone was urgent, and from the expression on her face, you would have thought Jane was a child who had taken a bad tumble from a bicycle or had a close encounter with a vicious dog.

"I was out," Helen said. "He left a message on the machine." She pushed something toward Jane—a slip of paper with a phone number on it. Jane looked at it blankly, as she had at first looked at Masha's letter blankly, unable to take in its meaning. "I tried your cell," Helen said, "but it must have been turned off."

"I forgot to charge it," Jane said. Then her heart seemed to stop beating, and her skin went cold. The area code was 608—home—but the number itself was unfamiliar, ending ominously in a triplet of zeros. She knew what it was, what it had to be, as Helen, obviously, had also known.

She was in the kitchen now. The phone was in her hand, the plastic receiver once white but gone gray with fingerprints and grime, sticky with jam.

"University Hospital," said the voice on the other end.

Jane's heart thumped and her fingers felt stiff and clumsy. Words tumbled out, fragmentary, confused. Her voice seemed to have become detached from her, struggling on its own to convey the necessary information like the frantic body of a decapitated chicken. "This is Jane Levitsky. I got a message. My husband— I don't know— I'm not at home. Shaw, that's the name. Maisie Shaw, Margaret Shaw. Would they be in a room? How do I . . . ?"

The voice on the other end was calm, as though Jane had asked for the billing office. "Yes, Mrs. Shaw. Just one moment, please." The tapping of computer keys. Then, "I'll connect you."

There wasn't any air. Jane felt her heart in her throat, a tightness, a suffocating pulsing. She thought, *So this is what people mean when they say that.* Then the connection was made, there was a ring, and the phone was picked up.

"Hello?"

It was Billy's voice.

Jane worked to push some words out of her mouth. "Billy—it's me. I got your message. What happened? What's wrong?"

"She's okay. Jane? She's going to be fine. Okay?" Billy's voice was loud, distinct and definite. Stern. "She was coughing. A lot. She was having trouble breathing. Not— Just lying there, trying to breathe. She won't, they said there won't be—the doctors. Any brain damage."

Jane could not speak. All she could hear of what Billy had said were the two last words. "Is she okay?" she asked. And again, "Is she okay?"

"She's right here. They put her in an oxygen tent for a while. She has some kind of virus with initials. Respiratory something."

"Is she all right?" Jane asked again. She felt if she asked it enough perhaps Billy would say something that would make her believe his answer. What this might be, she could not imagine.

"She's all right. Jane? Listen to me. She's all right. She just, she has to stay here a few days. I think—"

She interrupted him. "I have to go. If I leave right now— I think there's a bus at seven."

There was, but Jane didn't catch it. Helen drove her to the station. She got a neighbor to watch the kids and drove Jane into town, but it was rush hour. The traffic was terrible. Five minutes late and the bus had gone. Jane wanted to scream. She wanted to throw herself to the floor like a toddler herself. She wanted to propel herself by the force of her will backward through time. If the neighbor had gotten there a little faster, if they hadn't missed the light at McCormick Boulevard, if the sun hadn't fallen at the angle it did, its glare creating havoc at the entrance to Lake Shore Drive!

If she hadn't found the letter, she would have been back at Helen's house a few minutes earlier.

It was no good. There was nothing she could do except buy a ticket for the nine-thirty bus and sit on a molded plastic chair to wait, her suitcase between her knees.

"Come back to Evanston," Helen urged. "Have dinner with us. I'll get you back here in plenty of time."

Jane shook her head. She could barely speak. "I'll stay here," she said, and Helen kissed her, a light, dry kiss, full of regret, like a moth brushing against her cheek, before disappearing back into her incomprehensible life.

Jane was hungry, but getting out of the chair seemed impossible. Her limbs were heavy and unwilling. When she saw the pay phones against the wall, however, her muscles seemed to come to life all by themselves, propelling her up off the seat and across the floor.

The phones were filthy and defaced, studded with chewing gum. The first had no dial tone and the second would not accept her phone card, but using the third she finally got connected to room 3308 and listened as the phone in Maisie's room rang and rang without anyone picking up. What did that mean?

She sat down again. The fluorescent lights buzzed, a baby cried, an old woman shuffled across the floor dragging her belongings behind her in a bulging garbage bag. Jane, who under other circumstances would have looked away, stared. The homeless woman was stooped over, not tall to begin with, her long white hair knotted and wild. She wore a faded, shapeless cardigan over a long skirt that dragged behind her with a horrible swishing sound as she went, sweeping the filthy floor. She looked up and saw Jane watching her, changed direction and hobbled over to where Jane sat, stopped in front of her, and held out a dirty purse. Jane saw how hollow her cheeks were, although her stomach seemed to bulge under the layers of clothing. She had no eyebrows over her yellow eyes and she smelled like hard-boiled eggs and filthy wool, thawing mud and decay. Jane fumbled in her black leather satchel for her wallet and pulled out a twenty-dollar bill. She knew it was bribery—attempted bribery of a God in whom she did not believe. Of Fate. Of the hag, Baba Yaga, spinning out the length of each life in her hut behind her fence of bone.

The old woman looked at the money. She looked at Jane with her yellow eyes. Jane looked back. She thought of the slow stream of pilgrims who came to Dve Reckhi and were offered shelter in the kennels, of Karkov's Snake Woman walking the dirt road, her clothes yellow with dust, her children crying for her, wondering where she was.

Russian women fended off witch's curses with milkweed collected on Saint Nicholas Day, and by wearing belts, and with the juice of radishes or rainwater collected during a storm's first thunderclap. Jane reached into her purse again and found an emery board, a pack of gum, a crumpled tissue, and a flyer for a lecture on poetry of the Soviet era. She took the gum and handed it to the woman, her hand accidentally grazing the hag's bony, filthy hand.

The street woman grinned, showing her shriveled gums. She unwrapped three pieces, shoved them into her maw, and sucked, throwing the paper wrappers to the floor. Her toothless gums made loud, wet, slurping noises as she moved away, leaving in her wake the smells of urine and mildew. Jane thought of Baba Yaga's hut scurrying through the forest on hen's feet. Tangled rye was Baba Yaga's hair, blini shingled her roof.

Masha had written:

When I grow old, I will be a joyful crone. No children to look after, no husband, no household, no servants, no guests no carpets no stables! Only the flax to spin and the stove to feed. Only myself to please, and no fear of either life or death. Yes, old age is the recompense for enduring a woman's life! If one knows what to do with it.

But she hadn't even made it to forty.

The bus was nearly empty. Jane had a double seat to herself but she couldn't sleep. Out the window the sky was dark and dull, crisscrossed with the lights of airplanes. On the highway they passed an identical Van Galder coach going the other way, bound for Chicago, and as it flashed by, Jane felt she could see her former self inside it, yesterday's self, sharp and self-absorbed, thrilled with anticipation. How could that self and this one be the same? How could she have been so preoccupied with Masha's life when her own was breaking open?

But no, Billy had said that Maisie would be all right. He had said—what had his words been? There won't be any brain damage. Jane shut her eyes and tried to calm down. She opened them again and looked at her watch. It was 9:55. The bus was scheduled to arrive in Madison at one A.M. She knew she should try to get some sleep.

When one of her children was sick, Masha remained by the bedside day and night. When Vanyushka was dying, she nursed him round the clock. When Katya fell from her horse, when the twins had measles, when Kostya's delicate chest kept him indoors one winter, Masha was not off in Kovo or Moscow, but home at Dve Reckhi where she belonged. Or so Jane had always believed. She thought of the children in *Lady of the Snakes*—of Masha's real-life children—waking one day to their mother's absence. *In the morning, Tanya opened her eyes and saw the sun streaming in the window. It fell in a golden band across her bed, thick as a tree trunk. Something was odd.* That was how Karkov's final novel began. She thought of Joyce Winterson saying, "I always thought Maria Petrovna had a ruthless streak."

They were almost in Beloit now. Jane promised herself that if Maisie would be all right, she would work less and spend more time at home with her. She wouldn't travel. She would stay in Madison where she could see Maisie every day. But a high, single-minded, almost childish voice inside her head chimed in, *What about the letter, then?* The letter, tasted but not consumed? What about other manuscripts tucked away in odd corners and library shelves and the backs of closets all over the world—not just in Chicago but in New York, London, Moscow, Helsinki? Were they all to be lost to her now, lids closing them away in leaden chests without keys? Words she would never read until someone else found them, plumbed them, published them?

> From her bed Tanya could see dust motes floating in a band of sunlight. The air was hot. Usually her mother woke her early, when the sky was pale like an egg about to crack open and release the day. She turned her head and saw that her brother Fedya was awake. His round, pink face wore a worried look. His brow was furrowed and his gray eyes were like water in a storm. Beyond him, in the bed nearest the door, her other brother Ilya slept peacefully, curled up with his knees to his chin. He always kicked the covers off in the night.
>
> "Fedya," Tanya whispered. "Something's wrong."

But no, this was nonsense. This was melodrama. There was no God to receive Jane's bargaining, to let Maisie live or die according to what Jane would give up. If there were— If there were, she would give up anything, of course! Her own life! But that wasn't the way the world worked. She would not have to relinquish her work, Masha, her quest for tenure, giving papers at conferences. Her constituted existence.

She sighed, shifting on the hard seat. If she had been at home when it happened, what could she have done? Billy had been there. Billy had done everything she could have done. The bus sped north. It began to snow. The big wipers clacked and the tires hissed. Across the fields, distant lightning illuminated farmhouses and groves of stark, leafless trees that vanished the next instant into the purple darkness as though they had never been. Thundersnow.

Down in the kitchens and from out in the yard, Tanya could hear people shouting, pots clanging, dogs barking, footsteps running. In his bed by the door, Ilya woke up suddenly and, hearing the commotion, began to cry. It was as though the whole estate had awakened suddenly, like Ilya, into tears. Tanya felt that, as soon as she stepped out into the hall, she would be caught up in a whirlwind, as though the house had come free of its foundations. Her mother, with her calm gray eyes and purposeful footfall, was the steady axis around which the house spun. Her absence sent them tumbling through space.

In Madison Jane flung herself at the single waiting taxi. A man in a tweed overcoat cursed at her. From the back of the cab, moving down the empty streets, she watched as the big white flakes immolated themselves on the windshield and filled up the deserted hospital turnaround. The main doors were locked and she had to go in through the emergency room. The night triage nurse told her how to get to the pediatric wing.

Inside room 3308 it was dark. Gradually Jane made out the bed against the wall. Maisie was curled in the corner, knees to her chin. She wore a miniature hospital johnny that fell open to reveal the diaper underneath. The cotton blanket had been kicked aside. Tied to the metal bed frame was a bunch of Mylar balloons that rattled quietly as the air eased them back and forth. A cot took up most of the rest of the floor space, and Billy lay sprawled across it with his mouth open, snoring, all his clothes on.

Jane stepped quietly to the foot of the bed. Maisie's face looked tight and private. Wires emerged from under her gown and wound back to a big machine against the wall. What was it for? Maisie's chest rose and fell. She was all there: head, chest, legs, feet, fingers, and toes. Jane felt dizzy with relief. She sat down on the edge of the cot and put her hand on Billy's back, but he didn't wake up. She slipped out of her heavy wool coat, spread it on the floor, and lay down.

> Tanya stepped out of bed. The stone floor was cool under her bare feet as though the stones retained the memory of the cold, clear stream that had once poured over them. She went to the window. Out in the yard, a dog trotted across the dusty lane. Chickens pecked in the dirt. Old Alyosha sat propped under a tree snoring, his beard in his lap. Then the sudden sound of footsteps rang down the corridor and she heard her father's angry voice, shouting.
>
> "Zinaida Andreevna!" he called. "Alyosha! Where is everybody? Where's my wife? Hasn't anybody seen her?" Her mother's voice was always like the stream running over the stones, but her father's, raised in anger, rattled like hail on the nursery roof.

Sometime later Maisie's cheerful, imperative voice woke Jane. "Daddy!" Maisie said.

Jane struggled to open her eyes. A gray dawn crept in under the blinds, and she could hear carts rattling by in the hall, voices, the patter of soft-soled shoes. Billy lay asleep on the cot, snoring softly.

"Daddy! Daddy, wake up!"

Jane pushed herself up off the floor. Maisie opened her eyes wide at the sight of her and reached out her arms. Jane lifted Maisie up, wires trailing like tentacles. She clung to Jane, warm and fierce and heavy. "Mommy!" she cried happily. "Mommy, look at me! I'm sick!"

An orderly knocked on the door and wheeled in breakfast, French toast strips steaming under plastic wrap.

Billy opened his eyes. He sat up and yawned, stretching, filling up the small room.

"Look, Daddy!" Maisie said. "Mommy came!"

"Hi, Billy," Jane said.

Billy looked at Jane, his tight jaw tawny with stubble. "Just in time for the recovery," he said.

CHAPTER TEN

MAISIE GOT BETTER as quickly as she had fallen sick. During the morning she was quiet with tired blue circles under her eyes that matched Jane's, but at lunch she ate a whole cheeseburger and a plate of fries, and after that it was hard to remember—almost to believe—that she had been seriously ill. The supporting evidence was all around them in the form of the hospital and its busy denizens, the doctors and nurses and respiratory therapists who came in and out with their white coats and their stethoscopes. They checked the machines Maisie was hooked up to, checked Maisie's lungs for functioning as if they, too, were machines. Jane found that she had trouble taking any of it seriously. Maybe it was denial. She was hardly even frightened when, later in the afternoon, while Maisie was sleeping and Billy had gone home for a shower, one of the monitors began beeping piercingly, a beam of noise stuttering out through the room.

Jane looked at the machine. It was a heavy box like an old-fashioned record player, covered with dials and buttons and numbers and plugs. All the numbers, glowing green, had gone to zero. Heart rate: zero. Respiration: zero. A flat line.

Jane looked harder. There on the bed before her lay Maisie, manifestly breathing. Her hair was messy and her fingernails had Play-Doh under them and her gown had gotten twisted so the electrodes taped to her chest were clearly visible, the chest itself moving up and down. The sun streamed through the window that overlooked the parking lot. Somewhere a truck was backing up, its distant mewling a faint counterpoint to the deafening alarm emanating from the machine. For a minute, maybe two, Jane stared. She wasn't frozen with fear but rather suspended, expectant, as though some great change were about to take place and she was waiting to see what it might be.

A nurse arrived, walking fast in her white cross trainers, her turquoise V-neck bunny-printed blouse flapping. Without even glancing at Maisie, she pressed a button on the machine. The noise stopped. In the silence the low, background hum of the heating system seemed suddenly very loud. The nurse adjusted the electrodes on Maisie's chest. "These things are always coming loose," she said. The numbers jumped and Maisie, who had slept peacefully through the machine's siren, woke up and began to cry.

Jane sat on the bed. "It's okay," she said. Only now that it was over was she suddenly terrified.

"Mommy!" Maisie cried, burying herself in her mother's lap, her head hard and damp against Jane's stomach. Jane felt Maisie could tell she'd just stood there, that she'd done nothing at a moment that might have been crucial, although it had turned out not to be.

"I'm here, Maisie," she repeated. "I'm right here."

And still, all the time, a part of her mind was busy thinking about Masha and the letter and the story of *Lady of the Snakes*, a world away from this buzzing hospital with its wires and antiseptics and nurses dressed in cartoons. A world where a child as sick as Maisie had been would have died already, where desperate mothers clung to the most tenuous threads of hope: superstition and prayer. *The dry road ran up the hill.* This was the world that could create someone like the Snake Woman; that could value her. *A woman walked along the road carrying a basket.* Masha had lost her beloved Vanyushka; but Jane, because she lived in an age of medical technology, of oxygen tanks and antibiotics and bronchodilators, had been spared.

Billy came back a little later. He stepped into the small room like a storm cloud: big, brooding, smelling faintly sharp, like ozone. The sight of him made Jane extremely tired. The thoughts she had had so recently in Helen's kitchen—how lucky she was to be married to Billy, and how she was going to work harder to let him know she knew it—had dissolved in the face of his actual presence, and she felt her anger rising to meet his. She didn't know where it came from, but she could taste the bitterness of it in her mouth. He seemed to blame her for where they had ended up—this hospital room with its liver-colored floor and its hallways full of sick and injured children—and she supposed she blamed him, too. Or, if *blame* were too hard a word, they each took out on the other their fear and their hatred of the place.

Billy removed his gloves finger by finger, unbuttoned his big blue-black overcoat, but didn't take it off. "How are things?"

"Good," Jane said. "They say she's doing very well. She should be able to go home tomorrow."

"Who's they?"

"The doctor."

"Which doctor? Ratzenberg or Billings?"

"I don't know," Jane said.

"Old or young?"

Jane hadn't noticed.

Billy sighed. He looked up at the ceiling as though commiserating with an invisible ally there.

Jane shut her eyes and leaned back against the wall.

"What's wrong?" Billy said.

"Nothing. I'm just a little tired."

"Go home, then. Get some sleep. I'm here."

She looked at him. He looked back, irritable, impatient. She could see his hands balled up inside his pockets.

"Okay," she said. She stood up. They were face-to-face, six feet apart, but Jane felt she could barely see him. "I'll be back by ten."

"That's okay," Billy said. "I'm happy to spend the night."

"No," Jane said. "You slept here last night."

"I really don't mind," Billy said.

"That's nice of you," Jane said. "But I'll be back."

Billy exchanged a glance with the ceiling again. "Whatever you want," he told Jane.

On the drive home the city looked different, transformed by the snow that had fallen overnight. The trees looked softer, bulkier, while the houses seemed skulking and withdrawn under their white hoods. In the parking lots of stores and in the corners of gas stations, towering edifices of plowed snow stood like barrow mounds. What was she doing here? How had she come to be here, in this frozen place, when in California the bougainvillea would be spilling red and magenta over the arbors?

At home, standing under the snow-peaked overhang, Jane couldn't get the front door open. She put in her key but the deadbolt wouldn't budge. It took her a minute to understand that the door was already unlocked. She turned the knob. What was wrong with Billy, leaving the house open? Then she saw the figure on the sofa and jumped.

She had forgotten Felicia would be in the house.

Felicia wore ripped jeans and a heavy fisherman's sweater that reached almost to her knees. Her hair was pulled back in a tight braid, and her face looked particularly pale and freckled behind her gold-rimmed reading glasses. Books and papers lay scattered around her on the couch: *The Lime Trees*, Sigelman's 1971 edition of *Dmitri Arkadye-vich*, a stack of Xeroxed articles, and Jane's own Russian-English dictionary, which usually sat on the corner of her desk in her study. Felicia's well-thumbed and much annotated copy of *Lady of the Snakes*.

"Hi," Felicia said, closing the book she was reading around her finger to hold her place. "How's Maisie?"

Jane looked at her, curled on the couch like a cat. There was no reason for her not to be there, but it didn't seem right. The whole house seemed suddenly wrong, dusty and askew, the window frames too dark, the shades flimsy and tattered, the floor bare. Then it struck her: someone had put away the toys. The rug was an unbroken oval of blue, like a pond after somebody has drowned.

"Better," Jane said.

"I was worried," Felicia said. "It was so scary, watching her struggling to breathe."

Jane put down her bag. She took off her coat and hung it up. "Yes," she said. "I'm sure it was."

"Usually she's so animated," Felicia said. "I knew something wasn't right because she was just sitting there. It was so unlike her."

"I'm going upstairs to lie down," Jane said. "I have to be back at the hospital in a couple of hours."

Felicia blinked behind her glasses. "Will Billy be back later, then?" she asked.

Jane lay on the bed in the dark, unable to sleep. She knew she should get up, she should take off her clothes and get under the covers, but she was too tired. Too tired to get up and too agitated to sleep. Through the window she could hear cars passing, guttering through the slush. The room was stuffy. Someone must have turned up the heat. Behind her closed lids she saw Felicia, lying on the couch downstairs reading Jane's books, her hands all over them. She saw her unbraiding her hair until it fell across her shoulders like a shower of gold. She saw her stretch, saw the wool of her sweater slide across her breasts, saw her pale long bare feet, toenails painted orange, the silver ring on the left big toe.

It was Billy's sweater. Billy had lent it to Felicia when she had mentioned that she had neglected to pack anything warm. There was no reason she shouldn't be wearing it, but still, seeing her in it made Jane suddenly see things differently, the way an outsider might see them. The distant husband and the voluptuous, blond student. What could be more obvious than that?

But no. How far she had fallen even to consider it! Billy, distant or angry though he might be, would never stoop to that. It went against everything he stood for, against the entire way he saw himself: a decent man, an upstanding man. Honorable. No, Billy could be up-tight, judgmental, inconsiderate, but faithlessness was not among his faults. Not all men succumbed to blond young women. Not all blond young women were interested in seducing older men. Why should they be? Besides which, Felicia had a great deal to lose — the roof over her head and her Ph.D. adviser in one fell swoop. She was too smart, surely, for that.

Jane turned over. She opened her eyes and stared at the darkened door. What kind of thinking was this, weighing consequences as though that was all that would prevent the thing from happening? Who was she — who had she become — to think this way?

To distract herself, she fished her own copy of *Lady of the Snakes* out of her bag, which was lying on the floor by the bed, found the passage she had been thinking of in the hospital, and began to read.

The dry road ran up the hill with fields of wheat on either side of it. It was hot, and the young wheat waved in the hot wind as though struggling to get free, but the cracked earth held it fast by the roots. Grow, the earth commanded, and the wheat grew, fecund and bountiful. All summer it would swell, day after day, like a woman heavy with child, until the men lined up with their scythes in the fields and hacked it down.

The road itself was yellow, caked hard, and dusty. In rain it was worse, a river of mud. A woman walked along the road carrying a basket. Plenty of people walked up and down the road which cut through the countryside of Kovo, winding from town to town and within sight of a few grand houses: tradesmen and messengers; pilgrims with worn clothes and calloused feet, begging from house to house, some on the way to the distant monastery at Travenko, others, having found it not to their liking, returning.

The woman carried herself proudly, head up and shoulders back. Her hair was full of the dust of the road. Her clothes—not a peasant's clothes, not a pilgrim's—were dusty too, although well cut and in good repair. On her feet she wore a pair of stylish boots caked with the fine, yellow dust, and she limped a little as she walked, as though her feet bothered her. She looked like a lady, but no lady would be walking such a road alone, or looking rumpled as though she had been sleeping in a ditch, or be so conspicuously without a hat. She walked without turning her head, a big covered basket over her arm. She kept a steady pace, until all of a sudden she stopped and sat down by the side of the road. She set down her basket and pulled off her boots. She wiped her face with a handkerchief already stained with dust. She looked one way up the road and then the other and, having ascertained that nobody was coming, she pulled off her stockings as well. Then she got up and walked away, leaving her boots lined up neatly on the side of the road as though expecting someone—elves perhaps—to take them away and clean them.

The red sun was low in the sky when the woman came into the village—a few poor houses roofed with thatch, gray smoke rising like flights of pigeons from the stovepipes, dirty children shouting and throwing sticks. The woman went over to where the children were playing. As she approached, they fell silent and stared at her. One boy was taller than the others with thick, shaggy hair and eyes of different colors, one blue and one gray, like the same sky in different weathers. It was to him that the woman addressed herself. Her voice was clear and low and she spoke gently, in a way he was not used to being spoken to. He had to take a step closer to hear her.

"Is anyone in the village ill?" she asked.

"What?"

"Is anyone ill?" she repeated. "In your village."

"Only old Lyubov," the boy said. "She has the fever."

The woman nodded. She must have been tired after all that walking, but she still held herself erect. The children did not notice the dark stains on the road where she had walked. Perhaps she had stepped on a stone in the road and that was why her feet were bleeding. "Which house?"

The woman sat down in the dirt beside the hut. It was nearly dark now, the first stars lying scattered across the sky where Baba Yaga had flung them like so many handfuls of salt. More and more appeared until the bowl of darkness brimmed with a million diamonds. The horns of the waxing moon rose slowly in the east. After a long time, as though in response to a signal, the stranger leaned forward and undid the fastenings of her basket. She reached inside and took something out, then did up the fastenings again. The object in her lap was long as an arm and gleamed faintly in the moonlight—but darkly, not as metal gleams, although it was sleek and curved as a Cossack's sword. The woman held it up in both hands, and as she did, it collapsed in the middle like a rope and slithered slowly through her fingers. A soft hissing sound slipped from between the woman's teeth as she held the snake up to her face and brought it toward her, almost as though she intended to kiss it. The snake stared at her, motionless, its flat, pale snout turned up, the black slits inky in its golden eyes. Its forked tongue went out—once, twice, three times—and then it struck, its mouth open wide and its teeth bared, the hollow, poison-filled fangs aiming for her cheek.

But the woman was faster. Even as the snake was striking, her hand was reaching up to grab it, to hold it firmly by the back of the neck. The snake hissed, its mouth straining toward her, its tail thrashing back and forth, and then went limp. Gently, like a mother stroking a child, the woman traced the rough cross just visible in the scales on its head. The snake calmed. Its body relaxed, its mouth closed, its head bowed toward the dirt. When at last the woman put it down, it crawled docilely into a fold of her skirt and lay still.

Maisie was very pleased with herself when they brought her home, as though her recovery were a magic trick she had performed.

"Yesterday I sick," she said. "Today I better!" She skipped down the hospital corridor, holding Jane's hand.

Billy was waiting in the car on the other side of the automatic doors. Jane could see him sitting in the driver's seat, his form distorted by the double layer of glass, the car window and the thick hospital door. He looked smaller than he was, a fun-house Billy hunched like a mobster over the steering wheel. The sight unsettled her. She paused, and Maisie tugged on her arm to get her moving again.

The March air was cold and smelled of snow. Inside the car there was a sharper smell. Soap? Aftershave? Billy's hair was wet from the shower, his face closely razored, revealing the hard, clean plane of his jaw. Scrupulous. In the back Maisie ate a graham cracker and kicked the front seat. Billy drove fast down the slushy streets. The silence was icy, aching. Maisie began to hum.

Jane started to talk. "The doctor said that the virus Maisie had, the RSV, it's something you can only get once," she said. "Like chicken pox."

There was a pause. Then Billy replied, "People do sometimes get chicken pox a second time, though, don't they? Isn't that what shingles is? Or is it rickets?"

"I think rickets is what sailors get. When they don't get enough vitamin C. That's why they used to give them lime juice on whaling ships. But you're right, of course. About getting chicken pox twice."

Billy was silent.

"We always believe doctors, don't we?" Jane went on. "What they say. Just like Masha believed hot olive oil would cure a child's cough because the midwife told her it would."

Billy swung the Honda fast onto Monroe Street. The back end fishtailed as the car roared up the hill.

"Can I need another cracker?" Maisie asked.

Jane reached over the seat and handed her one. "Why does it bother you so much when I talk about Masha?" she said to Billy.

Billy said nothing for a minute. Then he said, "Why do you have to talk about her all the time?"

"I don't talk about her all the time," Jane said.

Billy stared out the windshield at the wet street.

"She's my work, Billy. I'm not supposed to talk about my work?"

"Yes, of course!" Billy said. "I just wish you'd talk about other things more. It would help convince me that your head is here, in this world. More than it's there. That you care about what's going on with us as much as you care about them."

"Of course I do!" Jane said. "Don't be ridiculous!"

"Do you?" Billy said. "Maisie was sick. You seemed kind of— I don't know. *Blasé* isn't exactly the word. Detached. Distanced."

From the back seat Maisie chirped, "I not sick! I better!"

"I have not been blasé about Maisie being sick!" Jane said. "I was terrified!"

"I not sick," Maisie repeated. "I said good-bye, tent." She meant the oxygen tent. "Good-bye, hop-sital!"

"You weren't here," Billy said. "I couldn't reach you. You didn't return my calls! It was frightening, goddammit!"

"I forgot to charge my phone!" Jane said. "I'm sorry! You didn't say she was sick in the message you left on Helen's machine—how was I supposed to know?"

"I better," Maisie reminded them yet again. "Dat nurse tole me— I'm *all* good!"

They had reached the house. Billy parked and switched off the car. Jane got out, opened the back door, and unstrapped Maisie from her seat while Masha's letter sat perfectly still and silent in the vault of the Newberry Library, like a star at the center of a solar system.

Sigelman knocked on Jane's office door. He wore a rumpled shirt under a brown suit jacket and his half-bald head reflected the overhead lights. "Come have lunch with me," he said. "I'm on my way now."

Jane opened her mouth to decline, but what was the point? He wanted to have lunch with her; she would have lunch. Nothing in her life was very much fun right now, but this might be.

"Have the mushroom strudel," Sigelman suggested when they were seated in the narrow upstairs restaurant on State Street. "It's very good."

"All right," Jane said.

"It always makes me think of that scene in *The Lime Trees*," Sigelman said. "The one where Sergey and Irina go mushroom hunting in the forest."

Jane, who had been examining the menu, looked up. "He carries the basket for her, and their hands touch as she lifts the cloth to drop the mushrooms in," she said.

Sigelman smiled, a real smile instead of his usual wolfish grin, and quoted in Russian: "'The brush of her small, smooth hand against his large one, hardened by work, made her feel nearly faint. Her cheeks reddened and she could not look at him but lowered her eyes to the forest floor, scattered with pink and white wildflowers. As she struggled to regain her composure, a slow bee buzzed its way into the mouth of a wild geranium, brushing pollen from a neighboring flower against the stamen and collecting nectar on its hungry tongue.'"

"Poor Irina," Jane said, impressed, despite herself, at his recall.

"Poor Sergey, I should think!"

"Sergey's dead. He doesn't know the difference. Whereas Irina is left alone, her last hope of marriage gone."

"They should have been more careful picking the mushrooms," Sigelman said.

"Yes," Jane agreed. "They were fatally distracted by lust."

The waitress brought a bottle of wine and uncorked it. Sigelman waved her away, poured the wine himself, and raised his glass.

"To your career," he said.

Jane could see the way he must have looked decades before, a dashing young man from behind the Iron Curtain with a way of looking at you that made you feel revealed, as though you were a text he were explicating.

"Thank you," she said, and they drank.

"So," Sigelman said. "How was Chicago?"

Jane put her wineglass down. "How did you know about that?"

Sigelman shrugged. "It is a secret?"

"No."

"Well, then. Was it a good trip?" His pale eyes watched her blandly. Gray pebbles.

Now it was Jane's turn to shrug. She took another drink of wine. It was dry and cold and faintly acidic, and it tingled as it went down her throat. "All right," she said. "I'd hoped to spend the whole week, but as it turned out I only got a couple of days."

"I heard your daughter was in the hospital," Sigelman said. "What a scare! But she's all right now?"

Jane looked the tablecloth, concentrating on not starting to cry. "Yes. She's all right."

"Such a frightening thing," he went on, leaning toward her. "Of course you had to come right back! I'm very glad to hear she's all right."

"Thank you," Jane said. Part of her thought he was snowing her, practicing his charm out of boredom, perhaps, or just to keep in practice. What did he care about Maisie? But another part of her felt that the warmth and sympathy were real. *See,* she wanted to say to someone—Shombauer perhaps, or Helen. *See, he's not so bad!*

The food arrived. The mushroom strudel was delicious, and Sigelman told a story about a nephew whose appendix had burst when he was thirteen. "I went to visit him in the hospital," Sigelman said. "He was all right by then—convalescing with the TV on and everything. Absolutely fine! But my sister, she was a wreck. No sleep for a couple of days and worried sick, and her English wasn't so good, either. The hospital terrified her, she couldn't understand half of what anyone said.

"So I told her, 'Go home!' Joseph was fine. 'Hannah,' I said, 'you need some rest. I'll stay with him.' Not that he needed anyone to stay with him, a big boy of thirteen. At that age I was already cutting up meat at the butcher—ha!" He looked at her to see what she thought of the picture of him at thirteen in a bloody butcher's apron.

Jane smiled and cut another bite of strudel. "Go on," she said.

"So, I promised I would stay with him. And Hannah went home, and I sat down next to Joseph and I told him I wanted to get him something, something to entertain him. Because he was going to have to stay in the hospital another couple of days for the doctors to keep an eye on him. 'Joseph,' I said, 'what can I bring you? Comic books or a Walkman, maybe?' This was 1982, more or less, and Walkmans were hot—all the rage, you know. But Joseph hemmed and hawed. He didn't want a Walkman, but I could tell there was something he did want. Only he wasn't saying what.

"He was a skinny kid, my nephew, growing like they do at that age, their pants always too short. And he had acne all over his face. And he was shy. Even with me, his uncle! So I tried to encourage him. 'Joseph,' I said, 'go ahead and tell me! You want a camera? A couple of record albums? How expensive can it be?'

"But he just shook his head. 'Uncle Otto,' he said, 'it's not something expensive.'

"So I said, 'What, then? Spit it out!' And he goes red as a beet, and he leans over to me and he whispers: '*Hustler*. That's what I want! Can you get me some *Hustler* magazines?'"

Now Sigelman began to laugh, a great hoarse guffaw that made people at the tables near them turn and look. "*Hustler* magazine!" he repeated. "Can you believe it? *Playboy,* he said—*Playboy*—that was too dull for him! He'd heard *Hustler* was so much more exciting." He laughed with his head thrown back, his wattles jiggling.

Jane had to laugh, too: it was such a Sigelman story. She should have guessed, she thought, what the punch line would be. "So did you get them for him?"

But Sigelman didn't answer. The story and his laughter had cost him breath, and he began to cough.

"Otto," Jane said. "Otto, are you all right?" She leaned toward him and he shut his eyes, which were watering now, two rivulets running down the loose skin of his cheeks, and he nodded, making a great effort. Conversation at the tables around them stopped, and the young waitress hovered nearby, unsure if there was something she should do.

At last he managed to bring the coughing under control. He opened his eyes and let out a long, phlegmy breath. "Sorry." He wiped his face with his napkin. He was sweating. He poured himself another glass of wine and drank it down. "I'm fine. Just this fucking cough I get sometimes!"

"Have you seen a doctor?"

"Sure I have," he said. "Fucking doctors. Johnny-one-notes. Why should I give up my one pleasure in life, just to hang around here for a few more years?"

Smoking, he meant. Jane finished her wine. "Somehow I think you have other pleasures, too," she said.

"Well," Sigelman said with what was either sincerity or mock sincerity—Jane couldn't tell—"there's always the work."

"The work!" Jane repeated, and she went to pour them some more wine to toast it, but the bottle was empty.

Sigelman gestured to the waitress for another bottle. "Are you going to tell me about this trip of yours or not?" he said to Jane. "Surely it wasn't a total waste of time?"

Jane looked at him, at his gray, jowly face into which a bit of color had begun to return, his rumpled shirt with the sleeves rolled up, the age-spotted scalp with its wisps of white hair. Half a bottle of wine in her, she could no longer remember what she thought she was protecting by not telling him. Besides, she had to tell somebody. The words, unspoken, felt electric in her mouth. "Actually," she said. "I did find something."

He leaned just perceptibly forward. "What?" he said.

"A letter," Jane said. "Wedged in the back of one of Maria Petrovna's diaries." She was gratified to see the gray pebbles of his eyes narrow. "It's from Karkova to her sister Varya. It's very strange and very interesting. It says she got up in the middle of the night and went down to the river and picked up a snake. She seems not to have returned home for several weeks after that."

Sigelman put down his wine glass. "Where did she go?"

"I don't know. She refers to peasants' huts, but she's not specific."

"It sounds like—"

"It sounds like *Dama Zmiev*. Yes."

Sigelman said nothing. He sat with his big brow furrowed, frowning. The waitress, who had long ago cleared their plates, now took the salt and pepper off the table, leaving the stained cloth bare except for the check.

"There are lots of references to snakes in her diaries as well," Jane went on. "Particularly in the later years. I hadn't noticed how many until recently."

But Sigelman wasn't interested in what was in the diaries. "Just the one letter?" he said. "Uncataloged?"

"Just the one. And even that I didn't get to finish! It was closing time, and I almost got into a tug-of-war with the desk guy. And then Maisie was sick."

It was almost two o'clock now and the restaurant was empty. Out on the street a bus roared by. Jane reached for her purse.

Sigelman smiled and leaned back comfortably in his chair. The web of red veins in his cheeks grew redder. "So," he said, "we think we may have uncovered a biographical basis for *Dama Zmiev*. But we don't really have enough information."

Jane, who had been fumbling for her wallet, turned and looked at him. "*I* think *I* may have uncovered!" she said. She stared into his baggy gray troll's eyes.

"Of course," Sigelman said. "You."

That night, after putting Maisie to bed, Jane went downstairs where Billy was watching the Bulls game. She sat beside him on the old brown sofa. "What's the score?" she asked.

"Bulls up by two."

"Close game."

Billy said nothing. The light from the television flickered across his face so she could see only intermittently how tense and unhappy he looked.

"Want a beer?" Jane asked.

Billy glanced over at her, surprised. "Okay," he said. "Sure."

Jane got up, went into the kitchen, came back with an opened beer. She handed it to Billy.

"Thanks," Billy said.

"You're welcome."

"You're not having one?"

"No." Jane pulled her legs up under her, turned her face to the television.

There was a pause. Jane tried to follow the game. Then Billy said, "Since when are you that kind of wife?"

Jane looked at him again. He looked like someone she used to know a long time ago. "What kind of wife?" she asked.

"The kind who gets up to get her husband a beer."

"I'm the same kind of wife I've always been," she said. "What kind do you want?"

The game went to commercial. Billy shook his head. "No," he said. "You're different."

"How, exactly?" Jane asked. She was curious.

Billy shrugged stiffly. "I think you used to be happier. Before," he said.

Before? Jane thought. Before what? Before Maisie was born? Before they were married? Before they moved to Madison and she had a job and he didn't? Suddenly she was crying. It was all too much for her: Maisie's illness and Billy's coldness and Masha's letter and her own seeming inability to do anything right. She hadn't even managed to finish reading the letter! Sigelman, she was sure, would never have left the way she had. Tears slid down her face.

Billy, who could never bear to see anyone in pain, put his arms loosely around her. Jane leaned into his chest and wept. "I'm sorry," she said. She couldn't stop crying. His chest was solid, and she would have known his smell anywhere. She wrapped her arms around him and held him tight, and he fell back against the cushions, and she lay on top of him and began to kiss him. She kissed his face, his stubbly cheeks, and the hollows beneath his eyes. She kissed his ear and felt him sigh involuntarily as she breathed into it, felt the hardening inside his jeans. She slipped her hands under his shirt. His skin was warm. She pulled his face around and kissed his mouth. His lips opened for her, his teeth grazed her teeth.

"Let's go upstairs," Billy whispered.

Jane reached down to find his zipper. His penis pulsed in her fingers and he groaned and reached inside her blouse.

"Jane," he said urgently. "Let's go up to bed."

She knew what he was thinking. Felicia could walk in any time, but Jane didn't care. She slid her skirt up to her waist and pulled her underwear off, and at last Billy stopped talking.

But afterward, when she lay with her head cradled on his chest, he sat up and gently pushed her off.

"Let's just lie here a minute," Jane said.

"Janie. Come on." Billy found his pants, buttoned his shirt.

Jane sank into the scratchy cushions of the couch and watched him.

He picked up her underpants and tossed them over to her. He glanced at the door. He ran his hands through his hair to smooth it.

"Billy," Jane said, letting the underpants lie where they had fallen. "I have to go back to Chicago on Saturday."

He looked at her in utter disbelief. "What?" he said.

"Just for the day. I found something when I was there. A letter. It could be very important." Jane was getting cold, but it seemed better to tell him while she was still naked. It was as though she wanted to make him see she wasn't hiding anything.

"What's important," Billy said, "is for you to be home for a while! At least until Maisie is a hundred percent better. Until things settle down."

"Yes," Jane said. "I know. But this is only for one day." Didn't he know she wouldn't do it if it weren't very important? "Let me explain what it is," she said.

Billy shook his head. "No, don't tell me," he said. "I don't want to hear about it." Then he turned around and walked up the stairs.

Jane sat up on her knees and called after him, "Next Saturday, then!"

But Billy didn't turn around.

Masha Karkova had written:

What happens between men and women changes everything, and yet it changes nothing. We remain two separate kinds, unknowable to each other, gazing at one another with suspicion and longing.

CHAPTER ELEVEN

JANE COULDN'T DECIDE whether it mattered if she waited a week or not—or to whom it would matter if it did. To Maisie, who seemed a hundred percent better, sleeping well and chirping around the house at Felicia's heels, saying, "You ready to play now, 'Lisha?" To Billy, as a demonstration of Jane's commitment to the family? To Jane herself, so she could say she was flexible, prove she was willing to listen to what Billy had to say? She didn't know. All she knew was that the atmosphere of the house was fragile, brittle. The wrong word—the wrong tone—made the air curdle around them. A week wasn't really a long time, even if it felt like it. So Jane beat back her impatience, taught her classes, and took the bus down on the first Saturday in April.

It had been a chilly, foggy morning in Madison, but in Chicago the trees were blooming white and pink in the sun. Daffodils swayed near the door stoops and along the sidewalks, and the air outside the bus station was mild, the sky a pure and soothing blue. It was such a beautiful day, and Jane felt such a rush of elation, that she decided to walk from the bus terminal, even though it would take a bit more time. Down Canal she strode and across Kinzie. She passed the Technical Institute, people out shopping or sitting on benches enjoying the weather. Her shoes began to pinch, and she wished she had worn different ones. She thought of the Snake Woman leaving her boots by the side of the road as though expecting elves to take them away and clean them. She thought of the letter: "I remember the first night when I awoke in the dark…" How did it go after that? Something about a voice?

The source of *Lady of the Snakes*, as Sigelman had said; but how much of a source? She'd been asking herself this question for a week and a half, but she was afraid to guess at the answer. Masha couldn't really have gone among the peasants as a curer and itinerant pilgrim—could she? Could she actually have left her boots by the side of the road and gone on barefoot with bleeding feet? Could she have carried snakes in a basket, later let them crawl over her naked body? Impossible. Yet didn't Masha speak in the letter of lifting a snake out of the water—or was it only that she had watched it slither out of the water? It was hard to remember. It was frustrating how the exact words eluded her, but in half an hour she'd have them before her again in all their inky precision. She'd copy them down, take them away with her, keep them close. She would change the face of Karkov scholarship, she thought! She, Jane Levitsky, wife of Billy, mother of Maisie, daughter of Saul and Pamela—she would make her academic career at twenty-nine. *I can see you want everything*, Felicia had said, and it was true: she did. She was determined to get it, too; for herself, but also for all the other women who would come after her. To stand in opposition to women like Helen, women like Shombauer.

She climbed the steps to the Newberry, showed her reader's card, and took the elevator up to Special Collections. She walked up to the desk and filled out and handed in her call slips, relieved to see that this reference assistant was a woman, not the open-faced young man she had tried to stonewall. She went over to a table and waited, laying out her notebook and pencils, her laptop, her index cards.

A short time later yet another reference assistant came by with the folders she had requested on a rolling cart, like dim sum. Jane's hands were actually shaking as she opened the heavy archival folder marked as holding the diary from December 1875 to September 1876, and it was hard even to turn the little book over to open the back cover. She did it, though, of course, and stared at the thick cream-colored paper of the back page (Masha often left both the first and last pages of her diaries blank), at the black stitching and tan leather of the binding. There was nothing there.

Jane's heart skipped and she blinked at the empty place where the letter should have been. Then, with clumsy hands, she flipped to the front of the book, and then quickly through it from front to back. When that, too, revealed nothing, she set it down and turned each page carefully, but there was still nothing—no folded pages, not even a scrap of paper—only Masha's clear, bold handwriting making its way across the bound vellum.

Jane knew she had the right volume, but she checked her notes anyway. Her head had clouded and it was hard to think clearly, so she did not rely on thinking but checked everything by rote, trying not to let herself panic, just mechanically doing each thing: opening each folder, turning each page of every volume (in case the letter had gotten put back in the wrong book), rechecking her notes as to which volumes she'd had out. When all of this activity still yielded nothing, she shut her eyes and put her head in her hands. Then, all at once, she realized what must have happened. A wave of relief poured through her. Only now did she feel how tense she'd been, shoulders hunched, neck stiff, heart beating like a gong. The letter must have been taken out and filed with Masha's correspondence, since correspondence was what it was. She took a deep breath, feeling her heart pounding still too hard and her arms trembling as she leaned her elbows into the wooden table. Then she pushed her hair out of her face, reached for yet another call slip, and began to fill it out.

But she stopped almost as quickly as she'd begun. The call slip asked for the year of the correspondence she wanted. Had the letter been dated? She thought so, but she couldn't quite remember. Had it been written the year that Masha had died—was that right? Everything seemed fuzzy, suddenly, her sharp memory failing like an old TV. She got up and walked over to the desk.

"I was here a week and a half ago," she told the reference assistant.

She did her best to speak slowly and clearly, but she was sure her voice was either too quiet or too loud. "I was reading one of the volumes of Maria Karkova's diary, and there was a letter stuck in it, tucked in the back. But today it isn't there anymore. I assume it got filed with her correspondence, but I don't know what year that would be."

The reference assistant was a tall young woman with caramel-colored skin and a long braid. "There'll be a separation record where the letter was, saying where it went," she said.

Jane shook her head. "No. There's not. There's nothing." She was beginning to panic again, and she looked up to where the bright blue sky was visible out the high windows. It was still a beautiful day.

"Just a minute," said the reference assistant.

She was gone longer than a minute, though, and when she came back, she had with her an older woman in a blue dress, reading glasses dangling on a string of turquoise beads. "I'm the public services librarian," the woman said. "Is there a problem?"

Yes, there was. There was definitely a problem. Jane explained it again, and the public services librarian echoed what the reference assistant had said, that there would be a separation record. "Perhaps you have the wrong volume," she suggested kindly.

"I've checked them all," Jane said more loudly than she meant to, and several people looked up from their work.

The public services librarian made a phone call. She sent the reference assistant to collect the documents Jane had been working with, and she herself took Jane to see the curator of modern manuscripts in his office. Now Jane could no longer control her panic. It reached through her with chilly fingers, wrapped itself around her stomach, and squeezed. Panic whispered maliciously in her ear, and she fought back with anger. She could almost manage to feel they were doing this to her on purpose. They had taken her letter and dropped it deep in the machinery of their bureaucracy; they were wasting her extremely limited time. She sat in the office of the curator of modern manuscripts, Stefan Valdes, and she told him what she had told the other two: the letter was there a week and a half ago, but it wasn't there now. She did her best to speak politely but firmly, the way she would have spoken to a bank manager whose branch had erroneously debited money from her account.

Stefan Valdes was a slender man in a blue striped shirt, his shiny black hair cut short, his square jaw closely shaved. He might almost have *been* a bank manager, except that when Jane looked more closely, she saw he had a tiny silver stud in one ear. "Dr. Levitsky," he said, "I have no doubt we will find this letter. I can see how concerned you are, but I assure you there isn't any cause for that. There are lots of places a letter like that might have got to. It might have gotten into a different folder you were working with—"

"I checked them all," Jane interrupted firmly. "Don't you think that was the first thing I did?"

He smiled and held up his palms, clean and pink as a cherub's. "It might have been sent to the Con Lab for preservation. It might have been set aside for reassignment to the correspondence series, though in that case—"

"In that case, I should have found a separation record!" Jane said, interrupting again. "Yes, I know. But I didn't find one." And now the terrible thought that had been attempting to squirm up through the fog of her distress surfaced at last. Who knew about the letter, after all, besides herself?

"I just don't understand how you could have lost track of it!" she exclaimed in order to push the terrible thought away.

"As I said," he repeated patiently, "I have no doubt we will find this letter. You pointed it out to the reference assistant when you returned your materials?"

Jane had known this would be coming. "He saw the letter," she said, stalling. "He knew of its existence."

"And you explained where you had found it? And that it seemed to you it was not where it was supposed to be, but that it belonged with the correspondence?" His silver stud winked accusingly in the bright light of the overhead fixture.

"No," Jane admitted. "I did not actually say that."

"Well, that's a shame," the curator said. He folded his hands on the desk in front of him, an ugly metal desk on which books and folders, glossy magazines and bundles of rubber-banded paper were neatly stacked. His hands with their scrubbed skin and neatly trimmed nails attested to his own fastidiousness, seeming to say that *he* would never have neglected to do a thing like that. "But I'm sure it makes no real difference. It may just delay things more than either of us would like." He proceeded to ask her questions about the letter. To whom was it addressed? Could she be sure Karkova had written it? Was there any indication of the date? How many pages? Was it handwritten? What kind of paper was it on?

Jane answered as well as she could, trying not to be distracted by the urgent parallel questions forming inside her head. What if the letter was lost forever? What if finding it took a long time? What if somebody had—? If Sigelman—?

No. No. It wasn't possible. Why would he do something like that?

But she did ask, when the curator had at last exhausted his questions, "Has anyone else looked at that folder in the last week and a half?"

"That's privileged information," Stefan Valdes said. "But I assure you that it's something we will look into."

Jane went back to the reading room. There were still volumes of journals she hadn't read. There was correspondence she wanted to see—Karkov's letters in the months after Masha's death, for instance. She sat at the square table in the bright room and read how, in March 1876, the ice had broken up early on the Vaza River, how swans and mergansers had already been seen. She knew she ought to type the passage about the birds into her "animals" folder, but instead she kept reading, her eyes skimming over the words as though all her good habits of scholarship had vanished along with the letter. She read about how the muslin Masha had ordered had come but was the wrong color, and about some problem having to do with Anton Bek, the young man who had taken over Masha's role as Grisha's copyist. Whatever it was, Masha was upset about it ("my head aches as though there were thunder, but the sky is blue as an egg"—an odd metaphor), but either she wasn't clear about what had happened or Jane was too distracted to follow it. She was thinking of the curator's clean hands and infuriating smile, about the letter, which had to be somewhere. Her hands trembled and she found she had turned two pages without taking anything in.

Jane gave up and returned her materials. She retrieved her coat and went outside. Across the street in Washington Square Park, red buds swelled on the branches of the trees, and the benches were crowded with people taking advantage of the warm weather. It was 2:30, and her bus didn't leave till 7:00. She needed to talk to someone who might understand. She sat on the gritty steps and fished out her cell phone, carefully charged this time.

At first it seemed no one was home at Helen's house. The answering machine tape began to play, and the boy's voice recited the litany of names: "Dr. Paul Williams, Helen Williams, Michael, Abby, and Leonora Williams are not available to take your call." Here was the family in all its orderly glory. Jane thought of the good dinner Helen had cooked, and the big house full of designated rooms, not just living and dining and bed, but the family room, the sewing room, the TV room. Jane (whose own answering machine said only, "We're not home right now," while something clattered and banged in the background) started to hang up, but all at once there was a beep and Helen's breathless voice said, "Hello?"

"Helen?" Jane said. Just the sound of Helen's voice gave her a rush of warmth. "It's Jane. I don't suppose you're free for a late lunch? Or coffee, maybe?"

"Jane!" Helen said. "How's Maisie doing? I was glad to get your e-mail."

"Much better," Jane said. "Thank you."

"I'm so glad!" Helen said. "I was so worried! But today, I can't exactly *go* anywhere, but you could come up here. I can feed you something, if you're hungry."

"I don't know," Jane said doubtfully. She couldn't bear to be in the library, but she didn't want to go too far away, either. She watched the people trickling in and out of the doors, some in sport jackets or colorful skirts and some in jeans, but all serious and pale, all scholarly looking with their worn-out satchels and their scuffed shoes, their look of not being aware of where they actually were. Did she look like that? "I don't want to disrupt your plans."

"Oh, please," Helen said. "I'm in desperate need of some kind of disruption!"

The Evanston house seemed smaller than Jane remembered it, maybe because it was so much messier. Shoes and boots and sweaters were strewn everywhere, library picture books lay open in heaps, action figures stood at attention behind barricades of battered cardboard blocks, and someone had apparently upended a jar of marbles all over the carpet.

"Don't even look," said Helen, holding a squirming Leonora against her shoulder.

"Ma-ba!" Leonora cried. "Ma-ba!" She tried to lunge for the floor and the winking marbles.

"Do you mind if we just leave the house?" Helen said. "There's a park a couple of blocks away, and the weather's so nice. It's been — you know — one of those mornings. Afternoons. I made you a sandwich, though."

"That was so thoughtful," Jane said. "I'll take the baby."

"No, she's a mess. Sticky, and she needs a bath, but I didn't have a chance — Michael! Abby! Get your shoes on!" She reached down with one hand and tried to unfold a faded umbrella stroller that was lying in the foyer.

"I'll get it." Jane opened the stroller and Helen put Leonora in it, buckled the straps, and stuck a pacifier in her mouth. Leonora spit the pacifier out and began to cry.

"Oh god," Helen said. "Would you mind just wheeling her up and down the front walk?"

At last they got everyone out the door. It was still too early for the first leaves, but rhododendrons showed bursts of purple on nearly every lawn, and daffodils and hyacinths encircled tree trunks with yellow and white and pink blossoms. A few people were out walking dogs or clearing last autumn's detritus from flower beds, and the shouts of children and the roar of traffic on the expressway carried clearly through the gossamer air. Helen pushed Leonora in the stroller, and Abby ran ahead as far as the next corner every time they crossed the street, but Michael dragged his feet and had to be urged to keep up.

"Is Paul working?" Jane asked. She was eating the chicken-salad sandwich as they walked.

"Conference in Seattle," Helen said. "Things get a little tenuous. But he'll be home tomorrow."

"One more person to take care of," Jane joked, licking her fingers. Or maybe it wasn't a joke.

"Yes," Helen said. "But I miss him."

The park was a large expanse of grass with a baseball diamond at one end and a playground at the other. The swing set was full, and some older kids were kicking around a soccer ball. Michael and Abby raced each other to the monkey bars. The sun was still warm, but the shadows of the swing set and the trees already stretched their long fingers across the grass. Leonora had fallen asleep.

"Thank god," Helen said. "She hasn't napped in days."

They sat on a bench and watched the children.

"Helen," Jane said. "I don't think I told you before, but when I was here a couple of weeks ago, I found something. Something potentially very interesting."

Helen looked at her, her gray eyes narrowed with attention and intelligence—the look Jane remembered from years ago. "What?" she asked. "What did you find?"

Jane told her the story, or what there was of it: the letter with its suggestion of Masha's adventure and of being the source for *Lady of the Snakes*, and how, when she had gone back this morning, the letter wasn't there.

"Oh, Jane!" Helen said. Her gray eyes left the children, now sitting on the top of the monkey bars, and looked fully into Jane's flushed face. "How thrilling! This never happens—this kind of discovery. You know that, don't you?"

And suddenly Jane believed that everything would be all right. The letter would be found, and it would cast a new and radiant light on everything. She beamed at Helen, intensely pleased, but to hedge her bets she said, "Right at the moment, it feels like it hasn't happened this time, either."

"I'm sure they'll find it!" Helen said. "In a day or two. I wouldn't worry. Didn't the curator tell you not to worry? What is it, Michael?"

The boy had appeared in front of them, his cheeks red and his long lashes damp. He kicked the dirt with the toe of his light-up sneaker. "Abby called me a word," he said.

"What word?"

Jane watched him stare at the ground, unwilling to say. He had his mother's face: the same thin jaw and gray eyes, the scattering of freckles.

"Tell me, Michael," Helen said.

"Dummy," Michael said.

Helen smoothed his hair away from his forehead. "You're not a dummy, sweetheart," she said matter-of-factly. "You tell Abby I said so."

"But she—"

"Tell her I said not to call names," Helen interrupted firmly. She turned him around by the shoulders and pointed him back toward the play equipment. "Go!" she said, and then, when he'd reluctantly obeyed her, "First children! So sensitive."

"Really?" Jane said. "First children?"

"Because we don't know how to bring them up yet. They're our guinea pigs, so they need an extra lot of patience, I always think. But let's talk about your letter! Tell me again. She was called to God— that's what she said?"

"I think so," Jane said. "I wish I could remember more clearly." She was thinking of Maisie. Would a second child be less difficult, then? Did Maisie need more patience than Jane was giving her?

"Like Joan of Arc!" Helen said.

"Don't people these days think Joan of Arc had schizophrenia?" Jane said. "Or epilepsy?" She felt doubtful again. What *had* the letter said, exactly? Had Masha literally heard voices? Suppose Sigelman had read it—was there something in it he wouldn't have wanted her to see? Had something been hidden that he wanted to keep hidden? Or was his problem Jane herself, that she might make a major contribution to the field he thought of as his own? The field he had, after all, created.

"Here comes Michael again," Helen said. "What is it, sweetie?"

"I want to go home," he said. His eyes were dark with emotion and he had bits of dead leaves in his hair. Jane could see he was trying hard not to cry, and her heart went out to him. Despite being brown-haired and skinny rather than chubby and blond, for a moment he reminded her of her brother, Davis.

"Oh, honey," Helen said. She opened her arms and gathered him in, although he was too big for it, her face relaxed and shining faintly with happiness despite her frown. Jane wondered if her own face looked like that when she held Maisie.

"What a good life you've made for yourself," Jane said softly.

"Yes." Helen rocked her son close, and the sight made Jane long for her own child. "But you know what I miss?"

"What?" The sun was sinking, now, into the branches of the trees, and the wind was picking up.

"It's embarrassing," Helen said. "I miss the way people used to look at me, when I told them what I did for a living. Some people. As though I might have something interesting to say. I miss that more than the work itself, though I do miss the work, too, sometimes! Reading. Thinking carefully about things. I don't think I ever think carefully about anything anymore. Anyway, isn't that awful?"

"No," Jane said. "It's not awful."

"Mommy," Michael said, "can we have pizza for dinner?"

"We had pizza last night," Helen said.

"I love pizza," said her son dreamily, his knobby knees folded under him and the crown of his head tucked beneath his mother's chin. "I could eat it every night."

Helen made a face at Jane over Michael's head. "Why do I even bother cooking?" she asked, but it was a reflex more than a real question.

When Jane got home, long past bedtime, Maisie was stretched out on the couch in her pajamas, watching a video while Billy studied at the dining-room table.

"Hello, sweetie," Jane said to Maisie. "I missed you!"

"This a good video," Maisie said, lifting her arms for Jane to pick her up.

"Is it?" Jane carried Maisie through the archway into the dining room. Her weight felt good in Jane's arms. It felt like ballast. "Hi, Billy," she said.

Billy rubbed his hands across his face and looked up. "You have a good trip?"

"It was okay," she said. "Kind of frustrating." He didn't ask her why, and she didn't tell him.

"I didn't realize how late it was!" Billy yawned and got up, and for a moment they leaned toward each other as if they might kiss, but then they didn't. "I'll put Maisie to bed," Billy said.

"That's okay," Jane said. "I've got her."

"No, I should have done it before."

"Don't worry about it. You did the whole day." It was ridiculous the way they were talking, like people trying to hold the door for each other: *After you. No, after you.* But they couldn't seem to stop.

Billy had to spend the whole next day in the law library. Felicia was off somewhere; she never watched Maisie on the weekends, anyway. Jane took Maisie to the grocery store and the video store and the park. She hadn't done any class prep at all, and she had to stay up very late that night putting her Monday lecture together and looking over student paper proposals to hand back and answering e-mails, and then on Monday she was so tired she couldn't think straight. She stumbled her way through class, and then she forgot to hand back the paper proposals and had to e-mail all the students to pick them up from her mailbox. Not that half of them would even bother. This was the price she was paying for Saturday. If she had read the letter, she supposed, it might have seemed well worth it.

In her office after class, she shut the door and put her head down on the desk. She was so tired she almost fell asleep like that, but a sound from the other side of the wall made her open her eyes again. Sigelman was whistling loudly in his office. It was a cheerful tune, possibly a march, surprisingly clear and on key. Spurred by the thought of him, Jane picked up her phone and called the Newberry. She asked to be connected to Stefan Valdes, and then she asked him if he'd found her letter yet.

"I assure you that we are working on this," he said, impatience creeping into his voice for the first time. "We do have quite a small staff, however."

Jane wondered if the impatience was because the letter hadn't, as he'd assumed it would, turned up quickly. "Mr. Valdes," she said, "can I ask you something? If it turns out you can't find the letter—that it's disappeared—is this the kind of matter you would report to the police?"

There was a long pause. Sigelman was still whistling. Jane wondered if he could hear what she was saying into the phone. She could usually hear when he was talking but not make out the actual words. At last the curator said, "Honestly, Dr. Levitsky, they would laugh at us."

Through the wall Sigelman had switched to a waltz. Putting down the phone, she thought of all the things she might say to him:

Remember that letter I told you about? Well, I lost it.

Did you by any chance go down to the Newberry and take (steal? hide?) my letter?

What do you think the chances are that the most exciting document you've ever touched would immediately and mysteriously disappear?

Or maybe, *The fucking bureaucracy at the fucking Newberry swallowed my goddamned letter!*

In the end, though, she couldn't bring herself to say any of these things. When, a few days later, he asked her (as she'd known he eventually would) when she was planning to go back to Chicago and find out what the rest of the letter said, she'd stood up very straight and told him, "Just as soon as I can find the time, Otto!"

"Time!" he said with a wolfish grin. "You have all the time in the world! I'm the one who's going to die soon." He looked very cheerful and solicitous in his canary yellow shirt, the cuffs flapping.

"That will be nice," Jane said. "You and Karkov can go snipe shooting together in heaven."

"I doubt," Sigelman said, "either of us will end up there."

CHAPTER TWELVE

THE LAST DAY of the spring semester dawned cold and blustery. Jane woke up with a feeling of relief. The year was almost over; she had almost survived it. The dark gray sky out the window, the sight of the arborvitae shivering in the wind, couldn't dampen her mood. She buried her face in the back of Billy's neck and wrapped her arms around him from behind. It seemed to have been a long time since they'd touched each other, but the days and weeks rushed by in such a fog that Jane wasn't honestly sure how long. "Billy," she whispered.

A sound sleeper, he lay still and unresponsive. She didn't know what she wanted to say, anyway, just to somehow share her gladness, to offer some reassurance, maybe. He still had exams to get through, but he'd get through them. Then they would have the summer. She was determined that the summer would be different: easier, happier, with more time for each other and for Maisie. She would ask Felicia to find a place of her own. She would think of the things she and Billy used to enjoy doing together. Maybe they would rent canoes at the boathouse at Wingra Park, put Maisie in a life preserver between them, and paddle out to where the water was calm and clear in every direction.

She went downstairs to the chilly kitchen to make coffee, came back up for her slippers, and heard Maisie singing to herself in her bed. Jane went into the room, and Maisie stopped singing and shut her eyes. Jane sat on the edge of the bed and put her hand on the birthmark on Maisie's shin, ran her hand down to her toes and squeezed her foot.

"Time to get up," Jane said. "It's going to be a lovely day."

"I sleeping," Maisie said.

"Okay," Jane said. "But you have to wake up soon."

She went back downstairs and made toast, emptied the dishwasher, threw out the soured milk and opened a new carton, put milk on the shopping list by the microwave. She took a package of chicken breasts from the freezer and put it in the refrigerator to defrost. Her mind whirred cleanly, knowing what had to be done. Her body, strong and efficient, executed tasks. The wind rattled the window as though it were early March.

Upstairs Billy was running the water. In this house the water moaned in the pipes whenever anyone turned on a sink or flushed a toilet. It made a melancholy human sound, almost like weeping. Not enough insulation in the walls, perhaps.

The moaning of the water stopped, and Billy came downstairs wearing sweatpants and a T-shirt, rubbing his eyes. His feet were bare. "It's freezing," he said. "Jesus—it's May!" His hair stuck up, dark near his scalp but nearly colorless at the tips, as though something went out of it as it grew.

"It's the last day of the semester," Jane said.

"It feels like January."

"In January it's still dark at a quarter to seven. The sun's been up for half an hour."

"What sun?" Billy said, looking out the window. He poured himself a cup of coffee and sat down at the table.

Jane waited until he had half a cup in him. She wanted to tell him how she felt they were emerging from some shared darkness, real or metaphysical. "The weather certainly is nasty today," she said. "But I feel as though I can feel the world turning. Do you know what I mean? As though I'm sitting on the top of the world and the seasons are moving through me somehow! The winter moving out and the summer moving in—you know? Because of the way the light is, maybe."

"Sitting on top of the world, are you?" Billy said. He opened the refrigerator and poured milk into his coffee. Jane was pleased that she'd thrown out the soured carton. It made her feel like a good wife.

Thump, thump. Maisie was hopping down the steps. She came around the corner, her blanket dragging on the floor. "Hungry," she said.

Jane got a bowl, poured cereal. "Swimming lesson today," she said, setting the bowl on the table. "Mommy's going to take you."

"No," Maisie said. "No swimmy."

"You liked it last week," Jane said. "You kicked with the kickboard, remember? And the water splashed up."

"Don't want to," Maisie said. Her face darkened.

Now the pipes in the walls groaned again. Felicia would be up soon. "Well, I think you'll have fun," Jane said. "Once you get there."

"No!" Maisie kicked the table and cereal splashed out of the bowl.

Billy picked the Cheerios up from the tabletop and ate them. "I'm sitting on top of the world," he said, "and I feel a storm blowing in."

Jane drove to campus, parked in the remote lot, and took the shuttle bus from there. Gray clouds gathered over the lake, low and dark. The water was the color of granite and the racing waves were topped with dirty foam. Wind ripped through the trees, tearing cherry blossoms from their twigs, filling the air with showers of petals, and bending daffodils flat against the grass.

In the lobby of Van Hise she ran into John Lewin, who was waiting for the elevator.

"Can you believe the weather?" he said as the doors closed. He rubbed his red hands together. "I didn't bring gloves."

Jane held up her own gloved hands. "I found mine in my coat pockets," she said. The wind had tangled her hair and numbed her ears.

"Eighteen years since I left Arizona," he said, "and I'm still not used to this god-awful climate!"

The elevator stopped at the fourteenth floor, and they got off together. Carmen Bilinsky, the Slavic religions specialist, clattered down the hall in high-heeled pumps with a mug of coffee in her manicured hands.

"I'm just warming myself up," she said. "It's like Siberia out there!"

"We should consider it a form of research," Jane said.

The others laughed politely. Or maybe the laughter was genuine; Jane couldn't tell.

"Well," John said heartily. "The last day of the semester. Congratulations, Jane, you made it!"

"I have two classes to get through first," she said.

"Oh, the first year," Carmen said. "How well I remember it."

"I was wondering if it was like childbirth," Jane said, "where you forget the pain."

"I wouldn't know about that," Carmen said.

The elevator doors opened again and Otto Sigelman emerged, wearing a heavy brown overcoat, his face flushed with cold. The few strands of hair on his head were in disarray.

"We'll have snow by nightfall," John said, clapping his hands together. "Six inches, I predict!"

"Talking about the weather?" Sigelman remarked. He strode past them, keys in hand, and disappeared around the corner.

"Are you going to be like that in thirty years, Jane?" John asked her with a smile. "Supercilious and grumpy?"

"A big-headed crab," Carmen clarified.

"Let's see if I get tenure first," Jane said lightly.

"Speaking of which," John said. "I haven't seen anything of yours in print lately. I trust you've been busy?"

Carmen was still looking down the hall where Sigelman had disappeared. "I thought when he retired we'd see less of him, but he's around as much as ever. Lingering, like a bad smell. And he's been whistling, too. With Otto that's always a bad sign."

"Whistling?" Jane said.

"Bustlingly secretive. Have you noticed?" She directed her question to John.

"I know he took a trip somewhere," John replied. "To see someone he was interested in. Professionally, I mean. No more young women!"

"I should hope not," Carmen said.

"To Chicago?" Jane asked. She shifted her shoulder bag to the other side and pushed her hair back out of her eyes, trying to look casual.

"To Iowa, I think. Some relation of somebody or other. Has he mentioned anything to you, Jane?"

"No," Jane said. "No, he hasn't." But she knew that Stephen Olen's son, Greg Olen, lived in Dubuque.

"He shouldn't be driving," Carmen said. "He's a heart attack waiting to happen! Even fifteen years ago his cholesterol was almost three hundred."

"They don't care about the whole number anymore," John Lewin said. "Just the HDL."

"Nevertheless," Carmen said, while Jane looked at her appraisingly. *Young women*, she thought, mentally subtracting fifteen years.

In her office Jane set her satchel down. Through the wall she could hear a file drawer slide open and then rattle shut again. A chair was pushed back; blinds rattled. The sounds of a restless animal, waiting to be let out.

She went out into the hall and knocked on Sigelman's door.

The clattering inside ceased.

She knocked again. "Otto," she called through the heavy blond striated wood. She looked at the nameplate on the door, dusty black with old-fashioned gold lettering. The new nameplates—hers, for instance—were dull brown, with plain, square white letters. She could imagine the sermon Sigelman would offer on this theme—how the profession had become debased, the professors dishonored; you couldn't even get a decent nameplate for your office anymore! Once, people like him had been revered, respected, left alone, no state legislature breathing down their necks about teaching loads. No students complaining about grades, homework, rising tuition. Was it all this that had embittered Sigelman, or was it something else? The bald fact that times changed, that his had come and gone? There were students working in Slavics today (as he must know, or at least suspect) who'd never heard of him, others who'd heard of him but assumed he was dead.

"Jane?" His voice was hoarse and muffled by the heavy door. "Jane *Levitsky*?" As though she were someone he knew only vaguely and hadn't heard from in a long time.

"Can I come in? Whatever you're doing in there, I promise not to tell anyone."

A chair scraped across the floor; papers rustled. "Just a minute," he said. He coughed, a drawer slammed shut. Jane rattled the doorknob.

At last the door opened. Sigelman stood in the doorway in his rumpled shirt, gray-faced. His shaved jowls sagged. "What do you want?" he said. He frowned at her and the jowls wobbled, but he stood back to let her in.

Something came over Jane as she crossed the threshold. A shiver of nostalgia and longing went through her, as though she had stepped back through the curtain of years. Not that Sigelman's office was actually very much like her father's study. It was darker, messier, the air stinking of tobacco and heavy with a kind of angry passion, whereas her father's had been calm, tranquil, solemn—the quiet center of the world. Still, the shelves were crammed with books in half a dozen languages, and more books lay in heaps on the floor along with papers, academic journals, piles of old, unreturned exams. Both rooms had Oriental rugs on the floor, but Sigelman's was red and gray and black while her father's had been blue and gold. In both, little jugs and wall hangings and paper knives—souvenirs of half-forgotten travels—stood dusty on shelves and windowsills, mostly concealed by more books. A lifetime's worth of books, treated with simultaneous reverence and disregard, as ubiquitous and precious as oxygen.

Jane lifted a pile of bound volumes of the *Journal of Slavic and Soviet Linguistics* off a chair and found a place for them on the floor. "The library's been looking for those," she said, sitting down and pulling her sweater closer around her. "They send out e-mails weekly."

Sigelman ran a hand along his head and looked irritated, as though he had expected to find more hair. "That's what you came in here to tell me?" He walked around his desk and sat down behind it.

"So," she said. "You went to see Greg Olen."

Sigelman grinned, suddenly pleased. He strummed his thumbs along the slats of his chair. "Rumors flying, are they? Is that what's got you bent out of shape?"

"I'm just taking a collegial interest," Jane said.

"Of course," he said. "Collegial." There was a tautness between them suddenly, a bright electric connection.

"So," she repeated. "What did he have?"

Sigelman lifted his hands and turned them over, showing her their emptiness. "Do you know that he fancies himself a writer?" he said jovially. "Everybody's writing novels these days, apparently."

"Really," Jane said.

"Yes," Sigelman said. "He wanted to talk to me about his craft. As though I would be interested in anything he had to say on that score, just because a trickle of Karkov blood runs in his veins!"

Jane said nothing, hoping he would tire of the subject.

"I mean," Sigelman said, "he never even met his great-great-grandfather! Karkov died in 1889."

Or his great-great-grandmother, either, Jane thought. She said, "I know when Karkov died."

"Who said you didn't?" Sigelman leaned back comfortably in his chair.

Jane tried again. "Did he show you any papers? Letters? Manuscripts?"

Sigelman opened a drawer, took out a cigar, bit it, tapped his pockets as though looking for matches, then put the cigar down on his desk. "I thought you were occupied with the archival material," he said.

"I am," Jane said sharply.

"And so busy," he went on, "that you haven't even gone back and finished that letter you told me about. Maybe your plate is already over-full." He smiled, a slow, galling smile. The cigar lay on the desktop like a dead mouse.

"I just wondered if anything you saw might bear on *Lady of the Snakes*. I know it's not your favorite work, but some of us would be interested."

"You know," Sigelman said, "I think perhaps you're right. I may have been underestimating it. *Lady of the Snakes!* The last book, after all. Perhaps a signal of a new direction. Almost an anticipation of modernism, if you look at it in a certain light. I've been thinking I should give it another chance. A little more of my attention."

"How generous," Jane said.

"I'm nothing if not generous," Sigelman said, picking up the cigar and rolling it lovingly between his fingers.

Jane could see he wasn't going to give anything away. Besides which, she had to teach in fifteen minutes and she wanted to check her e-mail to see if there was anything from Valdes. "That's what everyone says about you," she said, standing up to go.

"As long as they're talking," Sigelman said, showing his yellow teeth.

Jane went into her office, leaving Sigelman to lurk like a troll in his cave. Knowing whatever it was he knew, or not knowing it.

There were no messages from anyone at the Newberry.

———

When Jane left the building in the late afternoon, the snow had begun. Big wet flakes poured out of the clouds and stung her cheeks as she trotted toward the parking lot, too impatient to wait for the shuttle bus. Passing cars sprayed dirty slush onto the sidewalk.

At home Felicia was stretched out on the couch with Maisie in her lap, watching a soap opera. Stuffed animals, toy trucks, wooden beads, plastic bananas, and cardboard pizza wedges were scattered everywhere, and the smell of last night's macaroni and cheese hung in the air.

"Hi," Felicia said. "That's some weather out there."

"Oh, it's not so bad," Jane said, reminding herself that she had never specifically forbidden Felicia to watch adult television with Maisie.

"It's time to go to the pool," Jane told Maisie. "Let's go find your bathing suit!"

"No!" Maisie grabbed on to Felicia. "No swimmy!"

"She didn't have a nap today," Felicia warned.

Jane nodded, then pulled Maisie off Felicia and carried her upstairs. "Remember all the kids who were there last week? Kara and Benjamin. Who else? Zachary?"

"No swimmy!" Maisie cried, squirming and kicking.

Outside Maisie was further aggrieved by the weather. "Don't like snow!" she wailed while Jane struggled to strap her into the car seat.

"No," Jane agreed. "Neither do I. Not in May, anyway." She wasn't wearing boots, and her shoes were soaked through. Snow clung to all the windows and would have to be scraped off. She could dimly perceive that the sensible course of action was to skip today's lesson, but she felt she had already committed too many resources to turn back now.

When they got there, Maisie refused to go near the water.

"Come blow bubbles with us!" the swimming teacher said. She was a blond high-schooler in a red bikini that covered almost nothing. "It's fun!"

Maisie buried her face in Jane's soft stomach and refused to answer.

"Let's ride on the float," the swimming teacher said. "Don't you want to ride on the float?"

Maisie pressed harder into Jane's middle as though trying to get back inside.

"Come on, silly goose," Jane said impatiently. "Just stick your toes in." She picked Maisie up and carried her to the edge of the pool. It was clammy down here in the YMCA basement, badly lit with dusty, yellowish fluorescent tubes. The tile floor was a dull, muddy brown so it was hard to see the puddles scattered across it. A stand of scarred wooden bleachers was pushed up against one wall, and here the waiting parents sat, trying to keep their bundles of winter jackets and snack bags from falling through to the floor.

"No! No! No!" Maisie screamed. The other children looked at her with worried monkey faces.

"Maybe we better try again next week," the swimming teacher said. "It's better not to force them."

As though, at sixteen years old, she knew anything about children!

"We'll just sit and watch," Jane said. She sat on the bleachers holding Maisie tightly, rigid with fury. The other mothers looked at her, sympathetic or judgmental, it was impossible to tell. The one father in the group watched the swim teacher, whose breasts bobbed and swung, half-inside the two triangles of red cloth.

"Go home," Maisie said into Jane's coat.

"No," Jane said.

"Yes!"

"No. If you won't go in the water, fine. But at least we'll stay and watch."

"Home!" Maisie said.

Jane ignored her, but a few minutes later, when she felt a spreading wetness across her lap where Maisie's urine had overwhelmed the swim diaper, she was forced to admit defeat.

She couldn't get the car up the driveway. The pavement was slippery with new snow and the car kept sliding back down, so in the end she had to leave it on the street. Maisie had fallen asleep. Jane lifted her out of the car seat and hoisted her onto her shoulder. She carried her inside and up to her room, laying her on her bed with her snowsuit and boots still on.

The house felt cold and empty. Jane changed her clothes and went downstairs. She sat on the couch looking out at the snow, which blanketed the street and mounded on the parked cars. The tree branches and electric wires were heavy with it. The sky glowed strangely, orangish gray, and most of the houses were dark, though one or two lit up as she watched, as the people who lived there got home from work. Jane let herself float from minute to minute as the light drained from the sky. She felt out of time, unreal, disconnected from the clockwork of ordinary life. Her eyes relaxed and went unfocused, and the snow was like static on a television screen, the whole world whited out. Why, after all, should she ever get up? What if she stayed here on the couch in the dark forever, never rising to answer the phone or cook a meal or write a check? What if she never met with another student or presented another paper? What if she never found out what happened to the letter from Masha? What difference would it make to anyone?

And then, like a pathetic fallacy, she heard the weeping inside the wall behind her. But of course it was just the pipes, the water running—the basement shower, from the sound of it. She blinked and almost swam back up to alertness, but then she decided not to bother. She didn't care. Felicia could come upstairs, could even try to talk to her; it didn't matter. Of all the things unimportant enough to get up for, right now Felicia topped the list.

The snow kept falling. The shower stopped, and a little while later footsteps clattered up the basement steps. She heard the door that led into the kitchen open and slam shut. Someone came around the corner, but it wasn't Felicia. It was Billy, with wet hair, a towel around his waist, his clothes in his hands. He was whistling. He didn't see

Jane in the dark until he was almost in front of her, and then he stopped short. His face didn't change much that Jane could see, just went hard around the jaw. He didn't say anything, and neither did Jane. She felt a jolt of cold go through her, as though all the windows in the room had suddenly been thrust open. It was very quiet, and then she could hear the pitiful, watery weeping again as the basement shower started up once more.

Billy said, "I'll get dressed." He moved toward the stairs.

Jane said—or at any rate the words came out of her reflexively— "Don't wake the baby!"

He paused and looked at her. His face was stern and wild— strangely alive. It was as though the stiff mask of himself he'd been wearing for months had fallen away, and here he was now—Billy, whom she had missed without even exactly knowing that he was gone. "Maisie is not a baby," he said, and then he went upstairs.

Billy, whom she had loved.

When he came down again he was dressed in black pants and a black T-shirt. She almost commented on his bad-guy costume, but then she noticed her teeth were chattering. It was as if the air around her had gone sharp, a cloud of ice crystals through which she squinted, trying to make out what was going on. Her consciousness seemed to be shrinking to a single cold point, like a dead star, while Billy went around the room closing the shades and switching on lamps. He hung up Jane's coat. Jane watched him. She knew she had to gather herself together. She had to get up, to say something.

"You better go tell her to take her stuff and get out of here!" she said. It was the best she could do.

Billy went into the kitchen. She could hear him going down the basement steps. The thought of the two of them in that room together made her stand up. How could she have been so stupid? She went through the kitchen and down the steps, and there they were, sitting on the bed. Felicia was crying. Billy's eyes were red.

"You!" Jane cried, pointing at Felicia. "You have to pack! Get up! Stop crying—stop it!" Felicia stood up, but she was too slow for Jane, who went to the closet and started pulling clothes from hangers and throwing them on the bed. "Where's your suitcase?"

Felicia pulled her backpack out from under the futon frame.

"Five minutes!" Jane cried. She held her palm up with her fingers extended, the way she did to students taking an exam as the end of the period neared. Then she went back upstairs. In the bedroom with the door shut, she sat down, the heels of her hands pressed into her mouth, her teeth biting into the flesh. The taste of her own skin nauseated her. She cried, telling herself she had to stop before she woke up Maisie, but she couldn't stop, and, anyway, nothing was going to wake Maisie tonight. She slept on and on through Jane's sobbing, and through the footsteps downstairs and the sound of the front door opening and shutting and the car starting up on the street. Twice Jane got up and went into Maisie's room and looked at her, wishing she would wake up so Jane would have something to do. But she didn't. She slept all night in her wet clothes and her snowsuit and her felt-lined navy blue boots. Probably she would get a rash, Jane thought, which seemed to her just one more bit of unavoidable suffering.

Once Billy came up and opened the bedroom door. "Janie," he said softly.

"Go away!" she hissed. The sight of him made her feel physically ill, and she shut her eyes and waited until he was gone.

At last it began to get light. Gray dawn crept under the window shade. After a while Jane got up, went to the bathroom, and drifted automatically down the hall to her study, her hand trailing along the peeling beige wallpaper. At her desk she turned on the computer and waited for it to warm up. When she checked her e-mail, Stefan Valdes's name jumped out from the list of senders. The letters of the subject line—a maddeningly neutral "Inquiry"—shimmered on the screen. Jane double clicked and the message popped up.

Dear Dr. Levitsky,

I am sorry to have to inform you that we have reached the end of our investigation into the document we spoke of. We can find no evidence that such a letter ever formed part of our collection. As far as we are concerned, this matter is closed. I regret not having been of any further assistance.

Yours sincerely,

Stefan Valdes
Curator, Modern Manuscript Division

Jane didn't realize how much she'd been counting on a different answer until she finished—as though, if the letter had been found, every terrible event of the last twelve hours would have been reversed or somehow proved untrue. Instead this news—if it could be called news—only confirmed that her world had fallen apart. She felt nauseated again, bile shuddering upward, her whole body rebelling against what was happening. Billy and the letter had both been stolen from her. Without meaning to, she had allowed it to happen. She'd been distracted and trusting, and she had paid a steep price for it. She swallowed hard and tried to think what to do. She looked at the clock. It was only a few minutes after seven. She opened the bottom drawer of her desk, pulled out the telephone directory, and looked up an address.

Finally, now, Maisie woke and called out, "Mama! Mama! You didn't read me two books yesterday night!"

Jane stood up and stumbled down the hall, dizzy with exhaustion. "You fell asleep too fast," she said.

"No, I didn't!" Maisie said. Her cheeks were rosy and she smelled of sleep.

Jane took off her snowsuit and changed her diaper. She put her in clean clothes, kissed her, and held her close.

"Downstairs, Mama," Maisie said, wriggling. "Down, down!" She was bright-eyed and her curls were tangled and her lovely pale, plump stomach pushed out from under her shirt. Jane felt she couldn't bear to let her go, and at the same time all she could think about was getting out of the house, getting away from everything, even Maisie.

In the kitchen Billy was drinking coffee. He was unshaven and his hair stood up on end. He wore an old sweater that, although it was not the sweater he had given to Felicia, recalled it clearly enough to make Jane see how, if you had a gun, you could kill somebody.

"I want Cheerios!" Maisie said. "I want juice! What you drinking, Daddy? Can I drink what you drinking?" Jane put Maisie down and she trotted across the linoleum to Billy, who picked her up and perched her on his knee.

Jane turned away and stumbled out of the room.

CHAPTER THIRTEEN

OUTSIDE THE DAY was bright and the thermometer was rising fast. You could almost see the snow melting. It sank into the ground and spluttered down the streets into the gurgling storm drains. Jane had her keys in her hand, but she didn't want to take the car. She needed to walk. Her skin felt cold even in the sun, and her heart was icy. She kept her eyes on the sidewalk, cracked and stained, studded with old gum. That was life—filth and decay, things trampled underfoot. Everything else was false, like a dream of flying from which one must awaken to gravity.

She walked and walked, up Gregory to Commonwealth and across the railroad tracks. Then she turned west again, not toward campus but skirting it to the little lakeside neighborhood where once, a long time ago, assistant professors like her would have been able to afford a house. As she fell into a kind of trance of walking, pictures began to appear in her mind: Billy and Felicia naked on the futon downstairs, Billy's long body stretched out from end to end while Felicia knelt over him, kissing and sucking. Jane could picture her hair cascading over him, her smile as she offered him breasts that hadn't been thinned by nursing, lips that had been seasoned to perfection by other men. She pictured Felicia whispering in his ear, telling him how good he was in bed, how smart he was, flattering him with all the clichés of sexual attraction. Should Jane have done that? She had thought authentic, distracted love would be enough, but now she saw that something else had been required. Revealing clothes, long golden hair, lacy underwear. How appalling that these were the things men wanted after all! She thought of Billy's face, which presented itself to the world as a mask of composure, the way it melted during sex into neediness: eyes narrowed, mouth slackened. The way the skin on his neck looked when he arched back in pleasure, blue veins beneath pale skin. The private architecture of his jaw, no longer private now.

It wasn't even eight o'clock when she arrived at Sigelman's house, a square white clapboard colonial in need of a coat of paint. Overhead the wind swept the clouds through the sky so that the sun's brightness came and went in patches, the snow lightening and darkening, Jane's shadow appearing and disappearing in front of her as she stood, looking at the house. No path had been cleared yet from the street to the front door, and the newspaper still lay in its orange plastic wrapper in the melting snow. Jane did not so much gather her courage as realize she had nothing to lose, and then she picked her way carefully to the house, trying not to get her shoes too wet, and rang the bell.

For a while nothing happened. Jane could hear the wind in the high branches of the trees and the shouts of the children from the nearby elementary school. What was Maisie doing? Watching cartoons on the couch, her finger in her mouth? Self-comforting, they called it, and thank god for it. Maisie would need as many kinds of comforting as she could get. Jane swiped at her tears and brought her mind to focus again on the glowing orange circle of the doorbell. She rang it again, holding her finger on the button. She didn't care if he was still in bed. She didn't care if she frightened him. So much the better.

At last she heard sounds from inside the house: footsteps, a door creaking. "I'm coming!" Sigelman grumbled loudly enough for her to hear. "Who the hell is it?" He opened the door. He wore a maroon silk bathrobe over sky blue pajamas, his feet jammed into scuffed leather slippers, his wisps of hair sticking out in all directions. He held up his hand to shield his eyes from the light. "Jane?" he said.

"Can I come in?" Jane said.

His eyebrows lowered and the edges of his mouth turned down, and Jane was sure he was going to shut the door in her face, but she couldn't let that happen.

"Otto," she said, "let me in!" As though she, not Sigelman, were the big bad wolf.

"Jesus Christ—do you know what time it is?" he said. But he stepped back so she could enter.

The hall was dark, with worn carpeting and stained wallpaper, a staircase going up. Sigelman led her through the doorway into the long living room in which a couch and a couple of leather armchairs sat opposite a big table covered with papers. On the floor was a spectacular blue-and-yellow silk kilim rug, and the walls were lined with books, most properly upright but some sideways or backward, the ragged edges of their pages showing. There was, as well, a vast, dusty clutter of old objects: amber eggs, crystal vases, Russian icons, cloisonné candlesticks. Books and papers overflowed onto end tables, onto the straight-backed chairs and the ottomans, onto the beautiful rug. "Forgive the disorder," Sigelman said. "I seem to have accumulated enough artifacts to fill the tomb of a minor pharaoh."

"You're expecting to be mummified, then," Jane said.

"Oh, I'm mummified already," Sigelman said. "Embalmed in flattery."

He sat in an armchair, and she sat on the navy blue sofa that exuded the odor of cigars. "I hope you don't mind my saying so," he said, "but you look awful. Nobody died, did they?"

Jane pushed her hair back out of her face. *Tell him*, she told herself. The words stood on her tongue, waiting to be spoken: *You took the letter, I know you did.* Instead she said, "You don't look so great yourself."

Sigelman shrugged. "That's just how it is with me," he said. "I'm old. But you—what happened to you?" He sat forward, legs apart, elbows on his knees. He looked like he really wanted to know.

Now, in the face of his nonchalance, the words marched out of their own accord. "You took the letter," Jane said. She leaned toward him, fingers laced together, feet in damp shoes set firmly on the rug. "My letter."

For an instant Sigelman's face went hard, the muscles tightening under the loose skin, and she might have been afraid of him if she'd had any emotions left. Then he shook his head. "Jane," he said. "Surely you didn't come to my house at the crack of dawn, wearing the same clothes you were wearing yesterday, to make that ludicrous accusation. You should see yourself!" His gravelly voice was oddly soothing, and suddenly Jane began to cry.

"Oh, come on now," Sigelman said. "Don't do that." He rubbed his big hands together and sighed, and Jane wondered how many women he had watched cry over the course of his lifetime. Dozens, probably. Scores. She tried to stop. Any respect he might have had for her would be dissolving, sinking into nothing like the melting snow, but the tears kept welling and falling, welling and falling.

Sigelman got up from the chair and shuffled across the rug. Jane reached into her bag and felt around for a tissue but couldn't find one, so she sniffed hard and wiped her cheeks with her hands. Sigelman sat on the sofa beside her. She could feel the heat of him, heat radiating off him as though he'd just gotten out of the steam room. Then his hand was on her shoulder, and he pulled her into him and held her against his chest, against the maroon silk and the pale blue cotton. She could feel the strong, fleshy body beneath the fabric, the hardness of his breastbone, and the rolls of fat at the top of his stomach. "Come on," he said, his hand lightly patting her back. "What could be so terrible?"

Jane curled her feet, still in their shoes, up onto the couch. She sobbed into his chest. Tears and snot seeped into his bathrobe, which smelled of smoke and sweat, a sour smell, but not one that bothered her. She could feel how powerful he still was, and she could feel his confidence in that power. She knew it would do her no good in the long run, but right now being here in his arms was extraordinarily comforting, like being held by a god. "It's all right," he said, the words vibrating in his broad chest, the breath moving through him, in and out, with a catch and a rumble deep in his lungs. "It's all right. Things happen! You're a strong woman. Whatever it is, you'll survive it. You wouldn't believe, now, all the things you're going to survive."

When she was finally done crying, she sat for a long moment, her head aching, a dull lump in her chest, her nose dripping, not wanting to move. But it didn't feel natural anymore. She needed to pull the fig leaf of her dignity around her. She sat up. Sigelman looked at her with a half-amused expression. "Well," he said, "are you going to tell me?"

"My husband, Billy—he's having an affair." Her voice sounded small and petulant, full of phlegm.

Sigelman pulled a handkerchief out of his bathrobe pocket and passed it over. "Men do that sometimes," he said. "I wouldn't take it personally."

She stared at him. "Not take it *personally?*" she repeated, wiping her face.

"Look at you! You're young, you're beautiful. You could have any man you wanted." He smiled, confident in his own good advice.

Jane blew her nose and sat up straight. "You stole that letter!" she said. "Don't tell me you didn't, because I know you did."

For half a moment he looked taken aback, but then he laughed, a loud, deep laugh that filled the room. "Listen to you!" he hooted. "The husband is fucking some floozy, and she's thinking about Karkov! Very good, Jane, really. I'm impressed."

"Why did you take it?" she demanded. "What did it say?"

"Enough!" He waved her words away. "I admire your persistence, okay? But enough."

She sat up straighter. "Answer my fucking question!" She thought if she spoke to him in his own language maybe he would answer her, but he just looked pleased, as though she were a dog he'd trained to perform a favorite trick.

"I don't know what you're talking about, Jane," he said. "I've told you before I'm not interested in minor figures. Why would I even want Maria Petrovna's letter?"

"I don't know why," Jane said. "You tell me."

"I don't need to tell you anything," Sigelman said. "I could use some coffee, though. You want something to eat?"

"Don't change the subject!"

"I'm going to make some anyway. I get migraines otherwise." He got up with a grunt and lumbered out of the room.

When he was gone, Jane shut her eyes and put her head in her hands, every ounce of energy used up. She lay down on the sofa. He was like a brick wall. He was like a mountain, and she was like a moth fluttering in the wind. She was more sure than ever that he had taken the letter, but she didn't see how she was ever going to get him to admit it. She should get up, she thought, leave the house—flee before he came back. But where would she go? Not home. She couldn't go home. There wasn't anywhere she could go, and anyhow she was so tired.

After a while he came back into the room carrying a tray with two steaming mugs of coffee, cream and sugar, spoons, and a plate full of supermarket cinnamon buns he had heated in the microwave.

"Come on," he said. "Sit up. You have to eat."

Jane sat up and leaned wearily against the back of the couch. "I'm not hungry."

"Come on!" he repeated impatiently. He pushed one of the mugs toward her. "A little nosh," he said. "A little sweetness to counteract the bitterness of life." He took a bun in his big hand and bit half of it off, slurped down coffee, made noises of pleasure in his throat. He ate the rest of the bun in two more bites, all the time eyeing her with those bland gray eyes, eyes the color of tap water. He drank some more coffee and sighed. "Jane," he said. "You know what? You're not the first person in the history of the world whose husband has thought the grass was greener, and you sure as hell won't be the last. You want to do something about it, do something! Go out and get the bastard back if you want him, or say good riddance and find yourself some-one new. Life is cruel—people are cruel. Terrible things happen. When I was a boy in Hungary, people were starving. Those who had food died of influenza or pneumonia. My older brother, Georg, died of tuberculosis when I was ten. And then the Nazis on top of all that! I learned early that you have to find your own pleasures. Why pass up a pretty girl or a cinnamon bun when you might die tomorrow? So do me a favor and don't take yourself so seriously for five minutes, okay? Eat!" He pushed the plate toward her.

Jane took a cinnamon bun. It was sickly sweet, gooey on the out-side and dry in the middle, but she ate the whole thing and washed it down with coffee. She licked her fingers. Suddenly she was ravenous. She took another bun from the plate.

"Good," Sigelman said gruffly. "Good." Then he took another bun, and they sat and ate without talking, the only sounds the plate sliding on the tray, the chewing and swallowing, and the water rush-ing in the gutters as the snow melted off the roof.

When the plate was empty, Sigelman said, "There. That's a little better, isn't it?"

Jane did feel a little better, but at the same time she felt worse. She was bloated and sticky, jittery from the caffeine on top of the lack of sleep. Her head ached and her stomach ached and she had no idea what to do.

"I'm so tired," she said.

"Come on," Sigelman said. He stood beside her, holding out his hand. "You can sleep in the guest room."

She looked up into his inscrutable face, all sagging skin and red-veined eyes. "Thank you," she said. She took his hand. It was rough and dry like a stone, and so big her own hand disappeared inside it.

He led her up the stairs to a small room at the back of the house with a window overlooking the yard, where the snow was already slumped and puddling on the grass. There was a single bed with a green quilted spread, and a picture of a horse over the bureau.

"Sleep as long as you want," he said.

When he was gone, Jane pulled down the shade, kicked off her shoes, and crawled under the spread with her clothes on. Her head pounded. Billy had fucked Felicia, and Sigelman had stolen her letter, and at the same time he had comforted her and given her refuge. Her hands and face were sticky, and she thought about looking for the bathroom, but the spread was heavy and warm and her mind was beginning to drift and she felt nauseated from all the sugar, and she wanted only to lie still. So she lay in the bed that was too soft and smelled faintly musty, and she tried to sleep. She missed Maisie. She wondered how she was ever going to be able to take care of her again, where she would find the strength. She wondered how what was happening now would shape Maisie's life—scar her, perhaps, as Jane's own parents' divorce had perhaps shaped or scarred her. Had Saul leaving Pamela set in motion a chain of events that ended here in this unfamiliar bed? Or no—that might not end here at all but years from now, when Maisie chose the wrong man or no man, left a marriage or was herself left. Jane began to cry again. People said children were resilient, but she didn't know. The only thing she knew was that she couldn't spend another night under the same roof as Billy. Her life was a train wreck and bodies lay scattered everywhere. She thought of Sigelman, who had grown up with people starving and dying of tuberculosis, and then the Nazis. She knew her own problems paled to nothing when viewed historically, but the thought only made her feel worse. The world was so full of horrors, it was a wonder anyone was ever happy for ten minutes at a time. Happiness seemed beyond her now or behind her, something that required far too much energy to sustain. She couldn't imagine how people managed it.

———

Sometime later Jane woke up feeling terrible. Thinking she was home in her own bed, she sat up and swung her feet, but unexpectedly there was a wall there and she hit it hard. A wave of nausea surged through her again, and she lay down to wait it out, then realized she couldn't and sat up again too fast, remembering at last where she was. She was dizzy and a loud buzzing filled her ears and everything started to go black, and then she vomited all over the bed.

Immediately she felt better physically, although the unpleasantness of her situation was strikingly clear. She had managed to miss the blankets, and she got quickly out of the bed and stripped it before the vomit could soak through to the mattress. Bright light streamed in around the curled edges of the shade, and when she looked at the clock on the bedside table, she saw that it was almost noon. The house was quiet. Jane opened the shade halfway and looked out. The snow was already patchy, revealing glimpses of yellow-green lawn, a thick hedge of scraggly, leafless branches, and the narrow driveway with a car-sized patch of bare pavement, two ruts in the slush leading away from it down to the street.

Still, she called Sigelman's name when she stuck her head out into the hall, just to be sure. No answer. She found the bathroom, washed up as well as she could, rinsed her mouth, brushed her teeth with her finger. She looked terrible in the medicine chest mirror, her face gray, her eyes bloodshot, her hair greasy and matted. She looked quickly away and sat on the edge of the bathtub, thinking how lovely a bath would feel. But first she had to do something about the sheets and the mattress pad (thank god he had a mattress pad). Gingerly she picked up the bundle and carried it down the stairs. She went through the dining room, which looked like it was never used, into the kitchen: worn linoleum, an old gas stove with crud baked onto the burners, a sticky-looking square wooden table piled with dirty plates and glasses. She stared for a moment in confusion into the broom closet before she found the door she was looking for.

The steps led down to a large, low-ceilinged room carpeted in dull beige and lit with fluorescent bulbs. It had a huge oak desk covered with papers, and a new computer with a flat-panel monitor, and piles of computer disks and music CDs and an out-of-date calendar, and a blue china bowl holding paper clips and bits of lint, a large roll of clear pink packing tape perched on top of everything. Along the back wall was a row of gray metal filing cabinets and unvarnished wooden bookshelves stacked with journals and unlabeled file folders and half-used reams of computer paper and a few plates covered with crumbs and jam. Jane wondered why, having the whole house to himself, Sigelman would put his office down here. She wondered whether the letter would be somewhere in one of those many drawers or file folders, or secreted away between the pages of a book, or even hidden in a locked safe behind one of the reproductions of Russian icon paintings that hung on the paneled walls—Christ on the cross, the Virgin with her head bowed, a saint she didn't recognize in a blue robe, everyone with divine light springing in gilt needles from their heads. Or maybe they weren't reproductions at all, but real.

There was a door in one wall of the room, and Jane opened it and found herself, as she had hoped, in the unfinished part of the basement: concrete floors, dusty pipes, furnace rumbling in the corner. An old bicycle, an ancient freezer, cardboard boxes marked, in faded letters, with words in a language she took to be Hungarian. Under the small window she was relieved to see a washer and dryer connected to a stained slate laundry sink. She carried the sheets over and started the washer, got the load going. Water poured in through the pipes in a great gurgling roar. It made her think of the sound she'd heard yesterday, water rushing in the pipes in the wall of her house, and what it had signified. She felt ill again. She shut her eyes and sat down on the dirty concrete floor, rested her cheek against the metal of the washer, but Billy and Felicia cavorted naked behind her lids, entwined in each other's arms, so she opened them again. It was hot in the basement, and the cold metal felt good against her skin. In a minute she would get up and do something—take that bath or lie down and sleep some more so she didn't have to think. She listened to the water and looked around her at the various pipes, enumerating them to herself. That one brought cold water in from the street; that one carried hot water up from the heater; that big waste pipe went down into the sewer system. There was a strange metal box tucked up against the sewer pipe, reflecting the fluorescent light. It was the kind of box her mother used to keep on the front stoop of the house on Euclid Avenue for the egg man, back in Jane's early childhood. Amazing to think there had been egg men once, even within the span of Jane's own lifetime! He had brought, not just eggs, she remembered, but bacon, too, and breakfast sausages, which her mother had fried up in those long-ago days before people had heard of cholesterol. The days when her parents' marriage had seemed as solid and permanent as the house itself, as the Berkeley Hills it was nestled in—though of course the hills lay directly on the Hayward fault and were as fragile as anything in the world.

Jane wondered what, if anything, Sigelman might use it for, this old-fashioned box in the unfinished basement next to the sewer pipe. She looked at the pipe, as thick around as the trunk of a good-sized tree, through which all the waste in the house flushed away, coffee grounds and dirty bathwater and excrement. And then from nowhere, Shombauer's voice was in her head. *Worthy only to keep company with shit,* it said, and suddenly Jane's heart was racing and her breath came in fast shallow gasps, and she looked wildly around to see if she was still alone. But the house, except for the rumbling of the furnace and the rhythmic sloshing of the washing machine, was silent. She leaned against the washer and pushed herself up, crossed the room to the box, and opened the lid. The metal was cold and grimy, and the hinges squeaked as the top came up. Inside, there was a large shoebox, grimy and dented and wound around with tape. Hardly knowing what she was doing, Jane reached in and lifted it out.

The box had a distinctive smell, not musty, as might have been expected, but earthy, like mushrooms or like moss growing on trees. There were two layers of tape: an older layer of thick, silvery duct tape that had been snipped open, and over that, now fastening the lid to the box, several rounds of packing tape that glowed oddly in the dim basement light. It was, she saw, the clear pink packing tape of the kind she had seen on Sigelman's desk. She tested it with a fingernail. It was shiny and dust-free, obviously put on recently. She thought of Pandora and also the Japanese fisherman of the folktale, and how they had both been warned. But there was no question of not opening it. As Sigelman himself had said, she might die tomorrow. She found a screwdriver in a heap of tools in the corner and used it to cut through the tape.

Inside, the yellowed, heavy paper of the past, three separate bundles of it. Three letters, though the envelopes were gone. The one on top lay slightly askew, and it looked flatter or cleaner—some subtle difference Jane couldn't quite pin down that made her sure it had been recently placed on top of the others. It was so impossible—that she had found this, that she was here to find it—that for a moment she knew she must be dreaming. That seemed no reason, however, not to continue. She unfolded the first bundle of paper, sat down on the floor (the clammy, gritty surface of which seemed to undercut the idea that she was dreaming), and began.

June 11, 1884

Dear Varya,

I received your letter yesterday, and although I thank you for your kind offer, I cannot spare Katya just now. It is true as you say that she has been through a difficult time these last months—largely through my own fault, as no one knows better than I! But it seems to me that to send her away just at the moment is not the best course. We have wasted already too much time each trying to make his own way through the darkness, and now I feel strongly that we must hold together. Nor can I satisfy your other concern and account to you for my recent illness or what you call my "peculiar behavior."

You inquire as to whether the "entire incident" has passed from my mind, but it has not. In fact, every detail of those days seems burned into my memory, and I am convinced I will never forget a moment of it. I do not, of course, talk about it with anyone, but it haunts me — as though it underlies everything as I move about the house. I seem to feel the hard dirt road under my shoe at every step. I remember the first night when I awoke in the dark and the room seemed to pulse with the sound of a voice so deep it was beyond hearing, except as a kind of distant thunder. I rose from my bed and drew the curtains. The light of the full moon flooded in, and so I did not need even a candle to dress.

Outside it was cool and the wind moved the new leaves of the birches. I walked across the lawn and out into the meadow and down to the river in the dark, my feet seeming to know where they would go. It did not feel like walking, but rather as though I were gliding through the whispering grass. Yes, yes, the grass said with its ten thousand tongues, as I moved through it in the dark down to the water's edge.

At the river, the water was black and gleamed like obsidian in the moonlight. I sat down on a rock and watched it — moving and yet seemingly still, like the earth itself, which feels solid under our feet, yet which we are told is actually a sphere of rock and fire spinning through space. I thought how cold the water would be if one plunged into it — a searing cold like fire that would cleanse me at once of misery and mortality — and for a moment it seemed that this was what had called me out of my warm bed — the dark voice of the river.

After I had sat there for some time — minutes or hours, I could not say — I saw something rising out of the dark water. It was like an emanation of the water itself — a gliding blackness which slid up

onto the bank and paused, then coiled and lay still. It was a snake—
a large one. Probably it and I, if laid side by side and nose to nose,
would have covered just about the same amount of ground.

It seemed to me that the snake was watching me—waiting to
see what I would do. It flicked its forked tongue in the moonlight as
though it would taste what sort of creature I was. It raised its head
and, although remaining as silent as the moon, it seemed as though
all the sounds of the night—the wind in the grass and the creaking
trees and the cold water flowing over rock—were funneled through
it, and I picked it up and put it in the basket I was carrying. The snake
was heavy and silken like a woman's breast—and yet strong and
muscled too, like a *muzhik*'s back. And so I felt that I had found what
I had come to the river to find.

I don't know how to describe my state of mind at that time, how
crushed I had been by death and by duties, by the hundred mouths
and hands reaching for me every hour of the day! And then, freedom—my burden of griefs falling away like a shed skin, the moon
shining and the river flowing and my mind like a swept room.

I got up and carried the basket down the road toward Kovo.
When I grew tired, I lay down in a field. I had never slept outside before and the smell of the earth damp with recent rain was sweet to
me as I lay in the grass under the brilliant stars.

It was a kind of madness, I suppose, as though my mind had broken under the weight I had been bearing all those years, a mountain
on my back. And yet it was also a kind of blessing. An ecstasy.

But you may believe me, Varya, when I tell you it will not be repeated. Nothing in this world could compel me to leave my children
again—nothing but that which I dare not name. If the worst happens, I beg of you in the name of God, look after them! They have
borne enough already. We have not been the closest of sisters, but
the children have your blood, too, Varya. Make of them what you
will—society ladies and members of the Horse Guard—I don't

care! Only comfort them, and try to love them a little. Kostya's health is delicate, and the twins must not be allowed to tyrannize everyone. Katya especially needs a kind hand to guide her. I don't know what she may have told you about this business with her father and that young man, but I gather from your letter perhaps too much. You may guess what the effect of the knowledge of this and other such — occurrences — has been on me over the years. The shame and revulsion, the recriminations, the cold sheets, the crockery smashed on the floor. I have pleaded with him, I have wept silently at midnight. I have torn out my hair. But nothing changes! I can change nothing in the end it seems except my own feelings. And so, inch by inch, I have dragged myself out of the quicksand, more or less. I have come to some sort of dispassion, if not exactly peace.

But let us not speak of this anymore.

God keep you, Varushka.

Your sister,
Masha

Jane blinked. She looked up, looked around the basement again — washer agitating, furnace chugging, dust, cardboard cartons — then read the last long paragraph again. Young man? What business with Katya's father — with Karkov — had caused Masha to plead and weep? Jane could think of only one thing, but then sex — sex and infidelity — were on her mind. Surely it wasn't possible that some (all?) of Karkov's dalliances were not with peasant girls but peasant *boys*? That was what the letter (she read the long paragraph a third time) seemed to say. No wonder Sigelman had taken it! It wasn't because of what it proved about *Lady of the Snakes* at all.

With confusion, excitement, and trepidation, she put down the letter and picked up the next. This one was also in Masha's hand, but addressed not to her sister Varya but her daughter, Katya. It was dated only "Spring, the Year of our Lord 1884."

Dearest Katya,

I hardly know how to begin to explain to you how it is that your mama has — it hardly seems credible even as I write it — run off and left those who have most claim on her. I love you, Katushka — you and your brothers — more than life itself! And yet I know how much it must have hurt you, waking to your mother's absence — as though the sun had decided one morning not to rise. I can only say I have felt it coming over me all spring, like the sap rising in the trees. I have felt it — and fought it — for your sakes, my dearest ones. But in the end I could resist no more than the tiny snail resists the ocean tide.

How different the world looks outside of the sorrowful boundaries of Dve Reckhi. All day long the countryside is mine and mine alone — the dusty road under my feet, the meadows blooming with flowers and the sweet smell of hay, the sun before me in the morning and at my back in the evening, and at night the yellow horns of the moon over my shoulder, lighting my path.

I know you, my dear, have had more than your own share of pain. First Vanyushka's death, and then this business with your father, and now my absence. I hope you can forgive God for taking your brother, and your father for what he cannot control any more than a plant can opt not to turn its face to the sun. The moth flies into the candle and is burned; we know its urge toward the flame to be a mistake, and yet it cannot help being attracted to the light! So it is with him. And the boy is gone. I trust there will be no others, for some time at least. This has been the pattern over many years, just as the pattern of the seasons follows heat with freezing. You should put it from your mind, my darling, if you can.

And God grant that you find it in your heart to forgive me, too.

I pray that you are well, and that you are working hard at your studies and especially at the piano. I know Vladimir Vladimirich is not all you would hope for in a music master, but you must make the best of it. God has given you a talent, and such a gift must be nursed like a baby, for to neglect it would be as sinful as to neglect one of God's living creatures.

Today it rains and I have taken shelter in this little church where the icons seem to turn their forgiving faces toward me. Yesterday, when it was fine, I walked up into the hills. The cliffs are parched and rocky there, and the dirt is the rosy color of the rising sun. I followed a path which rose and fell, now steeply, now gently, through mossy trees and across bare, pebbled slopes. After some time I reached a high meadow with sheep grazing and it seemed I could see all of God's creation before me — grass and trees and a little brook, its water bubbling and sparkling between its cool banks, and far below the *izbas* of the villagers and the domes of the distant church echoing the vast dome of heaven itself.

I saw a large sunny rock some distance off and thought it would be a fine place to sit and eat a piece of bread I had with me, so I started toward it. But as I approached I saw that the ground around it seemed to churn as though the grass itself were alive. I came cautiously nearer and saw that the earth was covered with snakes, which were emerging from a crevice beneath the rock! They moved slowly at first as they wriggled from the darkness into the light, and then as the sun touched them they began to twist and glide, spreading out in all directions as though the field were a great lake into which God had thrown a stone and the serpents the shimmering ripples. I stood transfixed, and occasionally one of the creatures would glide close by my feet, moving soundlessly through the grass on its way. I saw that the sheep were huddled together at the far end of the meadow, but I was not afraid. I knew God had not led me here to injure me, but rather to reveal the glory of his creation and lead me the next step on my way. I seized two of the adders as they passed near my feet and opened my braided basket and flung them inside. They were sleepy and slow moving — smaller perhaps by half than the grass snake I had already with me. Inside the basket they hissed loudly but the lid was tied on, and I was not afraid.

At night I dream I am back at Dve Reckhi and that Vanyushka is still alive. When I awake I am grief-stricken, but then I remember that Vanya is with God, and that God is watching over you as He does all of us.

One day, little bird, you will spread your wings. Until then remember how your mother loves you, and know that wherever God leads me—even unto the searing celestial blue of Heaven itself—I will watch over you.

Kiss your brothers for me.

Your loving,
Mama

The third and final letter was not written in Masha's hand, and it was shorter than the others. It was dated exactly two months before Masha's death.

June 2, 1884

Dear Aunt Varya,

Thank you for your kind letter inquiring as to the state of my mother's health. I am sorry you have got no reply from my father. He has been very distracted and anxious of late and spends most of his time out of the house. He prefers hunting with his dog to being here at home, or at least he says he is hunting but who knows what filth he is really up to. I told you what I saw in the spring and although it is true that Bek is gone, I do not see why he should be the only one. My mother says I should put it from my mind and I know she would not like me writing to you about it, but I must talk to someone! She does not seem to understand how serious and disgusting an affair it is. She says to trust in God, but what Papa did is against God. Well, Mama did not see what I saw, and in broad daylight, too! How she can stay under the same roof as him I cannot understand. And she will not let me go to you in Moscow, though I have begged on my knees.

At least Mama's health is somewhat better. The worst effects of the snake bite have worn off, and the doctors no longer fear for her life. The swelling has gone down and the fever has passed, and she is able to sit up in an armchair and look out of the window. How she came to be bitten by the serpent is still not clear, but she had developed a strange and frightening attachment to the creatures and had come into possession of some adders, the bite of which is known to be fatal. Why she felt compelled to carry them with her I cannot say, and she either cannot or chooses not to. Neither do we have any idea what she was doing in the Feska church where she was found half-dead with a clutch of letters in her shawl. I want to write that she has not been at all herself since they found her, but I wonder now who she ever was that she could do what she has done. Or Papa, either. Everything I thought to be true seems to me now to have been a lie, as though the world had turned itself inside out like a glove so one can see all the seams showing.

I will keep you informed of events here as best I can.

Your faithful niece,
Katya

Jane looked up. She seemed to have been reading forever. She knew it could not have been more than ten or fifteen minutes, but in that time everything seemed to have shifted. As Katya had written, the world had turned inside out, like a glove. She had thought Masha had sacrificed her life to her family, but in fact she had abandoned her children and wandered in some kind of ecstatic, dissociative state around the local countryside. She had thought Masha had been devastated by Grisha's infidelities with milkmaids, but instead it seemed she had accommodated what were apparently homosexual liaisons! Jane knew who Bek was: Anton Bek, who had apparently taken over from Masha not only as Karkov's copyist, but his sexual partner as well. That was the thread that held these letters together: the references to Karkov having what were presumably sexual encounters with boys. It was clear enough why Sigelman wanted to suppress them. What Jane was less sure about was why he hadn't just destroyed them. Was he unwilling to erase anything that had to do with Karkov, even if he didn't want anyone to see it? Or was it out of a kind of perverse desire to amuse himself—to follow through on the joke about sewage, the fact that these letters were written by Karkov's female relatives dovetailing perfectly, for him, with the nature of the behavior they alluded to?

And from where had Sigelman stolen the second two?

The washer jolted to a halt and suddenly the room was silent and still. Still trembling, Jane stood up and moved the laundry into the dryer. She had forgotten about Billy for the span of time she had been reading, but now she remembered again. Naked flesh, the coldness on his face this morning at the breakfast table. With an effort she concentrated on Masha, on Karkov, on the melodrama of a hundred years ago that was so much bigger and more complicated than her own tawdry but familiar story. She thought of what Sigelman had said: *You wouldn't believe, now, all the things you're going to survive.*

She thought she might manage going home. Maisie would have eaten lunch by now and gone down for her nap, her tangled hair splayed across the pillow. Putting the letters carefully aside, Jane went through the door into Sigelman's office and got the roll of packing tape. Tearing off long strips, she taped up the empty box so that you had to look very closely to see where the old layer had been split. She put the shoebox back in the metal egg box and checked the dryer, but the sheets were still damp.

Upstairs she put the letters at the bottom of her purse. She kept a little bound notebook in there that Billy had given her for her birthday, and she tore out one of the last remaining sheets and scribbled Sigelman a note thanking him for his hospitality. How wrong it was, thanking him and stealing from him at once! But everything was wrong today. It was hard to separate out any one wrong from the rest, and, besides, she only wanted to copy the letters. Then she would give them back.

She took a shower in the hall bathroom, but afterward she still felt dirty. She went back down to the basement and checked the dryer again. The sheets were only a little damp now, and Sigelman might be back any time, so she draped the laundry over her arm and went upstairs to make up the bed.

CHAPTER FOURTEEN

JANE WALKED back up the street toward her own house, but once she got out to University, she turned right instead of crossing over. She strode fast and kept her head down, fearful of running into anyone she knew.

At the copy shop, she eased the brittle pages open and slid them one by one onto the glass. She hoped the light wouldn't degrade the paper; if so, it couldn't be helped. Nothing, Jane felt, could be helped anymore. She was beyond weighing consequences or logically teasing out eventualities. Sigelman stole from the Newberry; Jane stole from Sigelman; Billy slept with a woman not his wife; Felicia slept with her adviser's husband. They were all the same, unable to keep their hands off things they had no right to. They were like children—worse than children. Maisie, at two and a half, knew better than to steal another child's toy. She didn't even take cookies from the cookie drawer without asking.

At the next machine, an older man in gray trousers and a navy blue sweater vest was trying to copy an article he had cut out of the newspaper and taped to a sheet of paper, but the machine kept spitting out blank pages. "Shoot," he said as yet another blank page slid into the sorter. "Jesus H. Christ!"

It sounded so quaint after Sigelman, this kind of language. But the man's face was red, his mouth set in a rigid line.

"You have to put the side you want to copy facing down," Jane said gently.

He jerked his head toward her. "What?"

"The page you're trying to copy," she said. "You need to turn it over." She picked up the sheet of paper and turned it over for him, shut the lid, and pressed the start button. A copy of the article hummed out.

He picked it up and turned to thank her. His eyes were two different colors, one blue and one brown. "Appreciate it," he said. "Don't know why I couldn't— Sometimes it's the simplest things!" Jane wondered if he had always spoken in this fractured way or whether it was part of the decrepitude of age, a process that seemed to be beginning in her as well, as though at thirty she had already left her youth behind her and begun the long, slow slide toward decay and death.

"Is that you?" Jane pointed to the headline—"RSE PRESIDENT RE-TIRES AFTER TWO DECADES AT HELM."

The man nodded. "Big mistake," he said, half smiling. "Retiring, I mean. Still, my wife says she likes having me around."

"That's nice," Jane said. "You always hear about the other way, wives complaining about their retired husbands being underfoot." She ran a hand through her hair, trying to fluff it, then gave up. Vanity would have to wait until she got out of this store, or maybe out of this whole squalid stage of her life: the cuckold stage, or whatever the word was when applied to women. Maybe there wasn't any word, which was even worse—to have become something for which there was no name, something beyond language. She turned back to her own machine.

"Deb's never been like other wives," the man said.

Jane looked up again. Without wanting to, she found herself wondering in what way his Deb was different—better, presumably—than other wives. "How long have you been married?" she asked and then wished she hadn't. She didn't want to talk about marriage. She didn't want to talk at all.

"Fifty-three years."

Was his tone regretful or proud? Maybe some of each. He looked like an ordinary man to her—on the street she would have passed him without a second glance—but obviously he had hidden qualities. Staying power. Good sense, intelligence, a prophetic vision of the future? She wondered what RSE was. She assumed he must have been a good president or he wouldn't have lasted twenty years. She guessed he was a good husband, but who knew? She wanted to ask him if he'd ever been unfaithful to his wife. She wanted to ask whether they still made love, and if so, how often. She felt she didn't know how other people lived, with what assumptions or intentions. She only understood characters in books, people made of words and ideas and hidden agendas rather than flesh and bone.

Instead she said, "Fifty-three years! That's a real accomplishment."

The man smiled. "What's that you're copying?" he asked.

She looked down at her stolen property. Her face got hot, but she found a handle of steely detachment within herself and clung to it. "Just some old family letters."

He squinted over, interested. "What language is that, Russian or something?"

"Bulgarian," Jane said.

When she got home, the car was gone. That was something to be thankful for. She knew she would have to face Billy, but she had a few things she wanted to get done first.

Inside, the house felt chilly and damp, and everything was in confusion. The living-room rug was scattered with plastic animals, zebras and lizards and cheetahs toppled on their sides as though they'd all succumbed to an epidemic. The couch pillows were scrunched and old socks lay on the armrests. Clothes were balled up on the chairs, and shoes and boots were scattered among dirty footprints on the floor. The table in the dining room still held what seemed to be the remains of Maisie's lunch: half a peanut butter sandwich on a plastic plate, a bunch of grapes that looked as though it hadn't been touched, another plate empty except for cookie crumbs. Jane picked up the remaining sandwich half and ate it. The bread was stale but the peanut butter was sweet and salty. She ate one grape, then three, then the whole bunch was gone. She wished Maisie had left some cookies. Going into the kitchen to get some seemed like too much work, and, besides, she had so many things to do.

She wondered if Sigelman had gotten home yet, and whether he could possibly suspect what she had done. She picked up her purse and took out the letters. She had made two copies of each, and now — like Sigelman before her—she had to decide where to hide them. She thought of folding them into the extra sheets they never used on the high shelf in the storage closet in Maisie's room, but she didn't want to involve Maisie in any way. She didn't even want to use the same parts of her brain to think about Maisie as she used to think about the letters. She considered and discarded several more hiding places: behind the cleaning supplies in the cabinet under the sink, in her underwear drawer, in a plastic bag in the backyard under a rock. At last she went up to the attic, opened a carton containing their camping stove and nested pots, and slid one copy inside a battered skillet. The other copy she would keep out of the house—somewhere secret and sensible, like a safe deposit box. The originals she filed in her desk under "Maria Karkova materials," right where they belonged. She had told herself she would give the originals back to Sigelman, but now she wasn't so sure. Should she give the Newberry letter to Stefan Valdes, even though he claimed it had never existed? And what about the other two? Unable to sort out these questions in her current state, she went into the bedroom, locked the door, stripped off her clothes, and threw them in the hamper. She pulled on sweatpants and a T-shirt and got into bed. It was almost four o'clock; where had Billy taken Maisie that they still weren't back? To the library? To the children's museum? Had she fallen asleep in the car as she sometimes did, and was Billy driving up and down the Beltline or out Route 18 toward Verona so that she would stay asleep? There was something soothing about aimlessly driving a car with a sleeping child in it, not deciding in advance where you were going, not knowing how long until you stopped, always something new coming into view—houses and parking lots and fields of corn that were left, almost immediately, behind.

Billy wouldn't have taken Maisie away, would he? Suddenly panicked, she got out of bed and opened the drawers in Billy's dresser, but there was no way to tell if anything was missing. She went down the hall to Maisie's room. She knew these clothes more intimately—the little T-shirts and miniature overalls and stretchy pants. Allowing for what was lying around in corners and slung over chairs or in the laundry basket, everything seemed to be there. Besides, Ducky was lying on the unmade bed, and Maisie wouldn't go to sleep without him.

Jane could see she wasn't getting any rest this afternoon. She wanted to call someone, someone who would give her sympathy, who would listen to what Billy had done with appropriate outrage. Her mother? Helen? Catherine, back east, whom she hadn't called once since she'd moved out here?

She thought about the letters again. So Karkov had slept with boys! She tried to think of male friendships or homoerotic tension among any of his male characters, but nothing came to mind. No doubt he had taken care to disguise any inklings in the writing. Still, she knew she would reread the books with interest. Sex always spiced things up, whether you liked it or not.

Suddenly Jane knew who she wanted to talk to. She went to her study, picked up the phone, and dialed. It rang and rang. Jane knew not to expect an answering machine or voice mail, but she couldn't seem to let the connection go, tenuous as it was—not really a connection at all, just an unrequited reaching out on her part, a link of the imagination.

And then, after fifteen rings—or maybe more, she had lost count—the phone was picked up. There was a rattling and a fumbling, a loud exhalation of breath. "Hello?" a voice said.

In the long period of ringing, Jane had forgotten what she was going to say. Now she had to fight the startled impulse to hang up.

"Professor Shombauer?" She forced the words out, stumbling over the syllables. "It's Jane Levitsky. Did I get you at a bad time?"

She could have been out and just got back into the house. She could have been sleeping or in the bath. Or maybe she'd been having sex—with a nice widower from the neighborhood or a colleague from a university in Europe visiting for a conference or (who knew?) a middle-aged woman schoolteacher with a pouf of white hair to match Shombauer's own. In her heart, though, Jane didn't believe Shombauer ever had sex with anyone, but rather that she drew strength from abstinence, like a priest.

"Jane," Shombauer said. "What do you want?"

What do you want? No preliminaries or niceties. Everyone always wanted something every minute, after all; why pretend otherwise? Jane felt a little better, a little calmer. Here was life cut down to the bone.

"I found some letters written by Maria Karkova," Jane said. "I found them in Otto Sigelman's basement. He stole them—or at least, one I know for sure he did, from the Newberry. He doesn't know I read them. I made copies. They prove that Masha's life was the basis for the plot of *Lady of the Snakes* and also that Karkov had sex with men."

That was it: a brief cogent summary, just the way Shombauer liked.

There was a long pause. Jane could picture her adviser in the high-ceilinged Victorian house with the fussy furniture and heavy oil paintings, the amethyst-colored decanter set on the octagonal coffee table next to the amber cut-glass candy dish. She could picture Shombauer's forehead slightly wrinkling, the corners of her mouth turning down, her fish eyes narrowing.

"Let's start at the beginning," Shombauer said. She spoke slowly, thoughtfully, so that Jane could picture the information filtering down through her mind, ordering and reordering itself as it fell so she could examine it from every angle, explore all the possible interconnections.

Jane tucked her feet up under her on the desk chair and looked out the window. The sun was low in the sky, and the long shadows of the houses and trees spread across the muddy lawns. A few cars splashed through the runoff down the street, but none of them was her car. What was the beginning? Her trip to the Newberry? Her questions about Masha's death? The week in college when she read Otto Sigelman's translation of *Dmitri Arkadyevich* for the class in which she'd met Billy? The spinning, magical silence of her father's study filled with books in strange languages she longed to decipher?

"I'm wondering what I should do with them," she said, declining for the moment to try to answer Shombauer's question. "I'm wondering, for instance, if I should go to the police."

"About Sigelman?" Shombauer snorted. "Unless he's much stupider than he used to be, they won't be able to prove anything! Say what you like about him, he knows what he's doing. Now tell me *everything.*" She stretched the word out, her German accent emphasizing the harsh consonants, giving the word a rough, pitiless overtone as though to imply that the world was, in all its expansiveness, a bitter place.

Jane knew Shombauer didn't really want to hear everything. She didn't want to hear about Billy and Felicia, or Maisie's illness, or Jane's sense that her carefully constructed life had melted away like the unseasonable snow. *You can't serve two masters:* hadn't Shombauer said so from the beginning? So again, instead of answering, Jane asked the question that was bothering her most.

"What kind of scholar would do what he did? He's covering up important information about Karkov! About his life and about his work. What happened"—here she paused, embarrassed to use the words that had sounded so ringingly in her head earlier, but she pressed on and said them— "what happened to our allegiance to the truth?"

Shombauer sighed, a long exhalation like water gurgling down a drain. "Jane," she said, not harshly or sadly but matter-of-factly, as though this was something everyone knew: "Fame and fortune—that's your answer! That's what it all comes down to in the end, for so many people, not just Sigelman. Maybe he's convinced himself that the world is the way he sees it, and no amount of evidence can shake that vision. Or maybe it's more cynical. It hardly matters. It is how it is."

Jane felt sure no one had ever spoken to her so plainly before in her life. In a minute, if she wasn't careful, she'd be crying again, and Shombauer didn't want to hear that, either.

"Besides," the older woman went on—and now Jane felt that Shombauer was speaking to her in a new way, a way she'd never spoken before, as though Jane were finally old enough to be let in on the family secrets: the crack-addicted cousin and the uncle with wives in two cities. The father who fucked the gray-eyed boy servant in broad daylight. "Besides, you have to remember that in many ways Sigelman *made* Karkov. Before Otto, no one read the novels! Even in Russia they had fallen into obscurity. In France, in Germany—it was the same everywhere. But Otto saw something in the work. And he saw something in the life that he thought people could be excited about—a large, bristly, enigmatic personality. And he had the energy to animate that vision, to make others see it. He had the instincts to know who to talk to and what to say, and he succeeded wildly! He rode Karkov to the very top, so that now he's taught in classrooms all over the world, and his name is sometimes mentioned—as it never was in his lifetime—in the same breath as Tolstoy's or Dostoyevsky's. Without Otto, I doubt Karkov's books would even be in print in this country, and you would be studying something else. Pushkin, maybe, or Goethe. Or maybe you'd be working in an office—who knows?"

Jane couldn't speak. Studying Goethe or working in an office, living in a different city. Married to a different man, mother of a different child! Or maybe no child at all, no husband. What if Sigelman had died of pneumonia instead of his brother Georg? What if the Nazis had put him in Mauthausen or Auschwitz?

"Jane," Shombauer said. "Are you there?"

"Yes," Jane said, rubbing the heels of her hands over her damp cheeks. Outside, the yard was engulfed in shadow. "Yes, I'm here."

It was nearly seven before the Honda pulled up the steep driveway. The car doors slammed shut, and then she could hear Billy and Maisie climbing the steps onto the porch and Billy saying, "Stamp your feet, Maisie! Stamp that muddy slush right away." He opened the door, and they came into the house. His face hardened when he saw Jane. His cheeks drew in and his eyebrows pulled together like caterpillars.

"Mommy!" Maisie said. "I goed to the zoo! I saw the tigows and the elephants!" She swung her arm in front of her face like a trunk, and then she ran over to the plastic animals that still lay toppled and scattered across the rug and began setting them upright. She was wearing a pink T-shirt with a kitten on it, and there was chocolate smeared on her face. Hungry for the weight of her, Jane got up from the couch and went over to her daughter and knelt down to hug her, but Maisie said, "Not now, Mama! Now I busy. I saw giraffes, too, like this one. And a crocodile and a big, big snake! Like 'Lisha's snake, only still alive."

A kind of electric shock went through Jane at the sound of Felicia's name. She'd known she couldn't wipe Felicia off the face of the earth just by wishing. She'd known she'd have to face her at work and probably even discuss her with Billy, but it hadn't occurred to her that Maisie would talk about her—that Maisie would miss her, even. That Maisie would need some kind of explanation of why she had disappeared. Jane stood up and looked at Billy, and he looked at her, and she tried to figure out what she could possibly say to him, here in the chilly living room in front of their child.

"So," Jane said. "You went to the zoo."

"Yes. It was such a bright day."

Then they were at an impasse again.

"They don't got rhinos at the zoo," Maisie said informationally, poking at a plastic rhino. "Too big. Bigger than elephants!"

Billy looked at his watch. "Half an hour till bed, Mais," he said.

"I'll give her a bath," Jane said. "Maisie, I'll give you a bath and read you a story, okay?"

"No bath," Maisie said. "I not dirty!"

"A nice warm bath with bubbles," Jane said, and just as she was bracing herself for a no-bath tantrum, a slog through tears and soap in the eyes and water splashed everywhere, Maisie looked up from her toys and said, "Okay! Rhino coming too. He *very* dirty." She picked up the rhino and ran lightly up the stairs.

Later when Jane came back down to the living room, Billy had put away the toys and folded the clothes and washed the dishes and was sitting at one end of the couch reading the sports section of the *Capital Times*. Jane sat down at the other end so that the piece of furniture seemed balanced between them like a seesaw.

"So," Jane said, "the zoo?"

"Jane," Billy said. "I'm so sorry." He looked at her across the endless expanse of couch. It was dark outside now, and he had turned on the table lamp. Jane could see him well enough to see that he didn't look all that sorry. Certainly not sorry enough.

"Did Felicia go with you?"

Billy's face furrowed and he looked down at his lap. "No. Of course not," he said. "Jane—"

But she interrupted him.

"You think that's it?" she said. "You say you're sorry and it's done?" The self-righteous anger felt good, and for a moment she was so glad to be able to indulge in it that she forgot how terrible she really felt— how terrible things really were. And then with a shudder, she remembered again.

"No," Billy said. "I don't think that. But I *am* sorry. I shouldn't have— I never— If I'd thought..." But none of these sentences seemed to be sentences he could finish. He lifted his hands as if to explain something, then let them fall again.

"If you'd thought what?" Jane said coldly. "That I'd be back early and catch you? You would have refrained that particular evening?"

Billy said nothing. She watched him closing up like a clam, drawing his shoulders in.

"You shouldn't have is right!" she went on. "My god, Billy—the babysitter? You couldn't come up with anything more banal than that? What about the secretary at that law firm you worked at, or did you ever consider one of those high school girls you used to teach?"

He was so still now he hardly seemed to be breathing. Then he made an effort and looked up at her.

"Jane," he said. "Janie." He reached a hand out toward her, but she was too far away. His arm looked weirdly disembodied, like an arm reaching out of a grave in a horror movie, and Jane recoiled, pressing back into her end of the couch.

He tried again, reaching out with words this time. Jane wanted to shut her ears against them, but instead she sat with her back still pressed painfully into the hard arm of the couch, and she listened as he labored to explain, his phrases heaving and sputtering toward her.

"Things had been so—so tense and wrong between us. You know they had! And you seemed as though you wanted— as though you didn't want... And ever since Maisie was born— Or maybe not then, exactly! But still, it felt almost as though, as though it didn't matter."

"*Matter?*" Jane jumped on the word. "How could you fucking my graduate student possibly, in any universe, not matter?"

Billy bobbed his head—a nod of agreement or a tremor, Jane couldn't tell. He brought his hands together and cracked his knuckles. The sound was very loud in the quiet room. "I don't know," he said. "I was just trying to explain." But she could hear the coldness in his voice now, underneath the sadness. He wasn't trying anymore.

How had it come to this? Certainly things had been tense and wrong. Certainly each of them had wanted and not wanted many things. But from there to adultery was still a giant leap, a leap that defied and outraged the imagination.

Billy moved toward her on the couch now. Bravely, he put out his hand again, and this time he touched her knee, though gingerly, as though he might get a shock.

She jerked her leg back. "Get out of the house!" she said, while the muscles of her leg vibrated and the recoil of his touch flew galvanically through her, her whole body jangling with heartache and disgust.

CHAPTER FIFTEEN

A WEEK WENT BY, and then somehow another week. On Saturdays, when Maisie went to stay with Billy at Vince's, the emptiness of the house was breathtaking. The air seemed to coalesce into a kind of sap in which it was hard to move. Jane sat at her desk with her notes on Masha's letters spread out in front of her. In the past she had been able to sink down into the work like a weighted diver into an undersea world, but these days she floated like a cork on the blind, salty surface. She didn't know what to do. The article she'd been drafting about nature writing, her idea about Karkov taking bits from Masha's diaries for his own use—all of it seemed dull and paltry compared to what the letters revealed.

Should she write an article, then, revealing Karkov's sexuality? Should she write about the origins of *Lady of the Snakes*? Either way she would have to disclose her sources, but she hadn't decided what to do about the stolen letters yet.

In the meantime, she had been trying to get in touch with Greg Olen. She was fairly sure Sigelman had been to see him, and everyone seemed to think he had inherited some family papers. Jane knew Sigelman would do whatever he had to do to get his hands on them. Maybe he already had; how would she know? Maybe the other two letters in the egg box had come from Olen. She had assumed, because the box was battered and the underlayer of silver tape so faded, that Sigelman had had them a long time, but really she had no idea. At Olen's house, no one ever answered the phone. She had left a couple of messages, but he hadn't called back. She couldn't blame him. His father had died and now people like her hounded him about his inheritance.

Weekdays Jane was busy with Maisie. The Chestnut Lane Children's Center—the day care she had liked all those months ago—had called with a last-minute opening, but she had declined it. "In the fall," she'd told the director, wondering even as she said it what she thought she was doing, what she was letting herself in for. While they'd chatted on the phone, Maisie sat blank-eyed on the couch watching television, her scabby knees hugged to her chest. Her feet were dirty, and her dimpled mosquito-bitten arms were brown from the sun. She watched a lot of television since Billy had moved out. Time limits were a thing of the past.

Would Maisie be better off at Chestnut Lane, where there would be other kids to play with, art projects, new toys, music time, story time, hot lunches? Jane didn't know. All she knew was that life was falling apart around her and she had to keep Maisie close. For once it wasn't the work that mattered. She watched herself letting it drift away as though from above, like someone having an out-of-body experience. Doubtless there was a price to be paid for this, but it had become clear to Jane that there was a price to be paid for everything.

So each morning they went to the grassy park that ran downhill all the way to the lake, and Jane pretended to be a stay-at-home mom. Yesterday the playground equipment had been crowded. Two girls in apple-green dresses with their hair French-braided rode the horse swings for twenty minutes while Maisie eyed them enviously. "Does your little boy want to swing?" called one of the mothers, a plump blond in a denim jumper, from a bench in the shade.

Maisie looked at the woman. "I'm not little!" she said. "I'm big!"

"Of course you are," the mom agreed. "You're a big boy!"

"Actually, she's a girl," Jane said.

"I'm sorry," the woman said.

"She has flowers on her sneakers," observed the woman beside her, who was thin, with pale skin, straight brown hair, and a big raspberry-colored straw hat.

Jane had spoken to these same women last week. Or maybe it had been a different pair. Park moms, as indistinguishable as the beady-eyed robins that hopped across the grass looking for worms. Jane felt they were watching her, watching Maisie, and judging what kind of mother Jane was. Unlike them, she had no peanut butter sandwiches, no apple slices, no honey-sweetened animal crackers (or even conventional ones), no stale bread saved for the ducks. She felt like a raven, solitary and conspicuous, among them.

At last the girls got tired of swinging. Jane helped Maisie up onto one of the horse swings. The sun, which had been up long before six, beat down from the clear blue sky, only a few weeks shy of the solstice. All day and deep into the night, it illuminated every blade of grass, blazed off every parked car, exposed every expression on every face just when Jane would have preferred the cool forgiveness of shadows and dusk. She shoved her sunglasses back up her perspiring nose and gave Maisie a push. Maisie's knuckles were white on the handlebars that protruded from the sides of the horse's face, and she hunched low over the plastic mane.

"How old is she?" the blond mom asked Jane.

"She'll be three in September."

"Oh, really? Is she small for her age?"

"A bit." Actually, Jane had no idea whether this was true. She had lost track of all the benchmarks. Billy would have known. Billy always knew things like that—what pressure tires should be inflated to, how long to roast a chicken, people's birthdays and how old they were going to be.

Maisie dragged her feet in the gravel, slowing the swing. She pointed to the roundabout, a metal platform with arched supports where the other girls were taking turns pushing and riding. "I want to go on *that*," she said.

"Maisie," Jane said, "you just got on the horsey swing."

The blond mom spoke to Maisie. "You like those girls, don't you?" She called over to her daughters, "Caitlin! Brianna! This little one wants a ride!"

Yes, Jane thought sadly, Maisie liked Caitlin and Brianna. She wanted French braids and an apple-green dress. She wanted to belong to a normal midwestern family, but instead, in an hour or two, she'd have to go home with Jane.

"She's too small!" the older of the girls called back. "She might fall off!"

"I won't fall off!" Maisie cried, wide-eyed and passionate.

"You might," the girl said sternly. "You could fall wrong and break your arm, like my cousin Emily."

Jane stepped over to the roundabout, grabbed one of the metal arches, and pulled it to a stop. The girls groaned. "Hop on, Maisie," she said.

Maisie trotted over in her baggy overalls and blue Keds and hoisted herself up.

"Hold on tight to this pole," Jane said.

The girl who had been pushing jumped on, too. The round platform was heavier than it looked, and Jane pulled hard to get it going, getting gravel in her shoes.

"Here we go!"

The older girls shrieked, and Maisie, watching them, shrieked, too. Her face glowed and the wind ruffled her short curls as she squinted into the bright sunlight. The big girls laughed, wisps of hair coming loose from their braids.

"Hooray!" the older one shouted, letting go of her metal pole for an instant to clap her hands and then grabbing on again.

"Hoo-ray!" Maisie shouted and let go, too.

Jane could hear, as if in slow motion, Maisie's shout of joy shift registers, twisting upward into a shriek of terror. She flew sideways through the air—through the dust motes and floating pollen grains and the heavy smell of the grass—and then she hit the ground with a thump. For a drawn-out moment, there was silence as everyone turned to look at her lying there, blue dust rising around her. Jane found time to be startled by quite how blue it was—almost the color of the lake when a storm was blowing in—before Maisie's voice cut the morning in two. She screamed, lying on her back in the gravel, her mouth a black hole edged with red. The next instant Jane was kneeling beside her, afraid to pick her up. She couldn't speak. Blood welled and dripped down Maisie's chin. Jane touched her chest. The denim overalls were hot. Was something broken inside, down under the cotton and the skin, inside the paltry lattice of bones? How could you know?

"Let me see her," someone said. It was the brown-haired mom with the raspberry hat. She was kneeling next to Jane now, brushing Maisie's hair back from her grimy face, her own face furrowed with concern and sympathy, and also with a kind of calm reassurance that seemed to say that, even in the chaos of emergency, there was a way to proceed. A path. "It's okay," she told Maisie. "I know it hurts. Can you move your legs for me? How about your arms? That's great, hon, just perfect. You're okay. She's okay," she told Jane kindly. "She'll be fine in a minute. Why don't you pick her up?"

Jane put her arms around Maisie, who was still screaming in loud, frantic bursts like a car alarm, and cradled her to her chest. "Where's the blood coming from?" she managed to ask.

"I think she bit her lip," the hat woman said. "And there's gravel in her hands. But that's the worst of it." She got up and grabbed her diaper bag, pulled out a wipe, and pressed it against Maisie's lip. Already, Maisie was recovering. She was looking out through the tears, anxious to see what would happen next.

Jane buried her face in her daughter's gritty, sweaty hair and tried not to cry.

"That was some fall," said the mother of the girls. "She was lucky. That's exactly how my niece broke her arm."

"I told her she'd get hurt," one of the girls said.

"Thank you," Jane told the hat woman hoarsely.

"I'm a nurse," the hat woman said. "This was scary, that's all. It wasn't bad."

Jane thought of all the things this woman must have seen: severed limbs, and babies drowning in air because their lungs didn't work, and the glassy faces of children whose parents had died in car accidents, but it didn't make her feel lucky. It just reminded her how many horrors waited with greedy fingers in the dark.

Maisie's crying began to subside. She twisted her head to look around and saw everybody staring at her. Then she took a breath and sobbed out, "I want my daddy!"

Jane felt her face go red. "Hush," she said sternly. "You're all right."

"Daddy!" Maisie wailed. "I want my da-ddy!"

Jane stood up, hoisting Maisie onto her shoulder. "I'd better get her home," she said.

"Can you manage?" the woman asked.

For once Jane was grateful she hadn't brought anything with her. "I'm fine," she said, grabbing hold of her stroller and pushing it one-handed up the hill. *Fine!* she thought. She struggled along the path, the stroller veering toward the grass, Maisie squirming on her shoulder while the park moms watched, doubtless wondering why a child would want her daddy when she had her mother right there.

One Saturday afternoon in the middle of May—Jane's third weekend alone in the house—she picked up the phone and dialed Greg Olen's number yet again. This time someone picked up.

"Hello?" It was a woman's voice, slightly harried, as though she'd been right in the middle of something when the phone rang.

"Hello!" A jolt of nervous excitement ran through Jane. "Can I speak to Greg Olen, please?"

There was a pause, and in the quiet Jane could hear a noise float through the line—a faint, familiar sound she couldn't place. A quiet, squeaking, hamstery sound.

"He's busy," the woman said.

It wasn't quite a squeak, though. A chirp? A chirrup? A snort?

"My name is Jane Levitsky," Jane said, trying to make herself sound pleasant and businesslike, warm and engaging. "Do you have any idea when I could reach him?"

"Can I ask what it's about?" the woman said. She had a musical voice, low but breathy, like the bottom range of a flute.

Chirp chirp, came the noise—or *shlup shlup*.

"I want to talk to him about one of his ancestors," she said, and then she supposed she'd better explain who she was. "I'm a Russian literature professor at the University of Wisconsin, and I've been studying the writings of his great-great-grandmother. That's what I want to talk to him about."

"Great-great-grandmother?" the woman repeated.

"Yes," Jane said. "Maria Karkova. Grigory Karkov's wife."

"She wasn't a writer." The voice on the other end was dismissive. *Squech, squech.*

"Can I leave my number?" Jane asked. "Maybe he could call me."

"I'm sorry," the woman said. "I really don't have a free hand right now."

What was that supposed to mean? Jane pictured her hands cuffed to the wall or else filled with something heavy and precious—towers of china plates and cups, perhaps. Or maybe she was merely washing dishes, her hands fishing around in soapy water, the phone tucked under her chin.

"Can you suggest a good time to call back?"

"I really can't," the woman said. "Greg is very unpredictable. Ouch! No, no, no."

The last few words were obviously not meant for Jane, who couldn't think of anything to say except "I hope you won't mind if I try again." But the line had already gone dead.

After she hung up, it came to her what the sound had been and why it was so familiar. It was the squeaky, lip-smacking sound of a baby nursing. She remembered, suddenly, sitting on the couch in the old apartment a few months after Maisie was born, with sleet coming down outside the window and a cold draft lifting across the room. She'd had her shirt up and her bra down, feeding the baby while on the phone with one of her dissertation readers, a man of about sixty with grown children.

"What's that?" he had asked in the middle of the conversation. "I hear a kind of funny sound."

"I don't hear anything," Jane had said. And she'd run her hand over Maisie's downy head in apology for denying her.

As if cued by the memory, the phone began to ring. Jane waited for the answering machine to get it. She watched the red light on the machine blink on, but she felt very distant from it. It might have been Mars appearing in the evening sky.

Her brother Davis's voice came through the speaker.

"Jane," Davis said. "Guess where I am? I'm in Madison for a conference! I've been meaning to call and let you know I was coming, but I guess I never got around to it. I thought maybe we could get together."

His voice sounded forced, halfhearted. No doubt he'd had to make himself call her, his little sister with whom he had once watched television, sat in the backseat on family trips to Portland or Mount Shasta, walked to the library. He had never minded being with Jane as long as talking was not required of him. Talking had never been his strong suit.

Davis recited the number of his hotel. In a moment he would hang up, and although Jane did not exactly want to talk to him, the idea of missing him entirely was worse. The air in the house was so thick with sadness it was virtually unbreathable. She jumped up and grabbed the phone. He was her older brother after all, and she loved him.

"Davis?" she said. "It's me."

Davis paused. "Oh," he said. "I thought you weren't there."

"No," she said. "Sometimes I feel that way, but no. I'm definitely here." She carried the phone to the back door and stood looking out into the yard. Her memory of their mother's garden on Euclid Avenue was suddenly sharp and clear. She felt she could see it like an underlay beneath her own—the dusty gray-greens and brilliant purples, the spiky succulent leaves of the yuccas and the tiny white fragrant blossoms of the jasmine vine almost visible below the sharp midwestern grass, the weeds so green they hurt your eyes, the wild blackberry brambles where the mosquitoes caucused.

"Well," Davis said. "Good." He cleared his throat.

She had rattled him. She was always doing that.

"So," she said. "A conference?"

"One of the APS divisional meetings. It's on recent progress in many-body theories," Davis said.

Jane had had many-body theories explained to her before, but she still didn't know what they were.

"Do you have time to get together?" she said. "What's your schedule?"

Out in the yard the insects droned. It was hot and still, the white sun pasted in the sky. The idea of anyone having a schedule, of any individual instant being differentiated from any other instant, seemed absurd.

Davis was already waiting at a table when Jane came in. She had chosen a slightly nicer place than Davis was comfortable with—she could see that in the hunched, fidgety way he sat in his chair—but she ignored it. When did she ever get to go out to dinner? The host led her to him across the room, and Davis half got up as she kissed his cheek. He smelled clean and musty at the same time. A faint astringent smell hung around him, too, which might have been skin cleanser or some off-brand of aftershave, but which Jane always associated with science.

"Hi," she said, sitting down.

"Hi, Jane," Davis said.

They looked at each other. Davis's face looked less round and more serious than Jane remembered it, and there was a little gray in his hair. Suddenly, Jane was on the verge of tears. It was so good to see him, her awkward, irritating, inward brother! It was good to be with someone with whom she knew exactly where she stood.

"I'm glad you called," she said sincerely.

"So this is Middle America," Davis said.

"Sort of. You know they call Madison the Berkeley of the Midwest."

Davis looked around. At the table next to them, two young women with blond, sprayed hair drank cheerful green drinks. On the other side, a man in a suit and tie was digging into a large pork chop.

"I guess this particular restaurant doesn't show off that aspect of our culture too much," Jane conceded.

"I guess not," Davis said.

They smiled at each other.

The waiter appeared. "Are you expecting someone?" he asked, indicating the empty place setting.

"It will be just the two of us," Jane said, a little more loudly than necessary. "I'll have a gin and tonic." She was feeling giddy, as though she were on a blind date and not yet sure who she would turn out to be tonight.

"Billy's not coming?" Davis said.

"Billy and I are no longer living together," Jane said, looking just past Davis's ear.

Davis blinked. "You're kidding me!"

"No, I'm not. Are you going to order a drink or what?"

Davis ordered a beer. When the waiter was gone, he cleared his throat and lined up the silverware carefully on either side of his plate. When he was satisfied with the arrangement he put his hands disconsolately in his lap. "What happened?" he asked, as though he had looked around for a way to avoid asking the question but hadn't found one.

Though she had been waiting for him to ask, Jane found she couldn't answer. "I don't know," she said with some agitation. "Men are pigs!" But looking at her unhappy, uncomfortable brother who'd never done anything cruel to a female in his life that Jane was aware of, she amended, "*Billy* is a pig. He had an affair with the babysitter, and I kicked him out!" It sounded so clear and straightforward when she put it that way.

"Does Mom know?" Davis asked.

"No," Jane said. "I haven't told her."

"She likes Billy," Davis said. He sounded faintly plaintive, as though someone had turned off the television show he was watching.

Jane was annoyed. So their mother liked Billy, so what? That was hardly Jane's problem. "She liked Dad, too," she said. "Once."

Davis nodded. "Dad's not a bad guy," he said cautiously.

"No, of course Dad's not a bad guy!" Jane said. "Except for walking out on his marriage!" Davis was fidgeting the spoon between his fingers now, and she felt a great, enervating despair. "And us," she reminded him.

Davis nodded again without looking at her.

"But Billy didn't walk out?" he said. "You told him to go?"

"I—" Jane stopped. She shut her eyes, opened them again, and tried to speak calmly, to explain the situation clearly. "He slept with my graduate student."

"I thought you said the babysitter."

"Yes! She was the same person!"

"I'm sorry," Davis said. He put the spoon gently back down on the tablecloth, beside the knife.

It wasn't at all clear to Jane what he was apologizing for—for upsetting her, or for not understanding what she'd said, or for the hard time she'd been through.

"Thank you," she said. "But you know"—she leaned across the table, wanting to make sure he understood—"it's not really like Mom and Dad. You know why? Because Mom just sat back and let it all wash over her. She took whatever he did to her, but I'm not doing that. She would have let Dad stay, you know, even after she found out about Pei. She would have put it all behind them and never breathed a word about it." She took a piece of bread from the basket, buttered it thickly, washed it down with gin. The butter was sweet and smooth in her mouth, and the drink tasted of juniper and limes. She felt better. She liked the way the silverware glittered on the white tablecloth, the dissonant harmonies of the jazz that spilled out of the wall speakers. "For Mom," she told Davis, though she had never actually thought about it before, "life was something that happened to her, not something she took charge of. But that's not the way it is for me."

"Well," Davis said uncomfortably, "good for you."

"You sound like you don't believe me," Jane said.

"Of course I believe you." Davis took a sip of his beer before putting the glass down precisely inside the ring of condensation it had made. "You've always been like that. You're a take-charge person. You were like that when you were six years old."

"Yes," Jane said with a stab of lonely pride. "Yes, I was."

When their dinners came, they ate in silence for a while, comfortably. Davis had ordered the trio of sausages and Jane had the sea bass, but otherwise it was not so different from eating TV dinners together in the kitchen of the house on Euclid Avenue.

Then Davis said, "Maybe this isn't the right time to say anything about it. But I have this, kind of, girlfriend." His voice seemed to expand and deepen as he spoke.

Jane put down her fork and looked at him. Her brother's face was contorted, jaw pulling one way, sparse eyebrows pushed down over his deep-set eyes, in what she saw was an effort not to look excessively pleased with himself.

"Davis!" she said, trying not to sound too surprised but still to sound happy for him. "That's great! Who is she?" They had ordered a bottle of wine and she poured herself another glass. It wasn't very good wine. Billy not only knew about birthdays and tire pressures, he also knew about wine. She squinted at the label on the bottle and tried to commit the name to memory so she would never make the mistake of ordering it again.

"Her name is Andrea," Davis said. "She works at a restaurant I go to a lot. The Blue Daisy. She's..."

Jane watched with fascination as Davis's eyes unfocused and grew dreamy. She'd never seen this particular look on his face before. It made him seem younger, like someone just starting out in life. "What?" she prompted. "She's what?"

"She's, about my height, I guess," Davis said. "Her hair is— Well, her hair is long. And her eyes... Her eyes are indescribable."

Jane couldn't help smiling. "Give it a shot," she said. "Blue? Brown?"

"That in-between color," Davis said. "Not exactly blue or gray."

"Hazel," Jane said.

"No, not hazel. Sometimes kind of green, depending on what she's wearing."

"That's the definition of hazel," Jane told him.

"Is it?" Davis looked surprised. "I always think of hazel as a kind of light brown."

"It's not," Jane said. "You've been mistaken."

"I think I've been mistaken about a lot of things," Davis said. "Andrea is always correcting me. For example, she drinks a lot of diet soda, and I told her it worried me because it wasn't healthy to consume so much saccharin, and she laughed and told me they don't use saccharin anymore. They use something called aspartame. Did you know that?" The elbows of his checked shirt were on the table now, and his face wore a look of happy bafflement, as though ignorance were the most delightful condition in the world. This was what love did, Jane thought. It took intelligent people and turned them into sheep.

"Yes," she said, "they haven't used saccharin for years."

"That's what Andrea says! *Decades*, she says. Why don't I know things like that? Ordinary things everyone knows?"

"You've been thinking about other things. Many-body theories."

He pushed a piece of sausage across his plate. "It worries me," he said. "It's as though I've been living on some other planet, and now I wake up and find myself here."

"Well, welcome," Jane said. "Welcome to the planet of aspartame." The planet of sex, she thought. Of betrayal and heartbreak. Why should Davis be spared any of that?

"I mean, why would someone like Andrea want to go out with an alien like me?" Davis asked his sister.

"That's the wrong question," Jane said. She took another drink of the wine, then pushed the glass away. "Maybe you should be asking yourself whether you want to go out with someone who corrects you all the time."

"I didn't say all the time," Davis said. "And I don't mind. It just makes me feel odd, that's all."

She couldn't stop herself from continuing to lecture him. Didn't almost five years of marriage give her that right?

"Why should you feel odd?" she said. "You should feel happy! Cared for. Does she make you feel cared for?"

Davis considered the question. "Mostly, she makes me feel normal," he said at last. "I don't think I've ever felt normal before."

Jane felt drunk. Her imaginary podium dissolved, leaving her unsure what to do with her hands. She groped for her napkin in her lap. "I'm happy for you, Davis," she said, relieved to find that the words were true. Sad as she was, she was still happy for him.

"Thank you," Davis said.

"I would toast you, but the wine's so bad. I'm sorry I picked such terrible wine!" She wanted to tell him how Billy always chose the wine but she felt too ashamed. She wanted to come around the table and embrace him, but they didn't do things like that in their family.

"I think it's okay," Davis said, meaning the wine. "The thing is, about Andrea and me. I just don't think it can possibly last. I'm just not the kind of person who has relationships. I'm too strange.

I don't know what people do." He was looking at his sister intently now. "What do you do?" he asked. "In a relationship? If you want it to continue."

"Oh, Davis," she said. "You're asking me?"

Sunday morning Jane woke up feeling sick, her head spinning. Five minutes later she was in the bathroom, vomiting up the gin, the sea bass, the wine. How much more pathetic could she get? She washed her face and went downstairs and made coffee and toast, but she didn't feel like eating anything. It was not quite seven: twelve hours to fill before Billy would bring Maisie home. She wandered out the back door and looked at the garden. The peonies had faded and the grass was overgrown, but something purple was opening in the back corner by the chokecherry tree. She walked out through the calf-high grass to see what it was. Irises, a thick clump of them, their succulent stalks standing as straight as ballet dancers, unfurling their cheerful flags amid the weeds. Beyond them, beyond the boundary fence, the black stones of the Moravian church looked cold even in the sun and cast a chilly shadow across the alley. The world seethed with contradictory indications.

At nine she tried Olen again. The phone rang for a long time before the woman answered.

"Hello," Jane said. "This is Jane Levitsky calling again, from the University of Wisconsin. Is this a good time to talk to Greg Olen?"

"Greg's working," the woman said. Her voice sounded flatter this time, less flutelike. Probably she wasn't getting enough sleep.

"I'm sorry!" Jane said. "I'm sorry to keep bothering you." She wasn't getting enough sleep, either. "You have a baby and everything. You must have your hands full."

There was a pause. "How do you know about the baby?" the woman asked.

"I heard it," Jane explained. "Through the phone."

"You did?"

"Yes. Yesterday when I called, you were nursing. I heard the sucking. I used to feed my daughter when I talked on the phone, too, so I know. It's impossible to get anything done with a baby! So many things you can't do at all, especially when you're nursing. My daughter used to nurse all day long."

"Caroline is a milk fiend," the woman said. "I think she would never stop if I didn't make her."

Jane's own breasts tingled painfully in sympathy. "It doesn't last forever," she said.

"I thought everyone liked nursing," the woman said tentatively. "The books all say how great it is."

"I didn't like it," Jane said. "But it wasn't so bad, once I got used to it."

Another pause.

"The thing about Greg," the woman said, "is that he hates to talk on the telephone."

Me, too, Jane thought. She didn't like nursing, and she didn't like the telephone, but both were sometimes necessary. She said nothing, however, waiting to see what the woman was getting at.

"Even if you call when he's around, he won't talk to you," she said. "Or if he does, he'll be as unhelpful as possible. If you want to talk to him, the thing to do is to drop by. Ring the doorbell. He'd like to be a recluse, but he can't resist a ringing doorbell. He even talks to Jehovah's Witnesses."

"Drop in?" Jane repeated. "Really?"

"Afternoons are good," the woman said. "Greg's usually around in the afternoons."

The empty day seemed to take shape suddenly. It sat up and thumped its tail, sniffing the wind.

CHAPTER SIXTEEN

JANE SAID, "It's nice of you to talk to me." She was standing nervously on the stoop of a run-down gray house on a quiet street pitted with potholes. In the doorway stood a man in his late twenties, wearing jeans and a pale green shirt patterned with jaunty, darker green zigzags. His black hair was thick and wavy, and his dark eyes gleamed irritably in his fine-boned face.

"You happened to catch me," he said as she followed him into the hall, which was crowded with shoes and newspapers and a big black old-fashioned baby buggy. Coats hung from pegs on the wall, and the air smelled of cigarettes. He led her into a small, sparsely furnished living room. Against one wall paperbacks crammed a tall, unvarnished bookcase—Kerouac and Nabokov, Karkov and Solzhenitsyn and Mailer. On top of the bookcase, a silver samovar gleamed in the cloudy light that drifted in through the windows.

"That's a beautiful samovar," Jane said.

"It was my great-grandparents'," Olen said, looking at the vessel with pride.

Had it been Masha's, then? Had she passed it down to her children, who'd carried it all the way to America, to the vast, fertile farmland of the Mississippi valley that was the counterpart of the endless wheat fields of the Russian provinces? Jane had seen a photograph once of Masha serving tea. Could she have been using this very samovar? Jane stared at it, well polished, shining here as it had shone, perhaps, on the sideboard in the long, elegant *zala* of Dve Reckhi. She wanted to reach up and touch it, but she didn't know if Olen

would like that. She looked at his pale face, his sharp nose and furrowed brow, searching for a sign of Masha—for Masha's ghost peering
out at her from his eyes. He looked Russian, she thought. There was
a kind of fierce imperiousness about him. You could imagine him
giving orders, drinking vodka, riding a horse in tall, gleaming boots.

On the wall next to the bookcase hung a group of small water-
colors, mostly in shades of rust and green and pale yellow. One was
of leaves, another of shapes like shadowy fish. A third seemed to be
paw prints in a warm, watery violet, as though a cat had stepped in
paint and then walked across the paper.

"Those are Susannah's," Olen said, seeing what Jane was looking
at. "My wife's." Of the woman herself there was no sign. Maybe the
baby was sleeping and she was taking the opportunity to sleep, too.
Maybe she was in a studio somewhere, contemplating colors of paint.
Olen sat down on a chair and indicated the futon couch for Jane.

"Who changed the family name?" she asked.

"My grandfather. He was the one who married Sonya, Karkov's
granddaughter." Olen's face softened slightly, his jaw relaxing and his
shoulders settling as though someone had put a hand on his back.
"He thought Olenin was too foreign for the midwest. He was an extraordinary man. Got himself out of the Soviet Union. He didn't want
to stay in Europe—it was too close to the old life. He had America on
his mind, and when he got here he made a new life for himself. Out
of nothing."

"But you knew who your ancestors were? On your grandmother's
side?"

"I knew my grandmother's grandfather had been famous.
Wealthy. A count." He smiled sardonically, leaning back in his chair
and tapping the floor with a leather boot. "That was more important
to my family than that he had been a writer. He had been rich, he had
passed on his wealth to his children, and then the Communists came
and stole it all. It was the same on my grandfather's side—the family
had nothing after that." He looked at Jane. "Nothing," he repeated,

making sure she got the point. "Cabbages and rags! I remember my grandfather talking about coming to this country and walking into a supermarket for the first time in his life. Shelves filled with goods! He had never seen anything like it. Canned peas, baked beans, frozen fish..." His black eyes looked past Jane as though he were seeing that store in front of him with its abundant cans, its schools of filleted, rock-solid fish. Jane thought of her own grandfather, her mother's father, with his skinny chicken neck and his Naugahyde slippers, sitting in his easy chair in Cleveland talking about why his father had left Vilnius.

"It was like that in my family, too," she said. "Desperation, that's what drives people to do something that hard. Leaving everything behind the way they did." She thought of Otto Sigelman, for whom that desperation had been a personal reality, not merely a family legend. Was he owed something for that? Did she owe him something? What, after all, was her own desperation compared to his? A lynx to a tiger, maybe. Still, there was no denying even a lynx's weight or the sharpness of its claws. It had gotten her here, after all, hadn't it?

Olen wasn't interested in Jane's family. He went on talking about his grandfather, staring into space as though he could see back into the past. "When I went to his house as a boy, the basement was filled with cartons of toilet paper and cooking oil. Canned tomatoes. He never bought one of anything. Two pairs of pants, exactly the same. Two blenders."

"But it was your grandmother who was descended from the Karkovs?" Jane prodded.

"Yes. She was born after they died, though. And in this country. She had no memories of them. But she was the one who gave me my first copy of *Dmitri Arkadyevich*, when I was fifteen. In English, of course."

"You've read the novels, then," Jane said.

Olen gave her a look. "I'm a writer myself, you know. I teach writing." He pulled a pack of cigarettes from his pocket. The sky outside the window had grown paler since Jane arrived, the robin's egg blue thinned as though with water.

"What have you written?" Jane asked politely.

Olen tapped out a cigarette and jabbed it into the corner of his mouth. "The publishing industry in this country isn't the way it was in Russia when my great-great-grandfather was alive," he said. "It's all about money now." The cigarette wobbled in the corner of his mouth like a gesticulating finger.

"Yes," Jane said.

Out on the street a car swept by, its tires purring on the asphalt. Somewhere in the house, a baby began to cry. Its voice drifted down through the ceiling, growing gradually louder. Olen ignored it. He found a book of matches on the side table, lit the cigarette.

"Want one?"

"No, thanks."

The baby's cries grew frantic, high gasping shrieks, each louder than the one before, until all at once they ceased, leaving the house ringing with silence. Olen took a drag on his cigarette and blew the smoke out in a fierce stream, as though directing it into the smug faces and short-sighted eyes of the editors who had rejected his work.

"Where do you teach?" Jane asked.

"DCC. Dubuque Community College. It's a decent job. I teach a section of fiction and also a section of lit, though I never got my Ph.D. Quit after a year—what bullshit it all was! My god." He spoke with a pleased self-righteousness, the sardonic smile comfortably back on his face. "Of course, that's what you do, isn't it? Critical theory. Murdering to dissect."

Jane returned his smile blandly. She liked him, despite his bitter, tough-guy pomposity. He was interesting, even if he wasn't very nice, and Jane had always felt more at home with interesting people than with nice ones. "I guess that brings us to the point of my visit," she said.

"Let's have a beer, then," Olen said. "If we're going to talk seriously."

"All right," Jane said.

"Susannah!" he called loudly.

The baby began to cry again. Footsteps clattered overhead.

"Susannah! Bring us a couple of beers, would you?" Olen shifted impatiently in his chair, rubbing a spot on the wooden arm with his thumb.

A minute later a young woman flounced into the room with a small baby in one arm and two bottles of beer, held by the caps, drooping from her opposite hand. She clanked them down on the low, chunky wooden coffee table that looked like someone's high school shop project.

"Beer," she said, obviously annoyed. She was very young, perhaps twenty-one or twenty-two, with bright, short, sunshine-yellow hair cut close to her head and dark, tired eyes. Sleepless mother eyes, Jane thought. She moved like a sleepless mother, too, weighed down with the stupidity brought on by sleep deprivation, under which a barely controlled agitation kept her moving. She wore old blue jeans and a tank top that rode up to reveal her soft, sagging, blue-white stomach on which the purple-black vein of the linea nigra was clearly visible. "Take Caroline," she said. "I'm in the middle of ten things, and she won't be quiet unless someone holds her." Jane saw that she could hardly bring herself to look at her husband, though he regarded her squarely with a complicated mixture of irritation and desire.

"I can't hold her," he said. "She'll scream." Jane thought he had wanted to rile his wife, that that had been the point of making her bring the beers instead of getting them himself.

"Just take her!" Susannah said. "You're her father, aren't you?" She handed him the baby, which, as he had predicted, began immediately to cry. The tiny face went from pink to beet-red, and the arms and legs flailed helplessly in the soft terry-cloth outfit of unisex turquoise green.

"Someone tell *her* that." Olen bounced his daughter up and down in his lap with exaggerated woodenness.

"Hi," Jane said to Susannah, doing her best to look as though she were oblivious to the scene playing out before her. "I'm Jane Levitsky. I'm—" *I'm the one you talked to on the phone,* she started to say, but she thought better of it. Maybe Olen's wife had told her to come just to disrupt her husband's day, or for some other reason Jane couldn't even begin to guess at. Who knew what went on in the private stranglehold of other people's marriages? "I'm here to talk to your husband about his great-great-grandmother," she said.

Susannah nodded.

Olen stood up now, came out from behind the coffee table, and walked the baby up and down the room. She quieted slightly, her cry ratcheting down to a stubborn whimper. "She hates me," Olen said half-jokingly, holding the baby out in front of him so he could look her in the face.

"Don't be dramatic," his wife said.

"She's a mama's girl," Olen said, "Aren't you, Caroline? Mama's girl!" He bobbed the baby up and down so that her head nodded as though in agreement. "See?" he said.

"Are these your paintings?" Jane asked Susannah. "They're beautiful."

Susannah turned her head and looked at the paintings as though surprised to find them there on the wall. A rectangle of sunlight fell across the pale washes of color, giving them an otherworldly cast. "Yes," she said. "They're mine."

"Your mama did those when she was a free woman," Olen told the baby. "Before she became enslaved."

"I don't paint anymore," Susannah said. She tugged her tank top down over her stomach, self-conscious now.

"I'm sure you'll get back to it when she's a little older," Jane said. She felt very experienced suddenly, as though her own life weren't a minute-by-minute procession of fires to be put out.

"No," Susannah said, looking at her husband. "Somebody's going to have to earn a living." Olen, still jiggling the baby, pretended not to hear.

Jane knew none of this was remotely her business. She was here to talk to Olen — to flatter him if she needed to, cajole him. But there was something fierce and exhausted about Susannah that moved her. She was far too young to be living this life. Jane had thought she herself had been too young at twenty-five! "Earning a living is one thing," she said. "But you need to keep doing what you love."

Susannah looked at her in surprise. She opened her mouth as though she were going to say something, then shut it again. It was a full, pink rosebud of a mouth — a girl's mouth — but her eyes were narrow and sharp.

"I love the idea of being supported," Olen said, gesturing with the baby, which he held loosely along his forearm, like a waitress carrying too many trays. "What are you going to do to support me, Susie?"

His wife shut her eyes, took a breath. Then she opened them again and said, "Right now, I'm going upstairs to do the laundry."

"We know what that means," Olen said, looking down and addressing his words to the child. "It means she's going to take a nap." To Jane's great relief, he tucked his arm against his chest, holding his daughter more securely.

"Goddamn it, Greg!" Susannah said. Then she caught herself. Olen laughed. Jane knew that rocky shore between teasing and accusation. She knew what it was like to be stranded on it, to see nothing but sharp shale wherever you looked.

Susannah left the room. Jane could hear her footsteps going up the stairs. A door slammed and a loud humming started up. The baby had quieted and seemed to be halfway asleep on her father's shoulder, but when Olen tried to sit down, she opened her drooping eyes again and protested in a piercing register.

"I tell you," Olen said to Jane, serious now. "It's hard as hell to get anything done with a baby around. She's up all night. She cries! I've hardly managed to write two sentences since she was born." He looked half-disgusted and half-admiring, like the victim of a clever and original practical joke.

"That's too bad," Jane said.

"Open the beers, would you?" he said. "I've got my hands full."

Jane twisted the caps off the two Leinenkugel's and pushed one closer to Olen. The light in the room had shifted now, and the sky outside the window was the thin, clear white of a blank sheet of paper. "So," she said. "Maria Karkova was your great-great-grandmother. She's the one I'm interested in, actually. I was wondering if you had any papers of hers. I was sorry to learn about your father. I did hear you had inherited some old documents of the family's. Though, of course, I might have heard wrong." She smiled and spread her hands, palms up, trying to look benign but not uninteresting. Worthy, but not threatening. She imagined Sigelman sitting where she sat now. What would he have said?

"Maria?" Olen said. He took a long pull on his beer, keeping the baby balanced against his shoulder. "Really? Surely there's more meat, not to mention glory, in pursuing the certified genius of the family." He jiggled the baby, who sighed contentedly, her limbs hanging slack inside the turquoise terry cloth. Impossible that Maisie had ever been that small or that oblivious!

"She interests me," Jane said. "I'd love to hear what was said about her in the family, if anything. Any stories that were handed down. It seems likelier that some of her papers were kept than his, don't you think? Precisely because he *was* the certified genius, so there would have been more clamor for his stuff." She waited, watching him narrow his eyes thoughtfully, take another drink of his beer.

"Papers?"

"Letters, shopping lists." Jane forced herself to keep looking at him. She had no idea what he might have. "As far as I know, all her diaries are in the Newberry, but maybe not. Maybe there were other volumes?" She could imagine Sigelman mentioning the same items—Sigelman slipping pages into his jacket pocket when Olen wasn't looking.

With his left hand, Olen picked up the cigarette that had not quite gone out in the ashtray. He took a long drag as the baby slumped like a small sack of grain under his right hand. Jane tried not to look disapproving.

"Do you know Otto Sigelman?" he demanded suddenly.

Jane shivered at the sound of the name as though the man himself were standing behind her, his shadow falling across the room, the whiff of his cigar intermingling with the stink of Olen's cigarette. "He's a colleague of mine," she said carefully.

"You know that he was here?"

"I thought he might have been."

Olen blew smoke back over his shoulder, away from the baby. "Thought?" he said. "You didn't talk to him about it?"

Jane shifted on the couch, picked up her beer, put it down again. The light continued to fade, though it was only early afternoon. The wind was moving in the leaves outside the window. "He wouldn't talk about it," she said.

"Your department isn't a happy community of scholars?" Olen took a last drag of the cigarette and dropped the butt into his empty beer bottle. Then he shrugged as though to say he didn't care one way or the other, but his face had the square, solid look of a closed door.

"No," she said. "Is yours?"

He smiled now, a lazy, charming smile. "No," he said. "Not exactly."

"Well, then." Jane smiled back at him. "You know how it is."

Olen's eyes glittered. "There might be something," he said.

"Something?" Jane's hands jumped in her lap. "Can I see it?"

"Listen," Olen said, leaning forward suddenly so that the baby startled and let out a squeak. He didn't seem to notice. "Listen—fuck it! I'll tell you what happened. Sigelman came here, just like you did. Gave me a whole song and dance! He wanted what you want—papers, papers. The past more interesting than the present, dead writers more important than living ones. All that crap. And I told him what I was going to tell you: you have cash, you can see what I've got! An entrance fee. A hundred bucks for half an hour. Hell, that's a bargain, vulture lawyers charge twice as much." He looked at her to see if she would object to this assertion, but Jane wasn't objecting to anything.

"He hemmed and hawed," Olen went on, "but in the end he paid up! Cash." He savored the word.

Jane nodded. She could picture Sigelman riffling through his billfold, thumbing twenties. "Go on."

"So I brought him some documents I do happen to have. And he sat here and looked through them, and when he was done, he shrugged and said none of it was worth anything. Nothing of any importance—nothing of interest! But then, the very next day, he left a message on the answering machine saying he had changed his mind. He wanted the papers after all. He wanted to *buy* them! He offered me a thousand dollars—as though I would sell off my heritage!" He glared at Jane through the haze of cigarette smoke as though to make sure she understood that he would never, never do that, that he wasn't that kind of man.

Jane nodded, but she felt cold inside, her stomach knotted up.

"So what the hell is going on?" Olen demanded, jabbing a long, pale finger at Jane. "That's what I want to know! What made him change his mind? Or maybe it was part of his plan all along, his way of thinking to pay less than if he'd seemed excited to begin with. Who knows with a sleazy bastard like that? So—this is my deal for you, Dr. Levitsky. I'll let you look at some of what I have for free. All right? Right now. Only you have to tell me what it is, and what the fuck you think he wanted with it."

"Yes," Jane said. She felt for him, for the conflict between his ignorance and his desire to look tough and knowledgeable. He couldn't even read Russian. Whatever papers he had were his property—his heritage, as he'd said—and yet to find out what they meant, he had to rely on strangers. "I promise," she said. "If I know, if I can guess what he might have wanted, I'll tell you."

Olen frowned. She could see that he hated this, but it was the best he could think to do at the moment. He trusted her, at least a little bit—at least more than he trusted Sigelman—and she was determined to try to deserve that trust.

"All right, then," he said. "Wait here." He stood up and looked impatiently around for a place to put down the now-sleeping baby.

"I'll take her," Jane said, and held out her arms.

Olen hesitated a moment, then passed her over.

The baby was warm. Her face tilted up toward Jane's as she slept. It was a squarish, pink face with dark lashes, very different from Maisie's, which had been peachy white at this age, large and round. Still, the sensation of holding an infant was intensely, viscerally familiar. It flooded back to Jane so strongly it was almost like a blow, making her want to cry out. Was this really what Maisie had been like—a small perfect bundle with tiny starfish hands? This baby was soft beyond description, utterly other and yet entirely human. What Jane remembered with her conscious mind was something else entirely: tears and kicking, and the stink of old milk, and the different, permeating stink of the diaper pail. Overhead she heard the clomp of Olen's boots. What would he bring her? What did he have, secreted away up there? She had no idea, but the knowledge that it was nearby, that she would see it, filled her with ripples of warmth. How could she have thought she could give this up—the electric current, the thrill of pieces coming together? How, even for a moment?

Olen was gone a long time. Jane didn't hear his footsteps anymore. The sun broke briefly through the clouds and then went away again, leaving the room dim. Jane could feel the air thickening and smell the cool, sharp scent of approaching rain. It was strangely calming, sitting still, holding a baby, as life went on elsewhere.

At last Olen came back into the room. He held a sheaf of papers in his hand. "This is a sample," he said.

Only a sample? "Maybe you should show me the whole thing," Jane said. "How do you know this was what interested him?"

"Let's go slow, shall we?" he said.

Jane passed him the sleeping baby, taking the papers in exchange. It was an oddly freighted moment, as though she were actually trading one for the other—a baby for some pieces of old paper in Cyrillic script. And then, as she looked down at the top page, a glass shade seemed to fall, shutting out everything else in the world.

The paper was thin and brittle, yellowed, and the handwriting was hard to read, but Jane could see at once that it was Masha's. It was not a neat copy but messy, with many crossings out and arrows leading to new sentences scribbled in the margins. The handwriting itself was loose and irregular, nothing like the careful characters Masha formed when copying out Karkov's manuscripts. The passage written here began in the middle of a sentence, obviously a portion of a longer document.

early in the morning up into the dry hills. The sun was up. The sun was nearly always up these days, crossing the searing sky in a slow, relentless arc, cloaking itself in misty gray for a short while only in the silent hours. The hills were patchy and scrubby, rocky in one place, covered with a tumbling carpet of white flowers in another. Berry bushes grew in great, prickly swaths, noisy with birds. The birds squabbled and nested, gathering twigs and straw, eating bugs. But it was not the birds she had come for.

Up and up she climbed, her skirt heavy with dew, her bare feet so calloused they barely felt the rocky trail beneath them. Here was a ridge, and here at last the great dead stump of a tree whose roots still spread across the ground and into it, reaching deep into the cold earth, disturbing it, forming crevices and chambers there in the dark. The low sun was hidden still behind an outcropping of rock, and she sat on the ground and waited for the warmth to reach it. Today was the day, she was almost certain. When the sun reached the clay and the clay warmed, the serpentine messengers of Baba Yaga would writhe and tumble

When she finished the first page, Jane glanced up at Olen, who was watching her intently while pretending not to. She dropped her eyes again before he could say anything, and she turned the page.

out of the earthen tomb and, like Lazarus, shed their old dead skins and be reborn.

On and on it went. It was *Lady of the Snakes,* there was no question about that, a passage from about two-thirds of the way through the novel when the Snake Woman goes up into the hills and watches the asps emerging from their winter hibernaculum.

Or rather, it wasn't *Lady of the Snakes* exactly, but a version of it, a draft. Jane was pretty sure some phrases were different, and the passage about the birds was new to her. There was no doubt in her mind, however, what she was looking at—Masha's handwriting, Masha's descriptions, Masha's experiences.

Lady of the Snakes was Masha's.

She looked up again at last. The paper fluttered in her lap as a breeze blew through the room, and she held the manuscript carefully in place, her palms against the edges, instinctively touching it as little as possible so the oil of her skin wouldn't degrade the paper. She tried to read Olen's expression, but she was too agitated to see or think clearly.

"There's more?" she asked.

He nodded.

"And what did Sigelman say? What did he tell you it was?"

"He said," Olen said slowly, "that it was a copy of *Lady of the Snakes.* Not particularly valuable, but of personal interest to him because everything in Karkov's hand was interesting to him."

Rage flooded Jane. She could feel her eyes bulge with it. Sigelman had found this and meant to hide it—to suppress it—to make sure no one ever got so much as a glimpse of it—least of all Jane! That no one found out that Grigory Karkov had not, in fact, written *Lady of the Snakes,* but that his wife, a nineteenth-century housewife, had.

He wanted to slam the door on Masha, to push her back into the dusty corners of literary history when she belonged, as Jane had always suspected, in the clear bright center limelight. And these faded pieces of paper proved it.

"It's not nothing," Jane said as calmly as she could manage. "In fact, it could be very important."

"What is it, then?" he asked, his black eyes fixed on her.

"It *is* a manuscript of *Lady of the Snakes*. It's a draft—maybe even a first draft, with changes and corrections. What's interesting about it is that it's in Maria Karkova's handwriting, not Grigory's."

"You mean, he dictated and she wrote it down?"

"No. That's not what I mean. They never worked like that, and even if they had, he would have made the corrections and emendations himself. What I mean is, she wrote it!" The words sailed across the room, filling it with light. Jane sat up straighter in her chair.

"But she wasn't a writer," Olen said.

"I think she was." She knew it was true—knew it absolutely—the knowledge going deeper than the sum of the reasons she'd given him, though as explanations they were good and sufficient. You couldn't look at the manuscript and not see whose it was.

Olen stared across the coffee table at the paper in her lap as though the force of his will could make the Cyrillic script give up its secrets.

"Can I see the rest?" Jane asked.

He looked back up at her, a new, angry glint in his eye now that he knew for certain that Sigelman had tried to make a fool of him. "Why did he lie about it?" he asked.

"Because he's a chauvinist bastard!" Jane cried, no longer able to control herself. "He doesn't want anyone to know!"

Olen reached out for the papers, still holding the baby in his other arm. "I'll have to think about this," he said.

Jane forced herself to pass them back, watched him grip them too tightly, crumpling the pages slightly. "Listen," she said urgently. "Sigelman has been known to steal documents he's interested in."

As though she herself would never do such a thing!

Olen looked a little calmer now that the papers were back in his possession. "Let him try," he said.

Lightning split the sky as Jane drove home toward Madison. Rain washed over the car in gray curtains, pushed aside by her wipers one moment only to fill the windshield again the next. She peered through the torrent of rain at what she could see of the road, black and slick and curving through the cornfields. White headlights coming toward her, red taillights marking the way ahead. The noise of the rain pelting her roof was so loud she could barely think. She kept seeing Sigelman's smile in her mind, his bald, spotted head. Masha's book, she thought. Masha's book! Masha had wrung the luminous sentences of *Lady of the Snakes* out of herself, had spoken honestly about the lives of the peasants she had lived among. She had made a mask of her own face, her own searching and losing and finding, and let it speak. Somehow, in the short months between her shameful return to Dve Reckhi and her death, she had found the energy and spirit—found the time—to write it.

And when she was dead, when her body was safely buried in the graveyard by the birch grove, Karkov had stolen her words and palmed them off as his own. Well, he had done that before, hadn't he? Jane had already proved that with the concurrences from the diaries. The only difference, this time, was the scale of the theft. What depths would men sink to in order to further their own careers, Jane wondered, speeding home through the silver needles of rain, furious and euphoric.

By the time she got to Madison, the downpour was over. The storm clouds had drifted away to the east. Jane parked the car on the street and went up the path into the house in the weak sunlight. Inside, the rooms felt warm. Jane went around opening windows, turning on lights. She made herself a sandwich and carried it upstairs to her study, where she got her copy of *Lady of the Snakes* off the shelf.

Then she sat and looked out the window at the thin trunks and drooping branches of the wild chokecherry trees disappearing slowly into the dusk, not eating, not reading. Just holding the book.

Suddenly, she was so exhausted she could not keep her eyes open. She pushed herself out of the chair and staggered into the bedroom, feeling as though someone had hit her over the head with a hammer. She lay down on the unmade bed and shut her eyes. The only other time she remembered feeling this fiercely tired was when she had been pregnant with Maisie. Even the fatigue of sleep deprivation was not like this, not so sudden and ferocious.

And then, as this thought drifted aimlessly across her mind, a jolt of adrenaline shot through her, making her open her eyes. Staring at the dusty blades of the ceiling fan, she thought about how strange her appetite had been the last few weeks, and how her breasts had been sore in a way that made her think she was about to menstruate, but how, now that she thought of it, she never had. She thought about her distraction, her depression, her inability to concentrate. She had thought these things were artifacts of what had happened with Billy. She thought about the episode of nausea at Sigelman's and the other episode early this morning here at home. She tried to remember the last time she and Billy had slept together, and then she did remember. It had been late March, downstairs on the living-room couch. And now it was almost June.

CHAPTER SEVENTEEN

JANE HAD OFFERED to pick Maisie up in the car, but Billy said he would bring her on his bicycle. Jane watched for them from the couch through the front windows—it was a beautiful evening now that the rain had cleared—and at last they came into sight around the corner. Billy was pedaling hard to get up the hill, while inside the orange trailer he towed behind him, Maisie rode in luxury. Jane went out to the porch, her heart seeming to rise and sink at the same time, as if it were a rope in a pulley. Billy parked the bike and helped Maisie out, and they came up the steps hand in hand. He was wearing bright blue cycling pants and a blue-and-white-striped shirt. The muscles of his thighs and biceps were clearly visible, and his hair was plastered with sweat. Jane felt the coldness settling through her as it always did now when she saw him, even though she could see how hard he was working to be the person she wanted him to be. He stood in front of her, awkwardly cordial, his eyes full of hope and despair.

Jane knelt down to hug Maisie, burying her face in her daughter's hair as much to avoid having to look at Billy as to feel the warm silky curls against her skin. There was no way of knowing what Maisie understood, but she had to feel the awkwardness. Jane pulled her up onto her hip, startled by how heavy she was. She had to brace herself against the porch railing, shifting her weight to counterbalance Maisie's. Maisie's growth was a clock, marking the brutal passage of time. Soon Jane wouldn't be able to lift her at all.

"Thanks for bringing her," she said.

"It wasn't a problem."

"I would have been happy to come and get her."

"I know. You told me."

"Well, I would have."

Billy turned away and looked out across the street at the familiar view of the brown-shingled Olson house, at the daisies and sweet peas in Mrs. Olson's yard, the view that had, until so recently, been his. "Nice evening," he said.

"Isn't it," Jane said.

"That was some rainstorm, though."

She watched him, trying to figure out what she felt. Angry, certainly, and vulnerable. How could things ever get back to the way they had been, even if she wanted them to? Jealousy was like a knife slicing her open. Was he still dreaming of those big, shapely breasts, the full, mobile, skillful-looking mouth? Had the sex been better with Felicia? Jane had watched herself, an hour before, change out of her baggy pants into denim shorts and a tight T-shirt, put the small gold earrings with the green stones in her ears, as though the way she looked might make a difference to anything.

Now she forced herself to answer his pleasantries with her own.

"Yes," she said. "A lot of rain." She blushed at the banality of this and at the chilliness she heard in her own voice. Maisie squirmed to get down, and Jane set her on her feet. She ran into the house and turned on the television, confident no one was going to stop her.

"Did you have a good weekend?" Billy asked.

It was on the tip of Jane's tongue to tell him she was pregnant, but she didn't dare to. For one thing, she wasn't even sure she was. Maybe she was just tired out from the strain, or maybe she was coming down with something. She thought about telling him about Masha, but wasn't it her preoccupation with her work that had alienated him in the first place?

"It was all right," she said. "See you Friday."

"I didn't say good-bye to Maisie."

He came into the living room and knelt down to kiss their daughter, who was sitting on the couch with her arms around her knees, her eyes glued to the screen. Her fingernails were dirty and there was a hole in her sock. "Have a good week, okay?" Billy said.

"Bye," Maisie said absently. Jane waited for her to grab him or to cry or to insist he take her with him, but she just sat, sucking on her index finger. She had shut down, apparently, which was a reasonable response to the way her world was lurching. Certainly it was easier to handle than hysteria, but Jane found herself wishing that someone here could manage to express an authentic emotion. If they couldn't be happy, wasn't it better to be grief-stricken, or furious, rather than frozen into expressionlessness?

Billy stood up and looked around the room. "The house looks good."

Jane made a show of looking around. "Does it?" she said.

Billy nodded. "You know what I've always liked," he said. He pointed to the plaster archway that opened between the living room and the dining room, and they both stood there for a moment, gazing at it. "It's so graceful." He ran his hand through his sweat-stiffened hair and sighed. "If anything happens," he said, still looking at the archway, "a clogged drain or anything, just give me a call. I can come over and take care of it."

Why was he being so nice? It was making Jane crazy. There he stood on the rug in his tight blue cycling clothes like a melancholy superhero, wanting to do good. She longed to say that she could take care of a clogged drain herself, but they both knew she couldn't.

"Thanks," she said.

The late spring light was fading as Billy climbed onto the bike and rode away. Fireflies blinked in the grass, and the house felt empty and still. A new program came on the TV, and Maisie settled in to watch it, and suddenly Jane knew why Billy was acting so nice. He wasn't trying to make a point, or put her at a disadvantage, or even atone for what he had done. It wasn't even necessarily because he still loved her. He was being nice because he *was* nice. He was, despite that one neon exception, a nice person, a decent guy. She thought of Greg Olen and the pleasure he took in annoying his wife. She thought of Otto Sigelman and Grigory Karkov. She thought of her father. She could not deny that she was drawn to men like that—men who weren't nice at all. Still, she had married Billy. She felt a sudden pride in that, despite everything.

All week Jane waited to hear from Olen, to see what he had decided about giving her access to the rest of Masha's manuscripts and any other papers he might have. But he didn't call. He had said he'd never sell his family heritage, but Jane was worried. He had a new baby to support, and a teaching job that sounded like it was only part-time, and there he was, sitting on a pile of gold. What if Sigelman called back and offered him ten thousand dollars or fifty thousand? What if Sigelman staked out the house and waited till no one was home and broke in through a back window? Jane could picture it—the shattered glass, the old man huffing in, black leather gloves on so he wouldn't leave fingerprints. She wouldn't put it past him.

She bought a home pregnancy test and it came out positive. She wasn't surprised, but still her hands shook as she stared at the stick, and when she tried to toss it into the trash, she missed and had to pick it up off the floor and place it in among the dirty tissues and slimy soap wrappers and used threads of dental floss. Even then it seemed to glow unnaturally—peacock blue—and she covered it over with some toilet paper so she wouldn't have to look at it. What on earth was she going to do?

She called her doctor, but panicked and put down the phone when the receptionist picked up. She tried calling Olen, but nobody ever answered. She thought about going to see Sigelman, but until she decided about the letters, it seemed better to avoid him. There was too much to think about, too many decisions waving frantic arms, like children competing for attention. It made her want to stay in bed all day with the curtains closed.

But she had Maisie, so she couldn't do that.

She started taking Maisie to a new playground. She didn't want to see those women again, the ones who had watched her let Maisie fall off the roundabout. This park was farther away, beyond walking distance—out past the bustling Monroe Street corridor where they lived but not so far as the new developments, cornfields until a year or two ago, where hordes of young families were buying up new construction. It was dull and square, planted with a few scrubby bushes. The new playground wasn't as nice as the old one, but perhaps because of its unfashionable intermediate location, it was usually empty, which Jane liked and Maisie didn't seem to mind.

Today, though, another mother and child arrived when Jane and Maisie had been there for about half an hour. The mother was a very young woman with straight brown hair, a sallow face, and a pierced nose with a diamond stud in it that caught the morning sunlight. She pushed a heavy stroller with a fat blond baby in it. Maisie was playing on the climbing structure, lying down in the plastic tunnel with only her sneakers showing. The baby gurgled happily and clapped its hands as the young woman undid the seat belt, lifted it out, and set it on the dusty grass. Impossible, Jane thought, to consider having another baby, another small person to watch over and carry around and feed and push in a stroller! Impossible—even as the creature inside her opened itself up like a dandelion. She watched the girl in the baggy jeans, sitting in the grass with her face to the sun while the baby blinked at something on the ground, its mouth plugged with a pacifier. The baby's skin was very fair. Jane worried that it needed a hat. She worried that the girl, the mother, wasn't old enough to look after it. What was she doing, having a baby at her age? How had it happened? Easy enough to imagine sex in a basement or a dorm room followed by denial and panic, but after the initial rush of disbelief, why hadn't the girl gone and had an abortion? If Jane had become pregnant at that age, she certainly would have; wouldn't she? Even now that was what she was going to do—wasn't it?

The baby pulled a handful of grass out of the ground. It dropped the pacifier into its lap and began to suck on its fist, trying to slurp up the grass.

"No, no, no," the mother said. "You're not a cow." She put the pacifier back in the little mouth and lifted the baby into the air and cooed to it.

Surely Billy would agree that a baby wasn't an option. Surely, on this issue, they would see eye to eye.

Still, safer not to tell him. At least not yet.

Once she had been sure they'd always see eye to eye about everything. She remembered picking him up at the airport when he came back from Japan years ago, how he'd looked coming through the doors from customs with his hair unevenly flattened from fourteen hours on the plane. He'd looked taller than she had remembered him, and handsomer, and when he saw her, his face seemed to come alive. When he held her, the body pressed against her was both familiar and unfamiliar, his face scratchy with stubble and his smell sour from traveling. She held on to him as tightly as she could, feeling that she had not known until that moment how much she had missed him. And she had thought: This is all I want, to be held by this man this way.

But of course, nothing was all anyone ever wanted; she had known that even then, at twenty-three, and she certainly knew it now. People were greedy, they wanted more and more all the time, as much as they could get. Life teemed with desire, and the world brimmed with the objects of desire, and you would never have everything you wanted.

Billy had wanted what he shouldn't have wanted; was that really what she was so angry about? So satisfying to say, as she had said to Davis: He fucked the babysitter. Nothing extenuated that. But the truth was bigger; the truth, as always, needed to be teased carefully out. Wasn't that what she prided herself on doing so well, teasing out the truth in all its complexity? Wasn't that what she had gone on about to Shombauer—the scholar's allegiance to truth?

Across the street a row of split-level houses crouched on their narrow lots wearing the blank, heat-stricken expressions of lizards. Maisie slid slowly down the slide. The baby pulled off one white sock and threw it in the grass. The mother picked it up and put it on again, scolding gently. "Your feet will get cold, Amy. You don't want cold feet, do you?"

The baby—Amy—laughed through the pacifier and pulled the sock off again. She sat solidly on the ground but didn't look as if she could crawl yet. Jane wondered how old she was. She thought of asking, but if she asked, she'd have to have a conversation. Still, she was likely to have to have one in a minute or two, whether she said anything or not.

How old is your daughter? the young mother would inquire. Or, *What's your little girl's name?* (Maisie's hair was growing out, and she was wearing a sky blue T-shirt, so she looked more like a girl than she used to.) Jane would answer, and the other mother would remark that Maisie was cute or a nice little girl. *Thank you,* Jane imagined saying. *Of course, she's having a hard time right now because I kicked her father out of the house for sleeping with the babysitter. Besides which, I'm pregnant again and I'm thinking of getting an abortion.* What would the other woman say to that! Exhausted by the very idea of such a conversation, Jane shut her eyes and lay back in the grass. The sun burned through her eyelids in a dazzle of white and red. The dry grass prickled through her clothes. Maisie could be running out into the middle of the street, but it didn't seem likely. *Yes,* Jane imagined the woman saying, *I had two abortions myself, before Amy.*

The imaginary reply was interrupted by the woman actually speaking, her high, childish voice floating on the hot air: "Thank you," she said.

Jane opened her eyes. Maisie was standing next to the baby, shyly holding out her sock. The mother took the sock from Maisie and put it on the baby's foot, and the baby peeled it off and threw it again as far as she could. It fell about four feet away, on a chalky patch of ground busily patrolled by ants. She had a good arm, Jane thought, for a baby.

"I'll get it," Maisie said, and she fetched the sock.

"What a helpful girl you are," the mother said, and Jane saw that it was true. Maisie looked very grown up, standing next to the baby. She looked like a serious, helpful, mature little person. It made Jane feel like crying. How had Maisie gotten so grown up without her noticing? She thought of the way, when she held Susannah Olen's baby, she had felt she had missed the entire pleasure of Maisie's babyhood. Was she, even now, repeating her mistake? Could she only really ever see Maisie in retrospect or in brief dislocations of perspective like this?

"What's your name?" the mother asked Maisie.

"Maisie," Maisie said.

The baby pulled off her other sock.

"That's a pretty name," the woman said. "Mine's Rosemary. How old are you, Daisy?"

But Maisie was overcome with shyness and couldn't answer.

"She'll be three in September," Jane said. She hadn't meant to say anything; the words just slipped out of her mouth.

Rosemary looked around in a friendly way. Dark acne scars showed through a scrim of foundation, and her diamond nose stud glowed blue in the sun. "She's a nice little girl," she said.

"And how old is your daughter?" Jane asked.

Rosemary looked confused, and then she looked alarmed. "Oh no!" she said. "I just babysit her." She put a hand on the baby's head to shush her as she began to whine for her missing sock, which had fallen next to Rosemary's heavy, denim-clad thigh. The baby couldn't reach it, and Maisie was shy about going that close.

"I'm only a sophomore," the girl explained, "at UW." She picked up the sock and handed it to the baby, who immediately tossed it away again.

Embarrassment lifted off Jane in waves, but she tried to smile. "Some people do have babies at your age," she said.

Then Rosemary said, "You're Professor Levitsky. I took your nineteenth-century Russian novels class."

Immediately Jane recognized her. Third row, two or three seats from the end, near the radiator. "Rosemary Watkins!" she said.

"That was a cool class," Rosemary Watkins said. "A ton of reading, though. I loved that one book, *Dmitri Arkadyevich*. It was just like a soap opera." The undeniable soap-opera quality of Karkov's masterpiece had often stood it in good stead where student opinion went. Jane could never decide whether the book was great partly because of this or despite it.

"I'm glad you liked it," she said, sitting up straighter as she tried to make the adjustment to something approximating her classroom persona. In the grass Maisie was patiently trying to put the baby's sock back on while Amy wiggled her foot and drooled happily.

"Of course, I have to admit I didn't finish it," Rosemary said. "But my friend told me what happened in the end."

What made people think they could say things like that? What grade had she given Rosemary Watkins? Maybe none of the students did all the reading—not a single one. Maybe the best you could hope for was that they read a little and didn't plagiarize.

"It's funny seeing you here with your little girl," Rosemary went on, holding on to Amy's hands and making the chubby arms wave in the air. "You know professors have real lives and families and stuff, but you just never really think about it."

"We're pretty much just like other people," Jane said, watching Maisie watch the baby, waiting for her to throw the sock again. How happy she looked, proud and purposeful, her life suddenly filled with meaning!

"If you ever need a babysitter," Rosemary said, "give me a call. I love little kids." She was good with the baby, Jane saw. She was gentle and patient, and just now she couldn't resist kissing the fat white belly, making Amy squeal with pleasure. Maisie looked on slightly mournfully, as though wishing someone would kiss her belly, too.

"Thank you," Jane said.

"No problem. School is so much studying and agonizing about tests and stuff. Being with kids helps you kind of keep it all in perspective."

Jane would need a babysitter if there was another baby. Or rather, not *if*, because wasn't there one already? Easier to think not if it wasn't you it was inside of, lodged like a fishbone. If you hadn't experienced the link between what had once been a faceless minnow and was now the solid child climbing up the slide, her face pink with sun and pleasure. Was Jane's new feeling more right than the old one, or was it merely more emotional, sentimental, stereotypically female? She didn't know. She wondered what Billy would think. She couldn't seem to get out of the habit of wondering that.

On Friday evening, when Billy came to pick Maisie up, Jane and Maisie were waiting for him on the porch. Jane felt nervous and tired, but she had made up her mind to talk to him. She stood with her hands on the porch rail, watching him ride up. He was wearing ordinary clothes today, jeans and a T-shirt rather than his stretchy cycling outfit. His face was brown from all the riding he'd been doing, and the sun was making his hair blond again, the color it had been when he was younger.

"Hi, Daddy!" Maisie called.

He waved. "Hi, Maisie! Hi, Jane." She could tell he was trying to keep his voice the same, but Maisie's name rolled easily off his tongue and hers clotted in his mouth.

"Daddy, I want my own bicycle!" Maisie said.

Billy glanced at Jane. "Maybe for your next birthday. A tricycle. Three wheels."

"On my next birthday, I'm going to be three," Maisie informed him.

"I know," he said.

"And then, three and a half," Maisie said. "And I'll have a chocolate cake." She bounced down the steps to the sidewalk and stood there in her purple cotton shorts, trying to figure out how many fingers to hold up for three and a half.

Since when, Jane thought, didn't she want vanilla? "Billy," she said quietly, while Maisie was busy with her fingers, "I need to talk to you."

Billy, standing on the sidewalk with his bike, looked up to where she stood on the porch. "Okay," he said.

"I thought maybe we could go down to the park."

They walked down the sidewalk toward the frozen custard place at the end of the road. Maisie danced ahead, and Jane and Billy came behind more slowly. Jane was intensely aware of the space between them. It was important to stay strictly on her side of an invisible divider, but not so far over that he would think she couldn't bear to be near him. The air seemed charged with electricity, as though she'd get a shock if she tried to reach across. She tried to rehearse in her head what she wanted to say to him, but the words rushed away.

At the counter they ordered cones, then set off through the park and down toward the lake, which glowed deep blue under the paler sky. Maisie's cone dripped and her face was brown and wet with chocolate custard. Jane slowed down to let her get ahead of them, but still she couldn't bring herself to speak. Billy watched the boats out on the water. The soft splash of oars rose up from the blue surface. Billy ate his cone very neatly, with careful swipes of his tongue. Again Jane tried to gather her words, and again they scattered, and so she opened her mouth and said the first thing that came into her head:

"Masha Karkova wrote *Lady of the Snakes*. I found a manuscript copy in her handwriting that proves it."

Billy did not respond right away. He stood where he was and licked his cone, almost as though he hadn't heard her. Then he turned to her and said warmly, "I always knew you would do great things."

Jane flushed with pleasure, and at the same time she was embarrassed that she cared so deeply what he thought. Up ahead Maisie was squatting under a tree poking at some rocks with a stick.

"Also," Jane said, "I'm pregnant. About eight weeks. Though you could probably do the math yourself."

"Oh my god," Billy said. Melting custard dripped onto his hand, and he tossed the half-eaten cone into a trash barrel. Jane, who was hungry, licked hers and waited for him to say something. Light drained from the sky, and the air was growing clammy if not exactly cool.

"Well?" she said. "I'm hoping you're going to say something more than that!"

Billy's expression was getting harder to read as the dusk deepened. "What do you want me to say?" he said. "What do you want me to do?" His voice was very sad. It was a voice Jane hadn't heard since the year his mother died.

"What do you *want* to do?" she countered.

Billy shook his head. "It's your call, Janie. "It's your—" He broke off. Body, he meant.

But this was not what Jane wanted to hear. "Yes," she said. "Thank you! But I'm asking what you want to do, I'm not saying I'll do it." It was only now that she saw what she wanted him to say—saw that she wanted him to take her in his arms with authority and tell her that yes, of course they would have this baby! At the same time she knew that if he tried to do that, she would fight him. Her pride would not let her agree with any suggestion he made, nor permit him to hold her. And not just her pride, but her shame, too—for how could she have let herself become pregnant at a time like this? How could she have become pregnant accidentally twice (for Maisie, too, had been unplanned)—how, in this day and age?

"But I don't—" Billy began (making no move whatsoever to put his arms around her), when he was interrupted by Maisie, still crouching under the tree, who began to shriek.

"Look, look, look!" she cried. "Mommy-Daddy, look!"

They ran across the grass, but she was all right; she was fine. Her chocolate-smeared face was ecstatic, and she danced in the grass with her hands clasped together, something they couldn't see held inside. At first she was too excited to show them, but at last she stood still and opened her hands to reveal a tiny snake, not much more than four inches long, with a greenish striped body, a red eye, and a tiny black forked tongue. Its jaws were open wide as though it thought it was a dragon breathing fire, but anyone could see it wasn't a threat to anybody, it was so small.

"It was under the rock!" Maisie cried. "I founded it!"

"Jesus," Billy said. "Maisie, let me see it."

Maisie had clasped her hands together again and held them close to her face. "Mine," she said.

Jane was afraid Maisie would squash the little snake in her excitement. "Yes, yours," she said. "Honey, Daddy just wants to look at it."

Maisie turned her back and peeked inside her cupped hands. She whispered something that Jane couldn't hear. It was getting dark.

"Just show me, Maisie, okay?" Billy said. "Turn around!" But she crouched protectively over her treasure.

"Maisie," Jane said. "It's late. We need to be going home."

Maisie turned her head and glared at her parents over her shoulder. "Which home?" she demanded. And then, "I'm *not* leaving Stripy!"

Jane felt extraordinarily tired. She could see Billy trying to control his own feelings—sadness, frustration, confusion, some complicated brew of those. "You can bring Stripy home, too," she said, not addressing the real question, just trying to get Maisie moving.

Maisie looked at her to see if she meant it.

"Come on!" Jane cried, as cheerfully as she could. She held out her hand, but Maisie couldn't take it because she needed both of her own to carry the snake. Still, she followed her parents back up toward the street.

"Are you sure this is a good idea?" Billy said to Jane, walking closer to her now in the near dark, his breath hissing in her ear.

"Compared to what?" Jane said. "No, of course I'm not!"

The sky was a purplish charcoal color now, and the first stars showed over the roof of the auto repair shop on the corner. They crossed at the light and walked up the hill past fireflies glowing in front gardens and televisions flickering in living rooms where no one had yet closed the drapes. "There's that old fish tank in the basement," Jane said. She pronounced the word *basement* very carefully. "We can put the snake in that."

"We'll have to figure out how to take care of it," Billy said. "What it eats and so on."

Jane thought they must both be thinking the same thing: that Felicia would know how to take care of the snake. The ghost of Felicia, glimmering faintly, seemed to float just behind them as they moved up the street. Now that it was dark, it was hard to stay strictly to one side of the sidewalk. Once Billy's arm accidentally brushed Jane's sleeve, and she stepped quickly onto the grass.

"It's too dark for you to bike," Jane said. "And anyhow, you'll have to take the snake. I'll drive you."

"Thanks," Billy said.

So Jane went down to the basement and unearthed the fish tank from the storage room and brought it upstairs, while Billy stayed with Maisie and made sure the snake didn't disappear under the couch or into the radiator screen. They put it on some newspaper in the tank, and Billy carried it out to the car. All the time Jane kept thinking how strange it felt to have the three of them working together as a family, and yet how natural and ordinary. As she strapped Maisie into her car seat and got behind the wheel, it was almost as if they were all going on a family trip together.

Masha had gone out and carried snakes; now Maisie had a snake, too. Because of Felicia—Felicia was the link in the chain. Her ghost had followed them into the car, would follow them forever, one way or another. If she forgave Billy or didn't forgive him, it wouldn't make any difference. But if she didn't have this baby—if she had an abortion instead—there would be a new ghost, a second ghost, haunting them.

"This thing I told you tonight," she said, heading out Johnson Street to the other side of the isthmus, "I know it's terrible timing."

Billy's hands gripped the sides of the tank. "It's not your fault," he said. Then after a minute he thought to ask, "How are you feeling? Physically, I mean."

They drove past the store that sold polished rocks, the coffee shop with the best peach muffins, the sandwich place they'd eaten at the day they'd flown out to look at houses. Less than a year here and already they had a history, as a family, in this place. "I've felt better," Jane said.

Billy spoke out suddenly in the dark. "I just wanted to say—again, clearly—how sorry I am for what happened. What I did. It was wrong: inexcusable, and I know that. I want to make sure you know I know that." His voice was tense and urgent but so quiet she almost couldn't hear him over the engine.

Jane turned on her brights, speeded up. She wanted to tell him not to talk about it. She wanted to just keep driving—all the way out to the edge of the city and beyond, the three of them shooting through the darkness together, not knowing where they were headed exactly and not caring. Instead, half a mile up the road, she slowed and turned down a side street. In the back seat Maisie had fallen asleep.

"So," she said. "Are you still seeing her?"

"No!" Billy said. He sounded truly shocked. "No, of course I'm not!"

Jane thought about that, waited to see how it made her feel. Better—a little better. But there was still something else she needed to ask.

"How many times did you sleep with her?"

Billy didn't answer for a minute. Then he said, "I don't see what good it does, talking about it."

"You brought it up," Jane said. "How many times?"

"Three," Billy said.

Three! It could have been much worse, of course, but still somehow Jane had expected him to say one, only one, just one time: an aberration. But three. That was enough to fall into habits, to develop a routine. Her hands grew hot on the steering wheel. She wondered whether three referred to the number of different times they'd been together or to the number of total times they'd had intercourse in, perhaps, a single night. Which was worse? "Why did you have to do it!" she cried, pulling up in front of Vince's house. She couldn't tell whether she meant the question rhetorically or not.

Billy hung his head—or else he was just looking down at the snake. "I'm a jackass," he said.

"No," Jane said, "you're not! That's why it's so hard to understand!" And for a moment, she felt better. She liked this—this intimate conversation in the dark car. It was painful, but it also felt true to her: honest. She felt she was on the verge of some kind of a breakthrough and she waited, hands still on the steering wheel, but it didn't come. It didn't come the next moment either or the moment after that, and by the time Billy opened the door and ferried first the snake in its tank and then Maisie into the house, the feeling had disappeared altogether.

CHAPTER EIGHTEEN

THE NEXT DAY, Saturday, Jane decided to go see Sigelman. She got into the car and drove over to Shorewood, where trees shaded the quiet streets and flowers bloomed in every yard, pink azaleas and bloodred roses, purple irises dripping white and yellow beards, magnolia trees heavy with waxy blossoms. The whole world teemed with growth and color while Jane, her hands icy, rang the bell and waited, rang it again. At last she heard footsteps and the door opened, but it wasn't Sigelman standing in the hall. It was Felicia, dressed for summer in yellow nylon track shorts and a red ribbed wife-beater stretched over her pear-shaped breasts. Her toenails were painted orange, and her hair was pulled back in a long, thick braid. Her eyes were a startling green behind gold-rimmed glasses, greener than Jane remembered.

Jane forced herself to speak first. "Hello, Felicia," she said. "What are you doing here?" A cool anger ticked through her, giving energy to her tight smile.

Felicia tossed her head so that her shiny braid swung. Her eyes glinted behind the glasses. "I was just doing a few things for Otto," she said. "He hasn't been feeling well."

Otto! Jane thought. She stood up a little straighter and narrowed her eyes, feeling her face harden.

"He's agreed to supervise my thesis," Felicia continued. "Of course, I've changed my topic slightly."

"Have you," Jane said, and then laughter, like a string of bubbles escaping from a bottle, burbled up from her chest. The world seemed suddenly sharp and obscene and hilarious. Even the pattern of blue chevrons on the wallpaper looked dangerously jagged. Felicia and Sigelman! "How nice," Jane said, struggling to control herself. "He's very brilliant, as of course you know!" Fury burned from her like a crown of light.

Felicia fixed her cold green eyes on Jane, then looked away and rubbed at a spot on the hem of her shorts with studied boredom. "Very brilliant," she echoed.

"Can I come in?" Jane said.

A flicker of irritation crossed Felicia's face. "He's sleeping." But just then footsteps rattled the ceiling, and someone coughed, and Sigelman's voice called down the stairs, "Who is it? Who's there?"

Jane and Felicia looked at each other, hard. "It's Professor Levitsky," Felicia called back up, still holding Jane's gaze.

"Really!" Sigelman sounded pleased. "Let her in. I'll be down in a minute."

Felicia stood back, and Jane stepped into the house and went into the living room. The drapes were closed, and the room felt chilly despite the warm day. Felicia followed her and went around opening the curtains as though she lived there, which Jane supposed maybe she did. "Felicia," Jane said. "Why did you sleep with Billy?"

Felicia stopped what she was doing. A complicated look crossed her face, part surprise and part satisfaction. "It was just sex," she said, the way Jane sometimes said to a complaining student, "It's just a B."

Dusty sunshine flooded in through Sigelman's windows, so much brilliant glare it was hard to see. There were so many possible responses to this absurdity, ranging all the way from hilarity to violence, that Jane hardly knew which one to choose.

"But he's my husband," she said at last, settling on artlessness, though she knew even as she spoke that it was pointless, that the fact of her marriage meant nothing to Felicia.

Felicia shrugged. "Nobody forced him," she said.

"Felicia!" Sigelman's phlegmy voice trickled down the stairs. "Pick up those things now, won't you?"

"I have to go," Felicia said. She turned her head and called, "I'll be back soon, Otto," and sauntered out of the house.

The door slammed shut. The house fell silent. Jane went to the window and looked out at the sunny front yard, at Felicia jangling the keys to Sigelman's silver Saab, her braid swinging like a filly's tail. If Jane had had a rock in her hand at that moment, she might have thrown it, but at the same time a cooler part of her head was already wondering how things would end for Felicia, whether her brains and body would get her to the top or not. Would some jealous wife or former lover shoot her down, wreak some clever or violent revenge? Would she fall in love? Was she capable of love? Jane remembered how good she had been with Maisie—patient and always striking the right tone. There was no making sense of people, she thought. People, in their contradictory muddle, were beyond her.

The car backed down the driveway and sped off down the street, sunlight glinting off the windshield. Jane hoped it would crash, go up in a plume of fiery smoke. She hoped it would drive away into the morning and never come back. But she knew she would never be rid of Felicia, or of the other Felicias of the world—the people who would take whatever they could get by whatever means necessary. The trick was to learn to live with them—live among them—without turning into one. Was she capable of that?

The stairs creaked as Sigelman descended. It took a long time for him to get down them, and then at last he came into the room and stood for a moment in the doorway, breathing effortfully, one hand on the jamb to support himself. Jane had seen him only a couple of weeks before, but he had changed visibly. He looked haggard and gray, and he seemed to have lost weight. This wasn't a virus or the flu. His flesh hung from his bones. Jane thought of the scene in *The Lime Trees* in which Sergey visits his brother Fyodor, who is dying of consumption:

His skin had the delicacy of tissue paper, so that it was hard to believe the bones would not break through at the slightest movement. His eyes burned like black fire in his skull as though all that remained of life in him was concentrated there, glowing and smoldering, fighting not to go out.

"I didn't know you were sick, Otto," she said.

Sigelman shuffled over to a rocking chair, moved a stack of papers to the floor, and sat down. Jane cleared a place for herself on the couch. She wanted to jump up again and open the windows or offer to make coffee—any excuse to get herself out of the room—but she forced herself to stay and look at Sigelman. She thought again of Sergey's horror at the sight of his brother and his amazement at his wife Natalya's apparent ease in the face of Fyodor's nearness to death:

> Women, Sergey thought, seemed to have a natural understanding in the face of death. They knew what to do, where to look, how to behave. Death was not for them—for his wife or his sister-in-law either, the pretty Yelena—the same horror it was for a man.

Shows what you know, Grigory Andrevich Karkov, Jane thought. She said, "What's wrong with you, Otto?"

He screwed up his face in disgust. "Let's not talk about illness," he said. "It's so boring." He looked at her to see if she would challenge this, his skin the color of wet cement, his legs in baggy trousers poking out from under his robe.

"All right," Jane said, happy to pretend he wasn't dying if that was what he wanted. The edges of her lips turned up, though less in a smile than in a look of grim determination. "Let's talk about work, then."

"Work," Sigelman agreed. "My favorite subject."

"I went to see Greg Olen." She watched Sigelman. His eyes flickered, but that was all.

"Did you," he said.

"He showed me the manuscript," Jane said.

Sigelman hesitated, as though deciding whether to deny he knew what she was talking about. But then he said easily, "I'm surprised. After all, I told him it was worthless."

"You lied to him," Jane said.

Sigelman leaned back in his chair and shut his eyes, rocking slowly back and forth like the old man he was. "Olen is an idiot," he said. "Oh, his pretensions! His embarrassing idea of himself as a *writer*. The blood of Grigory Karkov has been diluted in him to the consistency of grape juice."

"Maria Karkova wrote *Lady of the Snakes*," Jane said flatly, knowing that Sigelman knew this as well as she did, whether he would acknowledge it or not. "That manuscript proves it."

"Maria Petrovna!" Sigelman scoffed, opening his bloodshot eyes. "She was the wife of a genius who got tired of her! An unbalanced woman, writing her sentimental diaries, copying out his manuscripts, producing brat after brat. Is it any wonder she lost her mind in the end?" A smile twitched at the edges of his mouth.

"The manuscript is in her handwriting, edits and all," Jane said, refusing to acknowledge his taunts. She seemed to have found her footing again, to be picking her way carefully from one truth to another across a dark, swirling river, the next one clear in front of her, and then the next.

"Yes, yes. In her handwriting! Maybe he dictated his corrections and she wrote them down!"

Jane kept her eyes fixed on his. She thought about enumerating the evidence as she would when she wrote her article, but he knew it as well as she did. "Otto," she said, "you know that isn't it."

He coughed, and his face tightened. "Don't tell me what I know," he said.

"You were going to destroy that manuscript if he sold it to you," Jane said. "Weren't you?"

Sigelman raised his bushy eyebrows, their whiteness now yellowing like old parchment.

"If?" he said. "I don't know what you mean by 'if.' I'm quite sure he'll sell before the summer's out. He's rather desperate for money. It's just a matter of settling on a price."

She stared at him—old, ugly, sinister: a skull grinning. Yet burning still, his ardor not for truth but for victory. "He told me he won't sell," she said.

Sigelman shrugged. "Believe that if you want." His grin spread wider, the gray skin tight against the bone.

"You have no right to buy documents just to destroy them!" Jane said, feeling for the next foothold. "Or to hide them, either. You're a scholar. Your work is supposed to be in the service of truth!"

"Yes," Sigelman said coldly. "For me it has always been about truth."

"Then why did you steal that letter from the Newberry?" Jane said. "The one that says Karkov had a sexual affair with the copyist! Why did you steal those other two letters and hide them in the corner of your basement?"

Slowly the expression on Sigelman's face changed, the flesh growing even paler and grayer. "Listen to me," he said, and his eyes darkened and he leaned forward, gripping the arms of his chair. "You want the truth? I'll tell you the truth! Grigory Karkov was a great man—*that's* what the truth is! I've spent my whole life reading him, studying him. Appreciating him! I am his greatest reader and his most important champion. And you—people like you—you would give anything to tear him down. A great writer in a great tradition, but is there a place for that tradition anymore? You and your kind make your livelihood scratching away, nibbling away at all that like termites at work on a great house. All I have ever done in my life is make it clear that Karkov is one of the pantheon. And that is what I am still doing." Color suddenly flooded his cheeks—not a healthy pinkness but a bright, bloody crimson. He began to cough again.

"Karkov *is* one of the pantheon," Jane said. "I don't deny it. But you have no right to keep another writer from the place she's earned!"

Sigelman tried to answer, but he couldn't stop coughing. He tapped his chest with his gray fist. Frightened, Jane crossed the room and knelt in front of him.

"Do you need a glass of water?" she said. "Should I call an ambulance?"

He shook his head, held out his hand to keep her words at bay, and at last managed to quiet himself.

"Otto," Jane said softly, still kneeling at his feet, "you may not have all summer."

"You can't stop me," he said, but his voice was rough and weak.

"I took those letters, Otto," Jane said. "I have them now. The one you stole from the Newberry and the other two. Where did you steal those from?"

"I stole nothing!" Sigelman pounded his knee. "Galina Pisareva gave me those letters for love!" He sat back in his chair and gaped at her, his chest convulsing silently, trying to keep the terrible coughing under control.

For love, Jane thought. She knew who Galina Pisareva was—Masha and Grigory's descendant through their daughter, Katya. Had Sigelman really known her—sought her out, perhaps, for seduction, hoping there might be something tangible in it for him? Was he making the whole thing up? It hardly mattered now. "What do you even care if Karkov slept with boys?" Jane said. "Does it make him less of a writer? Less of a man?"

"*I* say what makes Karkov who he is!" he said. "That's how it's always been."

Yes, Jane thought, that was how it had been, but things were changing now. She remembered what she'd said to Billy on the morning of the day she'd discovered him and Felicia: *I can feel the world turning.* The world kept on turning all the time, but Sigelman had stopped, and he wanted the world to stop with him.

"Otto," Jane said. "You've done such great work. You made Karkov who he is! But you can't control everything forever."

He opened his mouth to speak, but the coughing overtook him again. It was as though he had said everything there was to say, used up his life's allotment of words, and now there was only this, the great, dry, suffocating coughing that went on and on, punctuated by strained, horrible gaspings for air. He was like an ancient star collapsing into gas and dust.

Horrified, Jane watched, sure that he was dying before her eyes. She had killed him. Feminist, historicist criticism as personified by Jane Levitsky had killed him! She knelt staring at him in terror and fascination as he heaved and gasped and choked and, slowly, began to breathe again. By degrees he began to recover. He mopped his face with the wrinkled handkerchief and sank back into his chair, eyes shut. She should have known he wouldn't die that easily.

Despite her dread of a second encounter, Jane knew she couldn't leave until Felicia got back. Sigelman seemed to have fallen asleep in his chair. Jane sat across from him on the couch with a Slavics journal from one of the stacks on the floor in her lap, but she wasn't reading it. She was listening for the sound of the car and to the ragged noises of Sigelman's breathing, making sure it didn't stop. She thought of Maisie in the hospital, wires snaking out from under her paper gown, all the lines on the monitors going flat. She thought of Sigelman as a child, so long ago in Hungary, his older brother dying of pneumonia. Had Sigelman watched his brother die? Had he seen the blue skin and heard the rattling breath and vowed that he would get away from there — away from the old world of disease, ignorance, and death? But now those three horsemen had hunted him down at last.

What a life Sigelman had lived! Sitting here in this dusty, suffocating house with its books and secrets and beautiful silk rug, Jane marveled at it, and at the same time she knew it wasn't the life she wanted. *They all died*, Billy had said, and one day Jane would die, too. But not like this.

At last the Saab pulled into the driveway. Jane went out to the stoop where Felicia stood, her arms laden with grocery bags and pharmacy bags.

"He's dying," Jane said.

Felicia's eyes slipped away from Jane's to the house with its handsome shape and shabby clapboards. "Maybe," she said.

"You can't take care of him," Jane said, hating everything about this—that Sigelman was dying and that she was trying to keep him from getting what he wanted and that she was going to have to deal with Felicia—possibly even be grateful to her. "We're going to have to figure something out."

Felicia shrugged her macramé handbag farther up onto her freckled shoulder. Her strong arms held the grocery bags, and Sigelman's keys jingled in her hand. Behind her a gnarled crab apple tree was in full bloom, pink petals sifting delicately down to the grass when the wind touched them. "How do you know what I can do?" she said.

What did she mean by that? "Is he paying you?" Jane asked. Her glance involuntarily followed Felicia's back to the house. Was Sigelman perhaps going to leave it to her in exchange for nursing him—was that the implication? Did she think he could will her his reputation, his role as arbiter of everything Karkov? It wasn't possible that she was going to take care of him out of affection or the goodness of her heart—was it?

"If I can do anything," Jane said at last, "call me."

Felicia walked past her and let herself into the house. "Okay," she said. "I know the number."

Jane drove away from Sigelman's house on a wave of sadness and relief, but if she thought she was leaving death behind her there, she was wrong.

That afternoon she tried Greg Olen again, and this time the phone was picked up after barely half a ring. Right then, as Olen's voice said a sharp "hello" into her ear, she might have guessed that something was wrong. But her mind was so much on Sigelman and the letters that all she registered was relief that she had gotten hold of him so easily.

"Greg?" she said. "This is Jane Levitsky. How are you?"

He didn't say anything, and in the silence Jane could hear the baby crying in the background, reminding her of the way she had heard it nursing the first time she talked to Susannah.

"I thought only your wife answered the phone," Jane went on lightly, though she was beginning to be aware that lightness wasn't the right tone.

"Susannah's dead," Olen said, in the voice of someone trying out the words without quite believing them. "There was a car accident."

For a moment Jane didn't believe the words, either.

"Greg?" she repeated in confusion, and at the same moment another voice, coming distantly through the telephone line, said, "Greg? Greg?" It sounded like an older woman, standing behind him, perhaps, in the cramped house.

"Greg?" Jane said again. "Are you there?"

But Olen must have let the phone drop.

"Oh god," she heard him say, very faintly, and then again more faintly still, while the baby's crying grew louder and louder like an approaching train, drowning him out. On his end someone hung the telephone up.

Jane put down the receiver in confusion and dismay. The room with its big, cluttered desk and brown rug and overstuffed bookshelves was exactly the same as it had been the minute before, but it looked slanted, askew. Only a week ago she had met Susannah Olen—had sat in her living room, had held her baby—and now Susannah was dead. A chasm had yawned in the middle of a straight road. It could happen to any of them, any moment. It had happened to Masha's family, and now, like a curse borne down the generations, it was happening again. Her eye caught on a Post-it on her desk where she had written the number at Vince Steadman's house, and without thinking she picked up the phone again and dialed. When Billy rather than

Vince answered, she wasn't even surprised. It seemed necessary and inevitable that he would.

"Billy?" she said in a cracked, frightened tone.

"What's wrong?" Billy said.

"Oh, Billy—something terrible's happened!"

Billy's voice took on the calm, panicked intonation of a man expecting the worst. "What?" he asked. "What happened?"

"Susannah Olen died!" Jane said, and she began to cry.

"Jane," Billy said after a moment. "Who's Susannah Olen?"

The fact that he didn't even know made Jane cry harder. "Billy!" she choked out. "Do you think you could come over?"

Half an hour later, he was at the door.

"Where's Maisie?" Jane asked as she let him in. It was strange letting him into the house as though he were a guest when he still had the key on his key ring.

"I left her with Vince," he said. "You sounded so upset."

Jane looked at the shirt Billy was wearing, an old purple oxford cloth one, and her fingers prickled with the remembered texture of the thick cotton. She knew exactly what Billy would smell like if she were close enough to smell him; she knew where her cheek would rest on his chest. She felt cold, and she was worried about the advantage she had given him by calling him and begging him to come, and so she began immediately to apologize, pushing him further away from her with every phrase. "I'm so sorry!" she said. "I shouldn't have dropped this on you. You don't even know the woman! I hardly knew her myself. I'm sorry to be such a wreck."

"Well," Billy said uncertainly, putting his keys and his wallet down on the end table the way he always had when he lived there. "Who was she?"

"A young woman I met," Jane said. "A young mother. Twenty years old with a newborn baby. It was a car accident."

"Awful," Billy said. He sat down, uninvited, on the couch. "Was she a student of yours?"

Jane shook her head and sat down on the other end of the couch. She felt so sad again that her self-consciousness evaporated. "She was an artist," she said. "A painter. She had been, I mean, before the baby, and I told her she would get back to it when the baby was older. But she didn't think so. And she turned out to be right."

Billy leaned forward and rested his chin in his hands. His long back curved and his shirt seemed to glow in the clear afternoon light.

"She should have had all the time in the world!" Jane said. "I could be hit by a car crossing the street tomorrow, and what would—" She was going to say, *What would Maisie do?* but instead she finished, "What would I have done with my life?" She was aware that she had shifted away from sorrow for Susannah to self-pity, but Billy didn't seem to hold it against her.

"You've done a lot already," he said.

"I feel as though I've been living in a cave. I'm thirty and I've spent my whole life in a cave!"

Billy shifted on the sofa. His jeans rustled against the rough wool of the upholstery. Jane was intensely aware of his body a couple of feet away from hers, of his thighs on the cushion and the way his damp hair curled at his neck. Her own body pulsed stupidly with desire. Was this the life force asserting itself in the face of death?

"I'm sorry you're so sad, Janie," Billy said simply.

Again her mind, following the lead of her body, switched gears, and she said as steadily as she could, "I don't know if I can forgive you for sleeping with Felicia! I know you thought that thing, that I had— And I do think that matters, and I think you deserve to be forgiven! I would like to forgive you, but I just don't know whether I can."

Billy was silent. Jane sat waiting as the refrigerator cycled off and the sprinkler watered the lawn next door and a dog barked somewhere close by.

"If there were anything I could do to take it back," Billy said at last, his voice low and tired, as though he'd said these things to himself a hundred times without it making any difference. "To make it not have happened. Janie, I'm so sorry. I know it doesn't change anything, say-ing that. I look at myself—think about myself—and I don't know how I could have let it happen!" He looked up at her, his eyes wet and his face so open, she felt that if she touched him, her fingers would pass right through. "In spite of what I thought. How could it have?"

"I don't know," Jane said. "How?"

"I was lonely," Billy said. "And she did all the work."

A long silence followed. Billy looked so alarmed that Jane could see he hadn't meant to say it, that the words had just tumbled out. Still, they had the authority—and the consolation—of truth. Jane could see it now, as she hadn't been able to before: Billy's loneliness. *Since Maisie was born,* wasn't that what he'd said the other day? Not her fault—not anybody's fault—but there it was. Love multiplied, but the hours of the day did not.

Jane couldn't speak.

At last Billy did.

"I love you, Jane," he said. "I would like us to go on together, you and me and Maisie. Especially now." Now that she was pregnant, he meant. He asked, "What do you want to do? About the baby."

Jane wished he hadn't called it a baby. "I don't know," she said.

"I wish you could forgive me," Billy said, not fiercely but sadly. She knew it wasn't fair of her to wish he would be fierce, but she did anyway.

"Don't you see that I would if I could?" she said. "Or that I would pretend to, even, if I thought it would work? But it wouldn't, because I'm still angry, and I know it would come out in all kinds of ways, whether I wanted it to or not!" She tried to think what to say next. The truth was, at that very instant, she didn't feel angry. It seemed to her that both of them were drowning in a puddle of fear and indecision, but she couldn't think of anything to do about it.

Billy looked at her anxiously. He looked exactly the way Maisie looked when she was worried—big eyes, tight jaw, thick lashes blink-ing. She reached out her hand and touched his arm very lightly.

"Maybe eventually that feeling just subsides, I don't know," she said. "Maybe eventually you get used to it, the way you get used to hot foods." She could feel the heat coming off him through the warm, worn cotton of his shirt. "Of course it's not all your fault," she said. "I mean, I know it's been a bad year. I know things weren't great, that there were problems, even before..."

"Listen, Jane," Billy said, and he seemed to sit up a little straighter now, as though her words had given him a small jolt of energy, "I know I'm the one who broke the rules. Listen—this is hard to say. But if you do manage to forgive me for what I did, and if we try to go on together as a family, I need you to find a way to be less—prickly."

Jane started to tremble, whether with recognition or anger she wasn't sure. "What?" she said.

"Like, dinnertime sometimes," Billy said softly. He sat very still, as though she were an animal he didn't want to frighten away. "Sometimes it's like you're a—dark cloud—sitting at the table."

Jane blinked and two tears fell onto the couch. "Dinnertime," she repeated. She could see the table hastily set, the stained place mats and the cheap paper napkins, Maisie overturning her cup. Just the thought of it exhausted her.

She let herself fall sideways onto the couch, the top of her head not quite touching his leg, and she began to cry. Even though she had said it wasn't all his fault—even though she knew it to be true—it was surprisingly painful to think about.

"Not all the time," Billy said. "I don't mean it's like that all the time."

Jane reached up and laid her hand on his thigh. "I'm sorry," she said.

"Really," he said, "it's a little thing."

Jane wiped her tears away with her other hand. "I wish we had a time machine!" she said. "I wish we could go back and start again!"

"Worse things always happen when you go back in time to try to fix things," Billy said. He covered her hand with his, and at the touch of it all the oxygen seemed to vanish from her body, leaving her breathless. "Cities in flames, species destroyed, rodents raging out of control."

Jane breathed in deeply. She felt her chest expand, felt a warmth moving down through her limbs with her breath. "I would take rodents raging out of control, if we could start again," she said.

"But not the other two?"

"Which cities?" Jane asked. "Which species?" Bravely, she pulled herself up so her head rested on his leg, and he began to stroke her hair. Her whole body was electric again. They stayed like that for a while, both of them motionless except for his fingers moving back and forth across her hair. Then she sat up, touched his face lightly, and kissed him. His arms went around her and his mouth pressed back against hers, and she remembered again when he'd come back from Japan and she'd thought she'd never want anything in the world except his arms around her. And even though she knew, before very long, there'd be lots of things she wanted again besides this, it made her heart light that, for right now, it seemed like enough.

Later, after Billy had gone back to Vince's, Jane remembered Susannah Olen, still as dead now as she had been this afternoon. No second chances, no starting over again for her, or for her husband, either. She went into her study, cleared off a space on the desk, found a piece of stationery, and began to write.

Dear Greg,

I was so sorry to hear about the death of your wife. Though I met her only that once, I could see what a vibrant and talented person she was. I particularly noticed her paintings, with their careful, almost quiet elegance and beauty. It makes me sad to think that the person who made them will never have a chance to pursue the evident passion she had for her art. I hope, as your daughter grows up, the paintings will help her to know, a little bit, the mother who was taken from her.

Please accept my deepest condolences.

Sincerely,
Jane Levitsky

When she reread the note, Jane wanted to tear it up. Such paltry words and conventional sentiments! It struck her as sickeningly facile, superficial, and at the same time awkward and labored.

Nevertheless, she folded the paper and put it into an envelope. What else was there to say, after all? There was nothing anyone could write or do that would make Greg Olen feel the slightest bit better. And surely some contact—some human contact—was better than none.

CHAPTER NINETEEN

 ABOUT TWO WEEKS after Billy moved back into the house, Jane received the following response to her letter.

Dear Jane,

Thank you for your note. You barely knew Susannah, and yet you recognized her gifts as so few did. Your words have meant a great deal to me over the past terrible weeks. Thank you for taking the time to write.

It strikes me, as well, that there is something you and I should talk over. I hesitate to ask you to drive all the way out here, but it does not seem to me like something to be discussed over the telephone, and I'm rather tied down. So, if you ever find yourself in the neighborhood...

Sincerely yours,
Greg Olen

That night when Billy got home from work, Jane showed him the note.

"Are you going to go?" he asked.

They were in the living room, where Maisie was playing with Stripy, who they kept well fed on a diet of crickets. At first Jane had been squeamish about holding the snake, but now she was used to it. It was, after all, only a very small snake—a garter snake, it turned out—a tame shadow of Masha's vipers or Felicia's python. She liked the way it slithered and wriggled in her hands.

Now it squiggled across the rug as Maisie erected a ring of wooden blocks to barricade it in. There were gaps, though, and Maisie had to keep grabbing it and bringing it back into the middle as she reinforced the structure with more blocks, small stuffed animals, books, and plastic trucks.

"Maisie," Billy said, "don't hold Stripy by the tail, please."

"Why?" Maisie asked as the snake dangled from her fingers, trying to loop itself up onto her palm.

"I think I have to," Jane said in answer to Billy's question.

"Because it's a living thing," Billy told Maisie. "Not a toy."

Maisie started to cry. "You made me cry, Daddy," she accused, big tears running down her face and falling onto the carpet.

Maisie had been especially volatile since Billy moved back, more prone than usual to tantrums and tears, which seemed wrong. Maybe she felt safe enough now to let her feelings out. Or maybe it was because she got less attention, Jane and Billy were concentrating so much on each other. Or maybe it was a stage that would have happened anyway. Whatever the reason, Jane hoped it would pass soon.

It was hot, the air thick and sticky, the bushes swarming with mosquitoes and the lakes stinking of algae. Maisie was always damp, her hair flattened in sweaty curls against her scalp. At night in bed with the window fan on high, Jane and Billy talked about installing air-conditioning. They also talked about leaving Madison: if they were starting over, maybe they should really start over. Jane could look for a job somewhere new.

Or if they stayed, should they buy a bigger house to accommodate a second baby? Somewhere in Verona, maybe, or Middleton, where prices were lower.

"It could be nice," Jane said one night. She was naked, flat on her back with one hand on her already bulging stomach. "New construction. New floors, new carpets, new drywall, new grass."

"Awful!" Billy said, his hand on top of hers and his head nestled into her neck despite the heat. "No history, no aesthetic value, no soul."

"No weeds," Jane said. "No rotting windowsills."

"You couldn't walk anywhere."

"I don't walk anywhere now," Jane said.

Billy rolled closer and wrapped his arm around her. "You wouldn't raise Maisie out there," he said.

"How do you know what I would do?"

"I know."

Jane made herself keep her mouth shut. It was true: she didn't want to move to the suburbs, or to leave Madison, or to buy a different house. But still, she wasn't quite content either, although she didn't know exactly what she wanted to be different. Maybe only herself— her greedy, rigid, irritable self. Or maybe the whole world with its eternal strictures: gravity, only twenty-four hours in a day. Death.

As she walked up the path to Greg Olen's door, Jane could already hear the baby crying. She was nervous, her palms sweaty—all of her, in fact, starting to sweat. The sun beat down on the brownish grass and the blistered concrete driveways. She hoped it hadn't been a mistake to come.

Olen looked older when he answered the door. His hair had been cut short, exposing his drawn face with its broad, lined forehead. His black glittering eyes had dark circles under them, and his skin was bristly with stubble. He was holding the baby tightly as she screamed, arching her back and then falling forward against his chest. The noise she made was piercing and harsh, ceasing only for a moment at a time while she gasped for breath, and then redoubling itself. Jane could not remember Maisie ever crying like this, but maybe it was the kind of thing that, for your own sanity, you forgot.

"This is a bad time," Jane said.

Olen hoisted the baby up onto his shoulder. "No worse than

most." He turned and walked back into the house, leaving the door open for Jane to follow.

Inside, the floor was littered with clothes, shoes, baby toys, newspapers. Dirty dishes crowded the dining table—half-eaten bowls of cereal, plates strewn with crumbs, beer cans, Chinese take-out containers. Baby bottles, crusts of bread, empty chip bags, crusting cups of salsa. Olen led her into the kitchen, where he sat in the tiny breakfast nook, pushing aside the clutter to clear a patch of sticky Formica. The close air smelled of garbage and old socks. Didn't this man have anyone to help him? His parents were dead—she knew that—but what about friends or neighbors or bustling women from church? Jane remembered the older woman's voice she'd heard through the phone. His mother-in-law? An aunt? Where was she now, whoever she was, in this time of calamity?

"She's been crying since four," Olen said, in the hyper-controlled voice of a man trying to keep himself from screaming. He stood up again and rocked the baby, shifting his weight from one foot to the other.

Jane watched him, trying to assimilate the picture he made, the desperado with the small pink bundle.

"Is she hungry?" Jane asked.

"She won't take a bottle."

"Is she sick?"

Olen glared at her but seemed unable to answer the question.

"Is she hot?" Jane stood up and moved toward him to feel the baby's forehead, but Olen took a step back.

"Don't touch her!" he said.

"Put your hand on her forehead," Jane said gently. "Maybe she has a fever."

Olen slumped where he stood, shutting his eyes. Then he opened them again and touched the child's head. The baby took the opportunity to try to propel herself out of his arms, and he had to lunge to hold on. Her screaming crescendoed.

Jane longed to get out of there, to scuttle out the door and home to her own healthy toddler, who only screamed every now and then, and usually for intelligible reasons. But she could see somebody had to do something, and there didn't seem to be anybody else. She could hardly even think about the manuscript. It was hard, when a baby was crying, to think about anything else.

"Is she gassy, maybe?" Jane persisted.

Olen shook his head blankly, as though he didn't understand the language she was speaking.

Did she miss her mother? That was the question that hung in the air, the question Jane couldn't bring herself to ask. She spoke quietly to Olen, trying to direct her voice under the baby's cries rather than yelling over them. "Listen," she said. "There are lots of reasons that babies cry. Maybe she's teething. Maybe she's just overtired."

"*She's* overtired!" he said.

"I could hold her, if you want," Jane offered. "I'd be happy to. And you could try to get some sleep."

He shook his head. It was clear he was afraid to let the baby go. She was all he had, after all: all he had left.

"How about this," Jane said. "There must be a drugstore nearby. Why don't I go pick up a few things, and when I get back, you let me try them." She felt that something had to be done, that almost anything would be better than nothing.

Slowly he nodded. "I guess," he said.

It was a relief to be out of the house, away from the noise and the mess. The hazy summer morning smelled of cut grass and, distantly, of manure. Jane got in her car, turned it around, and drove slowly down the street. Again she was tempted to keep on going, to drive right home and leave Greg Olen to his misery, but instead she turned at the corner onto the street where he had said she would find a drugstore.

Jane had always liked drugstores, the way they were crowded with such an odd assortment of things. Medicines and greeting cards: what did they have to do with each other? Toothbrushes and candy, cosmetics and laxatives. Surely cigarettes did not belong in the same store that filled prescriptions for Taxol. She cruised past the supplements aisle—garlic tablets and Saint-John's-wort and bee pollen extract—thinking of Masha dispensing King of Denmark's drops to her sick children. Tinctures of medicinal grasses, water sweetened with jam. Had they really come back to this after a hundred years?

Back at the house, she went in without knocking and followed the sound of crying up the stairs to the baby's room: cheap white crib, an old rocking chair, dust bunnies, the powerful smell of old diapers. Dirty clothes and towels lay damply on the rug. Olen had laid the baby in the crib and now stood watching her while she screamed and flailed, trying to shove a tiny snot-covered fist into her mouth. Jane came over and stood beside him. Then, boldly, she reached into the crib and laid her hand against the baby's cheek. Olen looked at her, but he didn't try to stop her.

The baby was warm, but not burning up. Not a fever, Jane was pretty sure. Or if it was, not a bad one. Not meningitis, for instance, or pneumonia.

"Hush," Jane said, stroking the child's head. She eased her finger into the screaming mouth, probed the gums. Startled, the baby quieted for a moment and bit down fiercely on Jane's finger. Jane could feel the nubs of teeth ready to push through on both the top and the bottom. She pressed hard, and the baby moaned and sucked.

"What did you do?" Olen demanded in the sudden quiet, caught between relief and alarm.

"She's teething, I think," Jane said. "Poor thing!" She felt calm and sure of herself. She knew infinitely more about babies than he did.

"How can you tell?" Olen asked.

She took his big hand and guided it into the baby's mouth, pushing his finger against his daughter's gums and the ridged enamel just beneath the surface. "Rub them. Babies like the pressure."

He did as she said. The baby stopped squirming and stayed quiet.

Olen looked at Jane with newfound respect and suspicion, as though she had clapped her hands and made it rain.

Jane produced the bottle of infant Tylenol she'd bought, undid its complicated wrappings, filled the eye dropper. "Have you ever given her medicine before?"

He shook his head.

"This is how you do it. Watch."

She lifted the baby out of the crib and sat in the rocker with the child on her lap, a powerful, unexpected feeling of tenderness washing over her—she was so tiny, and her skin was so soft. She bounced Caroline on her lap for a minute and touched her small fist. Then she laid her across her knees and went to work, holding the head in place with her left hand and pinning her arms and legs. Caroline began to scream again. Quickly, Jane took the eye dropper and squeezed the medicine into the back of the baby's mouth. The baby screeched in protest, then swallowed. Jane sat her up and gave her back to Olen. "Teething rings are good. You can put them in the freezer; the cold helps soothe the pain. Or you can take a washcloth, soak it in water, and freeze it. Let her chew on that." She handed him a tube of teething gel she'd bought. "Rub this on her gums every now and then."

The baby was still crying, but more quietly now. Olen held her in one arm and rubbed her gums with the other. Thirty seconds later she was asleep. The silence was a miracle, like the wind dropping after a hurricane. Olen laid her back in the crib, where she sighed deeply and settled herself into the mattress. He pulled a blanket over her, and they left the room.

The living room, although dusty, was neat, suggesting Olen had been avoiding it. The samovar, tarnished now to a foggy gray, still sat high on top of the crowded bookshelf, and Susannah's pictures still hung nearby on the wall, warm with watery, colored light. Jane saw Greg's eyes go to them and then look quickly away. He sank onto the couch. Jane sat opposite him on a chair.

"I didn't know about the teeth," Olen said.

"I have a toddler," Jane said. "I've been through it."

"Susannah took care of all those kinds of things." Olen kept his voice carefully neutral, as though they were discussing a distant mutual acquaintance.

"There are books," Jane offered. "Lots of books about taking care of children."

"Yes," he said dully. "I think Susannah had one, or some." He lapsed again into tired silence.

"Listen," Jane said after a few minutes. "I can go now, if you want me to. I can come back another time. You said there was something you wanted to talk about, but I guess it can probably wait."

He rubbed his eyes, rubbed his stubble with his palms, and then sat forward, his hands clasped between his knees. "Now is fine," he said. "I wanted to talk to you about the manuscript."

Jane waited. Her heart squirmed and wriggled in her chest.

"Since Susannah—" He stopped and then started again, his voice harsher this time and more determined. "Since Susannah *died*, it seems clearer to me than ever that I have to hold on to what I have. Keep things for Caroline. Whatever is left to keep." He looked hard at Jane, and she nodded. "That Sigelman is very persistent," he said. "He also has a lot of money."

Jane waited.

"Susannah didn't like him, though. When he came here to talk to me about the papers. Not that she cared one way or the other about the papers themselves. Susannah always laughed at what she called my obsession with my family. With the past. Old stuff, relics, junk, that was what she said it was." He watched Jane carefully as though looking for any sign that she agreed with Susannah, but of course Jane didn't agree.

"It's your heritage. As you said."

"She liked you," Greg said. "Actually. She thought you were okay. You must have said something she liked, I don't know what, but she said why didn't I let you look at the junk, if you wanted to." Greg passed his hand over his face and looked over Jane's shoulder toward the window, open to the oppressive afternoon.

"Greg," Jane said, "you decide whatever you decide—that's fine. But if you do want, or need, to sell the papers, I'd guess a library might buy them from you. Maybe even the Newberry, where most of the Karkov papers already are. Maybe not for as much as Sigelman would give you. But you don't need to accept the first offer you get."

Greg slumped lower on the couch, cracking his knuckles. He looked even more tired, if that were possible. His skin was ashen and his whole body seemed to sag, limbs heavy, muscles slack, as though gravity were stronger on his side of the room. At last he pushed himself up off the couch with a great effort and ran his hands through his shorn hair. "Wait," he told her. He crossed the room, almost stumbling with fatigue. Jane watched him go out the door, listened to his slow footsteps climb the stairs. She remembered the last time she was here, when he had gone away for a very long time and she had sat in this room holding the sleeping baby above whom fate had hovered invisibly with its knife.

This time he was gone only a minute or two. When he came back, he was holding a carton that, according to the legend on the side, had once held Crawford's Best pork sausages. He set it down on the coffee table. "I decided what I want to do," he said. "I pretty much decided before I wrote to you, but I wanted to see you again to make sure. I'm keeping the papers—fuck the libraries—but I'll let you look at them. You can see them now, and you can come back later and look at them some more. I imagine you'll want to take notes and stuff."

"Oh!" Jane said. "Thank you!" Her sudden joy seemed very wrong in this house of grief.

He waved her thanks away. "I'm going upstairs to lie down," he said. He turned and left the room again, leaving Jane alone with the box.

She waited until his footsteps had stopped. Then she knelt on the floor and pulled the carton to her.

Inside, there was paper, lots of paper. Thin, brittle, yellow sheets smelling of dust and age—sheaves of it, thick with ink. They crackled in Jane's fingers as she lifted a handful and scanned the top sheet with greedy eyes. Here was Masha's handwriting, familiar as an old friend, only more cramped than it was in the diaries. It was more slanted, too, scratchier and splotched with blots, as though her pen had pressed heavily at the same time as it raced along. Here were crossings-out— words, phrases, entire paragraphs slashed, new ones scribbled in the margins, between the lines, wherever empty space could be found. Jane ran her finger across a page as though it were written in Braille, feeling the warped, dry texture of it, like dead leaves.

Masha, she thought. Are you here?

There she sat on the floor, the work of one dead woman in her lap, that of another looking down on her from the walls. Upstairs, their survivors slept the deep, urgent sleep of the exhausted, while inside Jane a new creature stretched and bobbed in its saltwater cocoon. One day Jane herself would join the ranks of the mourned and moldering dead, but not yet. Not yet. Life loomed before her, steep and shadowy. She leafed through the pages of Masha's novel, too excited to read them carefully, wondering what else, if anything, she might find here.

At the bottom of the box, there was a letter, dated June 12, 1884. It read:

Grisha,

It is long past midnight, but I cannot sleep. The baby heaves and lurches inside me. I can feel its desperation, its sense of being locked up in darkness. It is longing to get out into the world where the sun shines and the flowers drink up its rays, and pale green seedlings, the sickly color of cabbage worms, transform themselves into radiance.

I think it will go badly with me. The child, like any parasite, will tear me apart to reach the light. I find I have some things I want to say to you first.

Grisha, do you remember those days long ago in Moscow, in my parents' house? The grand staircase, the carpets, the chandelier dangling from the painted ceiling. I remember, as a girl, waiting impatiently for the days you would come and talk with Papa—the air of *life* that used to sweep into the house when you came in, and the way your laughter rang along the halls. The way you smiled at me when I came downstairs to listen to the talk, me just eleven or twelve then with my big staring eyes and my skinny girl's body—so much like a boy's body, really. Me with my adoration.

Was that truly us? Is my memory correct? Or is it rather a dream, a spun-sugar fantasy bodying forth from my imagination the way those feverish, vivid pictures swirled around me as I lay on the cold floor of the Feska church? Never have I had dreams like those, Grisha, dreams of what I—or someone like me—might have done in another life. A holy woman, a woman filled up with God! A woman walking the roads, healing the sick, whereas all I do is lie in my cold, carved bed, my body swollen with a helpless creature conceived in what I think of more as an act of will than of love. If you read the scribbled sheets below, you will see what I'm referring to.

This life has not been the life I imagined when I was young. Well, nor has yours been, I expect. Maybe you wish you had married a stupider woman—a woman easier to fool anyway—who wouldn't have guessed what you were up to when you went out with your gun and came back only with that look on your face—dumb relief mixed with anger. I used to think the anger was born of shame, but lately I don't think that's it. I think you're just angry.

How often I have hated you for marrying me! Hated myself for not being what you wanted, even as I loved you—love you still!—have loved you ever since I was that foolish, dreamy, headstrong girl. God knows I have tried not to, but it seems I might as well try not to breathe.

Of course you have given me the children.

And then there are your books, which I loved and later resented.

I resented you for that rapt, private look on your face when you were deep in the writing, and for how you used me the way a painter uses a shivering model. Still, it has been an education.

Which brings me back to this mess of pages. Whether it is any good or not, I have no real idea. I think so—I hope so—but you will know better. And if it is—any good—Grisha, I give it to you. I know how you have struggled the last years, with life and writing, both. I have seen the pain etched on your face and watched as you tried to ease it, not always as others would have liked you to. But even if you haven't always been a good man, you have certainly been a great writer! I have no doubt your works will outlive us. And although the words have been stopped up in you for some years, I am confident they will flow again as they have before. If my pages can buy you some time and a bit of peace with the greedy world, I give them to you gladly.

I have never had any real ambition. I did not write what I have written with any thought of publication, but only because I could not help myself. It flowed out of my pen like blood from a slashed vein when God knows my attention was needed elsewhere. When the nurse banged on the door and I pretended to be sleeping, or I feigned not to hear the twins fighting or Nikolka wailing in the yard. So I know a little bit what it's like, Grisha, not to be able to help yourself.

Take this work. Give it your name, as you gave it to me. God knows I would never have written it if I had not learned about words what I have learned from you. In that sense you are its legitimate father—its genuine progenitor.

Masha

Jane sat back on the cold floor, reeling. Masha had seen Grisha clearly for what and who he was, and loved him even as she hated him. She had struggled to live the life she was given as well as she could, and out of that struggle had come the most amazing things: her flight from Dve Reckhi, the Snake Woman, these pages, and this extraordinary gift.

If my pages can buy you some time and a bit of peace with the greedy world, I give them to you gladly.

I know your words will flow again.

But his words hadn't flowed again, ever. They had died instead, as though her death had stilled them.

It's as though he needed Maria Petrovna for the novels, Sigelman had said once, he who knew Karkov better than anyone in the world.

I think it will go badly with me. Here was the end of Masha's life — here were possibly the last words she'd written — and still Jane did not know, not absolutely, how she'd died. Had the child, stillborn, literally torn her apart as she'd feared it would? Or was her fear of a different kind, a fear of the life that would await her after its birth, when she'd once again find herself bound to Dve Reckhi, mother of yet another new baby? Had it been — that prospect — too much to face? Jane imagined the swift-moving Vaza after a rain, the black sky sparkling with stars, the black river noisy with its hurry to get to the sea, Masha's legs soaked already from the long grass of the hissing meadow — tipping from one darkness into another — taking her child and her words with her.

Was the alternative any better? Masha in her bed with the child stuck inside her unyielding bones, a river of blood soaking the sheets, running in rivulets across the floor. Masha's face convulsed with pain, trying not to scream because of the living children nearby — or perhaps screaming anyway, beyond caring, or even beyond remembering that she had children. Was this better, death not chosen but blindly assigned by fate while every atom of her being struggled to live?

Jane sat on the cold floor with her face buried in her hands. Impossible to say which was worse — as impossible as to know which way it had happened. But it didn't matter, not now. Not ultimately. How

Masha died changed nothing. What mattered was how she had lived during the thirty-five years she'd had. What she had written, and how she had loved, with what courage and generosity. Jane knew she herself would never be capable of it.

Sounds from upstairs startled her, and she got up off the floor and dug in her purse for a tissue. The envelope she had brought with her was in there, too, and she pulled it out and set it on her lap as she blew her nose.

Olen came back into the room looking marginally less exhausted. "Well?" he said.

"There's some amazing stuff in here," Jane said. "Thank you."

Greg nodded, but he didn't ask what she had found. She could see it was all he could do to stand in the room.

"I brought you something," Jane went on. She picked up the envelope and put it down on the coffee table next to Masha's farewell letter. "The originals are in here, and also translations I did of them for you. I'll tell you the whole story sometime, but just briefly, there are two letters from Maria Petrovna and one from the Karkovs' daughter, Katya. I don't know who they really belong to. But you're the descendant. So I thought I would give them to you."

Greg glanced at the envelope. "Where did you get them?" he asked.

"From Sigelman," Jane said. "Without his permission."

Olen's face took on a new expression, as though Jane had suddenly become more interesting.

Jane looked at him: at his gaunt body and his purple-shadowed eyes and the white scalp showing through the buzz-cut hair. How was he going to manage? How was he going to keep things together, raise his daughter all by himself? For him, as for so many, there would be no choice between working and taking care of a child. He would have to do both, struggle through as best he could, and alone. Who was she, then, to feel that working and raising children at the same time was impossible, a mountain too steep to climb? Her heart stirred, her energy seemed to flow back to her, just a little. Who, after all, was to say what was impossible? We were born naked and we learned to sew clothes out of animal skins. We were earthbound and we invented the airplane, the rocket ship!

"I'll call you," she said. "About the papers, and to see how Caroline is." She picked up her purse and slung it over her shoulder. "Only answer the phone sometimes, would you?"

His mouth twitched ambiguously. Jane chose to believe he was trying to smile at her. He was doing what he could.

CHAPTER TWENTY

MAISIE DIDN'T WANT to go to the sibling class recommended by Jane's obstetrician. "I don't want a baby sibling," she said without looking up from her drawing. She sat at her little table under the window, bearing down so hard with her wide-tipped marker that the ink bled through onto the wood.

Jane lowered her swollen body heavily into the chair opposite her daughter. "Well, you're going to have one, Maisie. This class is going to be a lot of kids just like you, learning about what it's like to be a big sister."

"What about brothers?" she asked. "Don't they have to go? Why can't I be a brother?"

"Brothers, too," Jane said. "Big sisters and brothers, I should have said."

"Why didn't you?"

"Because. I was just thinking about you." She leaned forward to tuck a curl behind Maisie's ear.

"Why?"

"It's just one night," Jane said. "You'll see the place where the baby will be born, which is a lot like the place you were born."

"The hospital. I went there with Daddy when I couldn't breathe. They had French fries there."

Jane looked at her in surprise, though it wasn't really so strange Maisie could remember that. "Actually," she said, "it's a different hospital."

Maisie was three now, her vocabulary ballooning. She was taller, too, and had better control of her body. She was still stubborn but more able to express her obstinacy in words, so there was less screaming. And she was becoming interesting, argumentative, always looking for holes in what Jane said. This was its own challenge, of course, but one Jane felt better equipped for.

"What are you drawing?" Jane asked, spreading her legs in an attempt to better balance her bulk.

"This is an anaconda. It's a hundred feet long. It eats crocodiles. What do anacondas eat again, Mom?"

"Waterbirds, I think," Jane said. "Tapirs. Maybe crocodiles."

"People," Maisie said, her marker squeaking across the paper.

"No, not people," Jane said. "People are too big for anacondas."

"Too big," Maisie said. "Just tapirs and waterbirds and babies. Mom, what's a tapir again?"

"It's some kind of piglike thing. But, Maisie, anacondas do not eat babies. Nothing eats babies. Moms and dads and big sisters take good care of them."

Maisie put her marker down and looked at her mother. "Why?" she said.

Partly because the job was no longer so new, Jane found teaching easier this year. She had a better idea of what was expected of her, what the students could manage, and how to present her ideas in ways that made sense to them. She was beginning to see that she could challenge them and co-opt them at the same time, meeting them halfway even as she drew them toward her. She was beginning, too, to develop a more balanced, coherent view of Masha. She could see now that she had pitied and championed Masha for too long, creating, out of her own needs and wishes as much as out of the evidence around her, various Mashas of her imagination.

She drove to Iowa every few weeks to visit Olen, play with the baby, and sort carefully through the papers in the Crawford's Best carton. She read Masha's diaries again. She made notes for something that was too long for an article but might possibly someday be a book, tentatively titled *"Lady of the Snakes*: Maria Karkova and the Aesthetics of Attribution." Her own baby stuck its knee into her stomach, fluttered, turned over. She noticed and did not notice. Soon it would need her full attention: her arms, her voice, her wakefulness. But not yet. For now, shy vampire, it funneled her blood through its body, but otherwise it mostly left her alone.

She was just getting ready to go home from campus one afternoon when she heard someone out in the hall fumbling with the lock on Sigelman's office door. She hadn't seen him all semester. He had been ill, or at any rate reclusive, holed up at home, sending Felicia in to fetch books and journals. Jane sat another moment at her desk, assuming it was Felicia in the hall, but after a long minute had passed and the slow rattling of the knob went on and on, she heaved herself up out of her chair and went to see.

Sigelman stood hunched over his doorknob, his key grasped awkwardly in his trembling hand. What little hair remained to him had yellowed over the course of his illness, and his red-veined eyes blinked dully in the general direction of the keyhole.

"Otto?" Jane said. "Do you need a hand?"

He looked up at her and his thin, dry mouth compressed with determination. He fit the key into the lock and turned it. "No thank you," he said hoarsely. Jane was about to make some neutral remark when he straightened up, forced his lips into a cadaverous grin, and said, "What did you do to get Olen to go back on his word to me? Fuck him? Did you want to defeat a sick old man as badly as that?" He leered at her swollen abdomen.

Jane thought of Felicia's story about Sigelman from so many months before, the student raising her hand and saying, "I'm not used to that kind of language," and Sigelman replying, after a torrent of obscenities: *There, now you're used to it!* But you could never get used to Otto's pugnacity. To his meanness. To his conviction that his way was the only way.

Well, his way was crumbling now, and there would be no going back. Times changed, the culture changed. The canon changed. Fewer people read Grigory Karkov—Sigelman had said so himself. But Jane would bet that within a few years more people would be reading Maria Karkova than ever had before. If Jane had anything to do with it, they would.

And so she smiled at Otto Sigelman as the baby kicked and kicked again inside her, restless, energetic, alive, eager to get out into the fray. "Did you hear Greg Olen is publishing a novel?" Jane asked.

"Vanity press, no doubt," Sigelman said.

Jane laughed, suddenly glad to see the venom was still in him.

At the hospital they admitted Jane right away and took her up to the fourth floor. Everything seemed to happen very quickly. One minute she was taking off her clothes and the next she was crouched in the bathtub, her arms braced against the slippery rim, screaming. Billy held her steady. His shirt was splotched with water and the dark room stank of chlorine and antiseptic. The pain eased and Jane moaned with relief, resting her head on the cold porcelain. "I want the epidural now," she told Billy.

"I'll go tell someone."

But the pain was starting again. She could feel it deep inside her the way you feel the tracks tremble before the freight train roars into sight and flattens you. "Don't go," she begged him.

"But I—"

"Don't go!" You were supposed to breathe into the contraction but she couldn't breathe. The pain rose up all around her like a wall of fire, cutting her off from air and light.

The nurse was there, a big bosom in a white shirt. "Sshh," she ordered, holding a finger up to Jane's face, and Jane was silenced, a child before a stern teacher.

"She wants an epidural," Billy said.

"She's doing all right," the nurse said.

"No, I'm not," Jane whispered. The room, which had seemed dark a moment before, was suddenly too bright, the awful light ricocheting from wall to wall.

"Where's the doctor?" Billy asked.

"It's not time for the doctor yet."

An argument seemed to start up but Jane couldn't follow it. She was shivering and she knew if she didn't stay very still, she would vomit. The pain subsided only to roar up again, breaking over her like a wave in a storm, burying her, smashing her onto the shore, crushing the air from her lungs. She shut her eyes and tried to imagine herself somewhere else—a sunny garden, a forest glade, at home in bed. But there wasn't anywhere else. There was only here, this room, this cold tub, this awful light that shone straight in through the skin of her eyelids. And the pain. The next thing she knew she was standing dripping on a tile floor, and then she was in bed with a rough cotton blanket across her middle. A lot of people were in the room. "It's almost time to push," someone said, and she looked up and saw the doctor standing by her feet. She tried to smile but it came out more like a grimace. "Hi," she said.

The doctor wore a white hat and a green smock. Translucent rubber gloves sheathed her hands. "You're doing great," she said, and Jane felt better, although she knew she had nothing to do with it. She was barely there.

"Are you going to give me the epidural now?" she asked.

"You went too fast for an epidural," said a voice beside her ear. She turned and was surprised to see Billy's face. She had forgotten about him.

Only now that the pain was coming again did she realize it had been away, and she braced herself as it took her and wrung her out like the mangle women used to use for laundry. She would have thought she had no breath for screaming, but she was screaming anyway.

"Push!" the doctor said, and she pushed. Something moved inside her, shifting, the way the plates of the earth shifted against each other. The pain reached deeper.

"Again!" a voice commanded, and hands on either side of her held her legs wide.

"More, more! Good work. I can see the head."

How funny that they called it work. Work was sitting in the library with a pencil in her hand. Work was tapping the computer keys or standing in front of a classroom, talking. Work involved her mind, whirring. It required volition. She pushed. The baby moved through her, slowly, like a rose opening its petals. The pain was a crown of fire between her legs. Her body blazed. She groaned and clenched her teeth and pushed.

"Okay. Now stop," the doctor said, but she couldn't stop. Deep inside her something moved, like a bone dislodged from a throat.

In the spring of 1878, after Vanya was born, Masha Karkova had written:

> So many babies I have had now, and each one so different, his own person even from the moment of birth! This one is like a sparrow with his quick, darting eyes and his fragile bones, the sweet, musical sounds he makes lying in his basket in a sunny corner. In moments of despair I have felt each new child like another silken thread, binding up my soul. But on happier days I see each one—not so much as a new beginning, but as a new note in a complex harmony, adding depth and resonance to a tapestry that already exists.

And a few weeks later:

> How quickly he grows! The others are all so big and he longs to join them. He stretches his tiny legs, flaps his arms, desperate not to be left behind. Stay, stay, I cry. The others dart through

the meadow in the golden light. They can scurry and forage, they do not need me. It is only the little one and me floating together in a milky hum, a warm cocoon. A few months, and then he'll break free and crawl away. I will be alone then, my soul ringing with emptiness.

On a white, icy January morning shortly after the birth of her son, Thomas Levitsky Shaw, Jane Levitsky sat at her desk thinking of the different moods of motherhood—joyful, oppressive, tedious. Peaceful. Exhausting. Still, she felt good today. She felt awake and alert, full of a powerful, roiling energy. She had been thinking about the biographical introduction she would write for her book, and today, a Saturday morning with Billy and the children downstairs watching television, she sat at the keyboard and began to write.

In the early spring of 1884, a Russian countess rose from her bed in darkness, carefully skirted the maid sleeping on a mat by the door, and stepped silently out into the moonlit hall. It was cold, all the fires burned down. She walked down the corridor past the dimly visible portraits of her husband's ancestors, posed photographs of her children, gilded icons. Behind the door on the left, her eldest son and daughter slept in a little room with a vaulted ceiling and a view of the river. On the right, in the big nursery, the younger children slept with Marya L'vovna, their nurse. She could hear them breathing in the still night. Someone coughed—probably Konstantin, whose chest was delicate. He often coughed in the damp night air.

All her babies but one. Her sweet Vanya (called Vanyushka) was dead. They had buried him in December 1882, in the bitterest cold of the year.

Countess Maria Petrovna Karkova was a tall woman, her thick, chestnut hair held in place with many pins. Her gray eyes glowed with warmth and determination, with fire held in check. Picture her standing in the cold hall alone at midnight.

What has called her from her warm bed? What force is about to propel her out the heavy front door into the night?

Consider that here was a woman who had lost a child. For weeks after little Vanya's death from pneumonia, Karkova had refused to leave her room. Vanya had been her special one, her angel, with his dark curls and infectious laugh. He was by all accounts a warm, affectionate boy, the kind of child who seems to have an intuitive understanding of the emotions of others. When his mother was happy, he would tease her and beg to be tickled. When she was pensive or busy, he would sit quietly beside her, or trot unobtrusively at her heels as she went about her business on the estate, the great bunch of keys dangling from her waist, their noisy jangling a cheerful sound but also a warning to the household servants that they had better get busy. When his mother was sad, Vanya might sit in her lap or bring her a flower from the garden to cheer her up.

Vanya became ill the week before Christmas, 1882. Karkova, beside herself with worry, tried to hide her anxiety from the children. In her diary for December 22, 1882, she wrote:

> *I am ill, ill with fear and despair. How brave my Vanyushka is! How he tries to cover up his weakness, to smile and to chatter to me when I sit beside his bed. "Hush, starling," I tell him. "Rest." "Do not be sad, Mama," he says. "I will always love you, and I am not afraid, whatever may happen!"*

> *But how can I not be afraid? All night I am on my knees to the mother of God. She smiles her fixed, golden smile and looks down upon me with her sad eyes, as if to say, "I have lost my only son; why should you keep yours?"*

Maria Petrovna Karkova was a woman of many guises. At times she was the purely maternal figure her children knew—life-giving and generous, like the fertile earth of Mother Russia herself. In controlling the finances and overseeing the workings of Dve Reckhi, Karkova did what was at that time considered a man's job. In her careful renderings and descriptions of the wildlife of the estate, she exhibited a naturalist's eye. The mystical, gorgeously poetic entries in her diary are the work of a literary artist, but they only hint at the literary masterpiece she would produce in 1884. The months just preceding her death in August of that year would be the most surprising and creative of her abbreviated life. It was as though she stripped away the masks she had lived behind until then—wife, countess, mother, manager, nurse, diarist—and revealed her true face.

Well, Jane thought, flexing her fingers and leaning back in her chair. Wasn't there more to any of us than the face we showed to the world, or regarded every morning in the cloudy mirror?

There was a knock on the door and Billy came in. He was wearing sweatpants and a ripped T-shirt, and his hair stuck up unevenly.

Wasn't that the trick? Jane thought. To see past the masks we made for ourselves, deep into the humming possible?

"I came up to see if you were hungry," Billy said. "The rest of us are."

Jane blinked, pulling herself back into the room. "Does that mean I should come feed the baby?"

"Soon. I'm making pancakes for Maisie. Do you want some?"

Jane yawned and tried to tell if she was hungry. Billy came over and put his arms around her, and she leaned into him. He smelled of cotton and frying butter.

"Billy," Jane said into his solar plexus. "Can you see through my masks to who I really am?"

He pulled back and looked into her face. "Sure," he said.

"Who am I, then?" she asked.

"You know who you are," Billy said.

ACKNOWLEDGMENTS

So many people generously supplied much-needed information and expertise for this book. Scott Craven let me sit in on his class on terrestrial vertebrates at the University of Wisconsin-Madison. Sibelan Forrester provided Russian translations, recommended books, and read the whole manuscript for Russian-related errors (any errors that remain are mine). Alison Hinderliter and Sara Austin at the Newberry Library answered many questions about the workings of that wonderful institution. Greg Anderson, John Galligan, Linda Falkenstein, Julie Nishimura-Jensen, Lauren Shohet, and Jennifer Snead all provided useful information.

Thanks to Julianna Baggott, Amy Benson, Betsy Bolton, Fleda Brown, Sarah Coleman, Lisa Davis, Ann Packer, Matt Pitt, and David Scott for reading this manuscript at many stages. Thanks especially to my mother, Linda Pastan, who has read it almost more often than I have.

Thanks, too, to the wonderful childcare providers without whom this book could never have been written: Danielle Strawn, Becca Kavanagh, Joanne Muldoon, Trisha Barczewski, Red Caboose, The Eyman Children's Center, and Trinity Cooperative Day Nursery. My apologies to the city of Madison, which actually has an enviable number of terrific daycare centers.

My immeasurable gratitude to Henry Dunow and Rebecca Saletan for their patience, intelligence, and advocacy, and for bringing this book into the world.